Her Scandalous Rake

The Worthington Legacy
Book Eight

Marie Higgins

DRAGONBLADE PUBLISHING, INC.

ARE YOU SIGNED UP FOR DRAGONBLADE'S BLOG?

You'll get the latest news and information on exclusive giveaways, exclusive excerpts, coming releases, sales, free books, cover reveals and more.

Check out our complete list of authors, too!

No spam, no junk. That's a promise!

Sign Up Here

www.dragonbladepublishing.com

Dearest Reader;

Thank you for your support of a small press. At Dragonblade Publishing, we strive to bring you the highest quality Historical Romance from some of the best authors in the business. Without your support, there is no 'us', so we sincerely hope you adore these stories and find some new favorite authors along the way.

Happy Reading!

CEO, Dragonblade Publishing

Chapter One

I T WAS THE perfect night to escape.

The storm clouds gathered like an army on the horizon, swallowing the last traces of twilight. Darkness descended swiftly, blotting out the stars and smothering the moon. A cold wind howled from the east, carrying with it the scent of autumn decay and the promise of chaos.

Diana, Viscountess Hollingsworth, stood at the window, a dangerous smile curling her lips. She had been waiting for this night—for weeks now, the anticipation had gnawed at her like a hunger she could no longer ignore.

She turned from the window and moved with unhurried grace, gliding from the sitting room into the vast, dimly lit great hall. Her movements were calculated, and every step was designed to convey an air of effortless indifference. Let them think she was unaffected—above suspicion, even.

Her husband's servants scurried about, lighting the lamps, but the hush that fell as she passed betrayed them. They were gossiping again; she could feel their eyes on her back, hear the whispers they thought she couldn't.

It had been two months since they had found Ludlow, Viscount Hollingsworth, naked in the stables—stabbed through the heart. The stink of liquor and cheap perfume had clung to his body like a final insult. It was no surprise. After two agonizing years bound to his infidelity and cruelty, his death had been almost… predictable.

As Diana ascended the grand staircase, she passed a few servants along the way, offering them a curt nod of acknowledgment. They curtsied in return, their movements stiff and obligatory, but their eyes betrayed them. When they thought she wasn't looking, the condescension in their glares was unmistakable. It had been this way from the moment she married Ludlow.

Her husband had enjoyed belittling her in front of the household staff, making her seem like a petulant child undeserving of respect. And the servants, so blindly loyal to him, had lapped it up. Over time, their disdain for her had only deepened, solidifying like cracks in the foundation of her marriage. She could never fathom why they had been so devoted to a man who treated them with the same disregard he treated her.

She had expected things to change after his death. Surely, with him gone, their misplaced loyalties would dissolve. But the opposite had happened. Their hostility had only grown, festering in the silence of the halls, and now it clung to every corner of her home. It was suffocating, their judgment constantly pressing in on her. Some days, she could barely stand the sight of them. Living among them felt like living in a den of spies—waiting for her to falter, waiting for a scandal to confirm their low opinion of her.

Tonight, that would all change.

As she turned the corner at the top of the stairs, low voices floated out from the next room. Slowing her steps, she listened closely to what they were gossiping about this time.

"Mr. Brown, did you hear the authorities have been questioning Lord Tristan Worthington about his lordship's murder?"

Diana stopped abruptly, instinctively pressing herself against the cool stone wall, her pulse quickening. The hushed voices drifted from around the corner, their conversation just loud enough to reach her ears. She hadn't heard this particular rumor before, and it gave her pause. It was tempting to dismiss the gossip, to brush it off as idle chatter from bored servants. Yet experience had taught her differently.

As much as she hated to admit it, the servants often had access to the most accurate information—things that moved through the house unnoticed, like whispers in the dark. They were the eyes and ears of the estate, privy to secrets that even she, the viscountess, wasn't always aware of.

"Indeed, I heard, but they have no evidence, Mrs. Yearly. If you ask me, I think Lord Tristan is guilty. He had every reason to kill his lordship."

Diana took a deep breath, trying to steady herself as a wave of unease washed over her. The very idea of Tristan being responsible for her husband's death was absurd—preposterous, even. She clenched her fists, pushing the notion away. If Tristan had truly wanted Ludlow dead, he would have done it three years ago, when the resentment between them had first begun to fester. Not now, when the marriage had deteriorated into nothing more than a hollow pretense, and the bitter battles had lost their edge.

No, Tristan wasn't the type to wait. He was decisive, driven by impulse when pushed, and if he'd meant to kill Ludlow, it would've been swift and without hesitation. But as the thought continued to gnaw at her, she couldn't entirely dismiss the shadow of doubt creeping in.

"I agree," the servant continued, "especially after what had happened between the two lords before she married Lord Hollingsworth. Why his lordship married her, I swear I'll never understand."

"Then, Mrs. Yearly, you will be happy to know gossip is circulating about her ladyship lately. The magistrate should arrest her any day now."

Diana's heart sank as the unsettling thought settled deeper in her mind. She silently prayed the servants were wrong this time. The mere idea of Tristan being involved stirred a whirlwind of dread, but even more infuriating was the knowledge that the past still haunted her. The scandal from three years ago clung to her like a stain that refused to fade, no matter how hard she tried to move forward.

Why couldn't the *ton* let it rest? Society's sharp eyes had never forgiven her, and neither had the whispering voices behind the fans. The elite circles were like wolves—always ready to pounce on old scandals to keep them alive. It seemed time had not dulled their appetite for gossip, and her name still lingered on their lips.

As for the servants… A wave of frustration rose within her. Didn't they have anything better to discuss than recycled rumors and worn-out stories? Their prying eyes and wagging tongues had been a constant source of irritation, fanning the flames of her past and making her life within these walls increasingly unbearable.

"The magistrate has taken too long as it is," Mrs. Yearly said. "Someone needs to be arrested. Soon."

"I agree," Mr. Brown grumbled. "It was a terrible and unsuspected travesty. Someone needs to pay."

Doom closed in around Diana, heavier than it had ever felt before. The weight of uncertainty pressed against her chest, making it difficult to breathe. She knew exactly why no one had been arrested for Ludlow's murder—because there were too many suspects. Ludlow had spent years making enemies, leaving a trail of bitterness and anger in his wake. Among them was Lord Tristan Worthington, the man Diana had once believed would be the love of her life.

The memory of Tristan was a thorn that had never stopped piercing her. He was supposed to have been her savior, the one to rescue her from the misery of an unwanted betrothal. But instead of sweeping her away, Tristan had fled, like a coward, abandoning her to a fate she hadn't chosen. His deception had shattered her, and his lies had been the cruelest of all. He had never intended to marry her—he only wanted to compromise her reputation, to tarnish her future without a second thought.

In the end, he hadn't just broken her heart; he'd turned her life into a living nightmare. Her girlish dreams of love and escape had crumbled, leaving nothing but bitterness in their place.

Tristan hadn't been the prince she had once believed him to be. No, he had been the toad in this twisted fairytale, and she had been left to pick up the pieces of the life he had so thoughtlessly ruined. Now, the past she had fought so hard to bury was rearing its ugly head again, threatening to drag her back into the depths of scandal and betrayal.

The last she had heard, Tristan was to be married soon. The news had stunned her, though she had long since let go of any illusions about him. Still, a small part of her—perhaps the last remnant of the girl who had once loved him—hoped that he could find happiness, even if his betrayal had left her miserable. She was mildly surprised that the rumors of murder swirling around him hadn't frightened his fiancée, the widow Lady Fairbourne, enough to call off the wedding. It seemed not even the darkest suspicions could touch Tristan's charm.

Diana continued walking toward her chambers, no longer caring if the gossiping servants saw her or whispered as she passed. Soon enough, she would be out of this wretched house, and a new viscount would take her late husband's place. The very thought brought her a small flicker of relief. The sooner she was free of these suffocating walls and the memories they held, the better.

When she finally stepped into the room that had become her refuge over the last two months, the flicker grew. This space had become her sanctuary, the one place where she could let her guard down.

A maid stood beside the bed, carefully turning down the covers, her presence a quiet comfort. Only a few lamps illuminated the room, casting long, soft shadows across the walls, wrapping the space in a cocoon of privacy. Here, at least, the weight of the world seemed to lessen, and Diana could breathe— if only for a little while.

"One moment, please." Diana held up a hand as she hurried to the older woman. "Martha, this is not necessary. I shall leave tonight for an extended stay with my cousin."

Martha Whitehead's eyes widened. From outside, the wind picked up and howled through the closed window, rattling the pane. "Milady, it's too late to travel... and a storm is brewing."

Chuckling, Diana turned toward her dressing table. "I'm not a stranger to traveling in bad weather. I have lived in England all my life. I shall brave the elements and arrive safe at my cousin's house. Besides, it's only an hour's drive. All will be well, I assure you." She picked up her bonnet and placed it snugly over her ringlets. Hopefully the maid didn't know how far her grandmother's cottage *really* was. "I assume you have already packed my things?"

"But of course, milady. You instructed me to do it days ago. You just didn't know when you'd be leaving."

"Splendid. Please tell the footman to load the trunks onto the carriage. I shall leave as soon as he's finished."

Diana peered in the mirror and met Martha's reflection. The maid shrugged and smirked. "As you wish, milady."

As the thin, middle-aged woman rushed out of the room, Diana clutched her hands against a roiling stomach and silently prayed everything would go smoothly. She didn't know why she feared the worst, unless it was because her life had always been a pattern of mishaps. She didn't want anything to ruin this for her now.

Freedom was just hours away.

"EVER'ONE RAISE YER glass and toast ta Lord Tristan's nup... nup... shuls." Tristan Worthington slurred his words as he tried to ponder on what he wanted to say. Realizing his mind was too unclear, he laughed and stumbled against the man standing next to him, spilling his rum over the side of his tumbler.

The man rolled his eyes. "Worthington, will ye quit toastin' to yer own weddin'? We all 'no ye aren't gonna marry the lady."

Tristan scowled at the fellow. *What was his name...* "Ah, but my good man, ye're wrong. T'morrow afta-noon, I'll be there in church standin' next to my beautiful bride, Lady... er... Lady..." Tristan rubbed the throb growing in his forehead.

The other men who'd gathered in the tavern released a fit of laughs. One belched loudly and lifted his cup. "Worthington has fergotten her name already."

Blast it all! Tristan thought. What *was* her name? "Doesn't matter. I'm marryin' her t'morrow."

His legs wobbled and he plopped his butt down on the chair before he ended up on the floor like he had last night. Inwardly, he groaned. How many nights had he been visiting the taverns *toasting* his nuptials, anyway? Too many to count. Tomorrow his life—his very freedom—would end, no matter how badly he wished for a different fate.

You're making a colossal mistake, Worthington, came the warning from the back of his mind. Yet he figured by marrying the widow, Lady Jane, he would be able to put his past to rest once and for all, so it must be done.

"Ah-ha!" he called out loudly to his nameless associates. "I remember now. Her name is Lady Jane Fair... er... burn, or something like that."

Once again, the men erupted in boisterous laughter, their voices so loud it seemed as though the very walls might shake from the sound. Tristan winced, the throbbing in his head growing unbearable. His skull felt as if it might split open from the pressure, each burst of laughter like a hammer against his temples. He couldn't endure any more of this raucous celebration. His one thought now was to get home and sleep off his drunken stupor, especially with the weight of tomorrow looming over him.

He glanced down at his wrinkled, disheveled clothes, grimacing as he tried in vain to smooth out the creased fabric. It was a poor effort. He needed to change before morning; it wouldn't do to walk into the church looking like a man who had just crawled out of a tavern. His mother, in particular, would be watching him closely, and there was no way she would tolerate her son acting—or appearing—like a fool in public. She had endured enough from him over the past few years. He had already caused her so much worry, and her health had suffered for it.

Tristan's chest tightened with guilt. He owed it to her to look the part tomorrow, to be clean, sober, and properly dressed for his wedding. After all the disappointment he had brought her, the least he could do was stand at the altar as the man she'd hoped he would become—not the wreck he feared he still was.

Tristan's mother had always held high hopes that he would marry into a respectable family, especially after the turmoil that had consumed his life for the past three years. He had nearly lost everything—his life, his memory, and his place in Society. For two long years, he had wandered through a haze of forgotten memories, unaware of who he truly was, until his brother, Trey, had finally found him and brought him home. It had been a miracle, but the cost was steep. The person he had been before had vanished, leaving behind fragments of a life he barely recognized.

And then there was Diana.

The woman he had once believed he loved—the woman he had thought held his heart—was no longer a part of his life. She was the last vestige of the man he had been before the accident, before the darkness of those lost years. Yet her absence still haunted him, a ghost of what might have been. Tristan knew he had to move on, to finally put her behind him. Marrying Lady Jane Fairbourne was the only way to close that chapter for good.

She represented everything his mother wanted for him: stability, respectability, and a chance to restore the family's tarnished reputation. And perhaps, if he allowed himself to believe it, marrying her would be exactly what he needed to heal. He could start fresh and bury the memory of Diana once and for all, leaving the past where it belonged—in the shadows.

Chapter Two

"MILORD?" THE TOOTHLESS bugger next to him grinned. "Do ye need me to stand with ye for yer big day t'morrow?"

Tristan waved a hand through the air. "As much as the idea sounds appealin', I must decline." He lifted his drink to his mouth and finished every last drop before slamming it on the table. "My friends," he called out, "I shall take my leave now. The next time I come ta this fine 'stablishment, I'll be a happily married man." Well, he wasn't too sure about the *happily* part, but he most certainly would be married.

As Tristan stumbled out of the tavern, the men inside erupted into cheers, shouting his name and raising their cups in a drunken salute. He waved them off with a halfhearted grin, his steps unsteady as he made his way toward where his coach should have been waiting. The evening's revelry still pulsed in his veins, but the weight of tomorrow lingered heavily on his shoulders.

Lady Jane Fairbourne—his fiancée—was beautiful, of course, and wealthy beyond question, thanks to the fortune left by her late husband. Yet this was a marriage Tristan didn't truly want. For years, she had been paraded before him, a glittering prospect in the eyes of his family and society. But now, after so many tedious introductions and forced encounters, he was weary of her presence, tired of the expectations everyone had placed upon them. He had grown numb to the idea of finding a woman who could stir his heart. The hope for love had faded long ago, replaced by the cold practicality of duty.

What he wanted now was simple: to marry and start a family. And if Lady Jane was the one to help him achieve that, then so be it. Most couples of the *ton* didn't marry for love anyway, so why should he be any different? He no longer had the energy to chase after elusive dreams of passion or connection.

His vision blurred as he stopped and leaned heavily against the stone wall of the tavern, blinking to clear his foggy mind. The street before him swayed slightly, and frustration mounted in his chest. Where in the bloody hell was his coach?

He glanced around, searching the darkened road for any sign of it, but all he saw were shadows and the vague outline of a few distant figures. He cursed under his breath, pressing his hand to his throbbing temple. It seemed the night wasn't quite done punishing him yet.

He scrubbed his hand over his face, trying to think of where his driver had parked. "Ah, there it is!"

Taking slow, deliberate steps, Tristan advanced toward the waiting coach, his boots crunching softly against the gravel path. The cool night wrapped around him like a cloak, its chill biting at the edges of his composure. His breath came out in sharp puffs, ghosting in the air before vanishing into the darkness. Frustration simmered beneath his calm façade, bubbling like a pot left too long on the stove. He clenched his jaw, not at the thought of the night's obligations, but at the woman who awaited him inside that carriage: Lady Fairbourne.

No one could deny she looked every inch the ideal wife—polished to perfection, with grace that drew eyes and whispers wherever she went. She knew how to command attention, how to wield charm like a finely sharpened blade. Men trembled under her gaze, caught between reverence and desire. But as dazzling as she was, Tristan couldn't shake the hollow truth that gnawed at him. Beneath the elegant exterior and effortless allure, she was not the woman he had ever imagined standing beside him, sharing the small joys of life or whispering promises in the quiet hours of dawn.

A memory bloomed, vivid and unwelcome, slipping into his mind like the scent of jasmine on the breeze—unavoidable, intoxicating. *Diana.* The woman who had once been his future. The vision was so clear it stole his breath: her auburn hair cascading in perfect ringlets, catching the light as if spun from molten copper. Her heart-shaped face, once the center of his universe, smiled at him in a memory so rich that it almost felt real. For a moment, the chill of the night faded, replaced by the warmth she used to bring him.

He stopped in his tracks, momentarily paralyzed by the ghost of her laughter ringing in his ears. The way she'd lit up when she saw him, as if he were the only man who had ever mattered, made his chest tighten with longing and regret. He shook his head, trying to banish the thought like dust from his coat. But Diana lingered, her presence as stubborn as the ache that had taken root deep within him. Her memory was a tether, tying him to a time when he had believed in love—when he had believed in her.

Stars had danced in her green eyes, eyes that once seemed capable of holding the secrets of the universe. When she smiled at him, he could feel the world tilt on its axis, as if everything had been set right in those fleeting moments. No other woman had ever looked at him like that, with a gaze so full of admiration it had made him feel invincible. In her presence, he had been more than a man. He had been someone worthy of love, of dreams, of a future brighter than he dared to imagine.

A groan slipped from his lips, raw and low, as if dragged from the depths of his soul. He forced himself to move, but with every step, her image clung to him, as persistent as the frost coating the air. He had been a fool then, caught in the whirlwind of hope and fantasy. Diana had swept him off his feet, and he had fallen willingly, letting himself believe that love could conquer the inevitable storms life would bring. For a brief, shining moment, he had let himself dream of forever.

But reality had been ruthless. The fall from that dream had left him bruised and broken, his illusions shattered like glass beneath a boot. He had learned the hard way that love wasn't a shield against betrayal. Women were not faithful, and love was little more than a beautifully crafted lie. The scars from that lesson remained, etched into him like carvings on stone. Even now, the details of what had gone wrong were blurred, obscured by the fog of his damaged memory. His accident had robbed him of certain truths—but the pain had never faded.

And now, as he walked toward a future built on duty rather than passion, the ghost of his past followed, whispering reminders of what he had once hoped for and lost. The shadows of love and betrayal intertwined, tightening their hold on him as the night grew colder.

Yet, even without the clarity of memory, Tristan's subconscious clung to one bitter, undeniable truth: Diana had hurt him—deeply. Like a knife wound left to fester, the pain of her betrayal still pulsed through him, raw and unhealed. Whatever she had done, whatever words had been spoken or actions taken, had carved into him with ruthless precision, leaving scars that memory loss couldn't erase. Though the details were lost in the fog of his fractured mind, the ache lingered, a persistent reminder that the trust he had once placed in love had been shattered. And with it, any belief that it could ever be restored.

When he had first met Diana, she had been a storm—beautiful and wild, capable of overwhelming him with her intensity. He had been captivated, like a moth drawn too close to the flame. He had sworn the sun itself rose and set with her, blind to anything beyond the brilliance she radiated. Their stolen kisses, breathless and forbidden, had spiraled into something far more dangerous, something neither of them had been prepared for. In those stolen moments, hidden from the eyes of the world, he had felt untethered and free, like a man allowed, for the first time, to dream without limits.

But dreams have a way of curdling into nightmares. No matter how hard he tried to bury those memories beneath the weight of duty and cynicism, they clung to him like a ghost's whisper, haunting him in the stillness of night. He could still feel the warmth of her touch, hear the faint laugh she had when she teased him, and recall the way her lips had pressed against his with a mixture of fire and tenderness. Those echoes were relentless, slipping into his thoughts when he least expected them, dragging him back to a time when love had felt like salvation, not a curse.

And then fate, with its cruel sense of humor, had pulled him back into her orbit. Lord Hollingsworth—her husband—had been found dead, and in the blink of an eye, Tristan had gone from a man trying to outrun his past to one trapped in its unrelenting grasp. The accusations had struck him like a physical blow, stealing the air from his lungs.

He could still hear the hushed murmurs in the corridors, the venomous whispers of scandal as his name was tied to the crime. He hadn't killed Hollingsworth—he knew that much—but proving it to the rest of the world was a different battle entirely.

Bitterness coiled like a snake in his chest as he shook his head, trying to force down the surge of emotions clawing their way to the surface. His jaw tightened, the muscles working as he fought against the urge to lash out at the injustice of it all. What had started as a whirlwind love affair had turned into a noose tightening around his neck. Whether by accident or design, Diana had dragged him back into the storm of her life, and now he wasn't sure if anyone would believe the truth. He wasn't sure if *he* even believed it anymore.

His grip on reality, much like his memories, was slipping. And the more he tried to escape, the tighter the past seemed to hold on, suffocating him.

Well… time to pay the piper. Tomorrow he would marry Lady Fairbourne, and even if it killed him, he *would* put Diana's memory behind him.

Tristan staggered toward the coach, his vision swimming as the world around him tilted slightly off balance. He grasped the door handle with a grip that was both desperate and clumsy, yanking it open and hauling himself inside with more force than grace. His shoulder collided with the interior wall, and he let out a breathless grunt as he half fell onto the cushioned seat. The cold night air clung to his skin, but inside the coach, warmth enveloped him, wrapping him like a heavy blanket. Too heavy. Stifling.

He leaned back against the seat, exhaling sharply, his legs still trembling beneath him. Perhaps he should have waited for his driver to offer a steadying hand, but patience had abandoned him hours ago, somewhere between his last drink and the moment he stumbled into the shadows of the evening. His muscles burned with the effort of standing, and now that he was seated, his body sagged in relief, as though surrendering to exhaustion.

A sound tickled at the edges of his awareness—a faint, rhythmic scratching, like metal scraping against metal. It came from the far side of the coach door, just out of sight. Tristan frowned, squinting into the dim glow of the carriage lantern, but the alcohol dulling his senses kept curiosity at bay. He shrugged it off with a lazy breath, sinking further into the seat. Whatever it was, it didn't matter. His driver could handle it. Right now, all he cared about was making it home without passing out in the middle of the street.

The coach jerked forward with a sudden jolt, and Tristan's body lurched with it, nearly pitching him onto the floor. He cursed, muttering something incoherent, and braced himself against the seat with one hand while planting his feet firmly on the floor. The wheels rattled against the cobblestones, the familiar rhythm of travel slowly returning. He closed his eyes, leaning his head back, the gentle swaying of the coach working against him like a lullaby he couldn't resist.

The scratching sound faded into the hum of the night, forgotten as the warmth of the coach lulled him into a foggy sense of comfort. His mind drifted, not quite asleep but far from awake, teetering on the edge of oblivion. He tried to resist it, knowing that sleep in this state would only make tomorrow's wedding preparations all the more unbearable. But the weight of his eyelids was merciless, pulling him down despite his weak attempts to stay alert.

His thoughts wandered toward home, toward the soft mattress waiting for him—the only salvation he could think of to shake off tonight's indulgence. He could already imagine the plush pillow beneath his head, the heavy quilt cocooning him, shutting out the rest of the world.

But just as he was about to succumb to the darkness, the coach hit a bump in the road that sent him lurching upright, the jarring sensation shattering the fragile peace he'd found. He blinked rapidly, disoriented, his heart thudding against his ribs as he tried to regain his bearings. The ride had turned rougher, the wheels jostling and rattling as though the cobblestones had suddenly given way to uneven terrain.

Tristan sat up straighter, running a hand through his disheveled hair. His brow furrowed as he peered out the small window, but the landscape beyond was cloaked in shadow, offering no clues. He rubbed his face, trying to clear the fog from his mind. The coach should have been on the familiar, well-maintained streets leading back to his estate. So why did it feel as though they were traversing a dirt path riddled with potholes?

Had the driver taken a different route? Perhaps to avoid a roadblock? He frowned, the unease in his chest spreading like a slow-burning fire. Something wasn't right. The ride was far too bumpy, far too erratic. He tapped his fingers restlessly against his thigh as he strained to hear any noises from outside—the sound of the horses' hooves, the creak of the wheels—but all he heard was the rhythmic clatter of the coach's interior shaking with each jolt.

He leaned toward the window, pressing his forehead against the cool glass, his breath fogging the surface. Outside, the shadows shifted, but he couldn't make out any landmarks. The realization struck him like a splash of cold water—he had no idea where they were.

Growing uneasy, Tristan reached for the curtain and yanked it back, his fingers trembling slightly as he leaned closer to the window. The cool glass fogged under his breath as he blinked against the brightness of the full moon hanging high in the sky, casting its silver glow over the countryside. The earlier storm had passed, leaving behind a pristine night, but the serene beauty of the landscape did little to soothe the panic rising within him.

This wasn't the road home. And he had no clue where he was.

Chapter Three

TRISTAN'S PULSE QUICKENED, the dull thud of his heartbeat echoing in his ears. The familiar cobbled streets of the city had been replaced by a narrow dirt road cutting through open fields. The moonlight painted long, eerie shadows across the ground, and the trees that lined the path swayed gently in the night breeze, their branches resembling skeletal fingers reaching for the sky. With each passing second, Tristan's dread deepened, knotting tighter in his gut.

He squinted through the window, desperately searching for some sign that he was mistaken, that this was merely a detour. But the truth was undeniable—they had left the city behind entirely. The moonlit fields stretched endlessly, broken only by the occasional silhouette of a barn or a distant tree line. There was no bustling city noise, no distant glow of lanterns, no sense of home. Only the lonely hum of the countryside and the steady rhythm of the wheels grinding over uneven terrain.

"No," he whispered, shaking his head as if the motion alone could dispel the nightmare unraveling before him. His alcohol-addled mind fought to make sense of it, but clarity came crashing down in a wave of horror—they were heading in the wrong direction. Far from home. Far from safety.

Panic gave way to anger, and Tristan's jaw tightened as he pounded his fist against the roof of the coach. "Dudley!" His voice cut through the night like a whip, sharp and demanding. "Where are we going?" His breath hitched as he waited, straining to hear the familiar voice of his driver offering some explanation. But all he heard was the crack of the reins and the pounding of the horses' hooves—faster now, more urgent.

The coach suddenly surged forward, throwing him off balance. He slid off the seat and hit the floor hard, a curse tumbling from his lips as the impact jarred his senses. Gritting his teeth, he scrambled back up, gripping the edge of the seat for support. The vehicle swayed violently, nearly tossing him again, so he dug his fingers into the fabric of the seat.

What was Dudley doing? Why weren't they slowing down?

Determined to put an end to this madness, Tristan lunged toward the door and grabbed the handle, yanking it with every ounce of strength he could muster. The leather of his gloves squeaked against the cold metal as he pulled harder, ready to confront Dudley and demand answers. But the door didn't budge.

His breath came in ragged gasps as he tried again, shaking the handle, twisting and pulling. Panic swelled like a rising tide, drowning his initial anger. This wasn't a stuck latch—something was holding the door shut. His mind raced, frantically searching for an explanation, until a chilling sound reached his ears.

A faint, metallic rattle. Like chains brushing against each other.

His breath hitched, and he froze for a moment, the sound cutting through him like a dagger. Slowly, he leaned closer, listening. The noise was unmistakable—metal links shifting with the swaying motion of the coach. His fingers trembled as he tried the handle one last time, but it was no use.

The door had been chained shut.

A cold shiver crawled down his spine, settling deep in his bones. His breath quickened as dread wrapped around him, squeezing tighter with every passing second. This wasn't an accident. Someone had locked him in here, and whoever it was, they had no intention of letting him out.

Tristan's mind raced as he tried to think, to form a plan, but the fog of alcohol clouding his thoughts made it nearly impossible to focus. His gaze darted around the dark interior of the coach, searching for anything he could use—a weapon, an escape route, anything that could free him from this trap. But the space was suffocatingly small, and every second that ticked by seemed to drive the walls closer, trapping him like prey.

He pressed his palms against the window, his breath fogging the glass as he tried to peer outside. The horses galloped wildly, their hooves tearing up the dirt road, and the shadow of the driver's silhouette loomed faintly at the front of the coach. But there was no sign of anyone else. No sign of an accomplice. Just the eerie glow of the moon and the endless expanse of countryside rushing by.

Tristan's throat tightened as he realized how isolated they were. Even if he managed to force the door open, where would he go? The fields stretched endlessly in every direction, and the coach was moving too fast to jump without risking serious injury. But staying inside wasn't an option either. He had to act, and fast.

He pounded his fist against the door, the thudding noise reverberating through the cramped space. "Dudley!" he shouted again, his voice laced with desperation. "Stop the coach!" But there was no response. The horses didn't slow. The chains didn't loosen.

Sweat beaded on his brow as he leaned back against the seat, his mind spinning with questions. Who had done this? And why? His instincts told him this wasn't just a random act of sabotage— this was deliberate. Someone had planned this, and whoever it was, they had made sure Tristan wouldn't escape easily.

But Tristan Worthington had survived worse. If they thought chaining him inside a coach would break him, they were sorely mistaken. His fingers curled into fists as determination ignited within him, burning away the last remnants of drunken stupor.

He wasn't going down without a fight.

Tristan pounded again. "Hear me now. If you do not stop this vehicle immediately, I will have you thrown in prison for kidnapping."

He waited for Dudley to comply, but his wish was not granted.

This couldn't be happening. Worry tightened around his chest, constricting his breath as fear surged through him. His mind raced with possibilities. Would this disrupt the wedding tomorrow? Part of him, admittedly, wished for an excuse to delay it, but the thought of causing more worry for his mother tightened the knot of dread in his stomach.

He realized he had no other choice but to sit back and wait, helpless to whatever fate awaited him. Was this a kidnapping? Or perhaps the coach had spiraled out of control without the driver at the helm? But that thought didn't hold. If something had happened to the driver, the door wouldn't have been chained shut. No, Tristan was sure of it now: he was being kidnapped.

What felt like hours passed, though his sense of time was warped by the pounding of his head and the growing unease. The coach continued its relentless pace until, with a sudden jolt, it stopped. Tristan quickly glanced out the window, his heart pounding harder.

They had stopped deep within a forest, surrounded by towering trees that blocked out much of the moonlight. The dense foliage made it difficult to discern exactly where they were, but nestled among the shadows stood a small two-story cottage. It looked secluded, isolated, the perfect place to remain hidden from the world. The place was completely unfamiliar to him, as were the surroundings. For a fleeting moment, he imagined an elderly couple living here, tucked away in a private retreat far from Society's watchful eyes.

But something told him this was no cozy homecoming. The stillness around the cottage felt unsettling, the air thick with tension. Tristan's pulse quickened as he waited for whatever—or whoever—was about to come next.

The door rattled, the unmistakable clink of chains sending a chill down Tristan's spine. His heart rate increased as the door creaked open, and before he could utter a word, the sharp tip of a saber slid through the opening, gleaming in the faint light.

He froze, his breath catching in his throat. Every instinct screamed at him to react, but the sudden presence of the weapon held him still, the cold steel mere inches from his chest. Whoever held that blade had the upper hand, and Tristan knew better than to provoke them without understanding the situation.

"Get out," a voice commanded from the shadows outside the coach, low and unfamiliar. The figure holding the saber remained hidden from view, but the tone left no room for argument.

Tristan swallowed hard, carefully raising his hands in a gesture of submission. He moved slowly, his muscles tense, sliding toward the edge of the seat. His mind raced, searching for an explanation, a plan—anything—but all he could do was comply for now. As he stepped down from the carriage, his gaze darted toward the mysterious figure standing just beyond the door.

This was no accident, no out-of-control coach. He was caught in something far darker, and escape, for the moment, seemed impossible.

"Mark my words, my lord, one wrong move and I'll slice this blade clean through you."

A figure cloaked in a hooded black cape stood in the doorway, their face concealed in deep shadows. Tristan blinked, momentarily taken aback by the strangeness of it all. The person before him had spoken with a voice that seemed too young for someone so threatening.

Despite the menacing situation, Tristan couldn't shake the suspicion that his captor might not be a full-grown man at all. The tone—sharp, commanding—lacked the depth and weight of a seasoned adult. Instead, it carried the unmistakable timbre of a lad on the cusp of manhood, just shy of full maturity.

Tristan's mind whirled. Was he really being held at saber-point by a mere boy? It seemed absurd, yet here he stood, the cold tip of the weapon inches away, his freedom slipping through his fingers. He studied the cloaked figure, searching for any other clues, but the hood obscured any defining features.

"What is this about?" Tristan asked, his voice measured but laced with tension. He needed answers, and fast. "You've gone to a lot of trouble. What do you want?"

The figure remained silent for a moment, the blade steady, before finally responding, the young voice carrying an unsettling authority. "All in good time. For now, follow me—quietly."

Tristan's misgivings deepened. Whoever this was, they were clearly skilled enough to wield fear and authority, despite their youth. Resigned to his fate for the moment, he nodded. The figure motioned toward the dimly lit path leading to the isolated cottage.

"I'll cooperate," Tristan replied.

His captor wore the attire of a driver, except the clothes didn't fit him as well. Even the hat hung low on his forehead, and the brim cast shadows over the occupant's thin face. Tristan was certain he could overpower this one—yet his captor held a saber in one hand and a pistol in the other.

A gust of wind blew from behind, pushing Tristan forward. Drops of rain fell on him. When had the storm moved in?

"I assure you, my lord, I'm well-schooled in the use of a saber and pistol. One wrong move and it will be your last," his captor said loudly above the howling wind.

Tristan frowned. The odds of escaping were not in his favor. "I believe you." And he did. The other man's hands didn't tremble like someone who had never done this before. There was confidence in the way he spoke and in his movements.

The lad motioned toward the cottage as he tried to keep his hat from blowing off his head. "Enter."

Tristan held his hands up in surrender as he walked. He wanted to make the other person aware that he was unarmed and was no threat. "Can you at least tell me why you have taken me? What have I done?"

"You shall know when I want you to know, and not a moment sooner."

Tristan's mind raced, trying to piece together why anyone would want to kidnap him. He had lived a mostly unremarkable life, aside from his ill-fated connection to Lord Hollingsworth, who was now dead. He certainly hadn't made enough enemies to warrant such an elaborate scheme. He wasn't like his brother, Trey, who had left a trail of broken hearts and scandal in his wake. Tristan's only notable downfall, as of late, was his growing reputation as a drunk.

As Tristan stepped inside the small cottage, the door creaking shut behind him, he swept his gaze across the room, taking in every detail with practiced precision. The interior was modest but carried the unmistakable warmth of a lived-in space. Faded, patterned rugs overlapped across the wooden floor, softening the sound of his boots as he moved forward. The scent of burning wood mingled with the faint tang of herbs, as though someone had recently brewed tea that still lingered in the air.

A few lamps were scattered strategically around the room, their flames flickering lazily and casting golden halos of light onto the walls. Shadows danced across the wooden beams of the ceiling, creating an almost hypnotic rhythm as the light shifted with the crackling fire in the hearth. The fire was robust, its glow casting a comforting warmth that Tristan could feel even from where he stood. Above the mantel, a few simple trinkets sat—a wooden clock ticking quietly, a ceramic vase filled with dried lavender, and a stack of worn books leaning precariously against one another.

The furniture was functional yet inviting: a well-loved armchair draped with a knitted blanket, its fabric worn smooth in places from years of use, and a small wooden table bearing the faint rings of long-forgotten teacups. The walls were lined with shelves containing mismatched books, jars of dried herbs, and small knickknacks that suggested someone had taken time to make this place a home. It wasn't opulent or grand, but it had an understated charm, as though the space itself breathed familiarity and routine.

A flicker of hope sparked within Tristan as he took it all in. This wasn't the cold, barren hideout of a killer plotting his demise. No, this place carried the marks of someone who lived here day after day, tending the fire, sipping tea, and reading by lamplight. That detail, however small, made his pulse steady for the first time since the chains had rattled on the coach door. If his captors intended to kill him, surely they wouldn't have brought him to a place like this. Or so he desperately hoped. His instincts had failed him before—but tonight, he prayed they wouldn't.

However, any comfort he took from the cottage's atmosphere was tempered by the cold tip of the saber pressing against his back, reminding him that he wasn't in control. His breath hitched as the weapon prodded him toward a single wooden chair positioned in the middle of the room. Every nerve in his body screamed to resist, to fight back, but the blade against his spine kept him compliant.

He reached the chair, and, without a word, the figure behind him gave a final nudge with the saber. Reluctantly, Tristan lowered himself into the seat, still scanning the room for any sign of who might be behind this strange ordeal.

"Now what?" he asked, his voice betraying more frustration than fear.

The hooded figure stepped around him, still keeping their face obscured. "You'll find out soon enough," they said, their young voice carrying an unsettling calm.

The lad walked behind him, tied his hands and legs with a rope before standing again, and then moved in front of Tristan.

He arched an eyebrow. "Will you now tell me why I'm here?" He struggled with the ties, impressed with how well his captor—as small in stature as the man was—could bind so tight. "As you can see, I'm not a threat any longer."

The lad kept his head down, intentionally avoiding Tristan's attempts to get a better look. The cloak's hood cast a shadow over his face, further obscuring his features, and he stayed just far enough away to prevent any real recognition. Even so, Tristan could feel the weight of the boy's gaze, as if he were being studied, assessed for some unknown purpose.

Frustration gnawed at him. Under normal circumstances, Tristan considered himself a patient man, but his current situation had shredded any calm he might have had. He clenched his fists in his lap, fighting the urge to shout, to demand answers. This strange, drawn-out silence was testing his limits.

Finally, unable to hold back any longer, Tristan growled. "Enough of this. Who are you? What do you want from me?"

The hooded figure remained quiet for a moment, the tension in the room thickening. Then, slowly, the lad shifted, still keeping his face hidden, and spoke, his voice tinged with amusement. "Patience, Lord Worthington. You'll have your answers soon. But for now, it's not about what *I* want—it's about what *you* deserve."

The cryptic words sent a chill down Tristan's spine. Deserve? What had he done to deserve being kidnapped and held at sword-point? The realization dawned that this was far more personal than he had originally thought.

His captor folded his arms. "You, *my lord*, are in my control. I'm going to ruin you completely! The same way you ruined a certain woman three years ago."

Chapter Four

TRISTAN GLARED AT his captor, not believing this *person* had the audacity to kidnap him before his wedding and threaten him.

"Did you not hear me?" the lad demanded. "You are in my control now! What have you to say to that?"

Nodding, Tristan cocked his head. "I heard you. Pray, tell me how you plan on ruining me as you have threatened? Because I can assure you, I did not ruin any woman three years ago." There could only be one woman that could come close to being *ruined*. Diana. Yet he had never ruined her. Lord Hollingsworth had!

As the figure before him began to shed the layers of disguise, Tristan widened his eyes. His captor straightened, shedding the driver's jacket, revealing the unmistakable silhouette of a woman beneath. The bulk that had been gathered around her middle fell away as she released the tie, and the fabric of her dress fell down, swishing around her legs. With a final, deliberate movement, she removed the driver's hat, and a cascade of brown hair spilled over her shoulders.

Tristan blinked in disbelief, his mind struggling to catch up with the revelation. This wasn't the boy he had thought was holding him captive—it was a woman. And not just any woman, but one he didn't recognize.

He studied her face, but no flicker of recognition came. Her blue eyes, however, were unmistakable in their intensity, sharp and filled with an anger that made his skin prickle. Those eyes were shooting invisible daggers at him, and despite the confusion swirling inside him, he couldn't deny the sense of danger she exuded.

For a fleeting moment, he wondered if she had mistaken him for Trey, who had once led a scandalous life as a notorious rogue before settling down. Trey had surely broken enough hearts in his time. But the victorious grin curling at the corners of her full lips suggested she knew exactly who she had, and it wasn't Trey.

Tristan swallowed, his voice hoarse with bewilderment. "I— I've never seen you before. What is this? What do you want with me?"

The woman took a step forward, folding her arms over her chest, her smile widening as if she relished his confusion. "Oh, you've seen me, Lord Worthington," she said, her voice low and dangerous. "Perhaps not like this, but trust me, you've played your part in my story."

Her words sent a shiver down his spine, and a cold realization began to settle in his gut. Whoever this woman was, she was here for revenge—and it was deeply, disturbingly personal.

"I finally have in my presence the *honorable* Lord Tristan Worthington."

Inwardly he groaned. So, the idea of mistaken identity flew out the window. "Yes, you do. Now will you be so kind as to tell me your name?"

"Tabitha Paget."

"And now will you tell me how you know me, and why in heaven's name you thought it important to kidnap me?"

"I work for someone who hates you. You ruined her life, and now it's time to ruin yours."

Her? "Pray tell, who is this person you speak of? Are you certain I know her at all?"

She laughed. "Oh, you know her, I assure you."

A loud gasp pierced the tense silence, and before he could

fully register what was happening, another figure appeared in the doorway. She was dressed in a nightgown and white wrapper, her auburn hair cascading over her shoulders like flames. Her hand flew to her mouth, eyes wide with shock—eyes that struck him with an unsettling familiarity.

For a moment, Tristan could only stare, his breath catching in his throat. He recognized those eyes, the same eyes that had once gazed at him with admiration and affection. His heart faltered as realization dawned on him.

"Diana," he breathed, his voice barely above a whisper.

The woman standing in the doorway was none other than the woman he had once loved so deeply, the woman whose memory had haunted him for years. Her face was paler than he remembered, and her expression was a mixture of disbelief and horror. But what was she doing here, in this remote cottage, and why had she gasped so violently?

Tristan turned his gaze back to the first woman, the one who had just revealed herself. The triumphant grin on her lips told him that whatever was happening here, it was all connected. Somehow, these two women—Diana and the one filled with burning anger—were part of the same story.

The pieces of the puzzle began to click together, and Tristan felt a cold sense of dread settle over him. He was trapped in a web far more complicated than he had ever imagined, and it seemed the past he thought he had buried was about to resurface in the most dangerous way possible.

"Lord T—T—Tristan?"

Although he had seen her from a distance at some of Society's functions, he hadn't tried to even look at her during those times. But now… In a rush, all the memories he'd tried to forget three years ago came back to him. *The ball… the infatuation… the greenhouse. And that incredible, unforgettable kiss.*

He'd tried to forget how lovely Diana had been when he first met her, but it was nearly impossible. Now she was a luscious beauty. Shaking his head, he pushed away the thought. Thinking of her this way was *not* healthy. Something in his forgotten memory told him not to trust her.

Slowly, her gaze swept over every inch of him, taking in the sight of him bound to the chair, vulnerable and at her mercy. Tristan's breath hitched as their eyes locked in the heavy silence. It was as though time had collapsed in on itself, and for a moment, he forgot everything—forgot why he was here, forgot the chains that bound him, forgot even the bitter years that had passed between them. All he could remember was how she had once made him feel. How, three years ago, a single glance from her had turned his world upside down, reducing his mind to mush. She had bewitched him then, made him believe he was in love—helplessly, completely.

But not now. Not anymore.

He swallowed hard, trying to harden his resolve, to cling to the anger and betrayal he had nursed for so long. This was his chance—his moment to confront her, to finally dredge up the past and cast her out of his thoughts for good. He needed to tear down the illusions he had built around her, the fantasies that had lingered in his heart despite everything. Confronting Diana might be the only way to banish her ghost from his mind forever.

Yet the reality of it—the sight of her standing there, a mixture of pain and defiance in her eyes—shook him. The thought that she had gone to such great lengths to kidnap him, to drag him to this remote place, made his chest tighten. She was now his captor, a role he never could have imagined for her. According to her maid, she despised him, hated him with a passion so fierce it had driven her to this.

But as he looked at her now, with all the bitterness and heartbreak swirling between them, he couldn't help but wonder—was hate really all that remained? Or was there something more buried beneath the weight of their past, something neither of them could truly let go?

"Tabitha? What is he doing here?" Diana asked softly.

"Hmm, well, my lady, I took the coach into town to buy the

items you requested dressed as your driver, and when I saw *him*, and heard he was marrying Lady Jane Fairbourne tomorrow, I knew I must do something quickly."

The servant was no longer brave and superior as she'd been a moment ago. Now she acted like most maids should in front of their employer.

Diana groaned. "Oh, Tabitha, what have you done? You can go to prison for kidnapping a lord. We can *both* go to prison for this." She covered her face with her hands as her fingers rubbed circles on her temple.

"No, my lady." Tabitha rushed to Diana's side and placed her palm on her shoulder. "It will be his word against ours. Nobody saw, I assure you."

"Lady Hollingsworth," Tristan said once he found his voice. "What a surprise to see you—and in your nightclothes, no less."

Diana's hands dropped to her side as her perplexed eyes locked on his. "I'm quite certain it is a surprise, my lord, considering you probably never expected to see me again."

"I must admit, I hadn't." He flicked his gaze over the length of her. "Especially under such circumstances. Tell me, Lady Hollingsworth, why did you instruct your maid to kidnap me?"

"I didn't know of her plans," she said coolly.

He moved his focus back to the servant, his mind scrambling for anything that might entice her to release him. "Do you plan to hold me for ransom? I can tell you that my mother has a bad heart. If I am not at the church to wed Lady Fairbourne tomorrow, my mother's heart will fail. If she dies as a result of this wicked deed, you won't see a penny of my money. I beg you, for my mother's sake, please return me to the church posthaste. If you release me now, I promise not to tell the magistrate of the kidnapping."

"Ridiculous," Tabitha shouted. "The storm has grown worse since our arrival, and even if we left at first light, it would be impossible to return you in time. By then your *loving* fiancée's heart will be shattered." Anger sparked in the maid's eyes.

He seethed, finally hearing the rain pelt against the roof. No matter how bad the storm, he needed to leave tonight. "How much do you want?"

"My lord?" Tabitha asked with an arched eyebrow.

"Name your price. How much do I need to pay you to let me go?"

"I don't care about your money, my lord. If you must know, I don't plan on returning you at all." She moved in front of him and stopped. "Lady Hollingsworth and I don't want one shilling from you. We want revenge! I want to hurt you in the same manner you have hurt my mistress."

Tristan's attention jumped back to Diana, but she didn't make a move to stop her maid. He looked back to Tabitha. "You really want revenge? Are you planning to push Lady Fairbourne over the cliff, then? Pray, my dear, take me to the cliffs and shove me over instead. Perhaps you'll succeed where Lord Hollingsworth failed."

ANGER, HURT, BETRAYAL, and confusion churned within Diana, twisting her heart into a painful knot. Tristan's words echoed in her ears—*shoved over the cliffs?*—each syllable landing like a blow. What was he talking about?

Her mind raced, but her body remained frozen, rooted in place by the weight of the situation spiraling out of control. She should act. She *had* to act. Scolding Tabitha for her role in this mess was high on her list, but right now, all she could do was stare, her breath hitching as Tristan and the maid exchanged venomous words.

Diana's gaze flitted between them, her pulse quickening with every accusation that filled the air like sparks from a fire. What was she supposed to do? Tristan wasn't just anyone—he was the brother of a duke, and if he took his grievances to the magistrate, there would be no escaping the consequences. Both she and Tabitha would be dragged to Newgate in chains, accused of kidnapping a man whose name carried too much weight for them to evade justice.

Think, Diana. Think. She needed a plan, an excuse, a way to smooth over this disaster before it imploded completely. But her mind betrayed her, sluggish and clouded by emotions she couldn't suppress. Seeing him this close—seeing him vulnerable, angry, and wounded—was her undoing. The sharp planes of his face, the intensity in his eyes, the tension radiating from his posture—it all overwhelmed her.

Her chest rose and fell as she struggled to breathe evenly, to regain control, but her thoughts remained scattered, like autumn leaves in a gust of wind. The man she had once loved was here, mere steps away, but this wasn't the reunion she had ever imagined. Instead of reconciliation, there was chaos. Instead of understanding, there was fury. And she had no idea how to fix it.

"My lord," Tabitha continued, "you are making no sense at all. This *is* about revenge, but we will see it done *our* way."

"You cannot be serious," Tristan grumbled.

Tabitha laughed bitterly. "I am very serious, my lord. Men like you don't deserve happiness when you take it from others."

"Pray, what do you think to accomplish by kidnapping me?"

A grin stole across the maid's mouth. "I plan to ruin you just as you have ruined Lady Hollingsworth."

"Kidnapping is going to ruin my reputation?" He barked out a laugh. "I think you have figured this all wrong."

"Actually, I have planned this out perfectly," Tabitha snapped. "You see, your servants know you were hesitant about the upcoming marriage to Lady Fairbourne. Even the men you were drinking with at the tavern knew you really didn't want to get married. Because of that, no one will doubt that you fled your own wedding."

"What about my driver? Wouldn't he be able to confirm that someone else took his place?"

Tabitha shook her head. "Not when *you* were the one who climbed in the wrong vehicle."

Groaning, Tristan closed his eyes.

Diana gasped and stared at her maid. "Lord Tristan was *that* drunk?"

Laughing, Tabitha nodded. "Indeed, he was, my lady. When I saw him stumble out of the tavern and go to the wrong coach, I knew fate was lending me a hand." Her grin widened. "And earlier, before that happened, I snuck into his townhouse and left missives on his desk that will lead his family to discover the purpose for his absence."

She turned her focus back on Tristan, whose glare was now aimed at Tabitha. "The missive is from a woman you've been meeting secretly for the past few months." She shrugged. "What other conclusion could they come to except you ran out on your own wedding? The last I heard, a gentleman's reputation becomes tarnished by doing this."

"Tabitha?" Diana asked in a harsh voice. "I thought you told me you were going into town for some supplies."

A blush stole across the maid's face. "Well, to be honest, my main goal was to set up Lord Tristan and kidnap him. Can I help it if fate lent me a helping hand?"

Diana blew out an agitated breath as doom began to close around her. She needed to think of a way out of this mess, and soon! "But it doesn't hide the fact that what you did was wrong, and you could suffer greatly for this mistake."

"Forgive me, my lady. I was only trying to get back at him. I only had your best interests in mind."

Tristan's face hardened and anger darkened his blue eyes. "I see you have thought long and hard about your revenge. And Lady Hollingsworth, I commend you for finding such a loyal servant."

"Indeed, my lord. It wasn't until now that I realized what a godsend Tabitha is to me."

Diana's breath hitched as she stepped closer, daring to brush the lock of dark hair falling across Tristan's forehead with her trembling fingers. The moment her skin met the soft strands, memories crashed over her, drowning her in a tide of emotions she'd tried so hard to bury. It felt as if no time had passed, as if it were just yesterday that his arms had encircled her, holding her in a way that had made her believe the world could fall away, and they would still be safe together.

Back then, she had been so young, so naïve—so utterly captivated by him. She had believed in dreams, in whispered promises beneath the moonlight, in the magic of forever. But forever hadn't lasted, and the pain of that truth had shaped her into someone harder, someone who knew better than to believe in fairytales. Or so she thought.

But now, with her fingers brushing against him, her heart betrayed her. It fluttered wildly, refusing to obey the logic she had lived by for so long. She hated him. She had to hate him. The pain of their past—the betrayal, the heartbreak—was proof enough. And yet, in this fragile moment, with his warmth so close, the line between love and hate blurred, leaving her suspended in a dizzying limbo.

Her hand trembled as she pulled it away, her chest tightening with the confusion that swirled within her. How could he still have this effect on her after everything he'd done? After everything *she* had done? The answer eluded her, but one thing was certain: even now, standing on opposite sides of a battlefield they had created together, Tristan could still make her feel alive. And she hated that most of all.

"I've spent three long and miserable years wishing things were different," she confessed, "and in all that time, I had such wicked thoughts of how I could humiliate you as you have humiliated me."

The longer she toyed with his hair, the more the color in his eyes lightened, and the creases around his mouth relaxed. Could he feel the spark that had always happened between them when they touched? She hoped not.

"I heard you had left for Paris right after you and Ludlow were married," he said in a softer tone.

She withdrew her hand and stepped back. "I did, but just as I'd gotten used to the routine of having a life once again, something always happened to ruin it. There was always someone who'd heard about the duel. Ludlow seemed to blossom because of what happened, but I wilted like a poisoned flower."

He glanced around the room. "So where are we now? Who lives here?"

"This used to be my maternal grandmother's house. She died three months past. A fortnight ago, I decided to come here and stay for a while. Ludlow's murder was suffocating me, especially all the rumors."

"I heard you were a suspect," he said matter-of-factly.

She chuckled, but humor was the farthest thing from her mind. "And so are you. For that matter, half of the men he played cards with are suspects, as well as most the women he had affairs with."

He shrugged. "So, you live out here alone?"

"Don't sound so surprised. I've been alone since you publicly proclaimed to win my hand in marriage by dueling with Ludlow, and then ran away from the duel that morning."

"Ran away from the duel? No, Diana, you cannot believe that. Hollingsworth—"

"Lord Tristan, please say no more. I don't want to hear your lies." Pain clenched her heart—a feeling she was accustomed to. She should also correct him for being so forward with her name, but she enjoyed the way it sounded on his lips. She recalled when he'd used it before. *Diana, I want to hold you so badly it's killing me... Diana, your lips are like wine—so pleasing to taste...*

"Diana, please, you must listen. I don't know what—"

She stuffed a rag into his mouth, muffling the words. "Gag him, Tabitha."

"With pleasure, my lady."

Diana took a deep breath, trying to remove her traitorous thoughts. Her head felt ready to explode, and she rubbed her temples again. Tabitha fidgeted with the rag, but was finally able to secure it around his mouth.

What am I going to do now? Diana needed a clear head to think logically, because obviously Tabitha had not thought this out before she acted. Until Diana could figure out a rational plan, Tristan would just have to remain tied to the chair.

"I'm tired and I want to return to my room." Diana walked around him and tested the ropes on his arms and legs. "You shall be fine right here. I suggest you get some rest, too." Peeking over her shoulder at the maid, she motioned with her hand. "Come, Tabitha. Let us leave him to wallow in his pitiful state right now. Perhaps the morning will be brighter for all of us."

Tabitha kept the victorious grin on her face as she walked out. Before Diana could quit the room, she took one more look at Tristan. His eyes watched her as a frown deepened his expression. Being away from him for three years hadn't been long enough, because his sad, helpless eyes still tugged at her heart.

Chapter Five

Bath, England, three years earlier

"Your Grace." Miss Diana Baldwin bobbed a curtsy to the Dowager Duchess of Kenbridge—the hostess of the party who wandered through the flower garden, greeting her guests. The older woman was such a sweet lady, and Diana wished all women of the *ton* followed the dowager's example.

Beside Diana, her mother, Baroness Baldwin, sighed as they strolled along the pebbled path. "Oh, my sweet daughter. It is my wish that someday you will be as grand as the dowager."

She looked at her mother. The older woman's expression was marred with lines of worry. "Mother, I have been out for three Seasons. I highly doubt I'll catch the eye of a duke. I would just like to catch some man's eye before I become a spinster."

"I know, dear." Her mother patted Diana's arm. "I do think this is the year you will get an offer. Your father has been very selective in the past, but now he's finally decided that we need to get you married this year."

"I fear Father has waited too long. I don't think any man will want me now, especially not a duke."

"A mother can dream, can't she?"

Chuckling, Diana shook her head. She wasn't really discouraging her mother's dream, she just knew the older woman's expectations were set too high. "I shall be satisfied married to a baron, but what would please me more is being married for love."

"Oh, my dearest daughter." Her mother stopped and faced Diana. "Most of us grow to love our husbands after we've been married a few years."

This was one of those *rules* Diana didn't understand. Why was it acceptable to marry a complete stranger? Most of Society lived this way, but one of her childhood friends had parents who were truly in love. Inwardly, she sighed. That was the kind of marriage she wanted.

She and her mother resumed their stroll through the dowager's flower gardens, but Diana's mind wasn't on the lovely roses. Instead, she silently questioned why her father had been so picky. Every year since she'd come out, she'd had a few men ask her father for her hand in marriage. Her father always found some reason to turn them down. She prayed her mother was correct and that this year would finally be the year she married.

"Oh, look. There is Lady Hastings," her mother, Esther, exclaimed. "My dear, do you mind if I go speak with her?"

Diana glanced toward Lady Hastings and her ill-mannered daughter, Lady Jane. She had never liked the girl who was out for her first Season. As an earl's daughter, that girl had always worn her father's title as her own.

"That's fine, Mother. I want to rest a spell under the shade of this tree." She fanned her face. "I fear the sun is terribly hot today."

"I shan't be gone long." Esther hurried to the other women.

Diana perched on the bench under the wide tree and peered out across the yard. The dowager's weekend party guests were still arriving. Several men who didn't look familiar had walked past her, and she hoped for introductions soon.

Two of the dowager's sons walked by—Lord Trevor and Lord Trey—and she presented them with her best smile. Only Lord Trey returned the gesture. Then again, Trey didn't have a good reputation, and Diana would do well to stay away from him for fear of being ruined.

Walking up the lane from the road, three men caught her eye. She recognized two of them she'd met several times before, Lord Henry and Lord Elliot. They were with someone who looked oddly familiar, but she knew she'd never been introduced to him before. The tall man was quite handsome, if she dared admit, and extremely muscular. His over-jacket stretched tightly across his shoulders, and his breeches appeared entirely too formfitting and showed off his exceptional build.

Her cheeks heated. *Good heavens!* Why would she think such a thing? Yet it was hard not to, especially the closer the threesome came toward her and the more she could see of the stranger.

She straightened and folded her hands in her lap, adopting as proper of an appearance as possible. A bee buzzed by her face, but she dared not swat at it, although she couldn't allow it to sting her, either. The last time that happened, her face had swollen and she'd become sick. Trying not to be obvious, she blew at the bee, hoping it would take the hint and leave.

The closer the three men strolled, the more the bothersome insect irritated her. Still, she continued to blow at it, hoping it wouldn't sting her. The handsome stranger finally looked her way and grinned. Diana's heart flipped in a silly rhythm. She smiled back and inclined her head.

The small group walked right by her without saying anything, although the stranger watched her over his shoulder as he passed. Once they were out of her vision, she swatted the bee, and the insect finally left her alone.

Closing her eyes, she couldn't get the handsome man out of her mind. One way or another, she needed to get an introduction.

A burst of giggles brought Diana out of her daydream, and she snapped her eyes open. From around the wide tree, three girls sat on the wraparound bench. Sighing, Diana leaned back against the thick trunk and frowned. She didn't have many friends her own age here in Mayfair.

"Did you see that dress she was wearing?" one of the girls asked in a low voice. "Why, it's ghastly, to say the least. She wore that gown last Season, but it appears as if the sleeves are different. Even the color is fading."

"And what about her mother?" another girl piped up. "That woman sticks her nose into conversations that are not her concern. In fact, she interrupted me while I was walking with my mother not too long ago."

"How disrespectful," a third voice said. "Why can they not realize nobody wants them here?"

"Except the dowager Duchess of Kenbridge." The second girl snickered. "She is just too nice to turn anyone away. Pity she can't see the country paupers for what they truly are." She huffed. "You know, there is a reason the Baldwins aren't invited to most social events."

"Well, except for Miss Baldwin's older brother, Mr. Cole Baldwin." One girl giggled.

Diana's throat tightened, making it difficult to breathe. They were talking about her and her family! They had been talking about *her* gown!

She pulled herself tight against the tree, praying the girls on the other side wouldn't notice her listening. Nothing could move her away now, even if she didn't want to hear another degrading word they said.

"In a way," the first girl said, "I do feel sorry for Miss Baldwin and her brother. It's not their fault their father is a gambler and squanderer."

"Very true. It's no wonder their mother flaunts her daughter in front of all the eligible men. I heard that in order for their family to stay out of debt, Miss Baldwin will have to marry a very wealthy man."

The girls' laughter made Diana's stomach churn. Could what they were saying be true? Impossible! Her father wasn't *that* badly in debt, was he? And if so, why hadn't her mother said anything?

She glanced down at her day gown, picking at the sleeves. This had been new three Seasons ago. Every year since, her mother had done her best to make alterations, telling Diana she could still wear it after it was spruced up and nobody would notice. Perhaps her father's gambling had depleted the family funds after all. Why else wouldn't her mother buy new gowns for them? Mother made Diana think her father would come into a lot of money very soon. Had this been a lie?

"Oh, look," one of the girls exclaimed. "There's Lord Tristan."

Diana had no idea who Lord Tristan was, and at this moment, she didn't particularly care.

The other two sighed dreamily. "Oh, Jane, I'm so utterly and completely jealous of you. I wish Lord Tristan's family wanted him to marry me!"

Jane chuckled. "Well, it's true. Our families are trying to arrange a marriage, but Lord Tristan insists he's not ready to settle down."

"Well, if I know you, Jane, you'll convince him soon enough."

"Indeed I will," she gloated.

Rustling of silk faded from the other side of the tree, and Diana dared take a peek to see if the girls had left. They had. She breathed a relieved sigh then embarrassment washed over her. The weekend party had just begun, but she wanted to leave immediately. Feigning illness may be the trick in getting her mother to take her home. If others felt the same way these three girls did about Diana's family, she could not stay a minute longer. She didn't want everyone gossiping about them behind their backs.

She left the bench and hurried toward her mother, who stood next to Lady Greenly and Lady Sutherland. Now that Diana knew what others were saying about their family, she noticed the forced smiles the older women were giving her mother. Her heart wrenched. Did her mother know or even realize they were being made to look like fools at this gathering?

Slowly, she joined her parent and stood next to her. When there was a break in the conversation, Diana tugged on her arm.

"I'm feeling quite ill, Mother."

Esther frowned. "You do look a little peaked." She caressed Diana's cheek with her knuckle. "Perhaps you should go upstairs and lie down until dinner?"

"Well, actually, I was hoping we could return home," Diana answered softly.

Her mother snorted a laugh then quickly switched her gaze between the other two ladies before meeting Diana's eyes. "But my dear, we've just arrived. There's no reason to leave." She patted her daughter's hands. "All you need is to rest for a bit. I'm quite certain you'll feel much better by suppertime." She turned Diana toward the house and gave her a gentle push. "Now go up to our room and lie down. I'll wake you before the meal."

Disheartened, Diana trudged toward the house. How could she tell her mother what she'd overheard without causing any pain? And, if the gossip wasn't true, then what had her parents done to make people talk about them in such a way? Was this the reason her father wanted her married *this* Season?

As she turned the corner of the house, she ran smack into a hard, male chest. Strong hands gripped her arms to keep her from falling, and a scent of leathery musk enveloped her. Not believing any man could smell this good, she looked up into a pair of the most fascinating blue eyes she'd ever seen. The longer they stared at her, the more they twinkled.

Finally, when the rest of his face registered in her brain, she realized this was the man she'd seen earlier. It wasn't proper to meet like this, but she'd give anything to know his name.

"Forgive me, sir. I did not see you."

"There is nothing to forgive." He released her arms and took a step back. His mouth stretched into a grin. "I don't believe we have met."

"You are correct, sir. We have not been formally introduced."

He glanced around them and shrugged. "Since nobody is here to do that now, let me begin. I'm Lord Tristan Worthington. The Duke of Kenbridge is my father."

She curtsied. "I'm Miss Diana Baldwin. My father is Baron Baldwin."

He bowed. "Nice to meet you at last. I saw you sitting by the tree earlier, and I have to admit, you caught my attention."

Her cheeks grew warm as heat continued to spread through the rest of her body. "Thank you, my lord."

When his name was called, he turned toward the person not far from him. Lord Tristan lifted his hand. "I shall be finished momentarily."

She had a second to admire his profile: square jaw, clean-shaven face, and such a sweet smile and dreamy eyes. He looked back at her more quickly than she'd expected, and she feared he'd caught her gawking. Her throat turned dry and she swallowed hard.

"Well, Miss Diana Baldwin," he said, taking her hand and lifting it to those perfect lips, "I bid you farewell—at least for now. I hope we will meet again soon."

"Uh, yes. That would be lovely."

He walked away and she stared after him, still feeling the imprint of his lips on her knuckles and the heat from his stare. Perhaps this weekend party would turn out wonderful after all.

Chapter Six

"Everyone raise their glasses in a toast to welcome back those lords who have returned from their Grand Tour." Lord Felton lifted his glass and smiled.

The others gathered in the room cheered with lifted champagne glasses.

Tristan laughed and toasted, before gulping his drink. He was very delighted that his cousin, Lord Elliot, was one of those men.

But Tristan's mother's weekend party at the Worthington's estate in Bath wasn't about the lords who had returned as much as it was for persuading them to find a wife—as well as himself, he was sure. Nevertheless, he had enjoyed the event thus far. It'd been a while since he'd socialized with his grandmother and mother's friends.

Beside him, Lord Henry slapped Tristan's shoulder. "My good man, what plans do you have tonight? Are you really going to stay here at the party? A few of us were thinking of leaving later this evening and finding some wenches to entertain us."

Tristan laughed and glanced at his friends standing around him. "As much as that sounds like the safe thing to do, I shall stay. I don't need my mother put out with me again."

"Nonsense." Elliot flipped his hand in the air. "What she doesn't know won't hurt her."

"You don't know your aunt very well," Tristan told his

cousin. "My mother *always* knows when I'm not telling the truth. However, I assure you, I shall find something that will keep me entertained." He waggled his eyebrows. "So far at this gathering, I have noticed a few women who are unaware of my charm, and I find I'm most eager to show them."

"Well, I hope you don't expect us to entertain you, Worthington," Elliot said. "Both Henry and I have more pleasant matters to attend."

Mocking a bow, Tristan nodded. "I will leave you to your adventures. I assure you, I will find some way to keep myself occupied."

His friends laughed and walked away like strutting peacocks. Tristan shouldn't look down on them for what they had planned this evening.

Adjusting his brown coat, he strolled out of the room, nodding to acquaintances as he made his way toward the violins introducing the first dance of the evening. A few couples occupied the dance floor as a couple of eager young swains searched for a partner.

Tristan smiled and leaned against the wall. He enjoyed dancing, and especially getting to know the young ladies. He hadn't been a regular in Polite Society for a few years since he had been in Scotland visiting relatives on his mother's side, but he found it surprising that he didn't know very many people at his own mother's party.

From across the room, a light blue gown drew his attention. Lady Jane swept into the room, followed by two of her closest friends, Margaret and Lilly. Jane looked his way and smiled with shy demeanor. Tristan knew her well enough to know this was all an act. Jane was far from being shy. Fluttering her eyelashes and giving men that sensual pout made her extremely popular with the young swains.

He had once been fascinated by the woman, but when his mother and Lord and Lady Hastings started pushing them together, Tristan lost interest. Thankfully, papers hadn't been signed and no betrothal agreed to, however he knew his family was in hopes of a match with their daughter.

As he studied Jane and her followers, he couldn't help but notice the glares and smirks aimed toward someone only a few feet from them. Tristan switched his attention to the target of Jane's unscrupulous ministrations. Standing beside her mother was the same young lady he'd met earlier today. Miss Diana Baldwin.

A grin tugged his mouth wide. This afternoon had been entertaining when he watched her. At first she hadn't noticed him, but when she did, he detected a sparkle in her eyes. Then when she started blowing kisses his way…

He chuckled. When he'd seen her doing this, it had taken him by surprise. At first he thought her extremely forward, yet she didn't act as if she was purposely trying to flirt with him. That, in itself, made him more interested in her. When their gazes finally met, she had actually blushed! Now he wondered if she blew kisses to someone else, but he knew she hadn't.

Miss Baldwin fidgeted as she stood next to her mother, the young lady's eyes downcast as she clutched her hands in front of her. Beautiful auburn ringlets hung by her ears while the bulk of her hair wound in a coil at the back of her head, a light blue ribbon woven around it. The blue gown she wore accentuated her womanly figure better than any other woman here.

Indeed, she was a sight to behold, much lovelier than the other ladies. He didn't think it was her first Season, only because she didn't have that innocent, wide-eyed stare. There was something reserved about Miss Baldwin.

He glanced again at Lady Jane and her friends, still laughing behind their fans at Miss Baldwin. Did she know what the other girls were saying?

Anger rose inside him. Nobody should be the subject of ridicule. Jane and her friends acted as if they were still schoolgirls in the nursery instead of grown, *mature* women. He was certain they were acting this way because they felt threatened by Miss

Baldwin's beauty. Still, that didn't give them cause to make a spectacle.

He pulled away from the wall and walked toward the three, ready to set them straight. Before reaching them, he changed his mind. Perhaps words were not the key in helping these girls learn a lesson. Instead, he would *show* them how ridiculous they were being, and that men did *not* like a gossiping female!

Decision in mind, he turned sharply on his heel and headed toward Miss Baldwin. Just before he reached her, she raised her gaze and looked at him. Slowly, her eyes widened.

He stopped in front of her and bowed. "Good evening. Miss Baldwin, would you do me the honor of dancing with me?"

"Uh… um… well…" she stammered.

Her mother bumped an elbow into her daughter's side and smiled wide. "My daughter would be delighted, my lord."

He passed Miss Baldwin a charming smile, then said to the older woman, "My dear Baroness, the delight would be all mine."

The older woman giggled and fanned her face. Just then the music stopped and couples left the center of the dance floor.

Tristan offered a hand to Miss Baldwin. "Shall we?"

Hesitantly, she slipped her white-gloved fingers across his palm. Heat from her touch jolted through him, and he caught a quick breath. She must have felt it as well because her gaze bounced up and met his. Her cheeks bloomed with color.

He turned and led her to the middle of the floor, and on his way, took a peek at Jane and her friends. All stood staring at him with wide eyes of unbelief. He should snub them as they were snubbing Miss Baldwin, but he wanted them to see how he preferred to be with Miss Baldwin instead of them.

A heavenly aroma of flowers attacked his senses. He inhaled deeper. *Lilacs.* Not only did Diana's beauty take his breath away, her fragrance made him want to bury his nose in her neck and never leave.

The dance began and as they moved together in unison, her eyes stayed on him. She didn't look upon him as most women did. In fact, the way she studied him caused him to worry that something wasn't right. Was there food on his teeth? Perhaps he'd not used his linen napkin properly during the meal and food was on his face instead.

He gave her a charming smile. "Miss Baldwin, I wish you'd cease looking at me as if I have grown two heads."

That seemed to break the spell because she blinked and chuckled, appearing more relaxed.

"Forgive me, my lord. I didn't mean to stare so openly. Pray, don't think I am rude."

"I know you are not. But I'm curious to know why you act the way you do sometimes."

"Pardon?"

He chuckled. "Well, I must say you are a peculiar woman, but only in a good way, I assure you."

"Why do you think I'm peculiar?"

"Because one moment you are shy and innocent, and the next moment your gaze devours me while you blow kisses my way."

She stumbled but quickly righted herself. Panic crossed her expression for a brief moment. "Pray, my lord, what are you referring to? I promise you I have never *devoured* you with my gaze or blown kisses to you."

"Indeed, you say? Then tell me what is this gesture?" He puckered his lips, demonstrating what she had been doing to him this afternoon. "While you were sitting by the tree earlier today, you were doing this to me. Is that not blowing kisses?"

"Oh dear," she mumbled and closed her eyes for a brief moment as the shade of her face went scarlet.

"Tell me, Miss Baldwin, if I was mistaken."

She nodded and moisture gathered in her green eyes. "You are, my lord. I fear I wasn't blowing kisses to you, but trying to blow away the bee buzzing around my head."

Embarrassment swept over him, yet he knew she felt the same—if not worse—for his mistake. "Forgive me, then. I honestly thought..." He paused, not really knowing the words to say. Yet the more he thought about what she'd really done, and what he'd thought she was doing, the funnier it became. Soon a chuckle bubbled in his throat, and within seconds, she laughed with him.

"It is rather humorous, is it not?" she said. "In my attempt to make the bee go away without stinging me, I led you to believe I was being forward."

He threw back his head and laughed heartily, which eased the tension in their conversation considerably. When he looked back at her, she smiled with a gleam in her adorable eyes.

Tristan enjoyed her looking at him in this way. As with other young ladies, she didn't act as if she was trying to impress him, but instead, she was being herself.

He let his gaze roam over her face; skin that looked so soft, a perfectly shaped nose that wouldn't get in the way if he tried to steal a kiss, and lips so luscious he wanted to sample them. Why was he thinking about seducing her when he knew nothing about her? Quickly, he raised his eyes to hers and smiled. He wanted to know everything about this lovely creature who was more interesting than any woman he'd ever met.

"Tell me truthfully, my lord, is this the reason you asked me to dance?"

He shrugged. "Yes and no. When I first caught you flirting with me," he paused and winked, "I knew I wanted to meet you. I have never known a woman who was so bold, yet the more I studied you during the meal tonight, the more I realized you were not what you seemed." He took a quick glance around them at the other couples, then back to her. "I'm amazed your beauty hasn't made you more popular this evening."

"My beauty?" She laughed louder. "Indeed, you jest, my lord."

"I wasn't trying to make you laugh. I'm being very serious."

"Serious?" She arched her brow. "I think not. I'm quite certain you would have heard about the Baldwin family by now. If so, there's no way you could have made a comment like that and been serious."

Curiosity got the best of him, making him want to get to know her better. "The truth is I haven't heard anything about your family. I have been in Scotland visiting relatives, so I've been out of the area for a few years."

Her eyes widened. "You have? Well, I'm relieved to hear it."

"So tell me, what am I supposed to have heard about the Baldwin family?"

The dance ended, and he frowned. So did she, but then she had looked discouraged by his question, not that they had to stop dancing. He took her hand and led her away from the middle of the room, taking her back toward her mother. Miss Baldwin leaned closer to him and met his gaze.

"Trust me, you will hear something about my family tonight, but know this now. It's not true. At least I don't believe it's true. And…" She nibbled her bottom lip. "I thank you for the refreshing dance. I enjoyed getting to know you."

Her words made him that much more curious, and he wished he didn't have to leave her side. Yet dancing with her twice in a row would only start tongues wagging here in this den of gossipmongers. Neither of them needed that.

He stopped beside her mother, then took Diana's hand and bestowed a small kiss on her knuckles. "It was a pleasure, Miss Baldwin. I hope we can talk again very soon."

She graced him with a smile, but he could see it wasn't genuine because her pretty green eyes didn't light up. Did she think he was lying? Well, he'd just have to prove to her he wasn't.

Chapter Seven

DIANA SMILED. SHE couldn't help it. Watching Lord Tristan and remembering every little second of their dance together did that to her. Since he'd left her by her mother's side, Diana's heart hadn't stopped flipping and butterflies did their own ballet in her stomach. She had hoped he would ask her to dance again but so far he hadn't. It surprised her to see he only danced three more times and they were with older or married women.

The memory of his laugh sent tingles over her, and the way his blue eyes had darkened made her breathless. She should give up these foolish notions, but she couldn't. He was the only man who had made her heart sing within a few minutes of meeting him.

Throughout the rest of the evening, she'd kept her eyes on Lord Tristan as he moved from group to group conversing. Every so often, their gazes met. She should have looked away, but she couldn't. Not when his smile made her wonder if he was interested in her as she was in him.

After a while, her mother struck up a conversation with a couple of older ladies. The topic they discussed was mundane—that or Diana couldn't pay attention to them because she kept watching Lord Tristan. Either way, she refused to stand and listen.

She touched her mother's elbow to get her attention. "I'm

going into the other room to get a glass of lemonade."

"That's fine, dear." Her mother turned back to the other women.

Diana weaved through the crowded room, hoping not to run into Lady Jane and her friends. They had been talking about Diana this evening, she was certain. She may have not heard their words this time, but she could tell by the way they looked at her and snickered that *she* was their point of interest. Women like that sickened Diana. Was it any wonder she abhorred the *ton*? She preferred living in the country and not having to mingle with these haughty people.

"Miss Baldwin. Please wait."

Diana spun toward the person calling her, and groaned. Could she be polite while talking with Lady Jane? Or would Diana say what was really on her mind? She faked a smile. "Good evening."

The other woman lifted her nose as she looked down on Diana. "Are you enjoying yourself?"

Within seconds, Jane's shadows caught up to her, each had a trace of malice in their eyes.

Diana nodded. "Yes, I am. Are you?"

"We are having a splendid time." Lady Jane grinned haughtily. "The reason I stopped you is to inquire about your brother."

"Cole?" Diana asked. "What is it that you'd like to know?"

"Is he here with your family?" Lady Margaret Cummings asked quickly.

Diana shook her head. "He could not make it. There were other things he had planned this weekend."

Both Lady Margaret and Miss Lilly frowned. Jane merely lifted a thin shoulder in a shrug. "How unfortunate. I was hoping to become better acquainted with him."

"I'm certain he would have enjoyed that," Diana lied through clenched teeth. Vicious women like these three would have upset her brother so much he wouldn't have acted in a gentlemanly manner around them.

"Yes, indeed," Lady Jane said. "Well, I thank you for taking a moment to speak with us. I must be going now."

Jane and the other vipers sashayed back into the ballroom. Diana thanked her lucky stars she hadn't said anything rude, because Heaven knows she wanted to.

She turned and hurried to the refreshment table, hoping to get a cool drink soon because she needed something to calm her heated disposition. She fisted her hands at her side. Why couldn't she have made it through the evening without talking to those rude girls? And why was she the one being punished for something her father had *supposedly* done? She still didn't dare ask her mother. Diana didn't think she could bear bad news right now when this weekend had already started out badly.

When she reached the table, she hoped the footman would pour her a cup since she didn't have a gentleman friend to get her a drink. But before she could ask the footman, a masculine voice came from behind her.

"Here, allow me."

She jumped and looked over her shoulder. Lord Tristan stood entirely too close as he reached around her and took the cup from the footman. Tristan then presented it to her as if it were made of gold.

Her anger for Lady what's-her-name and her hen witted friends quickly left Diana as her heartbeat hammered with excitement. She took the drink. "Lord Tristan. What a surprise."

He smiled in that knee-melting, charming way of his. "I'm glad you think it is, because I have to admit, I was hoping for another chance to talk with you."

Excitement pumped through her faster. "You were? Why, I wonder?"

A corner of his mouth lifted higher than the other. "I'm completely bored at this party—to tears, in fact—and I want someone to cheer me up."

She laughed, and he joined her. "That shocks me, Lord Tristan, especially when I know how popular you are with the guests tonight."

"Still, it was all I could do to not fall asleep during each conversation."

"Oh, I highly doubt that, my lord."

"It's true. Not when I could keep company with you and enjoy the rest of my evening."

Sipping her drink, she studied him over the rim of the cup. Humor tinted his eyes, making them sparkle, letting her know he was jesting with her. Yet, he stood by her side instead of with his friends in the other room so there must be a little truth to his statement.

"So," he continued and held out his elbow, "I had hoped to convince you to take a stroll with me outside and free us from the hum-drum of this room."

As much as she wanted to, she didn't dare. Would it be proper? But of course it would. They wouldn't be the only couple outside strolling around the dowager's flower garden, Diana was certain.

She placed the cup on the table. Smiling, she hooked her hand around his elbow. "Lead the way, my lord."

Diana walked beside him, feeling like the grandest woman in the room—whether her gown was outdated or not. Not once did Lord Tristan act as if he was embarrassed to be seen with her. Surprising, since she figured he'd heard the rumors by now.

The moment they walked outside, she inhaled deeply, enjoying the fresh air. The moon was full tonight, and combined with the lanterns placed along the walkway, she was certain their stroll would give nobody reason to wonder if they were being proper or not.

He slipped his palm over the top of her hand as it rested on his arm. Her heart leapt and she looked up into his smoldering eyes.

"Are you feeling better, Miss Baldwin?"

"Immensely so, I thank you for asking."

"So tell me why a lovely lady like yourself hasn't been coerced into marriage yet."

She laughed. "It seems, my lord, that is a very interesting question—one I wish I knew how to answer."

"I would assume you would have a flock of men standing at your doorstep, waiting for the chance to woo you."

"You assume wrongly, then."

His gaze moved all over her. Tingles erupted inside her chest, creating sensitive bumps all over her skin. She wished he didn't have the ability to make her react in such a way, yet in a way she cherished this newfound feeling.

"Impossible." He shook his head. "Tell me truthfully, my dear. Why am I the fortunate man who gets to escort you outside tonight?"

She couldn't believe how sincere his tone of voice was. Perhaps he hadn't heard the rumors. No, that couldn't be right. Knowing Lady Jane and her friends, Diana was certain the whole party knew by now. "You are flattering me, my lord. I assure you, I don't deserve it."

They stopped by the tree where she'd been sitting when she first saw him earlier today. Even if they sat on the wooden bench, the lanterns surrounding the area would not make their time very private. Wasn't that what she wanted? Yet, the more she gazed into his sultry eyes, the more she wanted him to herself for a little while without curious eyes watching.

"Would you like to sit?" He pointed to the bench.

She grinned. "I hesitate sitting here with you, my lord. I would hate to be bothered by a bee again and have you believe I'm blowing kisses at you."

He tilted back his head and laughed. It made her happy to think she could do this. As she studied his handsome face, dark eyes, dark hair, and especially his tempting mouth, she realized no other man had made her feel so comfortable. And for certain, no other man had made her insides jump with excitement.

A movement from back by the house drew her attention when three women poked their heads out of the door. Diana groaned. Were those girls really trying to be her watchdogs?

Lord Tristan frowned. "What's amiss? You look upset." He swung his head in the direction she'd been looking. "Oh, dear. Lady Jane and her entourage," he mumbled.

"Lord Tristan, do you mind if we go someplace else? I really don't want to talk to them right now." She looked back at Jane. The gossipmonger and her friends had stepped out of the house and were coming in their direction.

"Your wish is my command, my sweet."

He took her hand in his and pulled her away from the lantern walk and in through the thicket of trees. He moved the branches away from her face and gown so she wouldn't get snagged. When they walked by a large tree, Lord Tristan pulled her in the back of it, pinning her against the trunk with his body.

"Shh…" He put his finger to her lips. He peeked around them toward the path they'd just left.

Diana heard Lady Jane's voice, but not her words—how could she when Lord Tristan's muscular frame leaned against Diana's so intimately. His finger still pressed against her mouth, and she dare not even breathe for fear she'd take in more of his intoxicating scent of leather and musk.

He pulled his attention away from the other women as they passed by, and stared into Diana's face. His gaze dropped to her mouth. Instead of moving his finger away, he tenderly slid it across her bottom lip. Her throat grew dry and her heart nearly beat right out of her chest. The sounds around them disappeared and all she could hear was her quick breaths—and his.

Good grief, what was he doing to her? And pray, why did she like it so much?

"I—I believe they are gone now," she whispered with much difficulty since her mouth felt as if cotton had taken up residency in her throat.

"Yes, I do believe they are."

He gave her a lop-sided grin that made her heart flip. Yet he didn't move. And Heaven help her, she didn't want him to move, either. She enjoyed this so much… too much.

Watching his gaze as it rested on her lips fascinated her, and gave her hope. Would he kiss her? It wouldn't be proper, that was for certain. But they were out here alone, and one little kiss wouldn't hurt.

The rhythm of her heart beat frantically against her ribs and she dared to move her head forward in silent encouragement. His blue eyes softened as his head tilted toward her.

"Diana? Where are you?"

Her mother's shrill voice broke the spell quickly. Tristan jumped back just as Diana pulled away from the tree. She moistened her dry lips with her tongue and tried to meet Tristan's eyes, but it was difficult.

"Perhaps I should take you back to your mother now," he said in a voice much deeper than she'd heard before.

"Yes, perhaps you should."

As they walked toward her mother who stood just outside the double glass doors, not another word was spoken. The awkward silence pierced through the air, making her very uncomfortable. Each step she took closer to her mother, Diana's heart sank. Could Tristan be regretting the *almost* kiss? His continued silence reaffirmed her worry.

When they neared and her mother saw Diana, the worried lines around the older woman's eyes and mouth disappeared. "Oh, there you are, my dear."

"Yes, Mother. I am here. Lord Tristan and I were just taking a small walk."

"Oh, how lovely." Her mother smiled at Lord Tristan. "Please forgive my interference, but I would like to introduce my daughter to an old friend I just saw at the party."

"That is just fine, Baroness." He bowed to her, then to Diana. "I shall take my leave now. Miss Baldwin, I hope to see you tomorrow during the morning ride my mother has planned."

"I shall be there, my lord." Diana curtsied.

With each step Tristan took away from her, loneliness grew inside her chest. What a wonderful man he was, and so willing to help her get away from Lady Jane. And even though Diana hadn't been with him for very long, their time together was well spent, and she realized she wanted to see him again… and be alone with him, even as improper as it was.

Tristan made her heart soar, and she enjoyed the elation shooting through her soul. The foreign feeling made her realize she wanted this always!

Chapter Eight

TRISTAN SQUINTED AGAINST the sun as it shined brightly toward the front of the house. He sat straight on his horse and waited as his mother's guests spilled out of the house and toward the stables where horses awaited them for their scheduled morning ride. He'd been waiting for ten minutes, but had yet to see the lovely Miss Baldwin or her mother.

Scrubbing his hand over his face, he blinked his tired eyes. Last night he'd lain awake thinking of Miss Baldwin. *Diana.* What a different woman she was… and what a relief! In just the little time they had visited, he had relaxed and didn't have to act like someone else around her. He enjoyed being himself, and he felt that she, too, had been herself around him. Unlike the pristine Lady Jane and her friends who sashayed around the dance floor last night acting as if they were the only women at the party. How he loathed women like that!

Diana Baldwin was a breath of fresh air, and she was exactly what he was looking for in his life. For the first time, he actually wanted to pursue her. He wanted to win her heart. The look of adoration that she had given him when he'd asked her to dance, and then later when he saw her at the refreshment table, was the greatest feeling he'd had in such a long time. He actually felt like her rescuer.

Three women walked out of the house in a rainbow of dresses, and as they came toward the stable, their high-and-mighty noses were where they always were… in the air, and their holier-than-thou attitudes were gleaming off their haughty expressions. He rolled his eyes. The more he compared Diana to them, the more they failed in comparison.

When they neared, Jane's smile broadened. "Good morning, Lord Tristan. How happy it makes me to see you here."

"Indeed? I wonder why that is since I live here."

"You misunderstood, my lord. What I meant to say was that I was hoping you would be here to ride with us."

"Of course I would be here. Where else would I be during my mother's party?" Jane chuckled lightly and the other two displayed faux grins. He motioned toward the horse. "Please find your mounts. We will be leaving for our ride soon."

"My lord?" Jane batted her eyes. "Will you help me mount?"

Tristan glanced at the stable hand that stood ready to help. "Lady Hastings, you already have someone to assist you."

He tried not to laugh at the displeasure on her face as the servant helped her on to the horse. If Tristan's mother would have heard and witnessed this scene, she would have boxed his ears for being so uncaring. But Tristan didn't want to give Jane any more encouragement than necessary.

He glanced back toward the house. Floating down the slope was a vision in a light gray riding habit trimmed with black lace. His heart jumped with happiness. At the back of Diana, her mother and another lady trailed behind.

Tristan jumped off his horse, and then motioned to the stable hand. Earlier, Tristan had prearranged to have the servant prepare one of his mother's mares—a beautiful white filly—for Diana.

As she neared, he heard the snickers from over his shoulder where Jane and her cronies were waiting on their horses. He threw them a glare, but they didn't see him. Their eyes were fixed on Diana as they whispered behind their gloved hands. He couldn't hear everything they were saying, but the words *outdated* and *riding habit* stood out. Jane growled in distaste and said, *why is she here?*

Tristan bunched his hands at his side. It wasn't his place to have them dismissed from the group, but he would inform his mother of the debutante's behavior and push his parent to have those women leave. Today, if he had his way.

He turned toward Diana as she neared. She smiled sweetly at him, and his heart melted. "Miss Baldwin, I'm so happy to see you this morning."

"My lord, you literally took the words right out of my mouth."

"I was hoping that you and your mother were going to ride with us."

"Well, I'm going to ride, but my mother is not a rider, so she'll not be joining us."

By this time, the older woman had caught up to her daughter. She curtsied to Tristan. "My lord, it makes my heart happy to see you."

"As does mine." He bowed. "Your daughter tells me you are not going riding?"

"No. I have never liked the sport, I fear, and I would only slow the riding party down if I went."

"Then you must allow me to watch over your daughter in your absence. I'll make certain no harm comes to her."

Diana's face brightened, but she didn't say anything. Her gaze switched from Tristan to her mother as if she eagerly awaited her parent's answer.

"Oh, but of course, Lord Tristan. It would be an honor to have you do this for me."

"It's my privilege, Baroness."

The snort of a horse pulled Tristan away from the women as the stable boy brought over the duchess's mare. Tristan took the reins from the servant then turned back to Diana. "I hope you don't mind, but I would like you to ride this one."

Diana's eyes widened as she gazed over the animal. Slowly,

she walked to the mare and ran her hand down the mane. "Oh, Lord Tristan. I couldn't possibly… This is a fine animal, indeed, but I fear the owner would not allow me on her."

He chuckled. "The owner is my mother, and I assure you, my mother will let you ride her." He put forth his hand. "May I assist you?"

Her cheeks darkened with color as she slipped her black-gloved hand into his. He pulled her around to the side of the animal before releasing her hand to grasp her waist. She placed her hands on his shoulders, and as he lifted her, she kept her sparkling eyes locked with his.

Heavens she was lovely!

Once she was settled on the animal, he moved back to his own horse. Her gaze had stayed on him the whole time. Once he mounted, he gave Diana a wink. "Are you ready?"

She gripped the reins. "Any time you are."

Without asking the other guests if they were ready, he urged his horse forward with Diana beside him. After a few minutes, he realized the group had followed. He just prayed that they wouldn't depend on him for conversation since he would be too busy trying to get to know Miss Baldwin a little better.

His mother's country estate covered many miles of God's beautiful land, but Tristan couldn't keep his eyes off the beauty next to him long enough to enjoy the scenery. They'd been galloping for a little while, so he slowed his horse to a trot, as did Diana.

"So, Miss Baldwin," he said, breaking the silence between them. "Where are you from?"

She smiled. "I'm from the Bristol area."

"Is that where you were born and raised?"

"Yes."

"Do you have any brothers or sisters?"

"I have an older brother—Cole. But I have no sisters."

"Tell me, have you been to many of these weekend parties? Or any other of society's functions?"

She nodded. "I have attended a few, my lord. Why do you ask?"

"I'm just surprised I haven't seen you before now. I have been back from visiting relatives in Scotland for three months now, but I don't believe I have seen you before."

"I know I haven't laid eyes on you before last night, either."

"I suppose our paths were not destined to cross until at my mother's party."

More color highlighted her cheeks. "You are probably right."

"Probably?" He laughed. "There is no *probably* about it, Miss Baldwin. I don't know if you realized this last night, but the stars were aligned perfectly, which is why we met. Why else did God send an angel to me?"

Her face turned a brilliant red. She glanced around them quickly. He did as well, forgetting that other people might overhear them. Thankfully, nobody was close enough to hear their conversation.

"Oh, Lord Tristan, you speak of such romantic notions, and I fear I am not the angel you think I am."

"Let me be the judge of that." He winked.

Just then, a few more guests rode closer to them. Diana cleared her throat and straightened a little more in the side-saddle.

"Lord Tristan, you had mentioned earlier that you were visiting relatives in Scotland."

"Indeed, I had."

"Where in Scotland?"

"The Lowlands—Edinburgh."

"Oh how lovely." She beamed. "You must tell me about your visit. I haven't been to that part of Scotland since I was a girl visiting my paternal grandfather."

As he told her about the areas he'd visited, and what new places had been built, her eyes danced with excitement. Once again, he'd forgotten about the rest of the riding party, and focused on Diana. He loved the way her face lit up and the musical tone of her laughter. He loved how her green eyes sparkled one moment before a dreamy expression covered her face, making him want to sigh with happiness.

She listened intently to his story and he felt like what he said was the most important thing in the world. When he was finished, she told him about her visits to Scotland, and as he stared into her exuberant face, he realized he could literally become lost in her eyes. *Become?* He was already there!

It took him a few seconds to realize she had stopped talking and was peering toward a brook. He switched his attention that way and noticed the other guests of the party had stopped their horses and visited near the water.

"Would you like to join them?" he asked.

"Indeed, I would. The water looks so peaceful over there."

Just as he and Diana reached the spot, he quickly pulled his horse to a stop and dismounted. After tying the animal to a nearby tree, he hurried over to help Diana down. As he lifted her off the horse, she held onto his shoulders and her body brushed scandalously close to his. A blush covered her face mere seconds before she pulled out of his arms.

Before he could think of anything to say, his name was called from behind him. Inwardly, he groaned. He knew that voice… the shriek of her tone… and especially the way his gut clenched. Lady Jane came to bother him once again.

Was it too much to ask for her to forget about him? He feared if she intruded upon his and Diana's conversation, he might not be so nice to Jane and her friends. Silently, he prayed that he'd be able to keep a civil tongue.

DIANA FROZE. WHY had she forgotten about those three women? So far this morning, Diana's day had been a dream-come-true. Yet now Jane and her friends were here to turn the morning into a nightmare. Even the irritated look in Tristan's eyes let her know he wasn't too happy about who would be meddling in their conversation.

"Lord Tristan," Lady Jane began sweetly. "I'm very glad that you stopped to visit with us. This has been the perfect morning for a ride, don't you agree?"

"Indeed, Lady Hastings." Tristan glanced at Diana. "The scenery could not be more perfect."

Heat climbed up Diana's face. All morning long his words had charmed her completely, but now that they were with mixed company, she didn't quite know how to act to his compliments.

Jane gave a forced laugh. "Yes, the scenery is most becoming." She turned her head toward Diana. "And Miss Baldwin, I'm quite surprised at you."

Panic started building in Diana's chest. "You are?"

"Of course, and I'm a little put out with you as well." She pouted and glanced at Tristan. "You have taken all of Lord Tristan's attention and you're not sharing him with the other guests."

Diana licked her suddenly dry lips, not quite knowing how to reply to that. "Well, I—"

"Indeed, you have put a spell on this Worthington brother and he has not found the time to visit with anyone else at the party." Lady Margaret lifted her chin arrogantly.

"Forgive me, I hadn't realized—"

"There is nothing to forgive," Tristan quickly added as he aimed his attention at Jane. "Miss Baldwin and I are getting acquainted. Is that a crime?"

"Of course not," Jane answered.

"Then I don't see what concern this is of yours." He glanced at Margaret and Lily. "Or yours."

"Then I suppose it is I who needs to apologize." Jane nodded at Tristan. "I was merely making conversation, and stating the obvious." She shrugged. "You and Miss Baldwin are causing many tongues to wag in gossip. It's not like you, Lord Tristan, to single out one particular woman at any social gathering."

"Especially one," Lily cut in as her gaze swept over the length of Diana in disgust, "who still wears a riding habit from two seasons past."

Humiliation washed over Diana and all she wanted to do was hide, or bury her head in the sand…or sink in the nearby brook and disappear. Once again, she didn't have a reply for that comment.

Tristan stepped closer to Diana. Lines of irritation creased his forehead as he slowly passed his scowl around to the other women, starting with Lily.

"It matters not how old or how new a woman's clothes are." He switched his focus to Diana and smiled. "Because if you ask me, Miss Baldwin looks lovely in whatever she chooses to wear." He threw a glare back at the other three. "A woman's sense of worth is not about her clothing or her upbringing. It's how she conducts herself in public and appears a true gentlewoman. From what I have witnessed from Miss Baldwin since meeting her, she has outshined all the women I have met at this party."

Tears of joy pricked Diana's eyes and she quickly blinked before anyone noticed. Her heart melted from his words, but really, her heart had been melting since they first met. She'd never believed in love at first sight, but now after meeting Tristan Worthington, she realized it was impossible not to have strong feelings for this man.

He turned toward Diana and offered his arm. "Miss Baldwin, shall we continue our ride?"

Smiling wide, she straightened her shoulders. "Indeed, we shall."

As he helped her back to her horse and helped her up, happiness burst in her chest. She wanted to pinch herself to make sure she was awake and had not been dreaming about what just happened. Never in her life had a man stood up for her in such a way. Truly, he was her knight in shining armor.

Chapter Nine

"HAVE YOU HEARD the latest gossip?"

Tristan stood next to his younger brother, Trey, as he watched the entryway into the grand ballroom. He'd only been away from Diana for a few hours, and already he couldn't wait to see her again and gaze into her emerald eyes and breathe in her enthralling lilac scent.

Shaking his head, he glanced at his brother for only a moment before returning his attention back to the corridor. "What a ridiculous question to ask. What makes you think I listen to gossip?"

"Normally, I don't either, but this time, it's about my brother so I decided to listen."

"Oh, really?" Tristan asked. "What are people saying about Trevor?"

"They aren't saying anything about Trevor, they are talking about *you*."

Tristan rolled his eyes before looking back at Trey. "I don't really care what people are saying."

"You don't? Not even when bets are being placed on whether or not you will become engaged before week's end?"

"Engaged?"

"Either that, or you will compromise the girl."

"Really, Trey. I cannot believe you listen to such gossip." He looked back up the corridor. *Where was she?*

"Are you saying you don't care what people are saying about you and Miss Baldwin?"

"Not in the least, and you should not care, either."

"If you say so." Trey pulled away from the wall. "But let me warn you, tread carefully. I have the title of a rake, and I know our mother wouldn't want two sons with that name."

As Trey walked away, Tristan nearly laughed. He wasn't a rake and would never become one. *If*, by chance, he compromised a young maiden, he would do the right thing and marry her. He had been raised to respect women. Trey had always believed he was too much like their father, which was why he was a scoundrel.

When a footman walked by carrying a tray of champagne glasses, Tristan reached out and took one. In one gulp, he finished the glass then replaced it on the tray. He resumed his position against the wall, and within seconds, saw the woman he'd been waiting for.

Heavens, she was beautiful. Lavender was certainly the color that enhanced her auburn hair and bright green eyes.

As he walked toward her, the violins announced the first dance. Finally, her eyes met his and she smiled... a smile that lit up her whole face.

He stopped in front of her and the Baroness and bowed. "Lady Baldwin. Miss Baldwin."

"My lord." Diana curtsied.

"Will you honor me with the first dance of the evening?" He held out his elbow.

"Of course." She hooked her hand around his elbow as he escorted her to the dance floor.

There was no verbal communication between them as they walked through the steps of the country dance, but the gleam in her gaze spoke volumes to him. The rhythm of his heart accelerated the longer he stared into her eyes... eyes that were filled with dreams. He didn't need to ask her if she wanted to take a walk outside with him, because he could see that she did. He didn't have to ask her if she would approve of spending some time with him alone, because he knew she was thinking about it now.

Unfortunately, he couldn't take her outside now. Because there was gossiping going around the party, he must stay inside and dance at least three more dances. Or two. Yes, two would be sufficient.

After the dance, he walked her back to her mother then turned to find another dance partner. The quicker he could get these dances over with, the sooner he could get back to Diana.

During the next few dances, he couldn't stop his gaze from wandering to her. No other man had asked her to dance, but at this point, Tristan didn't think he would like her being with another man. He didn't want any other man to look at her the way he does, and especially think about her the way he'd been since last night.

He chuckled to himself. What a strange turn of events. Never had he acted like a love-smitten young pup as he'd been acting since meeting Diana. Yet how else could he explain his foolishness? *Love?* No, he didn't think he was in love, but he did like her very much, and wanted to spend more time with her. He enjoyed the way she could make him laugh, and he never wanted it to end.

Finally, he'd danced with other women—older matrons, of course—before seeking Diana out again. Just as last night, he found her by the refreshment table. It was almost as if she knew he'd come there for her because when she saw him heading her way, happiness made her face glow.

"Miss Baldwin." He bowed.

"Lord Tristan." She curtsied. "You seem out of breath. Have you been dancing too much this evening?"

He leaned into her and lowered his voice. "Actually, I think I was out of breath hurrying over here to see you."

Her cheeks bloomed with color. "How shameful."

He winked. "I'm only being honest."

"I like that in a man."

"Just as I want a woman to be honest with me." He nodded. "And so that being said, I would like your *honest* opinion." He straightened. "Would you care to take a walk with me outside?"

"That idea sounds heavenly. I would love to take a walk with you."

"Splendid." He offered his arm, and she took it. Walking toward the door with her next to him made him feel like the grandest man on earth. It still surprised him that this woman could make him react in such a way.

Once they were outside, their footsteps slowed as they moved down the pathway lit with outdoor lanterns. The full moon also helped light the way, especially when he would soon take her off the lantern-lit path.

"Miss Baldwin, I have to tell you how much I enjoyed spending time with you this afternoon."

She looked up at him with twinkling eyes. "As did I."

"You kept me thoroughly entertained, and I thank you for that."

"Well, I did try my hardest, my lord."

"Please, call me Tristan."

She nodded. "And I give you permission to call me Diana."

He led her off the pathway and back toward the trees. Many shadows helped to make their walk more private, which was the very thing he was after.

"Will you be staying all day tomorrow? Mother doesn't have many events planned for tomorrow, but the party goes on all day."

Diana shrugged. "I don't know my mother's plans, but I do believe we will be staying."

"Splendid." He patted her hand still around his arm. "Because I want to spend more time with you."

"Lord... er, Tristan, I hate to confess this, but I do understand how Lady Hastings and her friends feel, because I don't know why you want to spend so much time with me."

He gave her a quizzical stare. "What kind of comment is that?"

"Hear me out first." She took a deep breath. "I'm sure by now you have heard the rumors I'd spoken of about my family, and yet still you are treating me as if I'm the daughter of a grand duchess."

"I hate to disappoint, but I have not heard any rumors about your family, and I don't care to listen to rumors, anyway. I have already made up my mind about you, and—"

The sound of his name being called from across the yard made him pause. He gnashed his teeth. *Why can't Jane leave me be for one night?*

Tristan swiped his fingers through his hair, taking in deep breaths as he tried to cool his anger. It surprised him how quickly *that woman* could irritate him. He glanced around them for a place to hide. Back behind the trees, sat a greenhouse. This would be the perfect place for them to go without being interrupted, especially when it wasn't noticeable along the pathway.

He grasped Diana's hand and tugged. "Come. I know where we can go that nobody will find us."

"Where?"

"It's my mother's pride and joy."

She nodded and followed. As he led the way, he still kept a sharp eye out for anyone who might see them. Thankfully the area around the greenhouse wasn't lit as well. Even inside the greenhouse the lights were dimmed.

He tested the handle and it opened. Breathing a relieved sigh, he walked them inside and closed the door.

"Will anyone be able to see inside if they pass by?"

"If we stand away from the lanterns, I'm sure nobody will notice us."

She nodded and walked around him as if studying each plant. Thankfully, she headed away from the lanterns.

"The Dowager Duchess of Kenbridge certainly has a lovely

greenhouse," she said.

"Indeed, my mother does."

"My mother keeps a small one at our country estate, but it's nowhere as grand as this."

He walked behind her, trying hard not to touch her because if he did, he'd surely pull her into his arms. "And where exactly is your country estate?"

She grinned at him over her shoulder. "I told you. It's near Bristol."

"Why do you do that?" He shook his head. "I have watched you closely these past two days—just as I know you have watched me—and I can tell you're a secretive woman. Your half-answered remarks are one of the reasons I want to get to know you better."

"Tristan, I assure you I'm not an intriguing person." She trailed her fingers across the table near the potted plants.

"You are wrong." He caught her hand. She stopped and met his gaze. "In fact, you have kept me enthralled all day today and most of the evening yesterday, and I would like to know why."

"I fear I don't know how to answer that."

He lifted her hand to his mouth and brushed his lips across her knuckles. "I'm happy to know that you are nothing like Lady Jane, but I want to know why. What makes you so different?"

There was a stretch of silence before the corners of her mouth lifted. "I would think it's a good thing I'm not like her. I can tell you don't approve of her, either."

Her comment caught him off guard and he chuckled. "How do you know that?"

"You forget, I have been watching you, and I noticed your subtle refusal when Lady Jane tried to speak with you. Tell me, Lord Tristan, was that my imagination?"

He took a step closer to her, and thankfully she didn't withdraw. "No, that wasn't your imagination. Her family and mine are close. Because of that, she thinks she needs to be seen with me during *ton* functions, which I refuse to do. When she sees me paying attention to another woman, she tries to stop it. Not only that, I cannot tolerate the way she thinks she's better than others. Since the party started, I've caught her glaring at you, and I don't like it. I can only assume she's jealous of your beauty."

"Tristan," she whispered, "you couldn't be more wrong."

"About what?"

"Lady Jane is not jealous of my beauty."

"She should be." He moved close—scandalously close.

From outside the greenhouse, women's voices were heard. He groaned, knowing exactly who had come looking for him. He pulled away from Diana, hurried to the door and locked it. From out the front windows, Ladies Jane and Margaret, and Miss Lilly walked by. He flattened himself against the door then motioned Diana to hide. She crouched low.

When the door handle jiggled, Diana's eyes widened. She released a small gasp but then quickly covered her mouth. He held his breath, hoping Jane and her friends would not become suspicious.

After a couple of minutes, Jane and the other two finally left. Tristan crept away from the door. When he reached Diana, he grabbed her hand and pulled her deeper into the greenhouse, farther away from the lanterns and stopped them by a thick wooden beam.

"That was close," he said.

"I know."

She sighed and relaxed her back against the girder, then chuckled. "Tristan, being with you has certainly been an adventure."

He smiled. "Shall I assume you are enjoying yourself, then?"

"Very much."

"Splendid. I'm certainly enjoying the evening."

A fly buzzed by her head, and he moved it away with his hand. The only discouraging thing about being this far in the shadows was he couldn't see the color of her eyes. But if he stepped closer... He followed his thoughts.

Her chest moved with quick breaths. She licked her lips, and he couldn't tear his eyes from that spot—except when the fly buzzed between their faces, pestering him once again. Just as he was ready to knock it aside, an idea hit him, making him grin. "Why don't you blow away the fly like you did the bee yesterday?"

She laughed and shook her head. "I fear if I do, you may get the wrong impression of my intentions."

"But my dear, sweet Diana. I'm led to believe your intentions are as wicked as my own." He arched an eyebrow. "Or am I misreading you?"

Even in the dim lighting, he detected a blush on her cheeks. He swept his knuckle across her heated skin to get his answer.

"Tristan," she said as she fingered one of the gold buttons on his over jacket. "I don't know why I'm here with you now. If we were caught, my reputation would be ruined."

"Then I'll make certain we are not caught."

The fly darted by his face again, and he tried to swat it. Soon, her hands were trying to make the insect go away as well. After missing their target, they started laughing.

"Hold still," he instructed, keeping his eyes on the fly. When it neared her hair, he batted his hand. Instead of knocking the fly away, he bumped her styled hair, making the pins fall out. Her locks tumbled out of the coil and hung around her shoulders.

"Oh, dear," she gasped and tried to fix it.

Mesmerized, he stopped her hands, lowering them to his chest as he held her palms against him. "Don't," he spoke in a deep voice. "I've never seen hair so beautiful before."

"Tristan, this is indecent." Her voice cracked.

"Please, allow me this one thing." He caressed her hair, running his fingers from the top of the curls all the way to the bottom where they rested against her arms. She inhaled sharply but didn't remove herself from his touch. "Your hair is so silky."

Her chest heaved with quick breaths. He ran the tip of his fingers up her hair once again, until it reached the curve of her neck before sliding his touch to her skin. Creamy, just as he'd imagined it would be. In slow circles, he rubbed his fingers along her collarbone. Her breaths grew quicker, as did his own.

"Tristan, I fear this is *very* improper." Her voice was abnormally low and so very soft.

"Diana, I want to hold you so bad it's killing me."

Closing her eyes, she sighed heavily. That's all the encouragement he needed. Cupping her face, he pressed his mouth against hers. Softly, he kissed her lips, gently urging them to part.

"Diana," he muttered, "your lips are like wine, so pleasing to taste."

Another moan rattled through her chest as she clung to his shirt. He pushed his body against hers, pinning her to the wooden beam. Diana slid her palms up his chest and linked her hands around his neck. Suddenly he craved her touch like nothing he'd ever experienced before.

Tristan didn't need to tell her what he wanted. It was like she could read his mind. She rubbed her hands over his shoulders, then around his back, pulling him closer.

"Oh, Tristan," she muttered against his lips, "I have never done this before."

He broke the kiss and trailed his lips down her throat. "My dear, sweet, Diana. Why can I not control myself around you?"

When he placed his mouth back to hers, the kiss turned wild. Never, had he experienced such desire for a woman, or had enjoyed kissing her so much.

Suddenly, the door rattled again as voices—both men and women—were at the greenhouse. Tristan stilled. Dread settled in his gut. *We're caught!*

Chapter Ten

TRISTAN PULLED AWAY from Diana and spun toward the door. Diana gasped and clung to his arm.

"Shh…" he told her. "Unless someone has a key, they will not be able to get in."

"What if it's your mother, or a brother?"

"Let's pray it's not."

Tristan held his breath and focused on the door. Several long minutes passed before the group outside the door moved on and he was able to expel a relieved breath.

"Oh, Tristan," she sighed and rested her head against his chest. "That was too close."

"I know." He wrapped his arms around her, kissing her head. "We must leave. I would not want anything to ruin your reputation."

Nodding, she looked up at him and smiled. "I thank you for thinking of me. No matter how tonight ends, I want you to know I have had the most exciting evening."

He grinned. "As have I—one that I shall never forget."

She moved away, but then he realized her hair was a mess. "Diana, wait." He pulled her arm until she came back to him. "We need to fix your hair."

"Oh, heavens!" She gasped and brushed her fingers over her glorious mass. "If I'm seen like this, my name would be ruined, indeed."

As best he could, he helped her wrap her hair back in the coil, but unfortunately, it wasn't perfect and he knew if anyone saw her this way, they would definitely suspect what she'd been doing.

"Diana, I'm sorry but I was never a good lady's maid."

She chuckled. "Well, that's a good thing, is it not?"

"I shall take you to the back of the house so that nobody sees you." He stroked her cheek. "Although I do not wish to end our evening this way, I think it is best."

"Yes, it is."

Side by side they walked out of the greenhouse. Tristan glanced around the yard to make sure there weren't others out here that would see them. Thankfully, the guests were further back toward the house.

He walked her to the house then took her to the servant's entry. "Just follow the stairs up to the floor where your bedroom is located and you should be fine."

"Once again, Tristan, I thank you for a lovely night."

She looked adorable in the moonlight, and although the urge was strong to take her back into his arms, he couldn't. Ruining her reputation was not a gentlemanly thing to do. "I will see you tomorrow at breakfast."

"Yes, you will."

He mocked a small bow. "Then until tomorrow..." He gave her a wink before turning to leave.

As he wandered back to his own room, his body still hummed with desire from that wonderful kiss. Diana was a very passionate woman. Her mouth and those tempting lips would be branded on his forever. Kissing her had been pure enjoyment and now he wished they were still in the greenhouse. Perhaps they should have been caught because then he would have to marry her.

Marriage? He stopped and brought his thoughts to a halt as well. Why would he think about marriage to her? Then again, the idea wasn't so terrible. He had wanted to marry a woman he could fall in love with. He had always wanted his wife to be a woman he could converse with easily and one who could make him laugh. And of course, she would have to be more beautiful than he'd ever beheld.

He grinned fully. This certainly fit Diana.

Chuckling, he started his trek back to the front of the house. By the time he reached the front door, the idea of proposing to Diana filled him with excitement. The more he fantasized about being married to Diana, the more pleasing it sounded.

THE NEXT AFTERNOON Diana stood in front of the full-length mirror in her bedroom and stared at the pale-faced, pathetic woman with red, swollen eyes. The last two days had been heaven on earth, and Tristan's kiss had made all her dreams come true... until early this morning when she was awakened and disaster struck. She should have known something bad would happen to her. It always had. There hadn't been a time in her life when things had gone her way. For once she would like to see that happen.

Bright and early this morning, her mother had got Diana out of bed with the most dreadful news. Her father had received an offer of marriage and had accepted it. Diana knew it hadn't been Tristan because her father was still in Bristol and Tristan was here.

Diana hadn't gotten a chance to say anything to Tristan before their trunks were packed and her mother rushed them out of the house before everyone had awakened.

Now, standing in her bedroom, she hesitated on going downstairs to talk to her father. She wanted to tell him to wait another day or two—that Lord Tristan might make an offer, but she feared her father wouldn't listen. Perhaps if she told him Tristan compromised her...

She shook her head. She couldn't lie to her father. Although, if she and Tristan had been caught while in their passionate embrace, her reputation would have been turned to ashes and Tristan would indeed have to marry her.

Oh, why didn't it happen like that?

Grumbling in distaste, she left the room. There was no enthusiasm in her legs as they carried her down the stairs toward the sitting room. Silence greeted her when she walked in and stood in front of her parents. Both of them wore wide smiles.

"Close the door behind you," her father said.

She did as she was told, then walked to the sofa and sat beside her mother. The older woman's eyes sparkled with excitement, which was something Diana didn't see often on her mother. Even her father's cheerful expression was foreign.

"Diana, my dear, I'm very happy about the offer that was made to me yesterday while you and your mother were attending the party."

Taking a deep breath, she slowly released it. "Who made the offer?"

"Viscount Hollingsworth."

Hearing the lord's name was like a slap across the face. *Lord Hollingsworth?* Why on earth would her father accept a marriage proposal for his daughter from a man like that?

Confusion filled her head and made her dizzy, and at the same time, her stomach churned fitfully. She'd met Lord Hollingsworth a few times over the years, and that's all it took to decide she couldn't stand the man. It wasn't his bright red hair or the red freckles splattered across his pasty face that she didn't like, nor was it that he was a good twenty years older than herself that made her feel this way about him.

In the few times they had conversed, he had never made her feel special—or even important. Instead, he made her feel as if she would be the most fortunate and coveted woman on this earth if she had *him* as her husband. He'd been so rude with his advances, and several times she had to tell him to leave her alone. "F-

Father, you must be jesting. Why, the man has not even courted me."

"I am most serious, daughter. Lord Hollingsworth has been enamored with you for a few years now. He has made an offer for you every Season you have been out, but I have respectfully declined, hoping to find you a loftier match. Your beauty is equal to at least an earldom."

Panic filled her chest. "Then why did you not decline him this time?"

"Because, my dear, I'm ashamed to admit that I'm in financial ruins. In the last year, I have had a run of back luck with... uh... business decisions."

"You've been gambling again," Diana said matter-of-factly.

Her father's face hardened. "Yes. I had one bad stretch at the tables and my markers were called in before I was prepared." He raked a hand through his hair. For a moment he looked so weary and vulnerable that Diana's heartbreak faltered a fraction.

"I didn't know how I was going to pay," he added with a shrug. "Lord Hollingsworth came to my rescue and paid my debts in exchange for your hand in marriage."

"What?" Her voice rose as she sprang up from the sofa. "He *paid* you to marry me?"

"Indeed, and that is why I accepted."

"But Father..." Her breaths became faster. "At the Dowager Duchess of Kenbridge's party, I met a wonderful man. Lord Tristan Worthington. We hit it off splendidly, and I feel he is going to talk to you soon."

Her father flipped his hand in the air. "I'm pleased you had a good time, but unfortunately, I have made my decision. I have signed the contract and you will marry Lord Hollingsworth within a couple of weeks."

"But Father, Lord Tristan's father is a duke—"

"The matter is closed," he snapped as his face growing red with anger. "If Lord Tristan would have talked to me sooner, I would have considered him, but as it is, I cannot go back on my word now. I do not want to hear another word about this. Is that clear?"

Tears built behind her eyes and her throat tightened with sadness. "Yes, Father."

He looked at her mother. "Esther, I want you to start planning your daughter's wedding immediately. Keep in mind that we don't have the funds for a grand affair, so keep the event simple."

"Yes, dear." She stood and yanked on Diana's arm. "Let's hurry. We have shopping to do."

Tears filled Diana's eyes, but there was no use in shedding them. In all of her life, she had never been able to sway her father. Once he made up his mind—that was final. Her heart sank in deep despair. No matter how she looked at it, her life was tortured, because marrying Lord Hollingsworth would eventually be the death of her!

TRISTAN HURRIED TO his brother's study and rapped on the door. Trevor would be awake by now because he'd always been an early riser.

"Enter."

Tristan's heart hammered in his chest so hard he feared he'd break a rib. He couldn't believe what he was going to do. Yet, it felt right.

Keeping his shoulders back and chin held high, he entered Trevor's study. His brother stood near the hearth with the poker in his hand as he broke apart the logs. Trevor glanced his way then returned his attention to the fire.

"Good morning, Brother," Trevor said. "I'm surprised you are not still asleep in bed at this hour."

"Too many things weigh on my mind." Tristan stepped closer, linking his hands behind him. "Before you act all domineering as the role of the oldest brother usually does by telling me how you think I should live my life, let me tell *you* how I'm going to live my life."

"Fine. Tell me."

"I am going to marry Miss Diana Baldwin."

Trevor snapped his head toward Tristan, his brother's eyes growing rounder by the moment. Seconds passed in silence. The only sound in the room came from the popping fire and crackling wood.

"What, pray tell, brought this on? When I spoke with you the other day, you were grumbling about Mother's party and wishing you could be doing other things."

Tristan smiled. "Indeed, I had grumbled, but then something wonderful happened to me when I met her. We had such a glorious time together getting to know each other. I haven't been able to get her off my mind, and I think…" he took a deep breath, "…actually, I *know* I want her as my wife."

"That is exemplary of you, Tristan. I commend you for making a most important decision about your future." Trevor placed the poker back against the wall of the hearth, and then turned toward Tristan. "I'm just very surprised at your announcement. I thought—as well as our parents—that you would marry Lady Jane."

Tristan arched an eyebrow. "True, our parents have been hinting strongly about me asking for her hand, but I just couldn't. I don't love her. I don't even like her much."

Trevor chuckled. "You were always the brother whom I believed would marry for love. Trey will never marry, I fear, and although I'm betrothed to Lady Gwendolyn and we barely know each other, I believe we will grow to love each other eventually." He shrugged. "But now I wonder if you indeed feel love for Miss Baldwin after only knowing her a few days."

Chuckling, Tristan turned toward the window, scratching his head. *Love?* He still wasn't sure if love was what he felt, but he couldn't deny how manly he felt around her. And although they had just met, their brief time together made him feel as if he'd known her much longer. They were destined to be together, he just knew it. "I have never believed in love at first sight, but when I first saw Miss Baldwin, there was something irresistible about her. I couldn't stop thinking about her. When we danced and we talked, I felt like I never wanted to leave her side. She was so natural. Not fake like the other women I know. Miss Baldwin is so very different from Lady Jane, and I really like the differences." A grin tugged on his lips. "So really, the thought of marrying Miss Baldwin does not frighten me in the least. I actually look forward to it."

Trevor laughed. "My brother—always the romantic." He flipped his hand. "Then go ask for her hand before she fears you have abandoned her. I heard she and her mother quietly returned home early this morning."

Tristan swung toward his brother. "They are gone?"

"Yes."

"They can't be. Diana told me yesterday she and her mother were planning on staying all day."

Trevor shrugged. "Well, apparently something changed the baroness' mind, because Mother told me that they had left."

Growling, Tristan pushed his fingers through his hair. "I need to find out where she lives. She never really told me."

"Then, I suggest you be on your gallant way and rescue the damsel in distress."

"Will you let our parents know where I'm going?"

"Of course."

Tristan spun around and rushed out of the room. When he saw the butler, he instructed him to alert the groomsman that he needed his horse saddled and ready posthaste. He ran back to his room to grab his jacket and riding crop, and then dashed back down the stairs and outside. Within fifteen minutes, he was atop his horse and riding toward Bristol.

Excitement built in his chest with the thought of seeing Diana again. She wouldn't discourage the idea of them marrying. The dreamy haze of her eyes when she stared at him, along with the way her mouth moved so seductively with his, let him know she was just as attracted to him as he was to her.

He rode his horse hard and fast, and soon he neared Bristol. The first person he asked when enquiring about the Baldwin's residence gave him directions. The manor wasn't as large as he'd seen before, and the place looked quite run down. It appeared that Lord Baldwin was having money problems. Tristan grinned. He would help his soon-to-be father-in-law out to help him repair this place.

Before Tristan rode too close to the front of the house, he dismounted, and walked slowly, eyeing the surroundings as he pulled his horse behind by the reins. From the back of the house, a woman strolled toward the rundown stable. Immediately, Tristan could tell it was Diana. Today she wore a copper colored dress trimmed with black lace, and on her hands were black gloves. Her bonnet was copper, but thankfully didn't hide her pretty auburn ringlets.

His heart beat faster and he quickened his stride to reach her. As he came to the front of the stable, he noticed her standing just inside, stroking her hand down the mare's nose. Her back was toward him, and her shoulders drooped.

"Oh, Chestnut," she said softly. "What am I going to do?" Her voice broke and she leaned her face against the mare's neck.

Tristan's heart clenched. He couldn't stand to hear her desolate tone. "Not to worry, my sweet. I'll make it right."

She jumped and swung around. Her eyes widened and within moment, color entered her face. "Tristan! What are you doing here?"

"I have come to rescue the fair maiden." He chuckled. "Actually, since you left without saying anything to me, I knew I must come find you."

She sighed heavily. "I apologize for our hasty departure, but my mother received a letter from my father who wanted us home immediately. I fear his news was dreadful."

He arched an eyebrow. "What news? Has he fallen ill?"

"Oh, Tristan." Tears spiked her eyelashes. "My father has signed a betrothal agreement."

Sadness—and panic—weighed heavily on his chest. Groaning, he scrubbed his palms over his face. He had to stop this. He couldn't let her marry anyone but him!

He stepped closer and touched her hand. "Who is the man?"

"Viscount Hollingsworth."

The man's evil face flashed through Tristan's mind. *Impossible! She couldn't possibly marry that vile man.* "You must be jesting. Hollingsworth is a deceitful, selfish man. Why would any father torture their daughter in such a way by allowing them to marry Hollingsworth?"

"I wish I knew, Tristan. I tried to sway my father this morning, but he will not relent."

Tristan hitched a breath. Anger and frustration sailed through him, making him want to lash out at someone—Hollingsworth in particular since he was the root of Tristan's turmoil right now. "That is utterly ridiculous! There must be a way to change your father's mind."

"My father wants us to wed within two weeks."

Suffocation choked Tristan. Hollingsworth couldn't have Diana—not when Tristan wanted her! Tristan took her hands in his. "Diana, I came here to ask if you would be my wife."

Tears slid down her cheeks and her bottom lip trembled. "If Hollingsworth wasn't in my life right now, I would happily accept." Her voice broke as more tears fell from her eyes.

"Surely, your father will listen to me. I am wealthier than Hollingsworth. I'm certain I could sway your father."

She shook her head. "I pray you can, but I fear the viscount is holding something over my father and is trying to swindle him in some way."

Cursing silently, Tristan pulled her in his arms. She clung to him like she never wanted to let him go. He felt the same helplessness and pulled her tighter in his embrace. She sobbed against his chest, which broke his heart that much more.

He kissed her ear and whispered, "Diana, you must trust me. I will fix things. Lord Hollingsworth will *not* marry you!"

Chapter Eleven

TRISTAN HAD NEVER felt this desperate before. All he knew was that it would kill him if he couldn't stop Diana from marrying Lord Hollingsworth.

He glanced toward her house. "Diana, please allow me to talk to your father. I will do all I can do to get him to change his mind."

She licked her lips and nodded. "Come. I shall take you to him. Let me warn you that he is a very stubborn man."

Tristan arched an eyebrow. "Then I should be able to understand him well since my brothers are also very stubborn."

He followed Diana into her house as she led him to the sitting room. It was obvious by the worn furniture, faded curtains and rugs that the Baldwins were in desperate needs of funds. Perhaps this was the key to getting Lord Baldwin to change his mind. Tristan could assist, and would gladly help as long as the lord gave Tristan his daughter's hand in marriage.

She squeezed his hands. "Stay here and I will fetch my father." She remained standing in front of him as her desperate gaze slowly moved over his face. "Tristan, I wish you luck. I shall pray you will know the words to convince my father to break the betrothal agreement."

"I will pray as well."

Releasing his hands, she turned and hurried out of the room.

Nervousness eased its way in Tristan's stomach. He flexed his hands, trying to think of the right words to say. *This must work!*

Never in his life had he imagined being in such a predicament. Although he figured he would marry for love one day, he had never imagined how much he would have to struggle just to keep that dream alive. Shouldn't this have just fallen perfectly into place?

After several long and agonizing minutes ticked by, footsteps thudded on the floor in the corridor, growing louder as they neared the room. Taking a deep breath, Tristan said a silent prayer that all would work out, and by the end of the day he and Diana would be engaged.

Diana walked in the room with her father. Lord Baldwin was a stout man, and not as tall as Tristan. A frown etched his expression and bushy auburn eyebrows were pulled together over a narrowed gaze.

Tristan gulped. Already things were not looking good.

"Father, allow me to introduce Lord Tristan Worthington." She met Tristan's eyes. "My lord, this is my father, Baron Baldwin."

Tristan nodded. "My lord."

The other man grumbled the same response.

Hope that Tristan had tried to keep in his heart began to sink. Fast. Regardless of the panic encasing him, he smiled his best at the other man. "Lord Baldwin, I am very happy to finally meet the man whose daughter has captured my interest." He took another breath, wondering why his heartbeat seemed to be running a race with his words. "The past few days at my mother's party, I had the privilege of meeting your daughter. I found her such a delight and—"

"You are too late, Lord Tristan," Baldwin barked. "She has been betrothed to the Viscount Hollingsworth."

Tristan gulped and quickly cleared his throat. "Your daughter has already explained this to me. However, I am here to see if I can convince you otherwise." He switched his focus to Diana, who bunched her hands at her side, appearing as nervous as Tristan felt. "Miss Baldwin and I have gotten to know each other, and I would very much like to marry her."

She smiled at him, but her lips quivered.

Tristan looked back at Baldwin. "I understand you have signed a contract with Hollingsworth, but—"

"Please, Lord Tristan," Baldwin grunted. "Do not make this any more difficult than it already is. The subject is closed. My daughter *will* wed Lord Hollingsworth."

Irritation expanded inside Tristan's chest and he wanted to shake Diana's father senseless. But he must remain calm. "My lord, if it's money you seek, I can assure you I'm quite wealthy—"

"Please, no more." Baldwin stepped closer to Tristan. Moisture glistened in the man's eyes as a different expression crossed his face. It appeared as if the man was silently pleading for help. "Lord Tristan, there is nothing I can do. However, if you can convince Lord Hollingsworth to break the contract, I will happily give you and Diana my blessing."

Something wasn't right here. Confusion swam in Tristan's head as he recalled Diana mentioning that Hollingsworth had some kind of hold over her father. Indeed, that must be the case because usually the father of the bride could break the marriage contract, yet Baldwin was reluctant to do so.

Tristan nodded. "That's what I'll do." He bowed. "Good day, my lord." He glanced at Diana and tried his best to give her a reassuring smile. "I *will* see you later with good news."

She brought her clutched hands to her chest and nodded. "I pray you will."

Instead of waiting to be shown out, Tristan hurried out of the house and to his horse, determined to find Hollingsworth and convince him to release Diana's father.

Although Tristan didn't know the viscount well, he knew that the man loved playing the gaming tables...and loved cheating people. Tristan would find that man even if he had to search all over England.

Thankfully, he found Hollingsworth at the second place Tristan looked. It helped that he knew people and had good connections.

When Tristan approached the table, a few of the other lords nodded greetings to him and motioned for him to join them. Hollingsworth glared, but didn't rebut the invitation. It shouldn't surprise Tristan that his younger brother, Trey, was here. That particular brother loved living up to his corrupted reputation.

After a few hands—and a few cups of port—Tristan relaxed and tried to get into the game although his mind scrambled to think of a way he could talk Hollingsworth out of marrying Diana.

Tristan laid down his winning hand and grinned.

Lord Harris shook his head. "I should have known Lord Tristan would take my money. It never fails when I play with a Worthington."

"Lord Tristan," Hollingsworth said, aiming his glare at him, "If I didn't know better, I would think you were cheating this evening."

The others in the room hushed as their hands stilled. Tristan had played cards with Hollingsworth several times before, and should be used to his sour attitude by now. Although Tristan should call the bugger out, he wouldn't... yet. "Then it's a good thing you know me, isn't it?"

Grumbling, Hollingsworth swiped his fingers through his bright red hair that in spots had turned to white. "Indeed, it's most fortunate I know you."

The other men at the table relaxed, but Tristan couldn't let the subject rest. He took another swig of his port before adding, "And it's a good thing you are into your cups a little heavy tonight, or I just might feel the need to call you out."

A few men gasped, but Tristan only heard the person sitting on his right. Slowly, he turned his gaze to Trey. The wide blue eyes of his brother were dark with anger, and silently he issued a warning. Trey had always been like that—thinking he needed to protect Tristan against men who were very much like the youngest Worthington brother. Tristan gave Trey a nonchalant shrug and returned his attention to Hollingsworth whose face was flushed.

"Shall we continue playing?" Tristan asked.

The others around the table chimed in with a positive response. Throughout the game, Hollingsworth continued to throw visual daggers toward Tristan, which he did his best to ignore. The fop had always been a bad sport while playing cards, and if Tristan didn't enjoy taking the lord's money so much, he would refuse to play with him most of the time.

Finally, Hollingsworth bowed out, gathered up the little winnings he had kept, and stormed out of the room. The other gents followed suit. Tristan stood, and so did his brother.

Trey reached his arms above his head as if he were stretching out kinks. "Well, Brother. I believe I shall retire as well." He clapped his hand on Tristan's shoulder. "But I'm happy to see you have won big this evening, and once again, brought with your company a bit of entertainment."

"Entertainment?" Tristan arched an eyebrow.

"Yes. You enjoy making the other gentlemen at the table nervous, including your own brother."

Scooping up his winnings, Tristan chuckled. "Well, someone has to liven up the game." He nodded to his brother, and hurried out to try and find Hollingsworth. He'd give the man every last thing he earned tonight if it meant winning Diana's hand. As he made his way down the steps of the building, a dark shadow against the building pulled his attention.

"Lord Tristan," Hollingsworth greeted in a not-so-civil tone.

"Hollingsworth." Tristan nodded. "I had assumed you were heading home to sulk."

"You thought wrong." The lord walked slowly toward Tristan, eyeing him carefully. "I'm not a man who sulks. Instead, I'm a man who gets even."

"Truly?" Tristan folded his arms across his chest. "What a

surprise. I hadn't heard that about you, Hollingsworth."

The other man's scowl darkened—if that were at all possible. "I'm warning you now. I will not tolerate a cheater."

"Ah, such a good thing to know about you." Tristan nodded. "I'm quite certain that particular trait will make you one trustworthy lord one day."

"Lord Tristan," he snarled. "I do not want to play another game of cards with you again."

"Why not, my lord?" Tristan frowned. "Don't you know how much I enjoy taking your money? Are you sure we couldn't just work this out?"

Growling, Hollingsworth gripped the lapels of Tristan's overcoat and shook him once. "Heed my warning, or you'll be sorry. If you don't do as I say, I might have to harm someone close to you just to teach you a lesson."

Whether the man was foxed or not, Tristan had enough of this imbecile. Breaking the hold Hollingsworth had on him, Tristan pushed the older man, causing Hollingsworth to tumble back a couple of steps before righting himself.

"Now hear this, my lord." Tristan sneered the last two words, hating that this kind of man had been born to noble parents. "I don't take kindly to threats, especially aimed at those I care about. So if you value your life, you will refrain from saying such things. Understood?"

"You doubt my sincerity?"

Tristan could tell Hollingsworth wanted more—and Tristan would indeed give it to him. "I'm a fair man, and although I'm not an avid gambler like my brother, Lord Trey, I do enjoy making bets. I have a wager for you, my lord." He held out the money he'd won tonight. "I will give you every last shilling here, if you withdraw your marriage offer to Miss Diana Baldwin."

It took only seconds before Hollingsworth's eyes widened and he laughed. "Oh, what a surprise this is! I actually have something Lord Tristan wants."

"I'm quite serious, Hollingsworth. Leave the lady alone. She does not want to marry you. She wants to be *my* wife."

Hollingsworth threw back his head and bellowed a laugh. "Oh, this is famous! Not very often do I see a time when a Worthington brother does not get what he wants." He flipped his hand. "Regardless, I can assure you, Lord Tristan, you have lost. Miss Baldwin and I *will* marry and there isn't a thing you can do to stop it."

Tristan's mind grasped for anything that might help him. "How much do you want? I will pay handsomely. I have spoken with the man earlier, and he will allow me to wed his daughter if I can get you to release him."

Hollingsworth shrugged. "If Lord Baldwin breaks the betrothal agreement, I shall see the man in prison and he knows it. I can assure you this battle I *will* win because I hold the trump card!"

As Hollingsworth walked away, Tristan's heart crumbled. What could he possibly do now to stop it?

"Tristan? What was that all about?"

Trey's voice yanked Tristan out of his turmoil, and he turned to look toward the building. Trey had been leaning against the side of the structure in the shadows. He pulled away and sauntered toward Tristan.

"I couldn't help but overhear what you and Hollingsworth were talking about."

"I'm sorry you had to hear that."

"Is there something I can do to assist?"

Tristan shrugged. "I want to marry Miss Baldwin and she wants to marry me, but her father signed a contract with Hollingsworth. Do you have any insane ideas on how I can stop her from marrying the wrong man?"

Trey chuckled. "I must admit, Tristan, I never thought I'd see you so adamant about a woman you just barely met. What happened with Lady Jane?"

"Nothing at all happened with her, nor will it ever. I want to marry Diana."

"Well, if it were me," he said walking past Tristan slowly, "and mind you, I will never be in your shoes, but if that were me, I would take what is mine without questions asked."

"But Trey, she's not mine."

Trey stopped, turned and looked over his shoulder at Tristan. "Then make her yours."

"How?"

"Elope. Go get her tonight and take her to Gretna Green."

"But can I?"

"What is Hollingsworth or her father going to do once she's married and you have consummated the marriage bed?" He shook his head. "Not one bloody thing! And although the elopement may dampen yours and Miss Baldwin's reputation for a while, people will soon forgive and forget, but at least the lady will be yours and not Hollingsworth's."

Hope sprang to life in Tristan's chest and he clamped his hand on Trey's shoulder. "What a brilliant suggestion. Has anyone ever told you how very clever you are?"

Trey's smile widened. "All the time, my dear brother."

Excitement rushed through Tristan once more, and he ran to his horse, mounted, and rode toward Bristol to finally rescue his fair maiden. He wouldn't get there tonight, but he would still take her to Gretna Green sometime tomorrow.

Chapter Twelve

DIANA'S STOMACH CHURNED with dread, her nerves fraying with every passing second. She had barely slept, her mind a relentless whirlwind of worst-case scenarios. All night, she had waited, hoping Tristan would come with good news. But as dawn arrived without him, her deepest fears began to take root, suffocating her fragile hope. What if he hadn't been able to convince Hollingsworth to release the betrothal contract? What if this nightmare truly had no escape?

By ten o'clock, her mother had dragged her into the nearest village for more shopping, an errand that felt like torture. She didn't want to see anyone—least of all the villagers who might greet her with cheerful smiles, unaware of the dread eating her alive. She couldn't bear the thought of meeting their gazes and acknowledging that she was destined to be the viscount's bride. Her pulse thumped at the very thought, her skin prickling as if she were wearing a dress made of needles.

As they moved from one shop to the next, Diana kept her head down, avoiding eye contact with the bustling townsfolk. In the dress shop, she stationed herself by the window while her mother haggled with the shopkeeper. The warm, musty scent of fabric surrounded her, but she hardly noticed. Her gaze kept darting outside, scanning the road as if Tristan might magically appear to rescue her.

She sighed, resting her forehead briefly against the cool glass. But then—movement. Her breath hitched as her eyes locked on a figure across the street, standing just inside the blacksmith's barn. A familiar shadow. A man facing the shop. Her heart stumbled in her chest, then began to race.

Tristan.

She didn't think. She couldn't. The need to see him, to hear those long-awaited words—*you're free*—propelled her forward with reckless speed. Her legs carried her before her mind could catch up, and she burst from the shop, dodging a startled vendor as she made her way across the road. The clatter of a passing horse and buggy barely registered as she darted between them, her skirts brushing the wheels. She was breathless, nearly to the barn door, her pulse thundering in her ears.

In just moments, she would see him. Just moments, and everything could change.

Entering the stable, she called out, "Tristan?"

The shadow moved toward the light. A strong hand grasped her arm and pain shot through her limb, making her cry out.

"No, my dear Diana. It's not your precious Tristan, but your fiancé."

The scent of alcohol from his breath made her gag, and she tried to pull away. Instead, he yanked her closer.

"Ah, my pretty Diana." His hand stroked her cheek. "You are going to make a fine, passionate wife, especially if you show as much interest in me as you do to Lord Tristan."

"Please, my lord." She struggled to get him to release her arm. "I don't wish to marry you. I will never love you. I love Tristan."

A fierce growl rattled through his throat and suddenly, both hands were on her arms as he roughly pressed his body against hers. "I care not about *love*. Only possession. You will be mine and there is nothing anyone can do about it."

"Y—y—you are wrong. Tristan promised he'd make things right." Fear shook through her body.

He cackled a laugh. "Oh, my dear Diana, how wrong you are to put so much trust in a Worthington brother. I can assure you, once Tristan realizes what kind of woman you are, he will turn and run far away from you and your miserable, penniless family."

"What are you talking about? He knows what kind of woman I am."

He stared into her eyes for the longest time before a smile snuck across his face. "Am I to believe that *you* don't even know what kind of family you have? If any true nobleman learned of your family's dark secret, I assure you, nobody would look upon you even if you were lying in the gutter and they had to step across you to get to the other side."

"Lord Hollingsworth, please." She struggled against him. "You are not making any sense. I don't know what you're talking about."

"Just know this," he said in a lower voice as he brought his face closer to hers, "once the secret is out, I will be the only man who will want you, and you will be happy that I'm such an understanding husband."

Behind her, a loud curse tore through the barn, cutting through the air like a whip. She spun around just in time to see Hollingsworth ripped from her side and hit the ground with a heavy thud. Her breath hitched as she took in the scene—Tristan standing over him, fists clenched, muscles taut with barely contained rage. His eyes burned with intensity, a storm brewing behind them, and for a moment, the barn seemed to shrink around them, suffocating in its charged atmosphere.

Diana sobbed with relief, tears blurring her vision as her knees weakened beneath her. He was here. *He found her.* For a brief, fleeting moment, she allowed herself to believe everything would be all right. But the weight of uncertainty quickly pressed down on her chest. Could she trust that Tristan's presence would bring the salvation she craved, or would it only plunge them deeper into this mess? Would he be her shield—or the spark that ignited an even greater disaster?

The tension between the two men crackled like dry wood catching flame. Hollingsworth groaned on the floor, rolling to his side, but Tristan didn't move, his fists still raised as if ready to strike again. His chest rose and fell with labored breaths, his knuckles white from the force of his grip.

"Tristan," she whispered, her voice barely audible over the pounding of her heart. She didn't know whether she was pleading for him to stop or for him to finish what he'd started.

His eyes met hers. Worry etched his expression. "Are you all right?"

"Y—yes. I thank you for saving me. Again."

On the ground, Hollingsworth muttered curses as he stood. "You have crossed me for the last time, Worthington." He aimed his curse toward Tristan as he jumped to his feet.

Tristan glared, his blue eyes as hard as steel. "I told you earlier, I would *not* let you marry Diana."

"And I told you that you don't have a choice!" Hollingsworth thundered as he rushed forward.

Growling, Tristan punched Hollingsworth in the nose, and the older man fell back to the ground.

She gasped and covered her mouth, but heard other gasps around her. Startled, she swung around to look behind her. Several people from the village had gathered. Embarrassment washed over her. Scandal was about to explode, and this kind of gossip would spread like wildfire.

Hollingsworth's evil laugh pulled her attention back to him. A trickle of blood dripped from his mouth.

"Lord Tristan, I grow tired of your attitude. This between us will end now." He swallowed hard. "Better yet, it will end tomorrow morning. At sunrise, I challenge you to a duel at Harvey's Cliffs. Be there with a second, or your name—and your family's name—will be reduced to that of cowards."

Tristan threw a glance over his shoulder at the crowd who was growing larger by the second, and then looked back at Hollingsworth. Tristan pulled his shoulders back and lifted a stubborn chin.

"I accept your challenge."

"And the winner will have Miss Baldwin as their wife," Hollingsworth added.

A cold hand wrapped around Diana's arm. Her mother stood beside her with a face void of color. "We are leaving *now!*" she grumbled.

"Yes, Mother."

Diana turned and looked back at Tristan, her breath catching as her gaze met his. A soft smile curved the corners of his lips, bracketing his face with warmth she hadn't realized how desperately she needed. He mouthed the words, *don't worry,* and in that brief moment, her fears unraveled like thread slipping from a spool. Her heart swelled, bursting with a happiness so pure that it momentarily drowned out the storm of dread that had consumed her all morning.

The silent reassurance gave her the strength she hadn't known she possessed. With renewed courage, she turned toward her mother, ready to leave and face whatever wrath her father would unleash once he learned of today's events. The road ahead was steep and uncertain, but Tristan's promise—unspoken yet deeply understood—gave her the resolve to move forward.

As they walked away, the breeze whispered through her hair, carrying the salty tang of the sea from the nearby cliffs. Harvey's Cliffs were notorious for duels, their jagged edges stained with the echoes of challenges fought and resolved. But Diana didn't tremble at the thought. Deep down, she knew Tristan would emerge the victor. He had never failed her before, not when it truly mattered, and her heart told her he never would.

With every step, she clung to that truth: Tristan was her anchor, her constant in a world of shifting tides. And no matter what awaited them beyond those cliffs, she believed she could count on him—always.

Tears spilled down Diana's cheeks, warm and relentless, as she stood by the window, staring blindly at the world beyond the glass. The muffled voices of her parents and Lord Hollingsworth filled the room behind her, discussing the details of her swift, inevitable wedding. Their words were like knives slicing through her composure, and she trembled beneath the weight of her despair.

She had waited all morning, clinging to hope like a lifeline, desperate to hear something—*anything*—about the duel. But when her father had delivered the news, it had hit her like a punch to the gut, stealing the air from her lungs.

Tristan didn't show up for the duel... Took the coward's way out... He's nowhere to be found.

The words echoed endlessly in her mind, a cruel refrain that refused to fade. She bit her lip until it hurt, trying to keep herself from sobbing aloud. She couldn't afford to believe it. She *wouldn't* believe it. Tristan had promised her, hadn't he? He was supposed to fight for her, to free her from the chains that Hollingsworth had tightened around her life.

Yet, where was he now?

Witnesses at Harvey's Cliffs had confirmed it—Tristan hadn't shown up. Only Hollingsworth had been there, standing smug and victorious. And Tristan, the man she had trusted with her heart, had vanished.

Abandoned her. Left her to the mercy of a vile, ruthless viscount whose interest in her wasn't love, but possession. She was nothing more than a prize to Hollingsworth, a trophy to be displayed. He didn't care about her hopes, her dreams, or her fears. He only cared about *winning*.

Piece by piece, her heart splintered, breaking under the weight of betrayal and shattered dreams. Tristan hadn't loved her—not the way she had loved him. She had been willing to give up everything, even prepared to elope with him if it meant escaping the suffocating future her parents had arranged. But he hadn't fought for her. He hadn't shown up.

He'd left her alone.

A sob finally escaped her lips, and she pressed her hand against her mouth to stifle it. The truth was unbearable, but she couldn't run from it any longer. Tristan was gone, and she was trapped.

In a way, Diana wanted to feel relief—relief that she had seen Tristan Worthington's true colors before she had married him. A coward. A deceiver. A man who had abandoned her when she had needed him most. Her mind whispered that she should be grateful, that fate had spared her from tying herself to someone so unreliable. But no matter how much she tried to convince herself, the ache in her chest wouldn't subside.

Her heart stubbornly refused to let go of him. Even now, with her trust shattered and her future slipping through her fingers, it clung to the memories of the man she had believed him to be—the man who had once made her laugh, who had stolen her breath with tender kisses and whispered promises of forever.

She hated him. She *should* hate him. But the truth burned like a brand in her soul: she still loved him, despite it all. And that love, unwanted and unbearable, was what hurt the most.

Tears blurred her vision as she stared out the window, her mind replaying moments that now felt like cruel illusions. She had imagined a life with him, had dreamed of a future full of adventure and freedom, away from the rigid constraints of duty and expectation. Now, that future had dissolved, crumbling like a fragile dream in the morning light.

Her gaze drifted to the road beyond the window, as if hoping, irrationally, to see him standing there. But there was nothing. Only the cold, indifferent world outside.

The bleak reality of her situation settled in her chest like a stone. She would marry Hollingsworth, a man who saw her as a possession rather than a partner. She would live a life dictated by duty, her hopes buried beneath the weight of someone else's ambition.

The thought suffocated her, and yet she could do nothing to change it. Tristan wasn't coming back.

Her heart had been wrong to believe in him. But even now, it refused to stop hoping. And that, more than anything, was the cruelest betrayal of all.

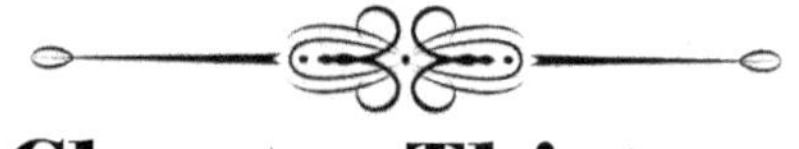

Chapter Thirteen

Three years later, back at the unknown cottage

TRISTAN'S BODY ACHED terribly, and his skin chafed from the rope burns. When he wasn't so mad, he'd have to compliment that maid for being so thorough with his bindings. But until then, he was content to be upset with her—and Diana—for forcing him to stay here.

The ladies had retired for bed hours ago and were probably sleeping just fine in their comfy beds while their prisoner was completely uncomfortable in this chair. He glanced over at the sofa only a few steps away from him. If only he could bounce somehow to those soft, inviting, cushions and lay his head on something soft, then he'd be able to sleep.

As well as he could using only his chin and shoulder, he tried to remove the gag. It moved a little, but didn't come off. Still, it was enough that he could at least lick his lips if needs be.

Using all of his strength, he concentrated on jumping in the chair. It took him a few times, but soon, he was able to move the chair—if only an inch at a time. That would be good enough for now.

He huffed and groaned as he forced his body to move with the chair, commanding the chair to move in the direction he wanted to go. Finally, when he got close enough to the sofa, he lunged. The chair tipped, and thankfully, landed on the cushions. Half of him was on the sofa, while the other half was still on the floor. It didn't matter, because at least his head had something soft to lay on now.

Exhaustion filled him and he took slow breaths, trying to relax. Too bad his mind wouldn't relax. He still wondered why Diana felt that what had happened between them three years ago was *his* fault. Her words had not made a bit of sense. If anything, he should loathe her, which he did. He just couldn't remember exactly why...

His memory hadn't fully returned, and that irritated him more than anything. It seemed that no matter how hard he tried to recall the past, the further away he was taken from the truth.

Slowly, he closed his eyes and listened to the rain pounding the roof in a steady rhythm. Soon, his mind drifted asleep. Diana's wide green eyes—passionate eyes—were in this thoughts.

Three years ago, he'd been crushed to discover she hadn't tried to stop the duel. Not that he wanted her to chase after him, but she didn't even voice her opinion or pretend that she cared. Many of the events that occurred before the duel were foggy, but he remembered feelings of despondency.

What had really happened that morning? Why couldn't he remember? When he'd finally started to remember his past, the deepening hatred for Diana stayed in his heart and wouldn't leave. He remembered being in love with her, yet was that feeling real at all? Could he have mistaken love for infatuation— or Heaven help him—*lust*?

As Diana stayed on his mind, a comforting sensation spread over him. When they first met, she'd been so adorable blowing kisses at him even though it was really to blow away the bee. Her eyes twinkled when she looked upon him while they danced. And her laugh was like Heavenly chimes in his ears. When she said his name, it was always followed with a sigh.

Then that dreadful day she'd learned of her betrothal to Lord Hollingsworth, her emerald green eyes had pleaded for help. His heart wrenched, and he'd wanted so badly to take away her pain—and his frustration. She'd made him feel like a man, more so than any other woman had made him feel.

Lord Hollingsworth was also in Tristan's mind. So forceful. So cock-eyed sure of himself that Tristan wanted to pummel the man's face. Hollingsworth knew he could make Tristan squirm, and that kind of feeling was *not* acceptable!

Slowly, the fog in his mind cleared.

The letter... Diana's letter.

Drowsily, Tristan shook his head, trying to remember more. The duel hadn't happened in the morning, but...

That night!

While he and Trey stayed at the local inn waiting for sunset to arrive that evening, a letter had come from Diana. His heart had thumped wildly, hoping that she wanted to meet him and perhaps they could run away to Gretna Green. Her letter had stated she wanted to meet him, but at Henry's Cliffs instead. She had exciting news to tell him.

"Tristan, this does not feel right," Trey had repeated as they mounted their horses and rode toward the cliffs.

Dusk covered the sky in blue and purple colors with a slice of red mixed in. Tristan wanted to share this beautiful evening with the woman he loved. "Nonsense, Trey. I couldn't very well meet her at her home. I believe she will be there waiting for me with her satchel packed and ready to leave for Gretna Green."

"I pray you are correct, but I have an uneasy feeling about all of this."

When they reached the cliffs, Tristan pulled his horse to a stop. Trey halted beside him. Shadows danced in the tall trees, most of the light from the sun had been removed.

"I'm telling you... something isn't right," Trey repeated in a low voice.

Tristan scanned the area and called out, "Diana? Where are you?" He dismounted and walked further.

The glade was peaceful and only the chirps from crickets were heard, and an occasional hoot of an owl. The waterfall shooting down the cliffs crashed at the bottom as it hit the rocks.

"Tristan, don't you feel it? The atmosphere here is too... eerie."

Apprehension washed over Tristan. "I agree, brother. Something is not right. Diana would have been here by now."

"I think we should leave. What if this was some kind of trap?"

Tristan glanced over his shoulder and arched his eyebrow at his brother. "Do you think Hollingsworth might have planned this and not Diana?"

"I do. Hollingsworth has never been trustworthy."

"He hasn't, but I'm not leaving." Tristan scanned the area again through a narrowed gaze. "If he is here, then I'll stay. Killing that man is the only way Diana and I can ever be together."

"Are you aware what kind of hero you'd be?" Trey dismounted. "I can count at least ten men who would be glad to see the bloke dead."

Moving further into the glade, Tristan kept his ears alert. If Hollingsworth and his second were here at all, they must have hidden their horses. Tristan took calculated steps toward the trees. "Hollingsworth? If you're here, come out and show yourself. Or are you a coward who hides behind the trees?"

Deafening silence filled the air.

"I don't feel right about this." Trey shook his head. "Tristan, get back on your horse—"

The blast of a pistol pierced the air. Immediately, the impact of the bullet hitting Tristan in the back above his left shoulder brought him to his knees.

Trey shouted a curse, terror laced his voice.

Pain like no other burned through Tristan's back as he fell facedown on the ground. Quickly the area soaked with sticky, blood. Dizziness assailed him, but he struggled to stand.

"Tristan, you've been shot," Trey said as he pressed his hands to the core of the pain.

"I'm fine." Tristan grumbled and shoved his brother away. He stood—unsteady—and glanced toward the area the shot had come from. "Come out and fight me like a real man, Hollingsworth!"

Two dark shadows by the nearest tree finally materialized into forms. The descending light from the sun touched them, and indeed one of them was Hollingsworth. Tristan didn't care who the other man was because he focused his hatred on the redhead holding the smoking pistol.

"Is this the way you have made it through life? Shooting people in

the back?" Tristan shook his head slowly, the dizziness becoming worse. "You have no right to call yourself a nobleman."

Hollingsworth threw down his weapon and marched toward Tristan. "I loathe men like you. All of you think you're better than the rest of us."

"I am better. I don't shoot people in the back. I face them like a real man." The pain in Tristan's back worsened, and numbness spread quickly through his arm. Still, if he had to fight this imbecile with his bare hands, he would. If only the dizziness wasn't consuming his vision right now.

Hollingsworth tilted his head back and laughed harshly. "My dear Lord Tristan. If you knew your efforts were wasted, you would think differently."

"What are you talking about?"

"Miss Baldwin." He stopped mere feet away from Tristan and folded his arms. "Have you not asked yourself why her father was willing to marry her off so quickly?"

The pain was too great to think. He shook his head. "I can only assume you are blackmailing him in some way."

"I paid off her father's debts. Did she tell you that? Diana knew that I would send her father to prison if he tried to back out of our deal."

Hollingsworth's words were muffled in Tristan's head, and slowly, he started piecing things together. "Diana knew I couldn't stop you? She knew there wasn't anything I could do to talk you out of marrying her?"

"Now you're getting it, Worthington. And here all along, I thought you were the dim-witted brother."

Tristan rubbed his forehead, the pain getting worse. In back of him, his brother was yelling at him to get back on the horse and leave, but all Tristan could do was stare in shock at Hollingsworth's confession.

"And that's not the best part," Hollingsworth snickered.

At this point, Tristan didn't really want to hear anymore, but the question came from his throat anyway, "What is the worst part?"

"Diana is now a ruined woman. Just this evening, I took my lusts out on her in her father's barn and she was unwilling to stop me. I suspect she will be giving an heir in nine months."

A loud curse rent the air mere seconds before Trey attacked Hollingsworth. *Trey pounded his fists into Hollingsworth's face, knocking the man to the ground.*

Tristan wanted to join in, but as he took a step toward them, he swayed. Suddenly, from out of nowhere, Hollingsworth's second plowed into Tristan. He lost his footing and landed on the ground. The other man's weak punches couldn't harm a fly, but in Tristan's deteriorating condition, he couldn't fight them off. Finally, he kneed the man in the groin, giving Tristan the room to stand. The man screamed like a little girl as he knelt on the dewy grass, holding his crotch and rocking.

Glancing at Trey and Hollingsworth, Tristan realized they were closer to the edge of the cliffs than they had been a few moments ago. Tristan broke into a run—as well as he could with the world spinning around him—heading to help his brother.

Hollingsworth threw a punch, knocking Trey down. The redhead blackguard then searched the ground for his weapon. Tristan prayed for strength as he bent and planned to bump his head right into Hollingsworth's chest.

Mere seconds before Tristan reached his target, Hollingsworth moved away. Suddenly, the ground beneath Tristan's feet disappeared. Like a bullet, he sailed through the air, down... down toward the turbulent waves below.

Coldness surrounded Tristan. He couldn't breathe. He whimpered and flayed his arms. They seemed weightless.

From out of nowhere a woman's voice soothed him. *Diana.* She urged him to drink tea. Yet his mind still swam with darkness. Within minutes his body relaxed and his mind drifted to a closure.

Chapter Fourteen

T HE NEXT MORNING, Diana was up early and dressed quickly so she could check on Tristan. Late into the night she'd heard him whimpering, and rushed to see what had ailed him, and then almost laughed to see him lying half on the couch.

Seeing him sitting, or lying there so helpless made her want to untie him, but instead she loosened his gag and gave him a sip of tea, urging him to drink. When he hadn't awakened, she threw a blanket over him and left him tied to the chair. She could tell he was having a bad dream because of the way his forehead creased and the moans that came from his throat. Even his head moved back and forth. After watching him a few minutes and realizing that he had calmed down, she had returned to bed.

She glanced at her clock and uttered a loud curse. It was nearly afternoon. Oh, why did she sleep so long? Quickly, she pulled a beige day dress over her head and tied a copper ribbon around her waist, pulled her hair back in a coil, and then hurried down the stairs. The scent of bread hung in the air and made her stomach grumble. Tabitha must be up and making something to eat.

Instead of going to the kitchen, she decided to check on Tristan first. Would he be awake? Then again, if he was, she was certain he'd be making a lot of noise right now. Fortunately, he was in the same spot where she'd left him.

Taking careful steps toward him, she didn't want to disturb his slumber. His eyes were closed, and his chin rested on his chest. The gag lay limp around his neck from when she'd removed it last night. She doubted he had rested any better than she had, being in such a cramped position, but although she'd lain on a nice soft bed, sleep hadn't come and she tossed and turned fitfully all night. Knowing that Tristan was back in her life kept her more alert than she wanted to be.

"Oh, what am I going to do with you?" she mumbled. She had thought of no solution for their problem.

She glanced at the window. It wasn't raining, and the sun was up. Still, as much as it had rained, the roads were probably very poor to travel on this afternoon. But if she untied Tristan, he would try to leave anyway… as stubborn as he was.

Walking toward the window, she tried once again to think of a way out of their mess. Keeping him tied up wasn't a good thing, but what other choice did she have? She stopped and peered out on the muddy ground as she recalled his confusing words last night. Why did the insipid man act as if he didn't know what she was talking about? She'd heard rumors that he'd lost some of his memory, but really, that was so far-fetched, she wasn't sure if it was true or not since there were so many rumors going around about him lately.

"Uh, Diana? Could you help me, please?"

His scratchy voice pulled her from her thoughts and she swung around. His head was turned toward her, but his body hadn't moved. "Lord Tristan, pray tell, what did you think to accomplish by moving to the sofa?" She walked toward him slowly.

"I was thinking to rest my head on something soft so that I could sleep." He grimaced. "Now I'm rethinking that decision since it's made my body that much more cramped."

She grabbed the back of the chair and pushed him to an upright position. "There. Is that better?"

"Actually, no. I would be much better if you untied me."

"I'm quite certain you would, but before I do, I need to ask you some questions."

He blinked his sleepy eyes as if he was clearing his vision. When his gaze finally locked on hers, he nodded. "Good, because I have some questions to ask you as well, but before that, might I inquire how long you and Tabitha are planning to hold me here?"

She didn't dare admit she had no plans—the right kind, anyway. But something in her heart encouraged her to just talk to him and try to work things out.

"I'm not quite certain, Lord Tristan. I haven't been able to speak with Tabitha about it yet. Last night I'd considered keeping you only long enough to make you anxious, but now..." She shrugged. "I rather enjoy torturing you, so perhaps we shall keep you longer."

"I do hope you will untie me before the torture begins. After all, your plan is already in affect, so even if I try to deny it, the damage will be done to my character. Why would I want to return home now anyway?"

She cocked her head, studying him. Was he playing another game? Then again, even if he did escape, his reputation would be ruined.

"Well," she stepped closer to him, sliding her fingers up his arm. Hard muscles flexed noticeably. He'd definitely not been this strapping three years ago. "I suppose I could untie you, even if the idea of keeping you bound and helpless sounds more and more pleasing."

He chuckled. "Oh, Diana, I never imagined your thoughts to be so wicked, especially from a recent widow."

Embarrassment washed through her as heat rose in her face. "You don't believe I could think of such cruel things to do to you?"

"Actually, now that you mention it, I suppose it's not totally out of your character to be so vicious."

She frowned, her heart dropping once again. Why did he continue to act as if *he* were the injured party? None of this made sense, and she was determined to get to the bottom of this.

HE COULDN'T RECALL the last time his body ached so much. He needed release. And now! In his current frame of mind, he didn't care what he had to do—or say—to make her release him. "Diana, if you will until me, I promise as a gentleman, not to run. I feel we need to talk about the past. That is the only way to understand each other."

She tilted her head and studied him for several minutes before nodding. "Fine, I'll untie you, but remember, Tabitha still has a pistol and won't hesitate to use it."

"I assure you there will be no need to use it on me."

She moved beside him and started untying the ropes. Closing his eyes, he inhaled her intoxicating scent of lilacs. Memories washed through his head, reminding him what had *really* happened three years ago. He shook his head and snapped open his eyes. Definitely, they needed to talk.

Slowly, the blood flowed back into his hands and feet, and tingled with awareness. Since he was still close to the sofa, he hopped on the cushions. A sigh fell from his mouth, enjoying the softness. "Ah, I thank you, Diana." He patted the empty space next to him. "Would you like to join me?"

"Not really."

He shook his arms then his legs. "Diana, I have realized that you hate me for some reason, and I cannot fathom why. The reason I told you I won't leave here is because I need to know why you feel this way about me. It hurts to know you think I've ruined your life."

She snorted a laugh before quickly covering her mouth with her hand. Most well-bred women would have scolded Diana for doing this. *It's not proper* they would have told her with their noses in the air. Yet he thought it adorable the way Diana did it—

so natural. His heart melted. Perhaps there was still the old Diana inside this shell of a woman after all.

"Oh, my lord, you are humorous. I'm beginning to wonder if there was something in that tea Tabitha made last night that I'd given you to make you talk this way. I fear you are not thinking straight at all." She shook her head. "I don't *think* you ruined my life. I *know*. And there is nothing you can do to make up for my misery, I assure you."

"First off, I'm in my right mind, and secondly—please call me Tristan. I recall a time when you were wrapped in my arms and whispered my name with much emotion it melted my heart." He quickly snapped his mouth closed. Good grief! Why had he said *that*? He couldn't bring up the past—not that part of their past, anyway.

She leaned back against the wall, folding her arms. Her gaze took on a seriousness he hadn't expected. Her adorable green eyes moved over his face slowly then came to rest on his lips. Anxiousness pumped inside him, and memories resurfaced once again. *This is not the time!*

"Indeed there was a moment in my life I sighed your name with feeling, but not any longer. I'm content now, living the life of a widow—or hermit, if you want to refer to me as—only because it's better than the ridicule I get when trying to associate with members of the *ton*. I've spent all these years with bitterness in my heart for what you've done, but now..." She released a deep breath. "Now I can live the rest of my life knowing you paid the price along with me for our actions those days at your mother's weekend party."

Her words still confused him. What about what she'd done to him? Why wasn't she remembering that?

"I'm sorry if you think me evil or vindictive, but what's done is done and there is no erasing what Tabitha did last night."

"I don't think you are evil or vindictive at all, Diana. Although bringing me down has brought great relief to you, I worry about what might happen if people found out you and your maid planned my kidnapping."

"They won't. Remember, Tabitha planned that all out before you climbed into the wrong coach. Nobody will think I had anything to do with forcing you here. They'll think you came of your own free will. It'll be your word against theirs."

He shook his head. "That's not what I meant. I'm worried about your reputation. What will this do to you?"

Her mouth stretched into a grin and she laughed. "Oh, Tristan. You have a short memory. I don't have a reputation, remember. Nobody will care, and what has happened here won't hurt or hinder me in any way. Polite Society might think I'm a little mad, but I can handle that."

"Do you want people to know we have been together since last night? Is that your plan? Do you want people to think you have been my secret love interest for a few months as Tabitha's missives have indicated?"

"I highly doubt anyone will think I'm involved at all."

He shrugged one shoulder. "They will if they realized I have been here in your grandmother's cottage."

"Honestly, Tristan, I don't think it will matter." She chuckled softly. "Although it would be most humorous, would it not? You, carrying on with the woman you ruined all those years ago? The *ton* would certainly never expect that. You would have the older matrons fainting dead away."

He couldn't stop the smile stretching his lips. "I'm sure you're correct. They wouldn't expect this from me. In fact, I wonder if Lady Fairbourne won't thank the good Lord she didn't marry me after this."

Diana tilted her head, her smiling slowly disappearing. "Do you love her, Tristan?"

The tenderness in her question twisted his heart. "You are the one who must not have a good memory. Have you forgotten I didn't like her much back when you and I first met? That, my dear Diana, has not changed at all."

"Why then did you want to marry her?" She moved to the

sofa and sat next to him, her eyes wide with wonder.

"My mother's health is declining. She often spoke of Lady Fairbourne and how she wished I would marry her. My brothers even acted like they would like me to settle down and raise a family. I've been a bumbling drunk since Trey and Judith found me two years ago, and I knew that wasn't the kind of life I wanted. I had no energy to court a woman the proper way, so I gave in to my family's wishes and proposed to Lady Fairbourne. I wasn't looking for someone to love, just someone to be comfortable with. Jane was without a husband, and because she still showed interest in me, I asked her to be my wife. I thought it was time to put the past behind me once and for all."

"I'm surprised some other woman hasn't sunk her greedy claws into you before now. You're a handsome and charming man who could have made any woman fall in love with you."

Whether she knew it or not, she'd given him a compliment. For someone who loathed him, she certainly didn't show it now. "You think I'm handsome? Charming?" Leaning toward her, he slipped his arm around her shoulders, gently pulling her forward. "You think I could get *any* woman to fall in love with me?"

She stiffened and placed a hand on his chest. Strange, but he thought she should have tried harder to keep him away, instead, he was able to pull her closer. Originally, he did it to tease, but now… now with her so very near, he breathed in her lilac scent as her silky ringlet hair rubbed his hand. His teasing mood had vanished.

"Tristan… please," she whispered.

It was all he could do to not kiss her, but he kept reminding himself this wasn't right. Every time he'd been with her before, the voice of reason had never won. Passion had. "Please what?" *Good grief, why had his voice dropped so low?*

"I—I didn't mean it like that." She gulped. "I didn't say what I did for you to do…*this.*"

Using his other hand, he swept his fingertips across her cheek, down her neck to rest on her shoulder. Her body remained stiff, although her breathing accelerated. She glanced at his mouth a few times, but switched her attention back to his stare. Panic laced her eyes, and he knew he definitely couldn't kiss her now.

"Forgive me, Diana." He pulled away completely. The warmth of her body left him in shock, like cold water being thrown on him. He forced a grin. "Besides, I was just teasing. I'm flattered you think I'm still handsome and charming."

Slowly, he stood and tested his legs to make sure they would carry him as he walked. Thankfully, the feeling was back in them. He walked to the window and looked out on the wet land.

"I said that because I wondered why you hadn't married anyone," she said softly.

A grin pulled at the corners of his mouth and he glanced in her direction. "I haven't married because you kidnapped me, remember?"

She rolled her eyes. "I'm speaking about before that. Why haven't you married someone before now?"

"Because I had loved someone at one time, and had been hurt. Terribly hurt. I hadn't recovered my memory from the accident, and I didn't know why I was such a bitter man. Now I do."

She scowled. "What do you mean you didn't know until now?"

"Because parts of the past were blocked from my mind. Last night I had a breakthrough and I remembered what had happened... what had *really* happened between us."

"Tell me, Tristan," she said rising from the sofa to walk toward him. Her forehead was creased with anger. "Because apparently your version of the truth and mine are completely different."

Chapter Fifteen

Never had Diana felt more puzzled than right now. And yet an inner panic began to grow in her chest. What if all these years she'd been misinformed and had judged Tristan too harshly?

Dryness had suddenly filled her mouth and she swallowed. No matter what was said, she was relieved to know the truth would finally come out. She'd waited three years for this.

"Last night while in my very uncomfortable position, I had a dream." He ran his fingers through his unkempt hair. "Actually, it wasn't a dream at all, but my mind was being opened. The fog that had covered my memory had been lifted. I now know exactly what happened."

Women's voices drifted to her ears from outside. Diana jumped from the sofa and ran to the window. *Visitors? Why on earth would she have a visitor?*

She turned to Tristan and grasped his hand. "We have company. You must hide."

He nodded. "I agree. Where?"

She pointed to the door. "Turn right and go down the hall. There's a bedroom on your left. Go in there and shut the door."

Within moments, his expression softened. His blue eyes nearly melted her. "Don't be long," he whispered before quitting the room.

Her heart hammered. What rotten luck! Just when he was going to tell her something she'd been waiting for so long to hear, her friend, Lady Dashwood, would pay a visit.

The front door swung open and Tabitha was chatting with Claudia as they entered the house.

Taking a deep breath, Diana smoothed her hands down her dress, hoping she didn't appear as rattled as she felt. She smiled at her long-time friend—the only person who had stood by her side in everything Diana had gone through. She moved to Claudia and gave her a hug.

"What a wonderful surprise." Diana pulled away and looked over her friend's dress. "You are simply stunning today, as always, and you always seem to have a new gown on every time I see you."

Claudia laughed. "And you are always so full of compliments." She lifted her chin and displayed a victorious grin. "As you probably can surmise, I'm quite enjoying being a widow and spending money my husband had never allowed me to touch while he was alive."

Diana nodded. "I understand you well, my friend. But tell me, why would you travel here when the roads are so muddy?"

"Diana, I would travel across all of England to come see my dear friend and check up on her. I want to make certain you are all right."

"But of course I am." Diana hooked her arm through her friend's. "I was just about to have tea and biscuits. Would you like to go with me into the kitchen and get some? Tabitha is a wonderful cook, and I'm certain you would enjoy her biscuits."

"That is a fabulous suggestion. Lead the way." Her brown eyes twinkled.

As they entered the kitchen, Tabitha's gaze darted around the room. "My lady, where is he?"

Diana's breath caught. Why in heaven's name had Tabitha said *that*? Quickly, Diana looked back at Claudia for her reaction. Her friend flipped jeweled fingers in the air and shook her head.

"Not to worry. Tabitha just told me about what she did to Lord Tristan, and I must say, what a brilliant idea Tabitha had." She laughed. "I only wish I could have thought of it instead."

Ease washed over Diana and she nodded. "I wish I had thought of it, as well." She met her maid's stare. "Lord Tristan was tired so I sent him to the back room to sleep."

"You untied him?"

"Yes. We can't keep him tied up forever, you know."

"But what if he tries to escape?" Tabitha's voice rose in a panic.

"Then he escapes." Diana shrugged. "The damage has already been done, and there isn't much he can do to repair it."

"Quite right." Claudia nodded, her black ringlets jiggling with the motion. "The whole town was abuzz this morning with talk of Lord Tristan skipping out on his wedding to meet up with his secret lover." She giggled. "I knew right away that I must come see you to find out if you knew anything. I'm very happy that my instincts were correct."

Claudia led the way to the table then sat. Diana followed. Tabitha prepared their teacups and brought them to the table.

"So I'm assuming everyone was in shock?" Diana asked.

"But of course they were. They didn't expect this kind of rash behavior from Lord Tristan." She sipped her tea. "Now the youngest Worthington brother, Lord Trey… before he married if he would have done something like this, society wouldn't have batted an eye."

"How right you are. But, what are they saying?" Diana asked, hesitantly. "Have they sent out search parties?"

"Not yet. Of course, I have heard a few people mention that they wonder if Lord Tristan is having some kind of memory lapse. But if you ask me, I really don't think that story is very believable, anyway."

Diana sipped her tea, watching her friend over the rim of her cup. Claudia was only a year older than her and married Lord Dashwood—a much older man—in her first season. Like Diana,

Claudia had been beaten by her husband.

"Why don't you believe that story?" Tabitha asked.

"Well, mainly because he's been doing so well since he returned from the dead, so to speak. He doesn't act at all like he has no memory." Claudia lifted the cup to her mouth and took a quick drink. "But if you ask me, I think his memory-lost story is not true, and just an excuse his family used to cover up what *really* happened when he didn't arrive the morning of the duel."

"Do you know what really happened?" Diana whispered. This subject had always been a hard one for Diana to discuss. She was still so very confused about everything that happened during that time. And to think, she'd find out as soon as she could get her friend to leave.

"That, my dear, is yet to be discovered." Claudia nodded.

"I heard he drinks himself into a stupor most nights," Tabitha added her thoughts. "Most of the servants at Lord Elliot's townhouse talked about the lordship's cousin, Lord Tristan, as if they didn't know anything else to talk about."

Diana rolled her eyes. "Well, those Worthington brothers certainly know how to stir up trouble and cause talk no matter what they seem to do."

"I agree." Claudia lifted her teacup and took another sip. "Their poor mother dealt with enough scandal while her husband was alive. I'm surprised the poor dear can still breathe."

Frowning, Diana remembered what Tristan had said about his mother's health issues. She touched Claudia's arm. "How is the Dowager Duchess holding up now? Have you heard?"

"I'm sorry to say, I haven't heard. I'm quite certain she will live through this tragedy. If she can live through all the scandal her husband brought on the family from his liaisons, and with Trey's rakish behavior, then to have Tristan disappear, the dowager is indeed a very strong woman."

"So do you think the dowager is all right?" Diana asked softly.

Claudia gave her a reassured smile. "I think she'll recover splendidly."

"Thank goodness. I would be very upset if something bad happened to her because of my grudge."

"Not to worry, Diana." Claudia patted Diana's hand. "What you and Tabitha did with Lord Tristan was perfect."

As the conversation continued, Diana prayed her friend was right. And she also prayed that she could stay focused instead of remembering that Tristan was just in the other room, waiting to tell her the truth.

TRISTAN STOOD NEXT to the door with his ear pressed against the wall. He was able to hear bits and pieces of the conversation going on in the next room. Thankfully, the women decided to adjourn to the kitchen to chat, or he wouldn't have heard anything.

It made him happy to hear concern in Diana's voice when she asked about his mother. His heart melted. Diana *did* care what happened to him and his mother. Even though she'd acted like she was set on revenge and didn't have a heart, she really had one after all.

When the ladies started discussing mundane things, he paced back and forth in the small room, eyeing the bed. He hadn't slept very well, and the feather pillows and heavy quilts beckoned him to lie down. But he fought the temptation. He didn't want to fall asleep, mainly because he was afraid Diana wouldn't wake him, and he definitely needed to talk to her about what he'd remembered.

But as the hours passed, his eyelids became heavy and he moved to the bed. As soon as his head hit the pillow, exhaustion took over and he couldn't open his eyes even if he wanted to. He drifted to sleep with Diana on his mind once again.

Jerking wide awake, Tristan's heart beat in a frantic rhythm as if he'd been running from someone in fear. He groaned and scrubbed his hands across his face, then threaded his fingers through his hair. *Where am I?*

Then he remembered. He ran to the window and pulled open the curtain. The predawn morning peeked on the horizon. He groaned. Diana hadn't come to wake him up after all. Well, at least he was still here and he vowed he would not leave until they had their talk.

He scratched his whiskery face. He needed a bath. His stomach grumbled. And food. But not quite in that order. Right now, he'd take whichever he could get first.

As he sneaked out of the room, his mind turned to what he had remembered yesterday.

Diana. The letter. The duel… and what followed.

Could Hollingsworth have been correct when he said he'd paid off the baron's debts and that Diana knew about it? Confusion filled Tristan, making his stomach churn faster. And had Hollingsworth taken Diana's innocence that very night and gotten her pregnant? If that were the case, it was no wonder Tristan had held such feelings of betrayal for her without knowing why.

But, Diana didn't have a child. If she had been pregnant, what happened to the baby?

No, that's not what happened. Hollingsworth didn't know how to tell the truth. So why had the man wanted to marry her so badly? And why had her father been so obliging to Hollingsworth?

The more Tristan thought of it, the more he wondered if Hollingsworth really had paid the baron's debts. That made more sense to why Diana's father wouldn't break the contract.

That dirty-rotten cheat Hollingsworth had planned on Tristan coming to meet Diana at the glade the night before the duel. If the viscount would have met him the morning of the duel, many people would have been there and seen firsthand who the coward *really* was. And yet now Tristan knew why there had been rumors about him jumping over the cliff, and not even showing up for the duel that morning.

Could that be the reason Diana had hated him so much and wanted revenge?

Taking a deep breath, he detected a faint food odor. It smelled pleasant, whatever it was, reminding him how long it'd been since he ate. Perhaps he would eat *before* bathing.

As he stepped into the corridor, he half expected Tabitha to rush toward him holding a pistol. It surprised him that he didn't awaken with his arms and legs shackled to the bed. Either that or she just didn't care if he escaped anymore.

Taking the lamp from the corridor table, he moved through the small cottage. No women's voices were heard this time. But if it were early in the morning as he suspected, then they would definitely still be in bed.

As Tristan moved down the hall, he hadn't realized until now how cozy the place looked. For some reason this style of home fit Diana perfectly. Although he couldn't remember what the outside looked like—and probably wouldn't have because it was dark when they had arrived—the interior wasn't as newly decorated as his mother liked to keep her houses. Had Diana's grandmother been wealthy? Wood décor was everywhere he looked, and so pleasing to behold. He would certainly not get bored studying each painting or furniture and admire the artists' touch.

Nothing looked worn or rundown. It just wasn't the fashion his mother enjoyed having in her homes.

Finally, he entered the kitchen. Slowly he walked through the room, admiring the shelves and cutting tables and the many stoves. In the corner sat a copper tub and his attention remained there. He hurried to the tub and pulled it out into the room a little more. Grinning, he couldn't wait for a nice relaxing bath.

The popping of wood jerked his focus to a large fireplace. Several large pots of water hung over the burning fire. Perhaps Diana or Tabitha was already up and preparing water for a bath. Even towels and soap had been laid out. Well, he'd show them that the early riser would be the one to claim the warm water first.

He tested the temperature of the water with his finger. Nearly what he wanted. Once he removed off his clothes. It didn't take long to pour the water into the tub before climbing in. The warmth from the water crept over his skin and soothed his nerves slightly. Since regaining some of his memory from those horrid two years of wandering to find his identity, taking a daily bath was the one thing Tristan enjoyed more than anything.

After he washed himself, he leaned back in tub to unwind. As he relaxed in the tub, he mentally planned out his morning. Once he filled his belly with food, he would take a tour through the house and acquaint himself with all the rooms. Hopefully by that time, Diana would be awake. They had so much to talk about.

Sighing in contentment, Tristan knew he'd made the right decision to stay here. With such a peaceful atmosphere, he was certain to clear his mind enough to remember all those events that were still trapped behind memory's door.

Whether Tabitha or Diana realized it, they had actually saved him when they kidnapped him. Marrying Jane would have made him more miserable than he'd been already. Living a life of misery was not an enjoyable way to live. His parents could testify to that.

He tilted his head back against the edge of the tub, and closed his eyes. From down the corridor, he detected soft footsteps. Finally, one of the ladies was awake. Tristan was quite certain they wouldn't like seeing their guest using the bath first...especially if they had drugged him last night which he suspected had happened.

The footsteps grew closer, and he struggled to open his eyes to greet whoever came his way, but it was too enjoyable to leave them closed. Finally, the headache he'd had since waking up disappeared, and he didn't want to do anything to bring it back.

Suddenly, a gasp ripped through the room, followed by a piercing scream from a woman. Tristan jerked upright, only to lose his balance and slip back in the tub, splashing water on the floor. By the time he adjusted himself, he noticed the woman.

My Diana.

He expected her to be in her nightgown and bare feet. Instead, she was fully dressed and even her beautiful hair had been wound in a coil as wisps of locks hung by her ears. Disappointment hung heavy in his chest. Although it would have been improper, Tristan rather wished she had been in a nightgown with her hair long and flowing. Instead, she stood across the room, her shoulders stiff as she presented her back to him. *Always the proper Diana.*

He cleared his throat. "Forgive me for startling you, my sweet Diana. I hope you don't mind that I'm taking a bath without asking permission."

"I, um… Well, I heated the water for whoever needed it," she said over her shoulder, but didn't look at him.

"So you are not put out with me for using it?"

She released an uneasy laugh. "Don't be absurd. It was for you or Tabitha."

He studied her stiff back still facing him. "Diana, why are you up so early? I thought I would have the house to myself for at least a few hours."

"Sorry to disappoint, but I'm an early riser."

He glanced over her body slower from the high neck dress with long sleeves, down to her boot crusted with mud. *Mud?* "Why were you outside?"

"I um… I had errands this morning, if you must know."

"So early? That's unheard of."

Grumbling, she glanced over her shoulder and looked at him. This time her face flamed red before she quickly looked away. "Unheard of by whom, my lord? Men or women?"

"Both, actually."

"Well, it's obvious you have never lived in the country."

"I have, but this isn't a farm so I doubt you were out milking the cow."

"No, this isn't a farm."

"So what were you doing?"

She grumbled louder and folded her arms. "It's none of your business, Tristan. Now just let the matter rest."

He arched an eyebrow. Although she was awake and had been doing *errands,* it was clear she wasn't a morning person. "If you wish."

"I do wish."

"Diana, I need to ask… why didn't you wake me last night so we could finish our talk?"

Her head spun around so fast when she turned and met his eyes, he thought it would roll off her shoulders. "Actually, we had gone into your room to wake you, but you were having a bad dream. Tabitha gave you a little tea with some sleeping draught in it to help you calm down."

"Pardon me?" He sat forward in the tub a little more. "You gave me a sleeping draught?"

She turned away from him again. "Only a little. Tabitha says it helps with restlessness."

"Then I thank you for helping me to sleep better."

She took a deep breath and exhaled slowly. "I shall leave now and let you finish your bath in private."

"Before you go," he said as she stepped toward the door. "Will you do me a favor?"

She took a quick peek over her shoulder again. Her face still flamed an adorable red.

"What?"

"Wash my back?"

"Augh!" She hissed and stormed out the door.

Laughing, he relaxed back in the tub again. It was rather fun to rile her, and especially see her cheeks bright with embarrassment. Spending the next few days with her would be quite enjoyable. Then again, that meddlesome maid was still here. Too bad he couldn't figure a way to get her to leave. Being alone with Diana was something he desperately needed.

Chapter Sixteen

"**D**ID YOU REALLY see him naked?" Tabitha asked, her eyes wide with shock.

Diana shook her head as she stood in the kitchen an hour later, helping her maid make breakfast. Heat climbed up Diana's face and she didn't dare look at Tabitha. Tristan's image—all wet and bare—was engraved in her mind and she feared she'd never be able to erase it. Every time she glanced at the tub, embarrassment flowed through her just the same as it had done when she first saw him this morning.

"Tabitha, he was in a hip tub, for Heaven's sake! I wasn't even that close to it, and all I saw was his chest and arms—and his bent knees, of course."

Tabitha laughed. "I cannot believe he thinks he lives here now."

Sighing heavily, Diana set down her fork and finally met her maid's stare. "What do you expect him to do? Stay tied up in the chair the whole time? Obviously, he couldn't even stay in his room last night."

"If we had it my way, I'd keep him tied up," Tabitha grumbled.

"Tabitha, really!" Diana shook her head. "So what are we going to do with him? We can't keep him here forever."

"As unbelievable as it sounds," Tabitha continued, leaning

her hip against the cutting table, "I don't think he wants to leave now."

"Neither do I."

"In fact—" Tabitha giggled, "I think he quite enjoys being here. I think he still has feelings for you."

Diana's face still burned with embarrassment. "If he does, then I pity the poor fool."

"Do you want me to take him back home? I can wear the same clothes I wore when I kidnapped him, and people wouldn't think anything differently when I drive into town."

Diana placed her hand over Tabitha's. "You should not be going into town at all. We don't need Lord Elliot seeing you by accident. I shudder to think what he would do to you if he knew you were here with me now. At night is different since you could hide better and dress in men's clothes, but day time…" She shook her head.

Tabitha frowned. "You are right, my lady. If I leave the house at all, it should be late at night when I can remain in the shadows."

"Quite right. Until Lady Dashwood finds employment for you in London or farther away, the best place for you to hide is right here."

"I thank you, Lady Hollingsworth. You have such a large heart for wanting to help me escape my nightmare."

"Think nothing of it." She smiled then returned to stirring the eggs in the pan over the stove.

"Did everything go smoothly last night?" Tabitha asked leaning closer to Diana as her voice lowered.

Diana took a quick peek toward the door, grateful it was closed. When she met Tabitha's stare, she nodded. "Yes, thank the Lord. Sally was beaten severely and I fear it will take her several days or even weeks to heal. Her soul, however, might take longer."

Tabitha blinked rapidly as tears filled her eyes. "I should have stayed there. I'm older and stronger than Sally. I could handle

Lord Elliot much better."

Diana clasp hands with her maid. "Don't say such things. No woman should have to endure such beatings, and no woman—even you—could have fought off Lord Elliot."

"What are you going to do, Lady Hollingsworth? Single-handedly rescue all the servants who are beaten by their masters and place them in other homes?"

"If I have to, yes."

"But Lord Elliot and other men like him will always hire more servants."

"Then perhaps the key is to get rid of those lords instead."

Tabitha's lips twitched before she laughed. "Oh, you are humorous and you have an evil mind. Is it bad of me to want to help you rid the world of men like Lord Elliot?"

Diana chuckled. "Not at all, so long as we don't really act upon our feelings, mind you."

"Of course not, my lady. Hanging is not something that sounds appealing at all."

"I agree. But Tabitha, I don't want to talk about this any further. Lord Tristan cannot know that Sally is here."

Tabitha narrowed her eyes. "Do you think he'll try to return her?"

"No. I just don't want him knowing what we are doing."

"He will not hear it from my lips." Tabitha nodded.

Diana turned back to the pan on the stove, stirring the scrambled eggs occasionally. Her heart wrenched with sadness for Sally's plight. The poor girl had been beaten terribly. One eye was swollen shut. Cuts and bruises from Lord Elliot's fists had marred the girl's face, making her unrecognizable.

Deep down inside, Diana knew she couldn't free every girl from a life such as this, but it shouldn't be for a lack of courage. While married to Ludlow, Diana had cried herself to sleep too many nights. The more she fought his vicious attacks, the harder he hit her. Finally, she'd lost all ability to resist. Thankfully, he tired of her quickly when she was that way, but it hadn't lessened the pain any.

Just as breakfast was done cooking, Tristan sauntered into the kitchen, appearing more handsome than ever. It wasn't the way he dressed that made him more attractive—since she hadn't thought to bring him more clothes—but it was the way his eyes sparkled when he smiled at her. His blue orbs nearly melted her to a puddle on the floor.

"Good morning, Lord Tristan," Tabitha greeted cheerfully.

Diana threw her maid a wary stare. Why was the girl acting in such a way… and flirty?

"It is a very good morning, Tabitha." He switched his eyes to Diana. "Here, let me assist you with those."

As he took the plates of food from her hands, his fingers brushed against hers. Heat coursed up her arms before spreading through the rest of her body. She didn't dare yank away from his touch for fear she'd drop the plates and the food would spill on the floor.

Her heart fluttered when she followed him to the table and sat. He took the seat right beside her. Tabitha turned to leave the room, but Diana quickly said, "No, Tabitha. Stay and eat your meal with us."

The maid's gaze moved between Diana and Tristan in hesitation.

Tristan nodded. "Indeed, come sit and eat with us."

Shock registered in Tabitha's face, her eyes widening. "As you wish." She fixed her plate then sat at the table.

"Tristan, I must say, you are remarkably chipper this morning," Diana started the conversation.

"I am, actually." His smile stretched. "This morning has been extremely pleasant thus far. Not very often does a lovely woman disturb my bath." His eyebrows rose suggestively.

Fire exploded in Diana's face. *Why did he have to say it like that?* "You know it was an accident—"

He held up his hand. "Nevertheless, I enjoyed it."

She threw him a glare.

Silence spread through the room, giving Diana time to collect her thoughts. Since she'd seen him all tied up in the chair, she hadn't been able to think of anything but their past. The moment she had heard Tristan fell over the cliff—and the rumors that circulated at the time—was when she'd stopped believing in love. Ludlow had married her a few days after the duel instead of the two weeks as she had been told, mainly because of the rumors. That was when the torture began. By that time, she had already realized there was no such thing as happy endings.

She still didn't know what had broken her heart more—Tristan's abandonment or Ludlow's abuse.

"Diana, my dear," Tristan said, pulling her out of forlorn thoughts. "Why the sudden frown? Are you not feeling well?"

She looked at him and attempted to smile. "I'm fine, I assure you." She quickly took another bite of her eggs.

"What are your plans for this morning?" he asked.

She didn't dare tell him she wanted to sleep since she'd been awake all night rescuing a beaten maid. "Nothing of consequence. Why do you inquire?"

"Because, I think we need to talk about our—"

From outside the thundering of horses' hooves shook the ground, and they all looked toward the window. Within moments a woman's shriek blasted from outside. Tabitha jumped up and ran to the kitchen door, pulling it open. The panicked voice of Lady Dashwood finally became recognizable as she called for Diana.

She moved away from the table and darted toward the door. Something was dreadfully wrong to have Claudia in such a dither.

"Oh good Heavens, Diana," Claudia began breathlessly. "I came as soon as I heard the shocking news."

Diana clutched Claudia's shaking hands. Her gut twisted and she wasn't sure if she wanted to hear what her friend had to say. "W—what?"

"Lord Elliot Henson was found murdered last night!"

Chapter Seventeen

T HE STATEMENT BOOMED through the room like a canon blast. Tristan sprang do this feet, knocking over the chair he'd just been sitting on. His cousin—Elliot? No, it couldn't be!

Gasps ricocheted off the walls. Tabitha slapped a hand over her mouth and Diana's face lost all color. She'd swoon any moment, he just knew it.

Taking long strides, he hurried to her side and touched her elbow. "Diana, I think you need to sit."

Staring at the wall, she shook her head. "I'll be all right."

"Lord Tristan is correct, dear," Claudia said. "You don't look well at all. Your face is white."

"No, I'm fine, really I am. It's such a shock to hear…" She took a deep breath. "Oh, dear."

Tristan didn't wait for Diana to ask for his help. He slipped an arm around her waist and led her back to the table. She followed without hesitation, leaning on him for support.

He switched his attention between the three ladies. Each one looked as desolate as the other. The news was devastating, and Tristan could hardly grasp the concept. He'd never approved of some of the things Elliot did in his life. The man was too wild.

Curiosity niggled at Tristan as he studied each of the ladies in the room, and he wondered how they all knew Elliot—enough to have the news of his demise affect them in such a way.

"Lady Dashwood," he asked. "What exactly did you hear?"

"Oh, it was just awful," she began as she took a seat next to Diana. "My cook had gone into town for supplies and heard the rumors. Apparently, Lord Elliot was found in the stable without a stitch of clothes with stab wounds all over his body." She squeezed Diana's trembling hand. "Just as you had found your husband."

Tristan nodded. Clearly the person who had killed Hollingsworth had taken Elliot's life as well. Another similarity between the two dead men where that they were both womanizers and loved to gamble.

"This cannot be good," Diana whispered. "People already suspect me of killing Ludlow. Now they are going to believe I killed Lord Elliot."

Inwardly, Tristan groaned. He'd almost forgotten that she was under suspicion for Hollingsworth's death just as Tristan was. A nagging thought pounded in his head. Would they suspect *him* of Lord Elliot's death as well? The only dealings he had with his cousin had been that they'd played cards on a few occasions. In fact, three nights ago, they'd had a futile argument during a game, but they were both drunk and hot tempered. Both of them were asked to leave the game. Tristan's friend, Lord Hawthorne, was given the privilege of escorting Tristan home that night.

Tabitha's grumble pulled him out of his thoughts. She stood, her hands bunched into fists, her lips tight in irritation. Her blue eyes blazed with fury.

"Well forgive me for not holding my tongue, but men like Lord Elliot don't deserve to live."

Both Lady Dashwood and Diana gasped. "Tabitha, really!" Diana scolded. "You should not speak ill of the dead."

"I meant every word," Tabitha countered. The hatred in her eyes made them even darker. "All that man ever did was drink, gamble, and beat his servants. The world is a better place with him gone."

Although Tristan agreed with the maid, he couldn't help but

wonder how she knew this about his cousin. He narrowed his gaze on her. The only way she would have known that about the man was if she'd been a servant in his home. So if she was the man's servant, what was she doing with Diana?

"Not to worry, my lady," Tabitha said as she stood behind Diana and rested her hand on her shoulder. "I will tell the authorities you were here the whole night." She glanced at Tristan. "He could even back up my story."

"I thank you, Tabitha," Diana said. "But neither of you know for certain that I was here all night since we all slept in different rooms."

"Diana, there is no reason the magistrate will suspect you." Lady Dashwood shook her head.

"Why can I not fully believe that?" Diana arched her eyebrow and glanced at Tabitha before moving her focus back to Claudia.

The other two women hung their head. Tristan found it strange that nobody answered Diana's question or at least tried to convince her otherwise. For certain, something was going on here that they didn't want him to know about. Curiosity got the better of him, yet he didn't dare voice his thoughts. He'd wait until he could get Diana alone and talk this out with her—and only her.

A small groan of despair came from Diana as she rubbed her forehead. "Let's pray that I'm not a suspect. I fear I wouldn't know how to talk my way out of this one." She looked up at Lady Dashwood. "I'm grateful you came here to let me know."

The lovely blonde woman nodded. "You were the first person I thought to tell when I heard the news."

"Please, return to your house and please keep me informed on anything else in regards to Lord Elliot."

"Indeed, I shall." Claudia met Tristan's eyes and nodded. "Lord Tristan, it was a pleasure to see you again. I hope all is well with your family, and your mother."

"The last time I checked they were doing splendidly." But the last time he saw them was the day before the wedding. It surprised him that Diana's friend didn't question him about his disappearance yesterday morning at the church. Obviously, she had known what Tabitha and Diana were up to the whole time.

"I shall take my leave now." Lady Dashwood stood. "I'll pay you a visit tomorrow."

Diana took a deep breath and met her friend's eyes. "I look forward to it."

Nothing was said after Claudia left. Tabitha cleared up the dishes and continued to clean the kitchen. Tristan stood. Diana's gaze followed him.

"Diana, would you join me in the sitting room? I believe the sofa would be much more comfortable to sit on than these chairs."

"You are correct." She stood. "I suppose we can have that much needed talk about our past now."

DIANA'S LEGS SHOOK as she walked into the other room. Between the lack of sleep and the shocking news, her body—and emotions—were a mess right now. A headache throbbed, but she couldn't let that stall her talk with Tristan.

She sat, and he scooted himself on the sofa right next to her. In a way, she wished he had chosen a different chair. Being this close to him played havoc with her emotions, and especially the feelings she thought had been put to rest.

He reached over and caressed the ringlet by her ear. "You still have no color in your face."

"Yes, well… when receiving such news that another man was killed the exact same way as Ludlow, it's no wonder I'm rattled."

"Very true."

She fidgeted on the sofa, uncomfortable with the awkward silence. "So Tristan, yesterday you had mentioned remembering something."

"I did."

"Will you please tell me what it was?"

"Remarkably enough, it was what happened the night before the duel."

"The *night* before? Pray, what could have happened that night?"

He arched an eyebrow. "I believe I already know the answer, but I need to ask you nonetheless… Did you send me a letter to meet you at Henry's Cliffs the night before?"

She creased her brow and shook her head. "Of course not. My parents had me heavily guarded for fear I was going to sneak out and meet you someplace so we could run away to Gretna Green."

"Just as I expected."

"Why, Tristan? What happened?"

"I had received a letter with your name on it. In the letter you stated that you wanted me to meet you at the glade. When Trey and I arrived and didn't see you, we felt that it had been a trap. We were correct."

Surprise flooded through her. "Hollingsworth met you the night before?"

"Yes. He was a coward and didn't want to meet me for the duel and have the crowd watch him die." He reached his hand over his shoulder and brushed his fingers across a section on his back. "Last night I had remembered exactly what happened at those cliffs, but it wasn't the bullet that had pushed me over as I had originally thought."

She furrowed her brow. "Did you… jump?"

He hitched a breath and stared at her with wide eyes. "Jumped? Are you jesting? You thought I had jumped off the cliff?"

She shrugged. "Well, there were so many rumors going around, I didn't know which ones to believe."

He studied her through hooded eyes, scratching his chin. "Will you tell me what Hollingsworth told you had happened?"

She sighed heavily. "He didn't say much. He rarely ever did, but when he showed up the next morning at the house and said you were a coward and didn't come to the duel, I feared the worst. But many people had gone to the cliffs that morning and they all had the same story—that you were not there." She swallowed hard. "Other rumors started spreading a week or so after it had all happened about you going to the cliffs before anyone else had gotten there to try and talk Ludlow out of the duel. When he wouldn't relent, you had tried to shoot him, but missed. When he got his weapon out, you fled and jumped over the cliffs."

Tristan cursed under his breath. "And you *believed* him?"

The tone of his voice accused her of something she should have known already. Before marrying Ludlow, all she knew about him was that he was a domineering man who took advantage of people—her father being one of them. After she married Ludlow she learned quickly enough that he was a deceiver. He'd hinted about her family having some deep dark secret, and all he was talking about was that her father had gambled away her dowry and left the family in financial ruins.

"It wasn't just him that told me, and I didn't want to believe, but others were there and could see you had not shown up for the duel. Then when you were found alive, Ludlow tried to convince me that you had faked your death because you owed him money. By that time, I was so confused about everything." She choked back a sob. "If only your brother had said something to me—or anyone—I would have believed. But he said nothing."

He huffed and leaned forward, loosening his cravat. "I want to show you something."

She held her breath. Why was he undressing?

Once he'd removed his cravat, he lifted his shirt over his head, and turned his back toward her. "Do you see that large scar on my shoulder?"

The scar was still puckered and slightly red. Reaching out to touch it, she stopped herself before her fingers could make contact. "Yes."

"This is where *your* husband shot *me*." He turned back to her and pulled the shirt back over his head.

She frowned, chiding herself for even believing that story in the first place. Yet, there was a part of her that hadn't believed at all. She'd just been waiting for Trey to tell her what really happened. "I'm sorry, Tristan," she whispered.

"What other rumors were going around?"

"Some say you jumped off the cliff while Ludlow was aiming to shoot you again." She shrugged. "There were even rumors that Ludlow and his second weren't even there—that you and your brother had been traveling abroad and came upon bandits that were being chased by the local military regiment and you were caught in the crossfire. They said you were close to the cliffs and when the bullet hit you, that's when you fell over the edge."

"I like that story better." He shook his head. "Nevertheless, Lord Hollingsworth and his second were the ones hiding within the shadows of the trees the night I received the letter. Trey had told me he didn't feel right about things, and urged me to get back on my horse. Just as I had turned to do that very thing, Lord Hollingsworth shot me. I couldn't even return a shot because I had no weapon on me at the time. Then we fought, and I fell over the cliff."

Tears burned her eyes and she blinked to keep from crying. "Forgive me for thinking you jumped or that you were a coward and didn't show." Without wanting it to, a tear slipped down her cheek. "I didn't want to believe that about you. I hadn't known you for very long, but the kind of man I'd come to know during that short time wasn't the kind of man who would jump—or run away." She cleared her throat when it began to crack. "Ludlow had also tried to convince me that you were a rogue just like your younger brother. Ludlow told me the only reason you were so determined to win me was because, because..." She took a deep breath, trying to steady her emotions.

"Because?" he asked softly as he brushed his thumb on her

cheek, removing a few more tears that had slipped free.

"Because you wanted to bed me. You were not used to giving up on a woman until after you had claimed your prize."

His jaw hardened. After a few moments of awkward silence, he exhaled slowly and withdrew his touch. "Why did you believe him?"

"I didn't believe him, but over the next couple of weeks the servants talked of this as well. People in town were also discussing your rakish behavior, especially because you had singled me out at your mother's party." She took a breath and continued, "After a while, I just finally accepted it as the truth. If only Trey had said something to me—or anyone—I would have believed. Why had your brother not come to tell me? Didn't he think I cared?"

Releasing a ragged sigh, Tristan pushed his fingers through his hair. "I had heard that Trey blamed himself for my death because he couldn't save me. Because he didn't try to stop the duel in the first place. I heard he was half mad with remorse that he kept to his room for months. The thought probably never crossed his mind to tell you. However, I do believe after Trey had tried to move on with his life, he blamed you."

She inhaled sharply. "Me? But why?"

"Because he figured you should have tried to stop the duel. He felt that you had encouraged the duel in the first place. Trey also felt that you should have confessed to being a compromised woman and possibly being with child."

His words vibrated through her so hard, it nearly shook her off the sofa. She jumped to her feet and stared at him. "*What?* You think I was in the *motherly way?*" She took a deep breath. "Why in Heaven's name would you believe that?"

He held up his hand in surrender. "Wait a moment before you get yourself in a dither, let me finish explaining."

"Oh! Please do."

He patted the empty space on the cushion next to him. "Sit back down, please."

Anger, hurt, and humiliation raged through her. Tears fell from her eyes for different reasons this time. Bunching her hands by her side, she glared at him. "You thought that just because I had allowed you to kiss me in the greenhouse, I had given other men the same privilege—and more?"

"Diana, please. Just sit down and let me explain."

She couldn't sit. She couldn't think. She couldn't even scream at the top of her voice how unfair life was. All she could do was… was… A sob tore from her throat and she covered her hands over her face. Diana didn't need to ask why he and his brother had thought this. Ludlow had ruined her reputation—and her life—in more ways than one.

Sobbing that she could not contain rushed forth. The palms of her hands dampened quickly from her tears. Frustration and helplessness had always been part of her life, especially after being forced to marry Ludlow, and she was tired of it. Tired of everything!

Strong arms wrapped around her shoulders and Tristan pulled her against his body. Warmth spread through her, comforting her more than she could have imagined. Gently, he urged her back to the sofa, where she obediently followed.

For years she'd been holding back her feelings, convincing herself there was no use in crying since it never solved a thing. Yet now as she sobbed against Tristan's chest, relief made her chest lighter, and that confused her. She couldn't understand the peace flowing through her, either.

He kissed her forehead and tightened his arms around her. "Please don't cry," he said softly. "It's tearing me up inside."

"Since your return from being um… dead, I have noticed you held bitter feelings for me." She sniffed. "Those times we had attended the same dinner parties, or the same balls, or I saw you in town, you glared at me." She lifted her head and looked at him. "I could never understand what I had done."

He ran the pads of his thumbs under her eyes, wiping away the tears. "When I returned to civilization, I had no memory of the duel. I remembered the days we'd spent together—and the time at the greenhouse—but not much after that. However, whenever I saw you, I did have a feeling of loathing… of hatred, but I couldn't make sense of those emotions. It wasn't until last night while I was dreaming that my memory opened up and led me through what really happened and what I had felt during those moments." Tristan leaned forward and kissed her forehead. "Hollingsworth had told me after he'd shot me that he'd forced himself on you earlier that evening and you were probably carrying his heir. He also mentioned that he had paid off your father's debts, and that you had known about it the whole time. Trey heard the same thing as I did, and I was never able to talk to my brother about Hollingsworth's accusations before I fell over the cliff." He caressed her cheek.

She sniffed back another sob. The pain in her heart made her chest feel as if a house was resting upon it. "Ludlow lied when he told you he'd compromised me. He didn't even touch me until after our wedding." She took a deep breath. "But he did pay my father's debts. I had known this, but I was too embarrassed to say anything to you. My father and I both thought that if you paid Ludlow back he'd change his mind and break the engagement."

Tristan nodded. "I think that was why I held so much anger and betrayal in my heart for you after my accident. I didn't know what it was, but now I feel that's what drove me to drink and turned me into a bitter man."

She wiped a tear sliding down her cheek. "I'm so sorry, Tristan. Ludlow had lied to both of us, and was determined to keep us apart no matter what the cost."

"So true. I just wish I could have stopped him. If I hadn't have gone to the cliffs that night to find you—"

"Shhh." She placed a finger to his lips. "We cannot relive the past. We must start over right now and move forward from here."

He shrugged. "You are correct, of course. I had wallowed in my heartache for too long. I had lost you, and I couldn't bear the thought of not being with you. Whenever I saw you in town, it hurt too much to look at you."

"Oh, Tristan." More tears poured down her face. "I never wanted to marry him. I hated him. He was cruel and always threatened me if I didn't do his bidding. It didn't take long for me to become bitter toward you for not... not..." She took a deep breath, releasing it slowly as she tried to control her emotions. "I had hoped that the rumors about you were false, and that you were somehow still alive so you could rescue me from my miserable life. I suffered so much abuse from that man. When I couldn't get pregnant, he beat me. When I disagreed with him over anything, he struck me and locked me in my room for days. Living with him was pure hell, and the whole time I kept imagining what *might* have happened if we were married."

"Oh, my sweet Diana." He kissed her forehead again and pulled her tighter as he brought her head to rest against his chest. "If I had known he treated you so terribly..." His voice broke. "I'm so sorry for everything. I had wanted to rescue you and marry you. We would have been very happy together, I know it." He stroked her hair. "And I would have never lifted a hand to you in anger like he had." He buried his face in her hair. "Oh, Diana, if I had known sooner what he'd done, I would have killed him by now." He kissed her head. "I promise you no man will *ever* lay a hand on you now that I'm here."

Slowly, the tears stopped and she wanted nothing more than to cuddle next to this strong man for the rest of her life. As she rubbed her cheek against his shirt, peace filled her. Soon her heart would mend, but it would take time. The best thing for both of them now was to heal—emotionally. Then, and only then, would they be able to trust each other and fall in love all over again.

"Tristan, indeed you are a wonderful man, just as I'd realized when we first met." She wrapped her arms around his waist and snuggled closer.

He relaxed back against the sofa, seeming content just to hold her. She'd waited for this kind of comforting feeling for too long.

Needless to say, it would be impossible to let him go now. But she must. There were still too many obstacles in their way, and until those were resolved, she and Tristan could never be together, and since that wasn't an option, she realized she must do all she can to right the wrong.

Being without Tristan was like a flower without sunlight. She would not be put through that torture again.

Chapter Eighteen

TRISTAN AWOKE, FEELING more alive than he'd been for a very long time. As he blinked, he realized he was still holding Diana while they slept on the sofa.

Smiling, he closed his eyes again and caressed her back and arm. Happiness spread through him. Having their talk made his heart light once again, and yet knowing how her husband had treated her, broke Tristan's heart. He'd always blame himself for not being able to save her. But as she'd mentioned before—they couldn't change the past now. All they could do was move forward, and he was definitely going to move forward. With her. They were both on the road to recovery, and soon, she would be back in his life forever.

A thought struck him, making him open his eyes. As long as they stayed in this cottage—their haven—out in the middle of nowhere, they were safe. But he needed to think of his family and to let them know all was well. Unfortunately, he had to talk to Jane to tell her and her controlling father, that there would *never* be a marriage between Tristan and Jane.

He didn't think his mother would be too unhappy about the news, especially when he explained that there was another lady in his life, one that he'd loved for three years now.

Looking toward the window, he tried to gauge the time of day by the sunlight. If his calculations were correct, it was midafternoon. He needed to return home before night fell upon them.

"Sweet Diana," he whispered and kissed her head. "Wake up, my dear."

A soft moan escaped her throat as she stirred against him. Slowly, her hand rubbed across his chest, and a smile gradually stretched across her face. *Adorable!*

"My dear, we have to wake up." He kissed her forehead again, letting his lips linger on her skin a smidgen longer this time. Inhaling, he breathed in her lilac scent, recalling now why he had always enjoyed walking through his mother's flower garden to the lilac bushes since he'd returned to civilization.

Diana's eyelids fluttered open. When she looked at him, her smile widened.

"Tristan."

He caressed her cheek. "Did you sleep well?"

"Remarkably well, thank you." She sat up and stretched.

He loved seeing her so relaxed and content.

"I don't think I have slept so well in a very long time," she said.

He winked. "Me, either. I have struggled to remember my past, which kept me depressed and drinking entirely too much. It was a nice little break for my mind to finally have undisturbed sleep."

He stood and stretched. Strange how his body wasn't even cramped for lying crooked on the sofa. Yet, she had been in his arms, which meant everything was as it should be.

"Diana, I hope you don't mind, but I really need to return home." A frown marred her expression, so he quickly explained. "I have no other clothes here. Besides that, my mother is probably very worried about me." He leaned over, grasped Diana's hands and pulled her up to stand by him. "There's something I have to do as well. I need to talk with Lady Fairbourne and her father to let them know there is not going to be a wedding. Ever."

Finally, Diana's smile returned which made her eyes sparkle. "That is a very good reason to return home."

Chuckling, he wrapped her in his arms. "Are you going to remain here or come back and live closer to me?"

"Ludlow left nothing to me in his will. Although my grandmother's cottage isn't legally mine, it's my brother's, he allowed me to stay here without question. Returning to Ludlow's manor is the last thing I want to do, but I suppose it won't hurt to go back at least until his cousin comes to claim the property."

"I will be nearby to protect you. I do wish we could live in this cottage forever. It's the perfect escape from society."

"That, it is."

"Perhaps we can meet here again in a couple of weeks?" He waggled his eyebrows.

She laughed and nodded. "I think that's a splendid idea."

Slowly, he traced his fingers over her beautiful face, over her creamy skin, her eyebrows, cheek bones, and down to her tempting lips. "I want to thank you for kidnapping me."

"You forget it was Tabitha who did the deed."

"True, but she would not have done it if she hadn't have loved you so much. *You* are why she did what she did, which was the best thing that ever happened to me."

"I'm so very relieved everything turned out the right way this time. You cannot imagine the relief flowing through me at this moment."

Tristan arched an eyebrow. "You don't think I can imagine it? I assure you, I can relate to that perfectly."

He dropped his lips to hers. The kiss was so very gentle, and yet passionate as it stirred emotions in him he thought he'd lost years ago. The newfound feeling thrilled him completely and gave him hope for a better future with her.

Reluctantly, he pulled away. Kissing her was so perfect he never wanted to stop. "My sweet Diana, I must leave now."

"I know."

"Promise we will see each other tomorrow."

She nodded. "I assure you, we will even if I have to pay you a visit just to make an excuse to be in the same room with you."

"You will always be welcome at my home." He kissed her mouth one last time then stepped out of her arms. "Do you have an extra horse for me?"

"I do. Take the black stallion."

"Until later, my sweet Diana." He bowed, turned, and quit the room.

It didn't take him long to get himself ready, saddle the horse, and leave. Diana and Tabitha stepped outside to see him off. Both women waved until he couldn't see them any longer.

He wasn't familiar with this part of England, but he knew the direction of Mayfair, so he rode hard searching for anything familiar that would let him know he traveled the right way.

A few hours later, he was home. Already he missed Diana and wanted to return to her grandmother's cottage. But he must remember he had other responsibilities first. Business first, play later.

He rode to the stable and dismounted. The stable boy rushed out, his eyes wide with surprise.

"Lord Tristan! You have returned."

"I have, indeed." He ruffled the boy's hair. "Is her ladyship still here?"

"Yes."

"Then I shall go straightway to see her."

He hurried into the house. As he passed a few young maids, they stopped whatever they were doing and stared agape at him. First he went to his mother's favorite sitting room, and when she wasn't there, he took the grand staircase two steps at a time, heading to her chambers. He opened the door and peeked inside. She sat in a cushioned chair by the window as she stared down at her flower garden, her expression laced with sadness. He'd only been gone a few days, but it seemed her hair held more gray streaks, and several new wrinkles marred her complexion.

Slowly, her head turned toward him. A gasp sprang from her

as she clutched her hands to her chest, tears filling her eyes quickly. "Tristan? Is that really you?"

"Yes, Mother." His wide strides ate up the distance between them until he knelt by her chair and hugged her. "I'm back now."

"Ohhh," she sobbed and clung to him. "I was so distraught. Nobody knew what happened to you or why you would not come to your own wedding."

"Forgive me for not saying anything sooner."

She withdrew and looked at him with confusion in her gaze. "Where were you? I heard you were kidnapped."

"You did?" He arched an eyebrow. "Pray, who would say such a thing?"

"Nobody knew for certain, but there was a man who'd come forth. Apparently, you'd been drinking with him the night before the wedding. He saw you climb into a carriage before someone chained the door closed and hastily rode off."

So someone had noticed... "It's nothing to worry about, Mother." He kissed her cheek. "I'm back now, and I'll set things right."

She swept her hand over his face and hair, then down to his shoulder and arm. "You appear healthy."

"I am just fine, I assure you."

"Were you kidnapped?"

"Yes and no." He shook his head. "It's a long story, but everything is as it's supposed to be."

A smile trembled on her mouth. "Thank the Lord." She wiped her moist eyes. "Have you heard the terrible news about your cousin?"

"Yes, Mother." He frowned. "I heard Elliot had been killed."

"It's such a tragedy, and my heart goes out to my brother and his family. I know how it feels to lose a child." She patted his cheek. "But I'm also worried about you. I heard you and Elliot had an argument the other night, and I fear the magistrate will suspect you just as he suspects you of Lord Hollingsworth's death."

"Cease your worries. I have witnesses who will say I was

nowhere near my cousin's home last night."

She sighed heavily. "Thank heavens." She dropped her hand from his check. "Have you spoken to Lady Fairbourne or her father yet? They are beside themselves with worry. Her father even sent out riders to find you."

"No, I have not seen them yet. I came here first." He glanced down at his wrinkled clothes. "However, I need a bath and to change before I pay them a visit."

She nodded. "You do that and I shall send notes to your brothers to inform them of your return." Sighing, she cupped his face. "I'm just so relieved you are home."

"As am I."

He kissed her cheek again, stood, then headed for his room. A nice warm bath, clean clothes, and a chipper spirit would get him through the rest of the day as he completed his duties. Jane and her father would be quite upset with Tristan, but he didn't care. All that was important to him was seeing Diana again.

It didn't take long to make himself presentable, and he left the house. During the ride to Lady Fairbourne's townhouse, Tristan rolled his thoughts around, trying to come up with the best way to tell her he didn't want to get married. Naturally she'd be upset—as her father would be—but Tristan would try to soothe their emotions as well as he possibly could.

He reached their place sooner than he wanted, and after giving his card to the butler was shown to the sitting room. Since the door was left open, the servants' whispers came from the corridor. Tristan couldn't quite tell if they were excited whispers, or panicked.

Time seemed to crawl, but soon heavy footsteps boomed on the floor in the hall. The square frame of Viscount Hastings came through the doorway first, followed by his wife and Jane. Tristan was relieved that they were all together and that he didn't have to travel to the Hastings' townhouse as well.

It was impossible not to notice the scowl the viscount threw at Tristan, but both women kept their eyes lowered. The women sat, but the viscount stood with his arms folded across his chest. Although Tristan was taller than the other man, the viscount came across as the authority figure.

"Worthington, I am in a foul mood, so say what you need to quickly," Hastings barked.

Tristan nodded. In any event, he hadn't planned on being here that long. "I am very relieved to see you and your wife here with Lady Fairbourne. I have come to speak with you all about what happened yesterday."

"Do you mean what *didn't* happen at the church?"

"Yes, sir. That's exactly what I meant." Tristan stole a glance at Jane who snuck a peek at him before lowering her gaze again.

"Well go on," Viscount Hastings urged.

"Because of circumstances I could not control, I was unable to attend the ceremony."

"We heard you were kidnapped." The viscount eyed Tristan carefully.

"I was."

"How did you get away?"

"I was released." Tristan sliced his hand through the air. "I won't go into detail, but during those hours I was tied up in a chair, I pondered my life and realized that marrying Lady Fairbourne would have been a terrible mistake."

Jane and her mother gasped. They both swung their focus to him.

"What are you saying?" Jane questioned softly.

He turned to her. "Lady Fairbourne, forgive me for putting you through this. I should not have asked for your hand in marriage."

"How do you know I would not have been happy?" Her voice cracked with anger.

"Because my parents were never happy in their arranged marriage, and I don't wish that torture on anyone."

Viscount Hastings stomped in front of Tristan again. "Do you think your apologies will help now? You are dragging my daughter into a scandal."

"Then tell everyone *you* broke the betrothal. Then only my reputation will be damaged."

Tears flooded Jane's eyes, all the while scowling at Tristan.

"And pray, Lord Tristan," she said in a tight voice, "what would be my reasons for wanting to call off the wedding?"

"It doesn't matter what reasons you give. Whatever it is, I will go along with it."

"But I don't want to give any at all. I still want to marry you."

"No, Jane. I shall not enter a marriage unless love is part of the deal, and I am not, nor have I ever been, in love with you."

Her bottom lip trembled as more tears streamed down her face. She turned to her mother and sobbed against the older woman's chest while she soothed her daughter.

Huffing, the viscount stepped closer to Tristan. The other man's expression was deadly. His eyes would shoot out venom any moment now, Tristan was certain.

"I warned you before that if you ever hurt my daughter—"

"Don't you understand?" Tristan asked, raising his voice. "I'm saving your daughter from a lifetime of unhappiness. Marrying me will make her miserable."

"All of this is because of Lady Hollingsworth, isn't it?" Jane shouted, pulling herself away from her mother and stomping up to Tristan.

"Pardon me?" he asked in panic. *How did she know Diana was involved?*

"You don't want to marry me because of Lady Hollingsworth."

"What does she have to do with any of this?" Tristan wouldn't give Jane the satisfaction of knowing the truth.

"I heard you were with her the past couple of days."

What on earth... That was impossible. Nobody would have known that information, especially when Tabitha was the one who kidnapped him! "I believe you have heard wrongly, then."

The older man's face reddened even more as he pushed his

finger into Tristan's chest. "If you don't marry my daughter, *you* will be the one miserable. I'll personally see to it, Lord Tristan."

Tristan shrugged. "Do your worst. I will not change my mind."

He turned back to the women, bowed, then walked past them and out the door. The viscount's threat didn't worry him in the least. Tristan knew the man over-reacted. Jane would find another willing soul very soon, he was certain.

As he mounted his horse, he breathed a sigh of relief. One obstacle down, others to hurdle, but they would be easy, he was certain.

DIANA'S COACH STOPPED in front of her home. *Ludlow's home,* she reminded herself. This grand estate would never be hers, and really she didn't want it even if she had that option. There were too many bad memories here. Evil lurked in every corner, and she still had nightmares that her husband's spirit would haunt her.

She turned to Tabitha who sat next to her and patted her maid's hand. "I hesitate to bring you in as my new maid. Ludlow's servants were very loyal to him since they'd been with the Hollingsworth family for years—although I don't know why—and they all hate me. I fear they will not like you because we are friends."

Tabitha shrugged. "Then we shall spend more time together, won't we?" She smiled. "I don't have a lot of friends, so I'll be fine. We shall get through this together."

"Yes, we shall. I pray our time here will not be long. The only reason I'm here is to be closer to Tristan."

Tabitha tightened the bows of her bonnet underneath her chin. "Do you anticipate him asking for your hand?" She winked.

Excitement rushed through Diana even though she shouldn't

feel this way. Just because they had talked about their past and he had kissed her so tenderly and passionately, didn't mean he would propose. As much as she wanted him to, she still feared that when he discovered she was barren, he wouldn't want her for a wife after all. Ludlow had wanted children, but she had never conceived, and he blamed her for not giving him an heir.

"Right now," Diana said, "I don't want to push Lord Tristan to do anything he does not want to do."

"Oh, he's sweet on you, my lady. He still has feelings for you, I can tell."

The footman opened the coach door and Diana climbed down first. Once Tabitha was out, she pointed to the trunks on the back, directing her gaze on him.

"Take Lady Hollingsworth's trunks to her room."

The middle-aged man glared at Tabitha, then switched his focus to Diana. She nodded. "Yes, Curtis. Do as Tabitha has instructed. She is now my personal maid."

His eyes widened. "But what will become of Martha White-head?"

"I'm certain we can find some other area for her to work on the estate. In fact, I believe she would make a wonderful housekeeper since Mrs. Newton has been very ill lately and is much too old to handle the manor by herself." Diana turned and headed toward the front door, keeping her chin up and back straight. She couldn't allow these servants to make her cower in any way. She was still the mistress of the manor until Ludlow's cousin, Mr. Tobias Lusk, came to claim it.

Entering the manor, she glanced over her shoulder at Tabitha who followed closely behind. Diana was grateful she would at least have a friend in this place, but she still feared someone would know Tabitha had worked for Lord Elliot. Diana could only pray that wouldn't happen because she did need an ally here, if even for a little while. It would make staying here that much more bearable.

"Oh my," Tabitha whispered in awe. "Your husband had

some lovely things."

Diana rolled her eyes. Slowing her steps, she waited for Tabitha to come closer. "Indeed, he did. He enjoyed showing off his wealth, and he treated these paintings, vases, and rugs better than he did his wife," she ended lowering her voice.

"When will his cousin arrive to take over?"

"I don't know." She shrugged. "Mr. Lusk has been notified of Ludlow's passing, but I have yet to hear when he will arrive."

The maid stopped, her gaze darting around the hall slower this time. "Perhaps we should sneak some expensive items out for you before he comes," she whispered. "After all, you have to live, too."

Tabitha's comment caught Diana by surprise, and she laughed. "Oh, Tabitha. Believe me, that thought has crossed my mind several times, but I talked myself out of it. Once I leave this place, I don't want anything to remind me of Ludlow."

"That's understandable."

From the kitchen, the staunch cook, Mrs. Jennings, walked out, her narrow gaze trained right for Diana. She gulped, not liking the way the older woman looked at her. Collecting her courage, Diana squared her shoulders and waited to see what the servant wanted.

"My lady," Mrs. Jennings said sternly, "I was not told you would be returning this soon."

Diana arched an eyebrow. "Is there a problem?"

"Well, not entirely. But yesterday you had visitors. Mr. Phillips told them we didn't know when you would return."

Diana shrugged. "I suppose if it were important to see me, they will return. Did they leave any kind of message with the butler?"

"No, Mr. Phillips did not have a message."

"Who was it that came?" Diana wondered.

The cook narrowed her gaze and lifted a haughty chin. "Mr. Phillips said that the magistrate and some of his men were the ones inquiring after you, my lady. The magistrate has some questions to ask you about Lord Elliot's death."

Diana's heart dropped as fear ran rapidly through her blood. The hint of brightness in her future quickly faded.

Chapter Nineteen

Heavy clouds filled the night sky, making the evening appear darker than normal as Tristan walked to the men's club where he and his brother, Trey, visited frequently. Although Trey would probably not be here, he enjoyed more spending time at home with his wife. Their good friend, Dominic, Marquess of Hawthorne, would probably be playing some card game, and winning. Tristan almost hoped to see his brother, Trey tonight. It would be easier to explain what was going on if both Trey and Nic were in the same room.

He hurried inside and gave his overcoat and top hat to the footman. Tristan strolled into the main room in search of his brother. Most of the tables were surrounded by men drinking and visiting. At first nobody looked at him, which suited Tristan just fine. Finally, one gent sitting at the closest table met Tristan's eyes. The man gasped and nearly spilled his drink as it fell from his fingers.

"Lord Tristan."

The trickle effect was rather astonishing. Once Tristan's name was spoken, gasps exploded around the room—his name on most everyone's tongue. Soon whispers overrode the gasps until the room buzzed with *Lord Tristan.* Surprised faces stared dumbstruck at him as if he'd risen from the grave. This expression was very familiar to Tristan since many had looked that way when he returned from the dead not too long ago.

He inclined his head briefly, but didn't say anything. As another footman walked by carrying empty wine glasses, Tristan said, "Excuse me, but can you tell me if Lord Trey and Lord Hawthorne are here?"

"Yes, my lord. They are in the blue room."

"I thank you." Relieved to hear his brother was here as well as their mutual friend, Tristan flipped a gold coin to the man before hurrying in that direction.

When he entered the parlor, his younger brother and Dominic were in conversation with two other gentlemen. Each man held a glass of wine. Tristan found it odd that they all wore the same, sour expressions.

When Tristan stepped further into the room, the floor boards groaned beneath his feet. Trey was the first one to snap his attention in Tristan's direction. His brother gasped, then sprang from his chair. The piece of furniture tipped over behind him and fell to the floor in a loud crash.

This sparked the other men into spinning around to look at Tristan. Their jaws dropped as shock registered on their wide-eyed expressions.

"Tristan!" Trey wrapped Tristan in a hug. When Trey pulled away, he glared through hooded eyes. "Where in the blazes have you been these past few days?"

Forcing himself to chuckle, Tristan walked to the table. It touched him to know his brother cared so much. Dominic jumped to his feet and shook Tristan's hand heartily.

"Thank the Lord you are back safe, my good man. Please tell us what happened. There was so much gossip we didn't know what to believe."

"Forgive me for worrying you all." Tristan glanced at the other two men and nodded. "Lord Gilbert. Lord Caldwell."

The men stood and shook Tristan's hand.

"I see you are not playing cards." Tristan motioned to the table. "It's not often I see Trey and Hawthorne in the same room without cards in their hands and a stack of bills in front of them."

"Tristan," Trey said with irritation in his voice. "Quit skirting around the question. Where were you?"

"We heard you had been kidnapped," Caldwell said.

"Indeed I was, Caldwell." Tristan sat then the other men followed as they gathered around the table. He studied Gilbert and Caldwell. The older men were friends of Hawthorne's family and had been kind to Tristan's mother. At times he wondered if these men were interested in her, yet they never let their feelings show. Tristan really didn't know if he trusted them enough to tell them what truly happened.

Clearing his throat, he drummed his fingers on the table. "I was kidnapped by a woman who thought to exact revenge when I had nearly ruined her reputation a few years back."

All eyes widened in disbelief. Seconds later, Dominic snorted a laugh and Trey shook his head.

"You must be joking," Trey muttered.

"I'm gravely serious, dear brother."

"How did you escape?" Hawthorne asked with a smirk on his mouth.

Tristan wagged his brows. "I charmed my way out if you must know."

He waited for their reaction, but it didn't happen as quickly as he figured it should. But within moments, they all barked with laughter. Grinning, Tristan relaxed in his chair.

"Who is the lady?" Gilbert asked.

Tristan held up his hand and shook his head. "I have already ruined her reputation enough. I shan't do anymore damage."

Caldwell arched a thick, white eyebrow. "I see you escaped unscathed."

"Indeed, I did."

Trey released a heavy sigh. Sitting back in his chair, he linked his fingers together and rested them on his mid-section. "I hate to be the bearer of bad news, but I fear you have returned home at the most unfortunate time."

Studying his younger brother, Tristan tapped his finger on the table. The sour look was back upon Trey's face—just as it had been when Tristan first walked into the room. "Why do you say that?"

"Because there has been another death—our cousin, Elliot. His life ended pretty much the way Hollingsworth had."

Tristan gave his brother a blank stare. "And pray tell, what does this have to do with me?"

"Have you forgotten? You are still one of the magistrate's suspects for Hollingsworth's murder."

"So." Tristan shrugged.

Dominic leaned toward Tristan and shook his head. "The suspicion has grown now that Lord Elliot has been killed. Several witnesses reported to the magistrate that they saw you and Elliot arguing a couple of nights before he was murdered."

Tristan scratched his chin. "But you were there, Hawthorne. You had to take me home from the card game because I was foxed. You know the argument didn't mean anything."

Dominic nodded. "And I have already told the magistrate this, but because you disappeared the night before your wedding and nobody knew where you were, you are still a suspect."

"Lord Tristan," Lord Gilbert spoke. "My cousin is one of the men working with the magistrate on this case. He informed me that your name is high on the suspects list. Unlike Hollingsworth, Lord Elliot didn't have that many enemies, but because you are linked to both men, the magistrate is going to start searching for more clues. Since your so-called kidnapping happened a day before the killing, that makes the magistrate more suspicious."

"What?" Tristan jumped out of his chair, standing above the other men. "My *so-called* kidnapping, you say? Indeed I *was* kidnapped. I didn't plan that, and I certainly didn't have any reason to kill Lord Elliot."

Lord Gilbert nodded. "I believe you about the kidnapping, but the magistrate will want to know who you have been with these past few days."

"I was with the lady who kidnapped me."

"Are you willing to give them her name?" Gilbert tilted his head, his eyes narrowing with distress.

Tristan scowled. "Of course I won't give them her name. As I'd mentioned before, I shan't cause scandal to her again."

Trey grasped Tristan's arm and glared into his eyes. "By not giving them the information they seek, that might be the very reason you'd get arrested."

Confusion swam in Tristan's mind. He understood the dilemma, but… No, he couldn't ruin Diana any more than he had already. "Then that's a chance I'll have to take."

"You are willing to be arrested for a crime you did not commit?" Trey's voice lifted in irritation.

Tristan nodded. "If that's what it takes, yes. I can only pray the magistrate will seek to find proof before they have a trial, because I can assure you, they will not find any."

Gilbert scrubbed his jaw. "I wish the higher courts believed in such a thing."

Across the table, Dominic released a ragged sigh and ran his fingers through his hair.

Trey groaned, rubbing his forehead and met Tristan's stare. "Then we need to have our older brother, Trevor, hire that well-known solicitor after all because I fear you will need him soon."

Dread squeezed Tristan's heart. Sadly, he knew his brother was correct this time.

Chapter Twenty

THE NEXT DAY, Diana sat as still as she could on her cushioned chair and waited for the butler to bring in her unwelcome guests—the magistrate and one of his men. Not more than five minutes ago, she watched from the window as their coach rolled to a stop in the front of the house. Fear leapt to her throat and stung her eyes. She couldn't tell them the truth about the night Lord Elliot had been killed. Good Heavens, they would think she had done the deed for certain.

Although she maintained a calm outward appearance, her heartbeat flipped with anxiety, and her palms were moist. Inhaling deeply, she realized her breathing had been altered, as well. Would they notice she was trying to hide something?

Slowly, she slid her palms on her dress to dry the wetness gathered, as she listened for their footsteps to sound on the floor in the corridor. The longer she waited, her stomach churned, and she wanted to scream with frustration.

Why would they suspect her murdering Lord Elliot? True, she had been there that night she'd rescued Sally, but the girl had met her out by the servant's door. Diana hadn't even gone inside the manor, and she especially had not been spotted by any of the nobleman's other servants since they were supposed to have been all in bed asleep. Not that Diana checked on every one, but she knew her servants—or Ludlow's—would have been asleep at that time during the night.

Finally, the sound she'd been waiting for came when several footsteps clamored on the floor. Taking another deep breath, she turned her eyes toward the doorway just as her butler showed them in.

The magistrate looked as if he were attending a social gathering, wearing a top hat, and his black coat stretched across his portly belly, and his black breeches looked just as snug. The man along with him wore a uniform—black jacket with golden buttons up the front and on the cuffs—and a black top hat and matching shiny boots. They entered the sitting room and then simultaneously removed their hats and bowed to her.

She nodded then motioned to the sofas. "Gentlemen, would you care to sit?"

"I thank you, Lady Hollingsworth," Sir Felix said and moved to the piece of furniture as the other followed. "I hope you forgive our intrusion, but we have some questions to ask you about Lord Elliot's murder."

"There is nothing to forgive. I will answer any question you have for me."

The other man gave her a smile, although Diana could see it was forced. Still, she regarded them with as much kindness and politeness as she could muster.

"How well did you know Lord Elliot Henson?" the magistrate asked.

She shrugged and folded her hands in her lap, hoping to stop the quakes threatening to become noticeable in her limbs. "Actually, I don't know him well at all."

"I believe he was acquainted with your late husband," the other man said.

"He very well could have been," she answered. "My husband had many friends, but that doesn't mean I associated with them."

"So are you saying you have never spoken to Lord Elliot?" the magistrate probed.

Diana shook her head. "I didn't say that. You asked me how

well I knew him, and I told you I didn't know him well." Perhaps she shouldn't have said it like that, but the two men irritated her more as the seconds passed.

Sir Felix scowled. "Pardon me then, my lady. Let me rephrase my question." He swallowed hard. "Have you ever talked to Lord Elliot?"

"A few times, yes."

The two men traded glances before the man with the thinning black hair straightened and looked at her. "Did you discuss anything personal?"

"Tell me sir, how could I discuss anything personal with a man I didn't even know well?"

"Lady Hollingsworth." The second man's voice nearly growled with malice. "One of his servants overheard you threatening Lord Elliot approximately two weeks ago."

Diana's blood turned cold as fear sliced through her. She couldn't believe someone had heard that conversation. "Tell me sir, did this servant tell you that I threatened his life? I can assure you I did not."

"Then tell us what you said," the magistrate said.

Trying not to show how rattled she was, she inhaled slowly and exhaled softly. "I had attended a gathering at his manor with a friend of mine, Lady Dashwood. I happened upon Lord Elliot and one of his maids during the event. They were in a room, and as I walked by I heard him yelling at someone. When I looked in the parlor, I saw him slap the woman across the face not once, but several times. Fear was evident in her eyes and the terror in her voice was unmistakable. I cannot bear to see anyone abused, so I snapped at Lord Elliot and reprimanded him for treating the poor girl in such a way—at a social gathering, no less." She took a deep breath and lifted her chin in defiance. "But not once did I threaten his life, even when he replied with some cruel words toward me."

The magistrate crossed his arms over his round belly and tapped his finger against his elbow. "Lady Hollingsworth, where were you last night?"

"I have been staying at my grandmother's cottage near Greenford for the past two weeks. One of my maids was with me, and Lady Dashwood visited me twice when I was there. I have only returned home this afternoon."

"Lady Hollingsworth?" the second man asked. "Are you aware that Lord Elliot was killed in the same manner as your late husband?"

She nodded. "Lady Dashwood told me, but if you must know, it's hard for me to credit."

"Why is that so?"

"Because I cannot imagine there is someone going around murdering gentlemen in such a way. It's very frightening."

Sir Felix nodded. "Indeed, it is. Lady Hollingsworth," he continued without hesitating, "how close are you to Lord Tristan?"

Fear clutched her throat, and she held her breath. How could she answer that question? Good Heavens! She forced herself to laugh lightly. "Oh, I'm quite certain you already know the answer to that. If you have lived around these parts in the past few years, I'm sure you have heard about the scandal that happened between Lord Tristan and myself."

Both men nodded, but it was the magistrate who continued his questions. "That is the very reason I ask, my lady. As you are probably aware, Lord Tristan is also a suspect."

"Yes, I heard the rumor."

"Well, we are now wondering if the two killings are connected—that maybe there is more than one person involved."

She didn't like the sound of that. "Pray, please cease confusing me in such a manner. What has this got to do with Lord Tristan?"

The magistrate's eyes narrowed and a wicked grin stretched his lips. "With all due respect, Lady Hollingsworth, we are wondering if you and Lord Tristan are working together on this—ridding the world of men who abuse women."

"Of all the insane, ridiculous notions!" Diana jumped to her feet. "You two must be out of your mind to think such a thing."

The two men quickly rose. "Lady Hollingsworth, were you not with Lord Tristan these past few days? Rumors have it that he was kidnapped and taken away from Mayfair by a woman set on revenge." The magistrate arched his brow. "And you just admitted to be at your grandmother's cottage for the past little while. I think this is too coincidental."

"Then you," Diana growled each word slowly, "are thinking entirely too much." Taking a deep breath, she concentrated on calming her ire. "Tell me, did you once stop to ask yourself that if I had kidnapped Lord Tristan and taken him to my grandmother's cottage, how would we have been able to murder Lord Elliot? Especially with his lordship's manor completely out of the way from my grandmother's cottage."

The two dolts exchanged worried glances before they aimed their attention back to her.

"Thank you, my lady." Sir Felix bowed. "You have been very accommodating. If we have any more questions, we'll let you know."

She walked to the parlor door, and motioned the butler over. "Mr. Phillips, please show these men out."

"Yes, my lady."

She stood by the door and kept her eyes on them as the butler led them down the corridor to the front door. Each step they took made her heart sink lower. Those two idiots couldn't possibly find any evidence that would link her to the murders, could they? Yet, her nightmare was hinting at reality. In her heart she *had* wanted her husband dead, and she *had* wished for Lord Elliot to have the same demise.

And what about Lord Tristan? How could anyone have known that he'd spent the past few days with her at the cottage?

Groaning, she rubbed her forehead, realizing that a pain in her skull had been there since she waited for the magistrate to arrive. The happiness she'd always wanted in her life was moving further and further away. Just as she felt Tristan would.

From one of the other rooms, the door slowly opened and Tabitha cautiously poked her head out. She took a quick glance up and down the corridor before straightening and exiting the room, heading toward Diana in an unhurried pace. When she reached the sitting room, they both entered as Tabitha closed the door behind them.

"How did it go?" Tabitha asked in a quiet voice.

Emitting a deep breath, Diana covered her face with her hands, her heart ready to break and tears to flow at any moment. "I fear I made them more suspicious. I could not lie to them, so I evaded their questions." Breathing slower, she dropped her hands and looked back at Tabitha. "However, I really think they knew what I was trying to do."

"Nonsense," Tabitha said as she patted Diana's shoulder. "Most men aren't that astute."

A smile tugged on Diana's mouth. She just couldn't help it. Sometimes Tabitha's clever comments made her laugh. "I had thought the same, but the magistrate and his man knew things they shouldn't have."

"Like what?"

"They suspected Tristan was with me at the cottage."

Tabitha scowled and folded her arms.

"Those two suspect that Tristan and I were working together to rid the world of people like my husband and Lord Elliot."

The servant arched an eyebrow. "Not a bad idea, if I must say."

Once again, Tabitha's comment caught Diana off guard and she chuckled. "As much as I feel the same, killing people is not the way to do it."

Tabitha shrugged. "Nice thought while it lasted."

Diana squeezed her friend's hands. "I'm just glad you are here to lend me support. Heaven knows Ludlow's servants would not care in the least what happens to me."

"I will always be your friend, Diana."

She released a sigh and tried to relax. "Tell me, did you get a chance to ride back to the cottage this morning to check on Sally?"

"Yes, and I'm happy to report, she's up and moving around, and her face is looking much better. It's not swollen any longer."

Sighing with relief, Diana nodded. "I'm very grateful for that. Maybe now Lady Dashwood can find employment for her."

Tabitha grew abnormally quiet as her expression took on a faraway look. She was thinking about something, and Diana didn't dare interrupt her friend's thoughts.

Tabitha tapped her chin as her gaze finally cleared. "Tell me, my lady, how well do you know Sally?"

Diana shrugged. "Not that well at all. I only met her the night I caught Lord Elliot beating her. Why do you ask?"

"Forgive me for wondering this, but is it possible that Sally killed Lord Elliot before you had rescued her that night?"

Diana's stomach churned with unease. That thought had crossed her mind a time or two. "I suppose it's possible, and I would not judge her if she had ended her employer's life." She shook her head. "However, we need to think bigger, here. Whoever killed Lord Elliot also killed my husband since both crimes were committed in the same fashion. However, I don't believe my husband was close enough friends with Lord Elliot to know his servants, and vice-versa."

"I suppose you are correct," Tabitha said with a sigh. "I was just trying to think of other people to help keep the magistrate from arresting you."

"I thank you, my friend, but we cannot blame the innocent. We must put our minds together and try to think of who might be doing this, because if the magistrate doesn't find any more suspects, he will surely arrest me or Tristan." A pain pierced her heart. She couldn't bear the thought of Tristan arrested. "But I need you to do something for me."

"What is it, my lady?"

Diana hurried to the desk in the corner of the room, found a piece of paper and ink pen. "I need you to deliver a note to Lord Tristan, posthaste." She sat and neatly penned a short missive. "I need to let him know what happened with the magistrate today."

"Why do we not just take a drive and see if we can run into him in Town?"

"Because until the true killer is caught, Tristan and I cannot be seen together. That will only make people more suspicious."

"That's understandable."

After she finished the note, she blew on the ink to dry it, and then folded it. As she handed it to Tabitha, she met her friend's gaze. "Give it directly to him and nobody else."

"As you wish, my lady."

Tabitha turned and hurried out of the room. Diana's eyes misted and she prayed everything would go according to plan. She must see Tristan, and the only way was after dark and after everyone was asleep, and the only place to meet was in her bedroom. They could ill afford having a servant—or anyone for that matter—witness their meeting.

Chapter Twenty-One

"BLOODY FOOLS!" TRISTAN grumbled as he stared blankly at the black and white chess pieces on the table in front of him. His opponent, Lord Hawthorne, sat directly across from him. Dominic had come over to try and talk some sense into Tristan, but instead, he convinced his friend to play a game of chess. Unfortunately, Tristan couldn't keep his mind on the game. Not when the magistrate had dropped by this morning.

"Worthington? Is the reference you made to *fools* aimed toward your chess pieces or something else?" Dominic had a hint of laughter in his tone, and sparkle of humor in his eyes.

Tristan shook his head. "I was referring to the magistrate and the idiot with him."

"Ah, now your words make more sense." Dominic nodded. "I must agree. Those two are fools, but fools who have solved many crimes before. Sometimes I wonder how they do it when they don't have an ounce of brain in their heads."

Looking up from the chess pieces, Tristan pierced Nic with a scowl. "Are you mocking me?"

"Hardly, my good man." Nic waved his hand in the air. "I'm merely agreeing with you in my own humorous way."

"Well, now is not the time or place for humor. I have much on my mind, and none of it is worth laughing over."

"That explains," Nic paused as he moved his white Knight

and took over one of Tristan's black Bishops, "why I'm winning."

Although Tristan didn't like losing, in this case he should just throw his hands in the air and admit defeat. Under the circumstances, there was no way he could concentrate on the game now.

"So tell me, what is it about their visit that has left you so upset?" Hawthorne leaned back in his chair.

"They tried to get me to confess the identity of the lady who kidnapped me, and even suggested the two of us were working together in Elliot and Hollingsworth's murders."

"Surely you jest." Nic's eyebrows creased. "Why would they say that?"

"Because they are bloody fools!"

Nic tilted his head as his gaze narrowed on Tristan. "Tell me truthfully and settle my mind. Was the lady who kidnapped you the same lady you had fallen in love with so quickly a few years past?"

Tristan couldn't tell his friend. Yet, Dominic Lawrence had always been a trustworthy fellow. Nic wasn't the kind of man who spread hurtful lies, either. "What would you say if indeed it was Lady Hollingsworth?"

Groaning, Nic rubbed his eyes and shook his head. "I would say my friend was not in his right mind." He met Tristan's gaze again. "Because I know for certain that you have feelings for Diana, and at this time in your life, that is not a good thing."

"What makes you think I have feelings for her?"

"It was obvious when you talked to us after your return the other day," Nic answered.

Shrugging, Tristan focused back on the chess set. "So what of it? Diana and I talked for the first time since my accident. We both discovered truths that were kept from us." He lifted his eyes to his friend. "And believe me when I tell you, she was not to blame in any of this. Not with what happened back then and certainly not what has happened to Hollingsworth and Elliot recently."

"Although you might think this way," Nic said, leaning forward, "the magistrate will see it differently. He will think Diana wanted her husband dead all this time because of what Hollingsworth did to her love for you. Now that you're back from the dead, the magistrate will think you and Diana killed her husband so the two of you could finally be together."

Tristan fisted his hands as anger shot through him. "That's ridiculous. They might think that about Ludlow, but what about Elliot? What could possibly be the motive for killing him? It's obvious that the two killings were done by the same person, so tell me wise one, what links us with my cousin's murder?"

"Perhaps Lord Elliot had seen the two of you kill Ludlow and was trying to blackmail you." He tapped his fingers on the table. "Tristan, you don't understand that there could be plenty of ideas the magistrate could create. The point is, you must *not* see Diana until after they have caught the true killer. Don't you see how dangerous that is not only for you but for her?"

Growling in frustration, Tristan pushed away from the table and strode to the window. Confusion clogged his rational thinking, and at the same time, loneliness clutched his heart when he imagined not being able to see Diana. He couldn't. He *wouldn't*. If needs be, he would find a way for them to be together, even if it meant returning to her grandmother's cottage. He would inform his family he was traveling abroad for an extended period, and Diana could just tell those who needed to know that she was caring for an ailing family member.

Worry eased slightly from his idea. If this was the only way, then he'd do it. He wouldn't allow Diana to slip through his fingers again.

The knock on the study door put a halt to Tristan's thoughts. "Enter."

Bentley, the butler, peeked inside. "My lord, you have a visitor. The young miss is delivering a note from her mistress, but she refuses to give me her name or a card. She says she has been tasked with making certain she hands the note to you and none other."

How odd, unless... "Bentley, show her in. I shall speak with her directly."

After the butler left, Tristan turned to Dominic who wore that worrisome expression Tristan was used to seeing lately.

"Do you honestly think that's a good idea?" Nic asked.

"If the messenger is who I think it is, then it's a *very* good idea."

"And pray, who do you think this young miss is?"

Without being able to help it, a grin tugged at the corners of his mouth. "The woman who kidnapped me, that's who."

Hawthorne's eyes widened. "Lady Hollingsworth?"

"No, it was actually her maid who takes credit for that."

When footsteps creaked on the floor outside the study, Tristan held his hand up to Nic, silently communicating with him not to say another word.

Just as Tristan suspected, the *young miss* that entered the study was Tabitha. She wore a brown cloak over her gray dress, and a matching gray bonnet. However, the hat was pulled low on her forehead as if she tried to hide her eyes. She watched Tristan until Nic rose to his feet. Tabitha stopped abruptly as her gaze flew to Hawthorne, and her eyes widened. In a flash, she threw her accusing glare back to Tristan.

"Nice to see you again, Tabitha." Tristan smiled. "Let me introduce you to my good friend, Lord Hawthorne. Hawthorne, this is Lady Hollingsworth's maid, Tabitha."

The interest in Nic's eyes was quite obvious as he skimmed his attention over Tabitha from the top of her head down to her shoes. A charming smile—the kind Nic enjoyed giving to women to make them weak in the knees—stretched across his face.

He bowed slightly. "A pleasure to meet you, Miss Tabitha."

Tristan was surprised that the maid's cheeks didn't flare with color like what happened to most women when meeting Dominic for the first time. In fact, she rolled her eyes and focused back on Tristan without even saying one word to Nic.

"My lord, I came here to deliver a note directly to you. My lady wishes that you tell *no one* about this note." She handed it to Tristan.

"I understand." He turned to Nic and said, "Lord Hawthorne, would you give Tabitha and I a few minutes alone?"

"Of course." He nodded to Tristan before turning to look at Tabitha. "Nice to meet you."

She forced a smile until Nic left the room and closed the door then she turned back to Tristan wearing a solemn expression. "My lord, Lady Hollingsworth assured me there would be secrecy about this meeting and the kidnapping. So why did you introduce me to Lord Hawthorne?"

"Calm yourself, Tabitha." Tristan walked to his desk and sat in the chair. "I assure you Lord Hawthorne is a man I can trust. He will not tell anyone about you coming here or about Lady Hollingsworth." He broke the seal on the letter and scanned the contents. Diana needed to speak with him tonight. It was urgent.

He glanced up at Tabitha. "Tell Diana I will be there."

"I shall." She turned toward the door and placed her hand on the door latch. "I beg you, Lord Tristan, please don't say anything to your friend. You might trust him, but I do not."

"Why is that, I wonder?" Slowly, he stood and walked toward her. "Have you met my friend before or had dealings with him?"

"No, but…" She took a deep breath. "Men like your friend are only a threat to women like myself. I may not know him, but I've heard of his reputation and it's not a good one."

Tristan wanted to laugh, but he refrained. "I certainly can't argue with you on that matter."

She curtsied. "Good day, Lord Tristan." She pulled the hood lower over her forehead, ducked her head and left.

Tilting his head, he studied her as she scurried away. Strange woman, especially when she tried her hardest not to have his servants look her way.

TABITHA RUSHED OUT of the townhouse, and breathed a sigh of relief to be out of that place. She couldn't have anyone recognize her or even *think* she looked familiar. That would certainly not be a good thing and perhaps ruin her life—especially when the wrong person saw her. But she wasn't out of danger yet. As soon as she stepped foot back into Diana's house, the immediate danger to Tabitha would be gone.

"What's your hurry, my lovely?"

The man's sultry voice turned her blood to ice. Yet at the same time, anger filled her and she wanted to tell the lord to mind his own business and leave her alone.

She glanced over her shoulder. Lord Hawthorne casually walked toward her from the side of the house, still wearing that knee-buckling grin on his nicely chiseled face. Curse the man for looking at her like that. He had no right. No right at all!

"If you will excuse me, my lord, I must be getting back."

"But Miss Tabitha, I'm certain your mistress would not scold you for talking to me for two minutes."

"Probably not, but I'd rather not take up your time." She continued to hurry, but his long legs had him catching up fast.

"I must admit Miss Tabitha, that you have me very curious about your behavior toward me. Pray, did I offend you in some way when we met? Did I say the wrong thing?"

Good grief! What was wrong with this man? Why didn't he take the hint? Huffing, she stopped and faced him, causing him to nearly bump into her. She had to tilt her head back to look into his face—a face that was too handsome to be real.

"If you must know, I would rather not converse with you. I'm in a hurry—"

"Just two minutes is all I ask."

He grinned at her again, and she wanted to slap it right off his face. "If I relent, will you then leave me alone?"

His eyes widened as did his mischievous smile. "Leave you alone? Why would you want me to do that?"

"Lord Hawthorne, I'm quite certain you have charmed many women, but I will *not* be one of them. Please save your efforts for someone who actually wants your attention. I, my lord, do not."

Not very often did she get to witness a titled man's jaw drop and his mouth gape, but this was one time she did. Surprise registered on his face along with bewilderment. She was sure he never had a woman say that to him before.

It didn't take long before he shook himself out of his stunned silence and straightened.

"Miss Tabitha, you intrigue me, and I find myself wanting to get to know you better, mainly because of your refusal to be courteous."

He cannot be serious! "Then what would it take for you to leave me alone? Would swooning at your feet and falling into your arms make you give up pursuit? If so, I would gladly do that now just to be rid of your persistence."

Lord Hawthorne chuckled and folded his arms across his chest. "So are you a woman who doesn't enjoy a man giving her compliments?"

She shook her head.

"Do you mean to tell me that if I told you that your eyes were as beautiful as the blue iris flower you would not like that? And if I told you that your face was lovelier than most women I have met—that it wouldn't make a difference to you? Indeed, you are an angel who has dropped from the heavens."

Against her will, her heart did a silly flip. Curse his hide! But she would gladly show him her devilish side—and she just might if he didn't leave.

Giving a nonchalant shrug, she said, "I'm sorry to say, but no, your words do not affect me. I don't have the time for flattery. You are wasting your efforts." She straightened her shoulders. "Now, my lord, I believe it has been two minutes and I must be getting back to my mistress." She bobbed a quick curtsy. "Have a pleasant day."

This time as she hurried away, he didn't follow. It took all of her willpower not to turn and look back, but as she reached the end of the walkway, she just couldn't help herself and peeked over her shoulder. Lord Hawthorne hadn't moved from where she left him, and when he saw her look back, his face beamed with happiness. *Oh great!* Now she knew she'd never be rid of him. Well, she would just have to try harder.

The closer to Diana's home, the more relaxed Tabitha became. She really didn't want to be around the Worthington family. Being right inside the dragon's lair frightened her nearly to death. And she wasn't an easy person to scare.

Yet she could never let them know her secret. Not now. Not ever.

LONG AFTER THE servants had retired for bed, Tristan crept out of his house. He wore black clothes and cape, hoping he wouldn't get noticed. The streets were dark as he rode his horse to Diana's house, and as he approached her estate, all seemed quiet. He tied his horse to the front gate and cautiously snuck to the front door. Just as the note indicated, the door was unlocked.

Once he stepped inside, he felt another presence. The dark corridor didn't show him anything, but he heard breathing. Seconds later, came the soft steps of a woman.

"Tristan?" Diana whispered.

A relieved sigh escaped his throat. "Yes, it is I."

A dark shadow moved in front of him and her hand clasped with his.

"Follow me."

Tristan twined his fingers with hers and followed. Together they tiptoed up the stairs and down another long corridor. When they reached a room, she opened the door. Inside one candle had been lit, which helped him to see slightly better.

Diana still wore a gown, but her hair had been brushed out of the ringlets and the tight coil she usually wore. With very little lighting, he couldn't see her beautiful eyes like he wanted, but he knew they sparkled green.

"I'm so glad you came," she said softly as she closed the door.

He moved in front of her and clasped both of her hands. "Nothing could keep me away." He wanted to take her in his arms so badly right now, but didn't dare. Being away from her these past few days had been torture, and he feared if he started kissing her, he would never want to stop.

"Your missive sounded urgent."

She nodded. "What I have to tell you is extremely urgent. It's about Lord Elliot's murder."

Tristan tugged on her hands and led her to the sofa against the wall near the window. He slipped off his cape and rested it over the back of a nearby chair before sitting next to her on the sofa.

"Has the magistrate talked to you?" he inquired.

"Yes, early this afternoon, in fact."

"Same with me." He rubbed his thumb over her knuckles. "And if they said the same thing to you as they did to me, then I certainly know why your note sounded so urgent."

"Oh, Tristan." Diana laid her head on his shoulder. "What are we to do? We were not working together to kill Ludlow or Lord Elliot."

"I know, but proving that to the magistrate might be quite a task for us."

She tilted her head to meet his stare. "Somehow they know I kidnapped you."

"Yes, they hinted that to me as well. They wanted me to confess that you were the lady who I was with, but I refused to give your name." He stroked her cheek. "I have done enough damage to your reputation, and I assure you, I won't do any more."

Sighing, she cuddled against his palm. "Oh, Tristan. We cannot go on like this, yet if we are seen together, people will become suspicious. They will think the worst."

She had been thinking what he had, but that didn't make it any easier to handle. Truth was, if he had to be without her for very long, he feared he would break down and let everyone know his feelings about this kind and forgiving woman.

"Diana, you might be able to go without seeing me, but I'm not that strong." He cupped her face and brought his mouth down on hers.

She responded quickly, meeting his kisses with a fierce urgency. Her hands clung to the front of his waistcoat before sliding up to hook around his neck as she pulled him closer.

Groaning with happiness, he wrapped his arms around her, keeping her in place against his chest. Her heartbeat thumped the same quick rhythm as his, and her heavy breaths were just as ragged as well.

It thrilled him to think her feelings mirrored his perfectly right now. Although he enjoyed what they were sharing, panic grew inside him and he wondered if he'd ever get to kiss her like this again. Three years ago when they'd been so passionate, something yanked away his happiness and left him in misery. He prayed that wouldn't happen again.

Yet somehow… he felt the worst was about to happen.

Chapter Twenty-Two

"OH, TRISTAN," DIANA whispered breathlessly against his lips. "I fear if we don't stop this instant, we might do something very improper."

Tristan's body shook with silent laughter, and she withdrew slightly to gaze into his shadowed eyes—eyes that she'd dreamed about for so long now that she still couldn't believe this was real. Smiling, she fingered the soft hair on his neck.

"My dear, Diana. I'm happy to know your thoughts are as wicked as mine."

"You were thinking the same thing?"

"I was thinking earlier that if I started kissing you tonight, I would never want to stop. After seeing your beautiful long hair flowing around your shoulders, I realized how I want you just like this, next to me and cuddling so personally." He leaned closer and rubbed his cheek against hers.

Happiness swelled in her chest. She'd waited to feel this way for so long. Unfortunately, as most of the events in her life, falling in love with Tristan wasn't right yet. There were too many barriers keeping them apart. Especially now.

"Tristan, whatever shall we do? We cannot see each other until they find the guilty person, yet staying away from you would be impossible."

"I agree." He kissed her lips again briefly before pulling back.

"But I do have a solution."

"Please tell. I'm all out of ideas."

"I propose we return to your grandmother's cottage. I shall tell my family I'm traveling abroad, and you could tell your staff that you have sick family and you will be gone for a long time." He grinned. "Nobody would know we were together."

She sighed and rested her head on his chest, sliding her arms around his middle. "That does sound Heavenly."

"Then do you agree that's our only choice?"

"Yes, I do. But I still fear someone will find out, and if there is another murder, the magistrate will continue to suspect us."

"We won't let that happen. We shall be very careful."

Diana lifted her head and looked into his eyes. "You are serious about this, aren't you?"

"Extremely." He cupped the side of her face. "We have been apart for too long. I refuse to let anyone—or anything—keep us from being together."

Her heart melted. How could it not from his sweet words? "Then when should we start planning our little holiday?"

"The sooner the better." He winked. "Actually I was thinking in a few days. You can leave first then I shall leave three days later. That way people won't suspect we have left together."

She nodded as calmness settled in her heart. She prayed he was correct that nobody would find out. Still, she must do something to try and discover who was really committing these murders. There was no way she wanted to keep her feelings from Tristan and everyone else.

For once in her life, she could see the end of a dreary tunnel, and she couldn't wait to get there.

THE PLAN WAS simple. All Tabitha had to do was take a few of Diana's trunks to the cottage, check on Sally, then return. Yet complications arose and by the time Tabitha was having the last trunk loaded, she was ready to scream with frustration. If it wasn't one of the horses losing a shoe, it was the footman dropping one of the trunks and breaking it beyond repair.

She'd wanted to leave early enough in the day so that she could return to the manor by nightfall, but now she would have to stay the night. Being by herself wasn't terribly boring, but conversing with Diana would definitely make time pass quicker.

Tabitha tightened the ribbons of her bonnet under her chin, and climbed into the carriage. Just as she settled herself on the seat, the vehicle jerked into motion. She'd brought a few books to read for her journey, but at the moment, she was too mentally exhausted to think about absorbing anything in the leather-bound novels.

Resting her head back against the seat, she closed her eyes, wanting nothing more to do right now but dream of her future. Or at least imagine what her future could be. Unfortunately, just as she was picturing a different world—one with happiness and solace—a man's charming smile and intense eyes popped into her head.

Never had she seen a more handsome man before—wide shoulders and chest, muscular legs, and blue-gray eyes that could melt a witch's heart. Not only that, but his husky laugh had made her heart skip a beat.

She growled and snapped open her eyes. Why was she thinking about *him*? The scoundrel shouldn't even be worth her time or worth daydreaming about. Men like him didn't have hearts.

From outside the carriage, someone whistled and the vehicle slowed. Mumbling voices were heard. Someone was talking to Mr. Coggins, the driver. Seconds later, the door opened and in jumped a man. She gasped and braced herself on the seat. In a split second, he had closed the door and sat next to her as the vehicle picked up speed. Familiar blue-gray eyes twinkled when he smiled.

"Where are we going, my lovely?"

When it finally sank in her head that Lord Hawthorne had invaded her space and privacy, anger overrode the shock pumping through her. She bunched her hand into a fist and punched his arm. "You cannot be serious. What in Heaven's name are you doing here?"

"I'm riding with you." He motioned his head toward the front of the carriage where the driver was. "Did you not hear me asking the driver if I could get in?"

"Of course not. If I had, I would have blocked the door to keep you away from me."

Sitting back in the seat, he stretched his long legs in front of him as he raked his fingers through his wind-blown hair. "You didn't answer me, my lovely. Where are we going?"

"*We* are going nowhere! *You*, however, will be getting out any moment or else I'll personally push you out myself."

His gaze skimmed over her arms then traveled down her dress. Chuckling, he shook his head. "I wouldn't bet on that. You do not appear to be that strong."

She rolled her eyes. "Are you sure?"

He shrugged and held his hands out, palms up. "Give it a try. I dare you."

Oh, the infuriating man! "Fine, you win. I cannot possibly throw you out, so I'll politely ask you to leave," she said, grinding out each word.

"All right. Go ahead."

"Go ahead? What are you talking about, sir?"

"You said you would *politely* ask me to leave." His grin stretched. "I'm still waiting for the polite part."

"Augh! What have I ever done to deserve this?" she muttered.

He leaned closer, gazing deep into her eyes. "You know, I don't believe I have ever seen such a vivid color of eyes in my life."

She arched an eyebrow. "You have never seen blue before?"

"Yes, but your eyes are more than that. In fact, I believe we shall name a new color right now—just for your eyes and your eyes alone."

"And pray, what would that name be?"

"Amazing."

Inwardly, she groaned. "You have got to be jesting."

"About your eye color?"

"Not that—about your choice of words. I believe, my lord, that you are repeating memorized phrases specifically used to charm a woman senseless."

He hitched a breath, placing his hand on his chest. "You wound me deeply, my lovely."

She growled. "Will you stop calling me *my lovely?*"

Leaning closer, his gaze rested on her mouth. He lifted his hand and gently stroked her cheek. Heat slipped from his fingertip and melded into her skin. *Good Heavens this is wrong!*

"I fear I cannot," he said deeply. "The sentiment merely rolls off my tongue, and stopping is furthest from my mind."

He was too close. Inhaling deeply only made her that much more aware of his intoxicating scent of leather and musk. Silently, she groaned, knowing she could *not* be taken by this man.

She pressed her palms against his chest—a hard frame, no less—and moved him away. "Lord Hawthorne, what have I ever done to make you want to pursue me like this?"

"I have not stopped thinking about you. In fact, you look very familiar to me, but I cannot think how I know you."

"You don't know me. So go away."

"But it's more than that," he continued without acknowledging her request. "I find you intriguing, and well, when I rode by Lady Hollingsworth's estate and saw you out front instructing the footman to load the trunks, I became curious. Especially when I never saw the lady of the home actually board the carriage."

"Lord Hawthorne, has anyone told you how insufferable you are?"

"Not at all, which is another reason why you intrigue me."

"Because you're not used to women shunning you?"

"Exactly."

She rubbed her forehead as the pounding that started when he flew into the carriage grew worse. "Please tell me what I can say to make you leave."

"What is it that you don't like about me?"

"You mean you don't know?"

"Humor me."

"Well, for one, I don't enjoy forward men. You are far too bold for my tastes."

Nodding, he scratched his chin. "And this coming from the woman who kidnapped my friend?"

Heat climbed her face that had nothing to do with her anger. "And secondly, I do not like that you have ignored every hint I've given to discourage you, yet you continue to pursue me."

"What can I say? I find you fascinating."

"And lastly, I do not like men who think that just because I'm a maid, that I'm a willing participant in their lusty adventures." Memories crashed through her head of Lord Elliot. Hatred for men like him made her so angry she could spit nails!

"You think that's what I'm after... a *willing* maid? Did you not hear me when I told you how interesting you are to me?"

She folded her arms. "Oh, I'm quite certain you find me interesting, but only for the bedroom. In reality, men of your station would never think of marrying a woman like me."

His eyes widened and he lifted his hands in surrender. "Stop right there. All I want to do is get to know you, and suddenly you are talking marriage?"

"Tell me I'm wrong, Lord Hawthorne. The only reason you want to get to know me is to charm me into having your wicked way with me."

He didn't speak, and silence stretched between them as the seconds ticked by. She knew she was right, and deep inside she wished for once she had been wrong. But she was old enough by now and been taught too many of life's lessons to know that fairytales never came true.

"You don't have to answer that, my lord, but please leave. I did not invite you to ride with me, so please be kind enough to go."

"Where are you going?" he asked.

"Away with Lady Hollingsworth to take care of her ailing relative." She lifted her chin. "That's all you need to know."

"Then where is Lady Hollingsworth? If you are traveling with her, shouldn't she be here?"

Tabitha fisted her hands, hoping he'd leave soon before she hit him. She moved her arm and pounded on the wall of the carriage and shouted, "Driver, stop the vehicle now."

Lord Hawthorne narrowed his eyes as the carriage came to a stop. She motioned toward the door. "Please leave now before I summon the watch."

He nodded. "As always, Miss Tabitha, it was a pleasure conversing with you."

He opened the door and climbed out. When he shut the door, she released a sigh of relief. Hopefully, from here on out, that man would stay far away from her.

DIANA DECIDED TO hold a dinner party for just her close friends. This would be her last appearance before she went away to help her sickly aunt—so her story would be. If she stayed completely away from her friends, they might suspect she had killed her husband. If they knew what had *really* happened, they would have hailed her a heroine because of what she had suffered being married to him.

Nevertheless, this evening she sat at the head of the table as she and six of her friends ate their dinner and chatted about useless topics. It was all Diana could do to keep the faux smile on her face as she sipped a glass of sherry.

After dinner, she led the ladies into the parlor where she'd previously had tables and chairs set up for a game of whist. It was hard to pretend to be enjoying herself, when all she wanted to do was leave this place and go to her grandmother's cottage to be with Tristan. Concentrating on the topic of conversations was also difficult, and she found herself glancing at the clock in the room more times than she should have.

Once, she thought she'd heard a man's voice at the front door, and her heartbeat thudded faster in excitement, hoping… praying it wasn't Tristan for fear people would speculate about their relationship. When she realized she'd been hearing things, her spirits dropped and it was even more difficult to smile.

She really needed to snap out of this melancholy mood before one of her friends noticed. Diana wouldn't put it past Lady Dashwood to actually say something, either.

Finally, when she could stand no more, she excused herself to visit the ladies retiring room. Up the smaller corridor was the room. A few maids were there, ready to assist. Diana wished to be alone, yet that wasn't proper without causing suspicion.

She didn't spend a lot of time in the room before she was presentable again, and when she walked out, she took slow steps, not really wanting to pretend to enjoy her friends' company. She must make some excuse to end the evening. Perhaps she would tell them that she had a long journey on the morrow, and she needed her sleep.

Shrugging, she rolled her eyes. At this point in the evening, she'd say anything to get her friends to leave. As she passed one of the empty rooms, the door was ajar and she could tell someone was inside. Curiosity had her stopping to take a peek.

Before she had time to think, the door widened and out from the darkness shot a man's hand, grabbing her and yanking her into the room. Her feet moved obediently—it was either that or fall on her face—and soon she was pressed up against a muscular body. Immediately, she knew his scent, and the way her body cuddled so well with his.

Diana glanced up into his shadowed face. "Tristan, what are you doing?" she whispered.

"How did you know it was I?"

She chuckled. "I assure you, there is no other man who wants to grab me and pull me into a room for some privacy."

He cupped her face with one hand. "Then indeed, I am the most fortunate man. I do not want any other man paying attention to you."

"You are too kind. But I think the other men will stay far away because they believe me to be a murderess."

"Good." He grinned.

"Good?" she gasped in shock.

"Yes. If they think that way about you, then I won't be competing with any other suitor this time."

She shook her head. "You were not in competition with anyone last time, either. If you recall, I was being forced to marry Ludlow."

"I do recall very well now, and I'm vastly relieved there is no other man in your life."

"You are the only one I want. Now and always."

She didn't allow him to make the first move. Lifting on her toes, she reached up to capture his mouth with hers. Thankfully his mouth had begun to descend and so she didn't have to reach very high.

His arms wrapped around her and held her tight as she slid her palms up his chest and hooked her hands around his neck. His lips moved perfectly with hers, so soft and gentle at first then a little more urgent. Her heart burst with love and acceptance, and she loved this feeling that hadn't been part of her life before.

She wanted more—much more. Never did she want to be separated from him again. If only fate would lend a helping hand this time. If only the real killer out there would get caught.

"Oh, Tristan," she sighed and broke the kiss. "We should not be doing this here. My guests are waiting for me to return."

He blew out a frustrated breath and leaned his forehead against hers. "I know, my love, but I couldn't keep away from you. I knew you had visitors this evening, and when I arrived, I begged Tabitha to let me see you—if even just a glimpse."

"Really?" Surprise jolted through her. "I thought I'd heard a man at my door, but then I realized it was only my imagination."

"No, it was I. When I saw you sitting in with your guests, I knew I had to steal a private moment to take you in my arms and share a passionate kiss."

"Three days," she whispered. "I will leave for the cottage tomorrow and then you will follow in three days, just as we had planned."

"I cannot wait that long."

Smiling, she stroked his cheek. "Neither can I, but we must."

"You are correct, my dear. I will try to have more patience."

She pulled away and squeezed his hands. "Let me leave the room first."

"I will."

Diana turned and stepped to the door, but the floor creaked as he stepped behind her and took her in his arms once again. Closing her eyes, she grinned as his chest pressed against her back. She rubbed his arms circled around her waist.

"Tristan..."

"Yes, I know. I had a moment of weakness. But can you blame me? I just enjoy holding and kissing you so much." He dropped a kiss to her neck.

"No, I won't blame you." She pulled away from him once again and peeked at him over her shoulder. "I'll see you in three days."

He nodded. "Three days, and not a moment longer."

Chapter Twenty-Three

TABITHA REACHED THE cottage just as the sun descended in the horizon. The long ride made her dreary, but her conversation with Lord Hawthorne made her emotionally weak. She kept reminding herself that he would only see her as a maid. Nothing more. It didn't matter if she was the bastard child of a nobleman, or if she perhaps had extended family with titles, she was too far beneath his station to live in *his* world.

She climbed out of the carriage and hurried into the house before the driver could bring in Diana's trunks. As Tabitha removed her bonnet, the stairs creaked, and she swung in that direction. Sally crept down the steps, her eyes wide with fear.

"It's just me," Tabitha assured her. "But go back up to your room before the coachman, Mr. Coggins, sees you."

Nodding, Sally quickly retreated.

Tabitha hurried to the front door and held it open for Mr. Coggins. She wondered how she could keep him from seeing Sally. Because it was too late in the evening for him to travel back to the estate, the man must stay at the cottage.

Without speaking to her, the coachman carried the trunks and set them on the floor. Obviously, he was one of Lord Hollingsworth's loyal servants because every time Coggins looked her way, he wore that same judgmental scowl as the rest of the servants wore.

"Thank you, Mr. Coggins. If you will excuse me, I shall prepare us something to eat in the kitchen."

"I thank you for your offer, Miss Tabitha, but I will not be staying to take the meal with you. I have a brother that lives not far from here, and I would rather visit with him this evening."

She didn't want to show him how happy that made her, so she tried to hold in her exhilaration. Nodding, she said, "As you wish. Have a safe journey to your brother's place."

He turned and left without replying, but that was all right with Tabitha. The quicker he was gone, the better. She followed him outside, and stayed until he climbed on top of the carriage, then steered the horses back up the road.

"Is he gone?" Sally whispered as she peeked out around the door.

Tabitha smiled at the other woman. "Yes, thank goodness. I worried he would not leave until morning. I would have been watching him nonstop then to make certain he didn't find you here."

Relief swept over Sally's expression and she smiled. Moving away from the door, she walked outside toward Tabitha. The reed-thin girl was probably eighteen or nineteen, but because of her thinness, Tabitha thought she looked much younger. Today her pale face actually held a little more color, and her blonde hair looked more yellow in the shadows.

"I would not have liked him here, either," Sally said. "These past couple of days, I have enjoyed coming out in the yard and partaking of this warm weather. It pleases me to smell the fresh country air and walk through the paths decorated by lovely flowers. After Lord Elliot's last beating, I feared I might not get through it alive."

When Sally stepped in front of Tabitha, she patted her friend's arm. "I would not have let him touch you one more time. Neither would Lady Hollingsworth."

Tears welled in Sally's eyes as she smoothed her hand over her brown dress, still sporting the rips that had happened during her last beating. Tabitha was thankful the other woman's face was not as bruised as before, and the cut on Sally's bottom lip was nearly healed.

"Seeing how you turned out," Sally said, "makes my will strong. Because you have endured, so shall I."

"And you will." Tabitha smiled. "Nobody should be put through the torture that we have. And God might strike me down for saying this, but I'm vastly relieved Lord Elliot has met his Maker. I assure you, God will not be merciful."

"I pray you are right. There were many times while he hit me when I wished I could… could…" She sobbed and brought her hand to her mouth.

Tabitha moved closer and put her arm around Sally. "You were not the only person feeling that way. I'm sure many of his servants wanted him dead."

"I'm truly grateful for all that you and Lady Hollingsworth have done. It's just very unfortunate that Lord Elliot had to die on the same night she rescued me. I hope the magistrate does not know she was there."

"I will do everything in my power to keep Lady Hollingsworth safe." Tabitha folded her arms across her chest. "What people don't seem to understand is that Lord Elliot deserved his fate. In fact, I think he should have gotten worse. I would have enjoyed driving a knife into his chest one last time."

In the stillness of the night, a noise was heard in the shadowy hedge other than the rustle through the leaves. It almost sounded like… a gasp!

Tabitha swung toward the hedge and fixed her stare on the dark shadows. "Did you hear that, Sally?"

"Hear what?"

"It sounded like…" She stepped closer as her heartbeat frantically pounded against her ribs.

"Like what?" Sally asked, her voice softer than before.

"I pray I'm wrong, but it sounded like someone is hiding in the hedges."

Sally released a panicked squeal and darted inside the house. Tabitha continued toward the spot where she'd heard the sound. The closer she came, the more her legs trembled. Yet, if someone were hiding—and listening—wouldn't they be trying to get away right now? The hedges remained unruffled and there were no other sounds. She stopped inches away from the greenery and peered as hard as she could through the darkness, but couldn't see anything.

Perhaps she'd been wrong. After all, it could have been a small animal. So then why did it sound like a man's gasp?

Shaking her head, she turned away and hurried back inside the house. Her imagination was playing tricks on her again. Why would anyone be this far away from the town without making their presence known? It definitely wasn't Mr. Coggins because he had traveled in the opposite direction.

She settled her panic and convinced herself it had indeed been a small animal. As she entered, she closed the door behind her. "Not to worry, Sally. I think it was a rodent."

"Are you sure?" Sally's voice came from the kitchen.

"I saw nobody trying to run, and I couldn't detect anyone still hiding. So yes, I'm certain it was a rodent."

Sally slowly exited the kitchen, running her fingers through her hair. "That relieves me greatly."

"Forgive me for frightening you."

"There is nothing to forgive. We all need to be very cautious. At least until Lord Elliot's murderer is caught."

"I agree." Tabitha rubbed her hands together. "Now, let's forget all of this nonsense and fix us something for dinner. I'm famished."

As she made her way into the kitchen, unease grew inside of her. Something wasn't right, and she couldn't shake away the feeling. From time to time throughout her life, she'd experienced these kinds of feelings. More often than not, she was right and horrible things had occurred. Now, the apprehension growing in her gut hinted of a danger that lurked in the future. One she could not control.

TRISTAN PACED THE floor in his study so much that he feared the rugs needed to be replaced. And to think he still had to wait three more days. How could he do it? Even now, the wait was killing him.

Since his return from the cottage after being kidnapped, he'd ridden his stallion by Diana's estate every day, but never saw her sitting by a window or outside. However, eavesdropping on his servants proved informative. That was how he'd heard about Diana's dinner party with close friends last night. And this morning, the servants had mentioned how they'd seen several trunks loaded on Diana's carriage.

Although he wanted to go to her now, there were still things he must do to ready his family and friends for his *traveling abroad* story. He must let his mother know so she wouldn't worry, and for certain he needed to let his brothers and Hawthorne know so they would not panic. Tristan would only tell his older brother, Trevor, the truth just in case the magistrate wanted to arrest him.

Deciding not to put this off a minute longer, he snatched his coat jacket off the back of a chair and left the study. "Gentry," he called out as he marched down the hall.

"Yes, my lord." The servant rushed out of one of the rooms.

"Please have my horse ready to ride quickly."

"As you wish, my lord."

Gentry hurried down the hall as fast as his boney legs could carry him. He reached the front door and opened it, but came to a halt. Standing with his fist raised to knock was Dominic Lawrence.

"Hawthorne," Tristan called and motioned his friend to enter. "What brings you to my door this morning?"

Dominic walked in, but he wasn't wearing his usual cheerful smile. Instead, worry laced his eyes and frown.

"Worthington, I need to speak to you in private."

"Certainly. Let's adjourn to my study."

As they walked to the study, Tristan noticed something else different about his friend. The dark circles under Nic's eyes, wrinkled clothes, and his unkempt appearance reminded Tristan of how *he* used to look after returning from a late night of drinking. Although—Tristan took a deep sniff—Nic didn't smell strongly of spirits at all.

Once they reached the study and Tristan closed the door behind them, it was Nic's turn to pace the floor with his hands clutched behind, resting on his lower back. His expression was unreadable, but Tristan could see there was much turmoil weighing on his friend's mind.

Tristan walked to his chair and sat. "I'm assuming you have heard bad news."

Nic stopped and faced him with wide eyes. "How do you know?"

Tristan wanted to chuckle, but refrained. "Because of the way you are acting."

Hawthorne nodded. "What I have to say is not good at all."

"Then please, tell me what is on your mind."

Running his fingers through his hair, Nic breathed in deeply then exhaled in slow measurements. His gaze dropped to the floor. "The other day when I met Diana's maid, the girl intrigued me, and I felt as if I knew her somehow." He shrugged. "She looks so familiar, but I cannot figure out how we met."

Tristan groaned and rubbed his forehead. "Stop right there." When Nic's eyes jumped up and met Tristan's, he continued. "Are you going to tell me you seduced Miss Tabitha into your bed?"

Confusion swept across Hawthorne's expression for a split second before he rolled his eyes. "Of course I didn't seduce her. What would make you think such a thing?"

"Because you have a way with charming women, and I noticed the way you had acted around her the other day." Tristan arched an eyebrow.

Nic flipped his hand in the air. "Well, remove that idea from your mind because it did not—and never will—happen."

Tristan couldn't believe how relieved he felt right now. He nodded. "Then pardon my intrusion. Please continue."

Clearing his throat, Nic straightened. "As I was saying, the girl interested me enough to watch her closely. Something just was not right about her. Last night I caught her in Diana's carriage with Diana's trunks, yet I knew Lady Hollingsworth was at that party which you had attended. When I talked to Miss Tabitha, my suspicion grew so I followed her to a place I have never been before—a few hours southwest of here. She arrived at a small cottage that sat on a beautiful piece of land surrounded by a magnificent grove of trees."

Tristan nodded. "That's the place she took me when she kidnapped me. It's Diana's grandmother's cottage."

"As it were, I continued to spy on her." He paused and cocked his head. "Were you aware they are keeping one of Lord Elliot's servants there?"

Surprise washed over Tristan and he blinked. "No, I was not."

"Apparently, Lord Elliot had beaten her severely, and Diana is now caring for her."

A smile stretched Tristan's mouth. Diana had such a loving heart. "That is something she would do."

"However," Nic said, folding his arms across his chest, "were you aware that Lady Hollingsworth had taken this maid from Lord Elliot's townhouse the very night of his murder?"

"Of course not. Don't be ridiculous. I was at the cottage during that time. There was no way Diana had taken this servant on that night."

"Well, she did. Both Tabitha and the servant girl had spoken about it while I was listening to their conversation."

Tristan's mind scrambled to remember details about that night. Wasn't that the night the women had given him a drink of tea laced with sleeping draught because he'd had a bad dream? Come to think of it, that next morning when he was soaking in the tub and Diana had walked in on him, he realized her boots were caked with dried mud and she looked tired.

Pain throbbed behind his eyes and he tried to rub it away. No! This couldn't be right. Nic must not have heard correctly.

"Tristan," Nic said as he walked closer, "I believe Lady Hollingsworth knows more than she has told you. From what I had overheard, I received the impression that Miss Tabitha killed Lord Elliot and Lady Hollingsworth knows about it." He placed his hand on Tristan's shoulder. "And if Miss Tabitha killed Lord Elliot, then she was the one who killed Diana's husband."

The confusion inside Tristan grew thicker and it felt like his head was being squeezed by giant hands. Not only that, but his chest tightened, making it harder and harder to breathe. If what Nic said was true…

"No!" Tristan pushed his friend's hand away, rose from his chair, and stormed to the window. The throb in his head had intensified. "What you say cannot be true. If Diana knew Tabitha was the killer, she would have said something to the magistrate." He swung and glared at Hawthorne. "Mine and Diana's reputations are at stake here. She knows neither of us wants to pay for a crime we did not commit." He raked his fingers through his hair as frustration built inside of him like a fierce volcano, ready to explode. "She wants to be with me as badly as I want to be with her, yet we both know making our relationship public is out of the question because of this very issue." He breathed deeply. "And if she has known all this time who the killer was, then she bloody well better report it to the magistrate."

Sighing, Nic leaned back against the edge of the desk. "Do you think Miss Tabitha is blackmailing Diana then?"

Once again, Tristan thought back to the time he was held prisoner, remembering the way Tabitha and Diana acted around each other. "No. Tabitha is not blackmailing. Diana loves her maid too much to be fearful of her, and Tabitha has too much respect for her mistress to do such a thing."

That conclusion meant only one thing. Diana knew who had

killed her husband and Lord Elliot and wasn't about to say anything. If Tristan got arrested, would she then speak the truth to free him? He wasn't sure he wanted to wait until that time came to know of her loyalty.

Chapter Twenty-Four

"I CANNOT BELIEVE she wouldn't tell me," Tristan whispered brokenly.

"There must be a reason."

Tristan shrugged. "The time we were apart, we each held onto the love we had once shared even though we tried to hide it those years. And now, when we can finally be together, she is the one stopping it, all because of her maid."

"Let's not assume anything yet," Nic said. "Because of what I heard Miss Tabitha and the other girl say, I believe Miss Tabitha is the killer. But I will continue to watch them both closely. Perhaps I'm wrong and Diana doesn't know—"

"Then we must find out." Tristan's heart broke—a feeling he had never wanted to experience again. "From what I have observed between Diana and her maid, they are as close as sisters. If she is protecting Tabitha, I want to know now—not after I'm arrested."

"But how can you find out? If she hasn't said anything to you..." Nic threw up his hands and began to pace. "Does she not love you more than her maid?"

"I want to think that," Tristan said in quiet tones as he stared blankly at the floor. "And I want to trust her. If I lose that trust, I cannot fully give her mine. And love without trust is no love at all."

Hawthorne stopped in front of Tristan. "What will you do now?"

"I don't know. I was actually going to join her at the cottage in a few days without anyone knowing I was there. But now…" He sighed heavily. "I will leave today. I cannot go on any longer without knowing the truth."

Nic gave Tristan a quizzical glare. "Are you addled? Why would you go now? What if Miss Tabitha makes you her next victim? And what if the magistrate finds you with Diana? He would certainly believe you two are in this together."

"Not if you go with me." Tristan nodded as confidence built inside him. "You must go with me, mainly so nobody gets suspicious. I need to talk to Diana in person, or at least hear it for myself that Tabitha is the killer. We need hard evidence to present to the magistrate to clear my name from their suspects' list."

Pausing, he scratched his chin as thoughts rushed through his mind. Silence filled through the room for the next several minutes while memories flitted through Tristan's head. All that he and Diana had been through, why did it have to end up like this? Why couldn't love win out for once in his life?

"I fear the only thing for me to do is go to see her today," Tristan said in defeat. "Even if it means discovering something I don't wish to hear."

Nic came closer and clasped his hand on Tristan's shoulder. "Give me time to return home and change before we're off."

"Yes, but hurry. I'm exhausted with all this worry. I want the truth out in the open once and for all."

Nodding, Nic turned and hurried out of the room. As Tristan watched Hawthorne leave, he prayed their plan would come about, and the real killer discovered. Tristan didn't know what he was going to say to Diana or how he was going to act, but one thing was certain—he couldn't trust her until she opened up to him about Tabitha. Until that happened, he couldn't fully give her his heart, either.

DIANA STARED OUT the window at the passing landscape, not really paying attention to the land she knew was so beautiful. Due to the pain in her heart, it was impossible to gaze upon such loveliness and smile.

The carriage wheel hit a rut and jerked her on the seat. She scooted back and made herself comfortable again. Yet deep in her heart the rut of despair could not be filled.

Pain squeezed her chest as she recalled the exchange she'd overheard between Mr. Coggins and Martha early this morning as the two servants loaded the carriage for Diana's departure.

After all these years of wondering why Ludlow's servants hated her, she finally discovered the truth.

Blinking back the tears stinging her eyes, their voices echoed in her ears—like a terrifying screech that would always be branded in her memory. They hated Diana because she had never given Ludlow a child. Apparently, Ludlow's father had a temper when he first married, but after Ludlow was born, the temper disappeared. The servants who knew Ludlow's family were in hopes that this would happen with Ludlow, but when Diana couldn't conceive, they blamed her. And ultimately, they blamed her for his death as well.

When she had realized she could not have a baby, a ray of satisfaction had glimmered in her heart. She didn't love Ludlow, and hadn't wanted his child. She didn't want a child to have to experience some of the beatings she had done during their years of marriage. Unfortunately, his judgmental servants couldn't see it that way.

Diana took a deep breath and slowly released it, hoping to calm her spirits. With any luck, Mr. Lusk would arrive at the manor while she was staying at the cottage. Then she would never have to return to the nightmare she'd endured for far too long.

Shouts from Mr. Coggins and the slowing of the carriage alerted her to her surroundings once again. *Home at last.* This cottage held such wonderful, tender memories of the times she spent with her grandmother. And now… Diana sighed and smiled. Now new memories would be made—happy and unforgettable.

When the carriage stopped, she opened the door and climbed down. Tabitha rushed out of the house and began issuing instructions to Mr. Coggins. Diana tried to ignore the suspicious glares from her disgruntled servant as he carried her trunks inside the house.

"Good day, Tabitha. I trust all is well with the place?"

Tabitha smiled brightly and nodded. "Everything is in order, my lady."

"Splendid."

Tabitha moved closer and touched Diana's arm. "When will Lord Tristan be arriving?" she whispered.

"Our plans were for him to arrive in three days."

"Sally and I have been cleaning a room and getting it ready for his stay."

"How is Sally faring?"

"She gets better and better every day. You can hardly see the bruises on her face."

Diana smiled and squeezed her friend's hand. "I thank you for everything. I do believe my life is going to change for the better now."

"Indeed it will."

It took a few more minutes for Mr. Coggins to finish unloading all of Diana's trunks, and Tabitha assisted as much as she could. By the disapproving glares from Mr. Coggins, Diana was vastly relieved she wouldn't have to deal with him much longer.

As she stood just outside the front door watching the man's departure, a cool wind blew against her. Gathering her cloak together, she glanced up at the sky. Dark clouds threatened overhead, hinting that rain would be coming soon. From the fierce rumbles in the air, she surmised today's storm would be long and bring plenty of moisture to the land.

She entered the cottage, and immediately, her mind returned to the last time she was here with Tristan. Finally, happiness had found her. She just prayed it would stay.

The stairs creaked and within seconds, Sally hesitantly stepped into view. Diana nodded and motioned with her hand for Sally to come closer. "Mr. Coggins is gone now. You will be all right."

Sally moved closer, her hands clutched against her middle. "I am very happy to see you again, my lady. Your presence here lightens my heart."

"What a sweet thing to say." Diana lifted Sally's chin with her finger and studied her. "You are looking much healthier, I notice."

"I feel much better." Sally smiled. "Soon I will be ready to obtain employment elsewhere."

Chuckling, Diana shook her head. "Let's not rush it. For now, you are welcome to stay here and assist Tabitha."

Diana removed her bonnet and gloves as she strode to the stairs. "But for now, I'm going to retire to my room to rest. I fear the journey—and the turmoil on my mind—have exhausted me greatly."

"We shall prepare a mid-day meal while you rest," Tabitha said cheerfully.

"I thank you. I don't plan on resting for very long, so please wake me when the meal is ready."

Just as she placed her foot on the first step, thunder boomed through the house, shaking the walls. Within seconds after that, rain pelted the roof, sounding more like rocks were striking the cottage. She groaned. Perhaps she wouldn't get any rest at all.

Once she walked into her room, she realized the howling wind was in competition with the hard rain to see which one could be nosier. She threw her bonnet and gloves on the vanity before flopping down on her bed. A lamp had been lit, but the dark clouds made the room much darker than Diana had expected.

She stood and went to the lamp to adjust the lighting. As she turned back to the bed and removed her cloak, a tree from outside knocked against the side of the house. Thunder boomed in the air again, but this time it sounded like men's voices, even Tristan.

Chuckling, Diana rationalized that because she wanted to see Tristan so badly, she could imagine him and actually *hear* his voice. These next three days were going to pass slowly, she just knew it. She couldn't wait to be in his arms again, gazing lovingly into his dreamy eyes, and hearing his husky tone.

Another sound ricocheted through the air and she swung toward the door, listening closer. Tabitha's voice was raised, but not with excitement, nor was it lifted in panic. It was more like she meant to warn…

Quickly, Diana rushed out of her room and to the top of the stairs. The voices were more precise now, and there were definitely visitors in the house. By the tingles running up and down her arms, she knew Tristan was here.

With her heart beating happily, she hurried down the stairs to greet the man she loved, but as soon as she rested her gaze on the people in the room, her feet skid to a halt. *Lord Hawthorne? What is he doing here?*

Both men were drenched from head to toe and shucking out of their soaked cloaks. Although they had removed their hats, each man's hair was saturated to their head. The rain pelting against the cottage reminded her of the storm swirling around them.

Diana took a quick survey of who stood in the room, and her heart sank when she noticed Sally still here. The maid stood in the corner of the room, twirling a blonde lock of hair around her finger as she stared at the floor, appearing as if she wanted to crawl in a hole and hide. Tabitha stood next to her—cheeks bright with fury—as she'd been talking, but upon seeing Diana, the young woman's chatting ceased.

Diana swung her attention back to Tristan. Although he smiled at her, his expression was faux. Distrust coated his gaze. Within a split second, her heart cried out as guilt swept over her like waves of despair.

She wasn't foolish enough to believe he was here for their secret get-away holiday, especially since he'd brought Lord Hawthorne with him. So then why had Tristan come, and in the rain?

Deep down inside she knew. Tristan was here for answers and nothing less.

Silently, she prayed he would believe her and understand when she confessed the truth.

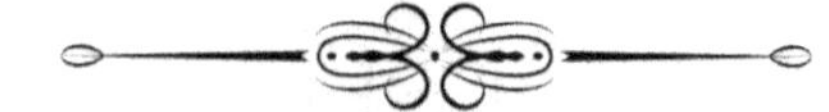

Chapter Twenty-Five

TAKING A DEEP breath, Tristan prayed for courage… courage to hold strong and demand to know the truth from Diana. He also needed the courage to keep his heart from melting every time he looked into her fascinating green eyes. Her lovely orbs had always had an enchanting effect on him that made him lose his mind several times since he'd first met her. How could one woman have this kind of control over his senses? If he discovered she was withholding the truth from him, his heart and mind wouldn't be able to take it.

A shiver ran through him that had nothing to do with the coldness seeping into his drenched limbs.

"Lord Tristan. Lord Hawthorne. What a surprise it is to see you here." Diana stepped toward them to take their cloaks. Tabitha rushed to help assist.

Tristan peeled his cloak off his shoulders and handed it to Diana while Nic did the same, giving his to the maid. Tristan moved his attention from beautiful Diana, past Tabitha and to the corner of the room.

A girl, slightly younger than Tabitha, stood still, acting as if she was afraid to move and appearing as if she wished she were a part of the wall. This must be the maid Nic had mentioned. Her pale face and downcast gaze let him know she did not want to be seen, and appeared to be frightened, like a mouse caught in a trap.

"Please come over here by the fire to warm yourselves," Diana encouraged. "Today's storm was certainly fierce and so very unexpected."

He followed her to the fireplace, watching her reaction closely. It was obvious by her wide eyes and over-exuberant greeting that she tried to turn an uncomfortable situation into a good one. She also fidgeted too much, which meant she was nervous... more nervous than she should be, in his opinion.

He switched his focus to Tabitha. The young woman acted the same way around Nic, except she didn't try to talk to him. Hawthorne, however, trained his suspicious gaze on her directly.

"Lady Hollingsworth," Tristan began and he rubbed his palms up and down his arms, trying to circulate warmth back in his body, "forgive us for this surprise visit, but it was most urgent that I speak with you. Regretfully, Lord Hawthorne and I had no idea we would be caught in the rainstorm, so I hope we have not burdened you in any way."

"Don't be ridiculous." Diana brushed her hand in the air. "You are always welcome here, Lord Tristan." She glanced behind Tristan at Dominic. "And you as well, Lord Hawthorne."

"You are very kind, Lady Hollingsworth."

"I fear," Diana continued, "that I don't have any extra clothes for the two of you to change into while we dry your wet ones."

"Actually," Tabitha hastily cut in, "your grandmother was a large lady if I recall, Lady Hollingsworth." She ran her gaze slowly over Nic, and Tristan was surprised to see disgust instead of interest when she looked at his friend. "So I'm certain if Lord Hawthorne wouldn't mind wearing a nightgown—"

"I appreciate your concern," Nic quickly replied, "but I would rather catch pneumonia than be seen wearing a lady's nightgown, or *any* gown, for that matter."

Tabitha glared at Nic, looking as if fire would shoot out of her eyes any moment. Tristan bit his lip to hold back a laugh. This was the first time he'd ever seen a woman not fall all over herself trying to impress Lord Hawthorne. This definitely couldn't be good for Nic's ego.

"Be that as it may," Tristan said, hoping not to encourage Tabitha and Nic into starting a heated argument, "I think standing by the fire will dry us quickly enough."

"Are you certain?" Diana asked in a tender voice. "I could find some woolen blankets and you two could wrap yourself in those while your clothes are drying."

He smiled softly at her. It was hard not to. "I suppose we could do that."

"Come," she said, turning toward the stairs, "you and Lord Hawthorne can use the guest bedroom to change. Tabitha?" She glanced at the maid. "Will you find me two blankets, and Sally will you get started on our meal? I'm certain the men are extremely hungry after their long excursion."

"As you wish, my lady." The women chimed together then moved out of the room, heading in different directions.

"Gentlemen?" Diana aimed her attention on Tristan. "If you will follow me, I shall show you to the chamber."

As Diana led the way, Nic nudged Tristan with his elbow then motioned his head toward the door Sally had exited and mouthed the words, *that's her.* Tristan nodded, but didn't say anything to his friend. Instead, he wanted answers from Diana first.

Marching ahead of him, he wondered what her big hurry was. He grasped her elbow in a loose hold, slowing her down a bit. She looked over her shoulder at him. "Diana, who is the new girl? She wasn't here before."

Her eyes widened and her attention jumped between him and Nic. "Her name is Sally. I thought she could help out Tabitha for a while."

"How very thoughtful of you." He really didn't know what else to say. Getting serious about a conversation at this point in the evening was useless. If he said something to upset her, she'd send him away, and in this downpour that wasn't such a good idea. It was best to prolong their much needed conversation until sunset. Diana wouldn't send him out of the house then. She was too much a lady to do that.

She led them into the bedroom before moving to the fireplace to lay some logs on. Taking fast steps, he hurried to her and grabbed the piece of wood out of her hand.

"Allow me to make my own fire," he told her. "It's the least I can do for showing up unannounced."

Her stare delved deep into his eyes before slowly moving over his face. "Tristan, why are you here? What was the great urgency to speak with me?" Her voice was low.

He shook his head. "Not now. There will be plenty of time for us to talk once I'm out of these wet clothes."

The shuffling of feet pulled his focus from Diana toward the doorway as Tabitha entered. She handed a blanket to Nic—almost shoved it at him, actually—then nicely handed Tristan a blanket.

"Thank you," he told the maid.

"I shall leave you to change now," Diana spoke calmly. "Just place your wet clothes outside the door and Tabitha and Sally will hang them above the fire to dry."

As Tabitha walked past Nic, she turned up her nose at him. Hawthorne gripped her arm, stopping her and piercing her with his hard stare. "I better not see burns in my clothes caused by your careless hand."

She arched an eyebrow. "Indeed, my lord, I had not thought of such a thing, but now…"

"*Tabitha,*" Diana warned. "I assure you, Lord Hawthorne, your clothes will not be burned."

When the ladies left and the door was closed behind them, Tristan breathed a ragged sigh. Although wet and weary, the worst of the evening was yet to come.

"By Jove, my good man," Nic said with a sudden cheerful voice, "I believe you put on a splendid performance."

Gritting his teeth, Tristan glared at his friend as he started to remove his neck cloth. Traveling to the cottage had been a long journey, and his friend's humor had grated on his nerves for the last time today. "Oh really? What gave it away? My sarcastic tone? The hard set of my jaw as I gnashed my teeth? Or was it the distrust that I'm sure Diana saw in my eyes?"

Nic tilted his head and gave Tristan a quizzical stare. "Honestly, was *that* called for?"

"What are you talking about?"

"I'm referring to your vicious attitude."

Blowing out a frustrated breath, Tristan finished removing the neck cloth and shrugged out of his waistcoat. "My apologies, my friend. I'm in a sour mood, and I should not be vexed with you. After all, if you had not overheard the two maids, I would still have my head in the clouds feeling an abundance of lover's bliss."

Nic scowled. "Are you saying I should have held my tongue?" He shook his head as he yanked off his waist jacket. "Forgive me for thinking that kind of news was important. All that was going through my mind was imagining the trouble you would get in if the truth wasn't discovered soon. I did not want to see that happen to you."

Tristan waved his hand in the air. "You misunderstood, Hawthorne. I'm grateful you told me, but at the same time, my heart is broken because the woman I have loved for so long is deceiving me. That is why I have a rotten disposition."

"Of course, Worthington. I understand. I shall try not to poke fun at your expense any longer. I cannot even imagine how you must feel right now."

"I thank you, Hawthorne. I pray you will never have your heart broken like this. Then again—" Tristan scratched his chin, "it would be a miracle if you ever gave your heart to a woman at all."

Nic laughed loudly. "That miracle will never happen, I assure you. I shall remain a bachelor for the rest of my life."

After removing his shirt, Tristan knelt in front of the hearth and threw the logs in. "You never did tell me why you are like this."

"What do you mean?"

He struck the flint. "Why are you so reluctant to fall in love?"

"Worthington," Nic said as he struggled to get his wet shirt over his head, "there are many things you don't know about me. Why are you so certain I have never given my heart to a woman? Perhaps I have been burned in the past, which is why I don't want to do it again."

The spark in the fireplace started. Tristan blew on it gently until a good fire began to burn. "Are you going to allow one woman to control how you feel for the rest of your life?"

Nic moved to stand by the fire. Tristan looked up at his friend's serious expression. Not often did Hawthorne show this vulnerable side to him.

Nic tapped his finger on his chin. "You know, I could say the same about you."

"Me?"

"Indeed. Have you not allowed Lady Hollingsworth to control your feelings? If we discover from our visit here that she has indeed deceived you, will your heart be scarred for life? Or will you eventually find another woman to love?"

Tristan stared into the fire. Numbness spread across him and he refused to think of the future. Nic was correct. Tristan had allowed Diana into his heart, and God help him, he never wanted to let her out.

"I just don't understand you, Tabitha. Why do you taunt that man so much?" Diana sat at the table peeling potatoes as her maids helped her prepare the meal. "Lord Hawthorne is a respected man… and a man many women would love to marry, I might add. I just cannot understand why you don't have dreamy eyes for him."

A loud unlady-like grunt came from Tabitha as she rolled her eyes. "*That* will never happen. Men like him are not worth my time. And honestly, the only reason I put up with Lord Tristan is because of you."

Diana set her knife and potato down before looking at Tabitha. "What do you mean *men like him*? Are you referring to rakes or nobility? Because Tristan has never been a scoundrel."

"Perhaps it's a combination of both that I'm disgusted with." Tabitha frowned. "Gentlemen think of themselves as holier-than-thou creatures who cannot even force themselves to speak civilly to someone who is beneath their station, and if they do speak, they treat us like our only purpose is to warm their beds."

Diana patted her friend's shoulder. "There are a lot of men like what you have described, but Lord Hawthorne and Tristan are not like that."

"I see them differently, my lady. They treat me differently when you are not around."

Narrowing her gaze, Diana shook her head. "Tristan has treated you in such a way, like he wants you to warm his bed?"

Tabitha cringed. "No, not that way, but he looks down on me as if I were nothing but dirt on his boots."

"Lady Hollingsworth," Sally cut in, "I must agree with Tabitha. Because we are not but mere servants, we will always be treated as such. Lord Elliot taught us that lesson well."

"Not all masters are like Lord Elliot." Diana cut up a potato, letting it drop into the pot. "In fact Tabitha, do you not remember how it was when you and your mother worked for my grandmother?"

"Yes, I remember. Working for her was pure Heavenly. Your grandmother was the sweetest woman I knew." Tabitha smiled at Diana. "And now I know that her granddaughter inherited her sweet nature."

"You are too kind." Diana's face grew warm with the compliment.

"But back then," Tabitha continued, "I worked for only a woman. After your grandmother died, I was sent to Lord Elliot.

That was the first time a man had been in charge of me." She shivered. "I never want to go through that hell again."

Diana touched her friend's hand. "Tabitha, not all men are like that. I assure you, Tristan and his brothers will never treat their servants with such disdain."

Tabitha set her knife down, narrowing her gaze on Diana. "Are you certain, my lady? I have heard talk from servants and they say the old Duke of Kenbridge was very mean to his servants and treated women like they were slaves."

Sighing heavily, Diana nodded. "Indeed, Tristan's father was a very inconsiderate, selfish man who loved to create scandal, but even the one son who we thought would turn out like him, Trey, didn't end up like his sire after all. Trevor and Tristan will never be like that, either. I stake my life on it."

"I'm comforted to know you have so much faith in them. However, they are but three men, and England is filled with men like Lord Elliot and Lord Hollingsworth."

Memories Diana tried to bury resurfaced. Scenes flashed through her head of Ludlow raising his hand to her when he thought she'd done something wrong. He even starved her on a few occasions, and those were the nice punishments he'd inflicted upon her. "Very true, Tabitha. I wish more men were like the Worthington brothers."

"As do I," Tabitha said with a frown. "Forgive me for speaking my mind, but I'm vastly relieved Lord Elliot and Lord Hollingsworth have been taken from this world. They both deserved to die for what they did to all of us. In fact, the thought of killing them with my bare hands had crossed my mind several times. I cannot tolerate men who treat women in such a way. They all deserve to die, or be punished severely."

"I agree," Sally muttered her response.

Diana carried the pot of vegetables to the hot stove before pouring water over them. "I believe there are many others who share your thoughts."

"Lady Hollingsworth? Did you ever think of killing your

husband?" Sally asked.

Diana walked back to the table and sat. She linked her fingers together and rested them on the edge of the table. Thoughts swam in her head, followed by the bitter feelings she'd once had. "Although I didn't think about doing the actual deed, I had prayed that something would happen to my husband to end his life." A tear slid down her cheek that she hadn't realized was there. "I hated myself for feeling that way, but when it finally happened, I thanked God that it had. I couldn't believe how *free* I felt, even when the magistrate suspected me of murder."

"For months I felt that way about Lord Elliot," Sally injected softly with tears in her eyes.

"As did I." Tabitha nodded. "And I was grateful this angel of mercy—" she touched Diana's shoulder—"came to rescue me."

Sally nodded. "That was also the day I will never forget." She sniffed and wiped her hand underneath her nose. "Lady Hollingsworth, you are truly my Savior for rescuing me from that monster."

When Diana smiled her lips quaked as she tried to hold back the sob rising in her throat. "I just wish I would have known about it sooner."

"You saved my life," Sally said.

"And mine." Tabitha wiped a tear off her face.

Diana stood and hugged Sally, then gave Tabitha a hug as well. Tears streamed down the servants' cheeks, and Diana's own cheeks were even wet.

Pulling away, she wiped her knuckles under her eyes to dry the tears before smoothing her palms on her apron. "Well, I think we should concentrate on getting the meal finished. I'm certain our visitors are famished. And we need to fetch their clothes and—"

Before she could finish, the floor outside the kitchen door creaked. Diana sucked in a quick breath and swung toward the door. Her heart dropped.

"What's wrong, my lady?" Sally questioned.

"I think someone is in the hall, coming."

Diana prayed she was hearing things because she didn't need Tristan or Nic overhearing and asking her questions later. Her mind argued that the men wouldn't leave the room wearing only a blanket to venture into a room with three women, yet... Someone was indeed outside the door. She could feel it as a dark cloud of doom settled over her.

Chapter Twenty-Six

TRISTAN HITCHED HIS breath. *We're going to get caught.*

He traded panic glances with Nic before motioning with his head toward the nearest room. As quietly as the two men could walk, they hurried on bare feet inside and closed the door. Tristan didn't dare make a sound. He even held his blanket around his shoulders tighter for fear of accidentally dropping the covering.

The squeak from kitchen door opening alerted Tristan that they had just barely made it before being spotted. Pressing his ear against the wooden door, he held his breath.

"Who is out there?" Tabitha's voice almost echoed through the empty corridor.

"I don't see anyone," Diana said as relief lightened her voice. "I suppose I was just hearing things."

"Most likely that is what happened," Tabitha answered. "The wind outside is still blowing strong. Perhaps that is what you heard."

"I certainly hope so."

As soon as the kitchen door squeaked again, Tristan quietly pulled up on the latch his hand had been gripping so tightly, opened the bedroom door, and peeked out. Tabitha and Diana had gone back inside the kitchen. His pounding heartbeat slowly returned to normal as he expelled a breath.

"Come," Tristan whispered to Nic, "let's return to the room before they realize we were listening."

Nodding, Nic pulled the blanket tight around his body and hurried up the corridor behind Tristan toward the stairs.

"That was a close call," Nic said as they reached the top of the stairs.

"Too close." Tristan glanced over his shoulder at Nic. "But when I have my talk with Diana and she asks how I know, I will tell her I overheard her in the kitchen. Although she insists on holding the truth from me, I shall not do the same. I plan on being completely honest."

"That's the only way to be."

"However," Tristan paused once they reached the room and entered, "I need you to keep Tabitha occupied. I do not want anything to interrupt my talk with Diana."

Nic rolled his eyes. "I shall try, but that woman can drive a man to drink, and I don't know how much alcohol Lady Hollingsworth has in this small cottage for me to consume."

"Then I suggest you ask her. You are very talented at holding your liquor and being charming at the same time." Tristan grinned.

"Do not make light of this, Worthington."

Fortunately, they hadn't waited for Tabitha to collect their clothes, laying out to dry themselves. Nic marched to the fireplace and adjusted his clothes that had been draped over the chair to dry. Tristan followed and copied his friend's actions. The quicker the garments dried, the more comfortable Tristan would feel.

"I have never met a woman like Diana's maid," Nic continued. "She acts as if I'm the one who is far beneath *her* station to even speak to me. When she does talk, nothing but disdain pours from her mouth."

"That is certainly out of the ordinary. Whatever have you done to vex her so?"

"Nothing, I assure you." Nic lifted his head and looked at

Tristan. "The few times I've talked to her, she has been this way." He shook his head. "I have never wronged her or caused her ill will, yet she treats me like I have made her life miserable."

"Indeed, that is very strange behavior."

"Quite right."

"As it were… will you still help me out by keeping her occupied?" Tristan asked. "I don't want her to accidentally hear her name in the conversation I have with Diana and come barging in to interrupt us."

"Of course. I just pray your talk with Lady Hollingsworth doesn't take too long. I fear I won't know what to do if Tabitha upsets me more than she has done already."

From out in the corridor, the stairs squeaked. Tristan swung his attention to the door. Mere moments later came a knock.

"Tristan? Are you still there?"

He walked to the door and opened it enough to poke his head out. "Yes, Diana." He smiled, although he couldn't feel the happiness inside him as he'd felt before when peering into her lovely face. "Where else would we be? There is no place for us to be since we are covered in blankets."

Her cheeks turned pink. "I suppose you are right." She folded her arms. "I just came to check on you to see if you were undressed so we could take your clothes."

"Actually, the fire is blazing well enough in here so we just draped our clothes over chairs and placed them in front of the hearth. There is no need to have Tabitha hang them up now."

"Splendid. I shall tell her to continue helping in the kitchen."

Diana didn't say anymore, and neither did she move. Her gaze studied his face slowly, and soon guilt laced her eyes. She stepped closer and touched his cheek tenderly.

"Tristan, something is amiss. I can see it in your expression." Her voice was low for their ears only. "You are worrying me by not telling me what is wrong."

"Shh…" He reached out and clasped her hand with his. "I will explain, but not now. Wait until my clothes are dry first and I can dress completely before we talk."

"I fear I cannot wait."

"And I fear my dear," he said with a chuckle, "that if I talk to you like this, my blanket might slip from around me and fall to the floor." He shook his head. "What a scandal that would be, surely."

The corner of her lips lifted into a smile, but it didn't reach her eyes. "I do understand your dilemma." She released a long breath. "I shall try to be patient. And while I'm waiting, would you and Lord Hawthorne like me to bring up some port for you?"

"Port?" Nic said from behind him in a most anxious voice. "You have port?"

Tristan wanted to laugh, but refrained.

"Yes, Lord Hawthorne," she answered in a louder voice.

"Then we shall certainly enjoy our port, thank you Diana." Tristan smiled.

She turned and headed back down the stairs. He watched her as long as he could until she was out of his vision. His throat tightened with emotion, yet anger flared inside him at the same time.

He closed the door and stormed to the bed before plopping down. His head pounded in frustration and all he wanted to do was shake some sense into her. Yet touching her would make him want to pull her against him, hold her tight, and taste her sweet lips.

"Do you think she knows?" Nic asked.

"Yes."

"What will you tell her?"

"I shall tell her what I suspect, what I feel, and what I think we should do about Tabitha."

Nic walked away from the fireplace and to the window where he leaned his shoulder against the wall as he stared out into the rainy evening. "What will you do if she doesn't agree?"

"I do not know," Tristan answered in a whisper as he stared down at the blue and brown quilt on the bed. "As much as I love her and want to spend the rest of my life making her happy, I cannot have lies between us. I want to trust her. I want to believe she loves me more than her maid." He looked up at his friend. "Is that selfish to think in such a way?"

"Not at all." Nic drew his finger on the windowpane.

"Why then do I feel so guilty for making her choose?"

Shrugging, Nic looked Tristan's way. "Probably because you are *forcing* her to make a decision. Yet, if you think about it, this is something Diana should have already decided. She knows right from wrong. If she knows Tabitha killed those two lords then Diana needs to do the right thing. Because Tabitha is her friend, Diana will need encouragement, which of course is where you will help out."

Tristan groaned and covered his hands over his face. "Why is life so difficult? Why can it not be perfect all the time?"

A chuckle came from his friend. "You are asking *me*? Sorry my good man, but I am not a man of the cloth who has all the Divine answers."

The hilarity of Nic's comment made Tristan grin and he dropped his hands. "So true. Out of all the professions in England, being a clergyman does not suit you, I'm afraid."

"I agree." Nic nodded. "So let's not speak of this again for fear I will receive this calling from God as punishment for all the women I've wronged in my life. That is certainly something I do not want for my future."

"The future," Tristan muttered as a frown reclaimed his face. "What I would not give to know the future."

"What we *all* would not give," Nic said then leaned his head back against the wall. "Did you ever picture your life would be this way when you were younger?"

"No. For years I knew I would be the one brother who married for love, but now I see my other two brothers have beaten me to it. The one thing that has been driving me these past few years—since returning from the dead—was knowing I did *not* want to turn out like my father in any shape or form. Father died not long after I had fallen over the cliffs. He died alone and had many enemies, pretty much like Lord Hollingsworth and Elliot. Women hated them and others looked down on them." He shook his head. "I do not want to end my life as they have."

"Perfectly understandable." Nic rubbed a hand over his arm. "Let's pray neither of us end up in such a way.

Sighing heavily, Tristan stood and walked to the hearth to check his clothes. They weren't as wet as before, but too damp to wear unfortunately. "At this point, I shall be happy to stay out of prison for a crime I did not commit. Proving my innocence is of utmost importance."

Nic folded his arms across his chest and lifted his chin. "Then starting tonight we *will* discover the truth."

THE SNAP OF a log breaking in the fireplace was the only sound in the dining room. Chatter around the table was kept minimal and abnormally quiet for dinner. Both Tristan and Lord Hawthorne were fully clothed and eating as if they were half starved. Diana could only pick at her food as she studied Tristan's withdrawn expression, her spirits sinking lower and lower. Even Lord Hawthorne acted as if he was not pleased with something.

Sally had taken her meal to her room for fear the two lords would recognize her somehow, although Diana didn't think they would. Still, she allowed the maid to hide out in her bedchamber instead of helping to serve them.

Tabitha acted as the dutiful maid and served Diana and the men, but before she could return to the kitchen to eat, Lord Hawthorne had invited her to dine with them. Even Tristan had agreed. Diana could tell the invitation had shocked Tabitha—just as it had surprised Diana. Tabitha had complied, and joined them at the table, but the conversations were kept very limited and not personal at all.

Tristan acted differently today than he had the last time he visited this cottage or the last time they had talked before she'd left to come here. Deep in her heart, Diana knew something was wrong. Very wrong.

Diana stared at her stew as she stirred her spoon around the carrots and potatoes, and hadn't looked up for a few minutes to see what everyone else was doing. It wasn't until Tristan cleared his throat when she finally lifted her gaze and met his.

"I must say, this is a very good stew. Compliments to the cooks."

Even though he smiled, Diana could see it was forced. Her heart clenched once again with worry.

"I agree," Lord Hawthorne added. "It's a shame Sally couldn't eat with us."

Something was definitely wrong! Diana could not believe Lord Hawthorne would say such a thing when he knew servants did not eat with their masters. "Well, Sally has been ill lately—"

"Sally is quite shy—" Tabitha said at the same time.

Both women quickly stopped and traded glances. Tabitha's eyes were wide and she snapped her mouth tightly.

Taking a deep, calming breath, Diana recovered as she met Tristan's suspicious stare. "Yes, Sally is a shy girl but she has felt under the weather lately." She glanced at Lord Hawthorne. "I thank you for inquiring about her."

Tristan set his spoon down and using a cloth napkin he wiped his mouth before placing it on the table next to the utensil. "Lady Hollingsworth? Are you ill yourself?" He took a quick glance at her bowl. "I have noticed you are not eating much."

"I'm quite fine, I assure you. I'm just not that hungry, I suppose."

"Then can I convince you to come with me into the parlor so we can talk in private?"

Her heartbeat raced, but not in excitement. *This was it!* He was going to tell her the dire news, yet now she realized she didn't want to hear it. If his news was going to break her heart, she would just as well not talk to him at all.

But curiosity got the best of her and she nodded. "I would be glad to accompany you, my lord."

He stood and walked around the table to her side and offered his hand. She graciously placed her hand in his and stood, gazing deep into his eyes—eyes that had no spark of love in them as they had only a few days ago. Tears burned behind her eyes and she blinked as she tried to keep them from falling. She walked beside the man who held her heart—and would always hold her heart.

Not another word was spoken as they entered the parlor and he closed the door behind them. Keeping her hand with his, he led them to the sofa where they sat together—the same spot they'd been sitting when they had their talk after Tabitha had kidnapped him.

He turned at the waist toward her, taking both of her hands now. His thumbs gently stroked her knuckles as his attention focused on her face.

If he didn't say something soon, she would not be able to hold back her tears. Yet he seemed content just to stare into her eyes and stroke her knuckles.

Swallowing the lump of emotion stuck in her throat, she took a deep breath for courage. "Tristan, the silence is killing me. Please say what is on your mind."

He nodded. "I will. I'm just collecting my thoughts."

"Tell me, have you changed your mind about me… about us being together?"

"No, I have not. Although, I fear *you* have."

She wasn't prepared to hear those words. She shook her head as a small throb started in her skull. "I don't understand. Why would I change my mind?"

Tristan didn't answer her right away, but once again he appeared deep in thought. Every second that passed made the creases on his forehead more profound. This time Diana let him think, all the while her heart raced with worry and she feared the worst. Had he found another woman to love? Was the scandal that had happened between them too much for him to bear?

Finally, after too much silence, Tristan expelled a heavy breath. "It has come to my attention that you might know the true identity of the person who killed your husband and Lord Elliot."

All the thoughts speeding through her head came to a sudden halt and she gasped. "Pardon me? You think I know who killed my husband? Pray, enlighten me, because I can assure you, I do not know such a thing."

The rubbing of her knuckles stopped, but he didn't release her hands. "Diana, please be honest with me. If we are to have a relationship it must be based on trust. You *can* trust me. I am nothing like Hollingsworth, I assure you."

Confusion filled her and she shook her head. "I fear your words are most alarming, and I know not what they mean. Indeed, you are nothing like Ludlow, and I can assure you that I trust you with my life and heart."

"Then why do you hold the truth from the magistrate about the killer? The longer you put off telling him, the longer we have to wait until we can be together."

She pulled a hand from his and rubbed the pound in her forehead. "Please, Tristan. Tell me what you are talking about, because you have me most confused. What am I withholding from the magistrate or from you?"

"The identity of the murderer."

Frustration filled her and made her jittery. She stood and moved toward the fireplace. "Do you not think I would tell the magistrate if I knew? I assure you, if I knew their identity, I would say something. I want to be with you without anyone being suspicious." Stopping, she looked over her shoulder at him. "Why do you believe I know this person's identity?"

"Diana, I overheard you speaking with Tabitha and Sally while you were cooking. I had come down from the room and heard you outside the kitchen door. I dared not enter because I could not believe what all of you were saying." Slowly he stood and made his way to her side. "Diana, I really think Tabitha is the one who killed your husband and my cousin."

Shocked, a loud gasp escaped her throat before she could stop it. "Pardon me? You believe Tabitha… *my* Tabitha is a murderer?"

"Indeed, the same. Is there another Tabitha?"

Although their conversation was not comical, she couldn't stop the laugh bubbling up from her chest. "You honestly think Tabitha killed Ludlow and Elliot? I can assure you, my lord, that you are sadly mistaken."

"You can *assure* me? How so, may I ask?"

Her mind scrambled for a reason to give, but she couldn't come up with one. She just *knew* her friend—a friend she had known for years and considered a sister—could not have done such a thing.

Or could she?

Shaking the negative thought from her mind, she frowned and glared at Tristan. "How dare you accuse Tabitha?"

"Oh, I dare." He raked his fingers through his hair. "Especially when I heard her confession of wanting to kill Ludlow and Elliot. You were in the room with her, did you not hear her say those very words?"

"Well, yes, but…" She shook her head. "She was not confessing to a murder, she was voicing her thoughts. She, along with Sally, has every right to hate men like my husband and your cousin. If I have withheld anything from you, it's this…" She took a deep breath and slowly released it. "Because of Ludlow's treatment toward me, I cannot abide men like that abusing their servants, or their wives. There are many of us in England, Tristan. Were you aware of that? Even Lady Dashwood was abused not only by her husband, but her father. Together Claudia and I have taken it upon ourselves to rescue these women from their most unfortunate situations. Tabitha and Sally are no more killers than Claudia and I are."

Tristan stared at her as his frown intensified. Anger filled her quickly as she continued, "Tristan, it hurts me that you cannot trust *me*. Do you honestly believe that I would become friends with a murderer? Tabitha may have hard feelings for men who beat women, but she is not a killer just because she has thought about it. I had thoughts about wanting my husband dead, so does that make me a murderer in your eyes?"

"No," he said in almost a whisper.

"So then why do you think that about Tabitha?"

"Because everything adds up," he explained. "Tabitha's anger toward men is the key, Diana. Have you not noticed how she acts toward Hawthorne?"

"Well yes, but that doesn't prove—"

"I have not met one woman who hasn't nearly swooned when Hawthorne smiles at them, yet Tabitha does the opposite of most women and throws perpetual invisible daggers at him. Not only that, but she is devoted to you. She will do anything to protect you, Diana... even kill. And because she was beaten, I would not judge her for wanting those men dead." He stepped closer. "Tell me, where was Tabitha the night Hollingsworth was found stabbed to death?"

Tears swam in Diana's eyes but she refused to let them fall. "She was here at the cottage. Two days prior to my husband's death, I had taken Tabitha out of Lord Elliot's house because he had beaten her severely."

"So, in her condition, would she have been able to travel without her master stopping her?"

Diana scowled. "You cannot be serious! Tristan, have you ever seen a beaten woman? Her eyes were swollen nearly closed, and she had bruises all over her body. She was as weak as a kitten."

Tristan exhaled a frustrated sigh and ran his fingers through his hair. "Oh, Diana, forgive me. I'm just trying to piece things together. I'm so sorry that Tabitha was hurt by my cousin, and I wish I had known so I could have stopped it." He shook his head. "I'm just trying to make sense of all of this. I have a gut feeling that Tabitha is the killer, she has motive, and I fear I cannot shake that from my mind."

She fisted her hands by her side as she thought back to that day. "You are just going to have to try, Tristan, because Tabitha did not do it!" A tear slipped down her face. Sadness washed over her, but not because she thought her maid guilty, but because she didn't know how to change his mind. "Tristan, how can I make you believe? Do you not trust *me*?"

He met her gaze and nodded. "I do, my sweet Diana, but I fear your love for the maid has clouded your judgment."

"I assure you, it has not."

"Then what do you want me to do?" he asked, his voice pleading.

"I want you to put this insane idea out of your head and help me try to figure out who the *real* killer is."

He reached out and grasped her hands, but she quickly jerked them away. Taking a step closer to her, he ran his palms up and down her arms slowly.

"I fear, I cannot. Deep inside me, I feel Tabitha is the one. Everything points to her." He stroked her cheek. "My love, can you not trust *my* feelings?"

"I have trusted you so far, Tristan, and although I will always love you, I fear I cannot let you turn Tabitha in to the magistrate. If you try, I promise, I will do everything in my power to stop you."

He remained silent, but his expression told her his thoughts. It was too late. She couldn't change his mind.

Heartbroken, Diana turned away. Obviously, his love for her didn't run as deep as hers. Now the question was, could she free him from her heart as he had done from his?

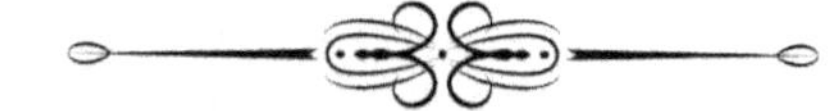

Chapter Twenty-Seven

NIC KEPT HIS wary eyes on Tabitha. After Tristan and Lady Hollingsworth had left the room, Tabitha started cleaning up the dishes and taking them into the kitchen. He didn't want her out of his sight, so he helped her. She arched a curious eyebrow at him, but didn't say anything as she went into the kitchen.

They were both far enough away from the parlor where Tristan and Lady Hollingsworth were having their talk that Tabitha couldn't eavesdrop on them without Nic knowing, and while she cleaned the dishes, he knew she wouldn't be trying to get away from him.

But she was nearly done, and he had a feeling that she would make her move at any minute now.

Once she wiped and put away the last dish, she remained by the cupboard with her back toward him. She didn't move, except for when she inhaled deeply. From this view, he couldn't tell if she was angry or just flustered. Knowing Tabitha, she was angry.

"My lord, I wish you would stop staring at me as if I were a dish of sweetmeats."

After they'd been in silence for so long, it was refreshing to hear her voice. "And how do you know I'm staring?"

"Because I'm not a fool, my lord. What else would you look at in the kitchen?" Slowly, she turned and faced him, but stayed by the cupboard. She folded her arms and arched an eyebrow. "I hope you don't think I'm going to stay and entertain you while Lady Hollingsworth and Lord Tristan are in the other room."

"Actually," he said rising from his chair, "that's exactly what I expect. The night is still early, and I don't wish to retire to my room." He shrugged. "So I suppose the two of us should do something to pass the time."

"The *two of us* will do nothing, my lord. My plans are to check on Sally and visit with her. What you do with your time is not my concern."

She stepped toward the door, but he quickened his step and reached the spot, blocking her escape. "Oh, my lovely Miss Tabitha. I have been looking forward all evening to spending time with you."

She rolled her eyes. "I fear that your idea of *spending time* with me does not meet with my approval. I know what you really want, Lord Hawthorne, and if you cannot recall our last conversation, let me remind you that I do *not* find you interesting in the least. Your twinkling eyes and knee-weakening grins will not charm me as they have done with other ladies."

Slowly, a grin stretched his mouth. He stepped closer to her, running the tips of his fingers across her cheek. "You think I have twinkling eyes and a charming grin, do you? How very sweet of you to notice."

Groaning, she smacked his hand away. "I did not mean it that way, my lord. Quit putting words in my mouth."

"Oh, my lovely, I don't need to put words in your mouth at all. You are doing just fine with that on your own. In fact, I still consider our conversations very stimulating."

Her jaw tightened and her fisted hands were turning white. "Please let me pass, my lord."

Nic struggled to keep a charming composure. It was hard to think of her as a killer when she looked so beautiful when angry. Her blue eyes were dark with passionate malice, yet he was still drawn to her. Heaven help him, he still wanted to see what it felt like with her locked in his embrace while he kissed her to distraction.

Good grief, what was he thinking? Indeed, she was a woman who would drive him to drink, and he had the sudden urge for a bottle of strong spirits right now.

"Could I indulge you to give me a few more minutes?" he begged, hating the fact that he'd been reduced to this level. "I really would like your company. I promise not to give you any of my charming grins, and I will try my hardest not to have my eyes twinkle." He tried to be serious, but it was in his nature to flirt with beautiful women.

She's a killer, he reminded himself. Unfortunately, his subconscious wasn't listening because he still wanted to hold her and see if passion was as evident in her kiss as it was when she argued.

Soon the lines of anger on her forehead and around her mouth disappeared and she nodded. "Shall we adjourn to the sitting room, then?"

"Splendid idea." He smiled and held out an arm for her.

Her attention moved to what he offered as a smirk tugged at the corner of her mouth. "Lord Hawthorne, you do not have to escort me. I assure you, I can walk to the room just fine on my own."

He opened the door and motioned his hand. "Then lead the way, my lovely."

As he followed her into the other room, he enjoyed watching the way her gray gown molded to her womanly curves. He admired the lift of her stubborn chin, and took pleasure in studying the way her brown hair swept up into a coil, leaving him ample view of her slender neck. A neck he wouldn't mind kissing.

Stop this! He silently scolded his thoughts as he searched the room for a decanter of spirits. Once she closed the door, she turned toward him but didn't say a word. As before, familiarity nudged in the back of his mind. He knew her from somewhere, and until he remembered, it would drive him mad.

"My lord, would you like a drink?"

Thought you'd never ask! "Indeed, I would, Miss Tabitha."

She moved over to the liquor tray and poured him a drink. "All Lady Hollingsworth has is port. I hope that will do."

"It will, thank you." He took the glass from her then nodded to the decanter. "Are you not going to have a glass?"

"Servants don't drink with their masters."

"Well, since I'm not your master and you did very little to conform with propriety, I think it's appropriate. Besides, this evening we shall be equals."

She chuckled and poured herself a drink. "Equals, my lord? I'm surprised at your behavior this evening. I'm most certain if your fellow comrades were here witnessing this, you would not be acting in such a way."

"True, I would not. But it's just you and I here now, so why can we not pretend to be civil to each other?"

Shrugging, she carried her glass over to the sofa and sat. He followed and sat beside her, drinking his port. Daintily, she sipped her glass as she looked at him from over the rim. In one word, she was *adorable,* and he wished he didn't think that way of her.

"Tell me, Miss Tabitha. Where did you grow up? Have I ever met you before?"

"Believe it or not, most of my younger years were spent right here in this cottage." Her gaze moved slowly around the room. "Lady Hollingsworth's grandmother lived here and my mother was her personal maid." She returned her attention back to him. "So unless you came here to visit, we would have never met."

"You said you were here in your *younger* years. What age were you when you left?"

"I was sixteen, my lord."

"So where have you been since then?"

She lifted the glass to her mouth again, taking her time in drinking the port. Nic wondered why she hesitated, unless she was trying to think up a lie.

"I was a laundry maid for a man who was cruel to me. After he died, Lady Hollingsworth took me in."

Tilting his head, he studied her. Up this close, he could get lost staring into her lovely eyes. "You are not going to tell me the lord's name?"

"No."

"Why not?"

"Lord Hawthorne, I can assure you we have never met before. I don't believe it's any of your business who I used to work for, and the only reason you ask is because you think you know me from somewhere. I can promise you, we have *never* met before. Because I was a laundry maid, I was never allowed to be around my master's guests."

Nic grumbled under his breath. Tabitha was more intelligent than he gave her credit for. But of course she was smart. Who else could have killed two lords without leaving a trace of evidence?

"Forgive me for upsetting you, my lovely. I fear I've been doing that quite a lot lately, and it's not my intention."

She arched an eyebrow. "Then tell me, Lord Hawthorne, what exactly is your intention?"

"Just to get to know you better." He set his empty glass on the table next to him.

"Why?"

"Because you intrigue me. Is that not enough reason?"

"No." She placed her glass on the small table beside the sofa before turning to look at him again. "Gentlemen like yourself have no business wanting to get to know female servants so personally. There is only one reason masters want to chum with us, and it's only for seduction. As I told you before, I will *not* allow that to happen."

"And as I told you before," he moved closer, sliding his arm along the back of the sofa until it touched her shoulder, "that is not my purpose. In fact, I'm getting quite annoyed that seduction is all you can think about."

"*Me?*" She gasped. "I assure you, that is not what I'm thinking about at all."

"Yet, every time we have talked, our conversations always end on this subject. Tell me why is that, especially if you never think about it as you proclaim."

"Once again, my lord, you are putting words into my mouth."

He dropped his focus to her lips and wished she would stop bringing his attention to that most tempting feature on her face. "Actually, I think you are trying to put ideas into my head, my lovely."

"I am not."

He met her heated gaze. "No? Then why are you talking to me like this? I never once mentioned seduction, and already in our short conversation, you have brought it up a few times."

"Lord Hawthorne, not only do I wish we could cease this most improper topic, I can assure you seduction is the last thing on my mind."

He narrowed his gaze on her and tilted his head slightly as he studied her. "You know, Miss Tabitha I believe you."

Her eyes widened. "You do?"

"Indeed, I think I have been mistaken about you. Now I can clearly see that seduction is not what you want at all. It's obvious that you are too frigid to be the kind of woman who is passionate." He nodded. "Now I see why no man has claimed you for his own yet."

She inhaled sharply and her whole body went stiff. "What?" she shrieked. "You cannot be serious."

"Oh, I'm indeed very serious. Everything is beginning to make sense." He gave a light laugh as he stood and walked to the liquor tray, tempted to pour himself another drink, but refrained for the moment. "You are the first woman I have come across who didn't enjoy my attention. Now I know why."

"That is *not* why!" She jumped to her feet and stormed toward him.

He held up his hands in surrender. "No need to get upset. It's all right to admit that you are not interested in men."

"For the love of—" She muttered something under her breath incoherently. "You are the most infuriating man I've ever met, and you are very wrong. I am indeed interested in men."

"Actually, you're not." He grinned.

Tabitha stomped her foot. "I am!"

"Forgive me for not believing, but you have shown nothing of the sort, my lovely."

Her face turned so red he thought it would explode. She grumbled again.

He'd give anything to know her thoughts right now. Taunting her this way was quite enjoyable, and yet, it was as if he wanted to goad her into doing something that only happened in his imagination.

Shame on him because he'd never had to sink to this level with a woman before. If teasing her and seeing the fire in her eyes wasn't so stimulating…

"You insufferable… jackanapes! If you weren't so thick-skulled, you'd see…" She gnashed her teeth. "Augh!"

He wanted to laugh, but he worried she'd catch on to his game. "Miss Tabitha, there is no need for name-calling. I promise I shall not speak a word to anyone about this discovery."

Stepping closer, she clutched his shoulders. "If I didn't hate you so much, I'd… I'd…"

"You would what, my lovely?" he said almost in a whisper, hoping she'd do what he wanted her to do.

Her gaze pierced his before it wandered over his face, coming to rest on his mouth. Dryness gathered in his throat, and he didn't dare move, especially when her angry expression slowly disappeared and was replaced with one he never imagined he would see on her.

Before he knew what was happening, she rose on tip-toes, wrapped her arms around his neck and kissed him. Stunned at first, he didn't know how to react, but within seconds, her body pressed more closely against his and he slid his palms around her back to bring her closer. He molded his lips to hers until they softened. At that moment, she relaxed and he had to tighten her in his embrace to keep her up.

Just as he'd imagined, her lips were soft and her kiss so gentle. Tilting his head, he deepened the kiss as his heartbeat knocked out a maddening rhythm against his chest. A heavy sigh tumbled from her throat, and she held onto him and met his urgent kisses.

Never in his life had he felt so alive and his heart raced so fast from just kissing a woman, yet he didn't want to stop to ponder these foreign feelings. Instead, he wanted to pick her up, carry her back to the sofa, and make them a little more comfortable as they continued kissing.

He broke the kiss to do what he'd just been planning, but when her hooded eyes met his, he practically melted from her smoldering gaze. Passion was evident in her sapphire orbs, and for the life of him, he couldn't stop staring. He'd once called her eyes *amazing* just to get her ire, and now he realized he'd been correct to label them such a word.

"Forgive me, my lovely," he said in a deep, soft voice, "because I was wrong about you. Very wrong."

A slow smile tugged at the corners of her mouth and for the first time, stars gleamed in her eyes. Her gaze dropped to his mouth again and she moved forward to kiss him once more, but just as her lips touched his, Lady Hollingsworth screamed *get out immediately* from the other room, followed by the loud bang of a door slamming. Both noises echoed through the house, shaking the walls.

Tabitha jumped back. Her face turning pale as her eyes widened. Her chest rose and fell quickly, and Nic was certain his breathing was just as ragged.

"I must go see to Lady Hollingsworth," she muttered in a tone entirely too sensual and unrecognizable.

"Indeed, you should," he said, although he really wanted her back in his arms.

Tabitha stood, having a staring war with him for a few earthquaking moments. Before too long she blinked, turned, and left the room.

Sighing heavily, he pushed his fingers through his hair. Something was definitely wrong with him. He knew Tabitha was the one who killed Hollingsworth and Lord Elliot, yet at this moment, Nic had wanted her more than he'd ever wanted any woman. No other woman had made him so breathless and confused at the same time. And none intrigued him as much. Yet, she would be arrested soon and placed in prison.

And possibly hanged.

And there wasn't anything he could do to stop it, even though he was halfway tempted to try.

Chapter Twenty-Eight

TRISTAN STARED AT the door for the longest time, praying it would miraculously open and Diana would rush back into the room and ask for forgiveness. She would tell him how much she loved him—much more than the devotion she had toward her maid—and that she would assist him in any way she could to put Tabitha in prison where the murderous woman belonged.

But his prayer went unheard. The longer he watched the door waiting for Diana to return, the more his heart ripped apart piece by piece and became heavy with sadness. Clearly, Diana did not love him as much as he had wanted her to, as much as he loved her.

Tears burned his eyes, but he refused to shed them. Anger was the emotion governing him as it forced him to march across the floor in haste, yank open the door, and leave. His wide strides ate up the floor as he hurried to the stairs and took two at a time on his way to the bedroom.

Inside the room he paced like a caged animal. Bunching his hands at his side, his thoughts tumbled with confusion and betrayal. This was the second time in his life he had allowed this woman to upset him so, enough he almost couldn't bear the pain. His chest weighed heavily with despondency and he scarcely could breathe.

He found himself at the window staring out into the night's

storm, but he didn't know how he got there. Nevertheless, he didn't want to move. His mind didn't want to think and his body stood stiff as a board. He wished his heart could remain as still and unaffected as the rest of him.

The bedroom door opened and strong footsteps walked in. Tristan didn't need to look behind him to see who it was.

"Worthington, what in the blazes just happened?"

It took Tristan a few moments to gather enough strength to talk. He didn't want his voice to choke and prove his vulnerability right now. "My hopes and dreams have been shattered, Hawthorne, that's what happened. Diana doesn't love me enough to turn her maid over to the magistrate. And because I wouldn't change my mind, Diana yelled at me to leave. Tonight."

Nic groaned and moved closer. "She cannot be thinking clearly. We would catch our deaths riding in this storm."

"I know."

"Did you tell her that?"

"No. There was hardly time." Tristan leaned his forehead against the glass. "Once she ordered us out of this house, she rushed out of the room and slammed the door."

"Then I shall go speak with her, because sending us out into this storm in highly improper and not cordial at all."

"We will stay in the stable with our horses. I've spent many of nights in the stable, and I'm still alive to talk about it." He glanced over his shoulder at Nic who stood with stiff legs and his arms folded across his chest as he scowled. "We will take some blankets to keep warm."

"I still cannot believe Lady Hollingsworth would even think of sending two gentlemen, such as ourselves, out—"

"Hawthorne, we shall be fine, I assure you."

Nic grumbled. "Tabitha must have some kind of hold over Lady Hollingsworth's mind to have a lady act in such a way."

"I know not, and right now, I care not." Tristan walked to the chair where his coat hung and shrugged into it. "Come, Hawthorne. It is time we take our leave."

"Did you say everything to Diana that you had wanted?"

"Yes, I believe so." He paused, trying to think of more to say since it seemed a struggle to do that now. "I thank you for keeping Tabitha occupied. I'm quite certain that was an unbearable task."

"Uh, indeed it was." Nic dropped his gaze as he slipped his arms into his coat.

Tristan grabbed the woolen blanket that he'd been wrapped in earlier while he dried. "This should be enough to keep us warm. Grab yourself a blanket, Hawthorne then let us leave this cottage for good." He turned toward the door. "I, for one, cannot wait to get back to speak to the magistrate about our suspect. I'm certain Sir Felix is intelligent enough to know when to make an arrest."

"I truly hope so." Nic took his blanket and folded it before heading toward the door.

Tristan nodded to his friend. "Hawthorne, I thank you for all you have done. You are truly a good friend. You have always been the one person my family has been able to count on for anything."

Nic smiled. "I appreciate your kind words. I have always felt part of your family—almost like one of your brothers."

Tristan took a deep breath and opened the door. The corridor was empty. Even the house seemed abnormally quiet. "Let us take our leave now and never look back. We did what we came here to do." Unfortunately, saying goodbye to his love for Diana wasn't part of that plan.

TEARS STREAMED DOWN Diana's face as she rocked back and forth on her bed, clutching a pillow to her chest. Tristan's accusations rang through her head and were permanently branded in her memory. Never would she forget the look on his face or his accusing words.

It had taken her a few moments after Tristan had blurted out his most disturbing thoughts before she found the courage to pick up her shattered heart and tell him to leave. Immediately.

He'd tried to talk some sense into her by grasping her arms and pulling her against his chest. He even had the nerve to kiss her, but she fought him and in the end, he withdrew. She was relieved to know he was the kind of man who didn't use force—not like Ludlow had.

As she had marched toward the door, his final words echoed in her ears. *Diana, know this now. I will not rest until Tabitha is in prison. That is the only way we can be together.*

Squeezing her eyes closed, Diana sobbed harder. Why had he hinted they would be together? Hadn't he realized he threatened to have an innocent woman arrested for a crime she didn't commit? Diana and Tristan definitely could never be together now that he had broken the trust between them.

Fast footsteps coming up the corridor made Diana look to-ward the door. Tabitha opened the bedroom door and hurried inside. Her face was flushed, and her eyes were wide.

"My lady, what happened?" She ran to the bed and wrapped her arms around Diana.

More sobs escaped her throat as she buried her head against Tabitha's shoulder. Tremors shook her body, and she couldn't control them. Her world was falling apart. Again. And once again, Tristan was the center of her turmoil.

Was loving him worth this much agony?

"Oh, Tabitha," she said in a shaky voice, "the worst thing has happened. I cannot trust Tristan any longer, and he definitely does not deserve my love."

Tabitha's gentle hand stroked Diana's head. "Tell me what happened."

It took her a few minutes to collect her strength to pull away, and when she did, she looked into her friend's worried eyes. "Lord Tristan and Lord Hawthorne think you killed my husband

and Lord Elliot." She sniffed. "When I defended you and told him there was no possible way you could have done the deed, Tristan wouldn't believe me. Can you believe he would do such a thing?" She wiped the moisture from underneath her eyes, but the tears kept falling in buckets. "I thought he loved me. I thought we would be happy together. Forever."

"Is that why you ordered him to leave immediately?"

"You heard that?"

Tabitha blinked and nodded. "I think everyone in the house heard, my lady."

"When I couldn't sway Tristan from thinking you were the one responsible for killing those despicable blackguards, I ordered him and Lord Hawthorne out of the house. I know the storm is still going full force around us, but right now I don't care. I don't want to see his untrusting face or hear his uncaring voice again."

Tears collected in Tabitha's eyes and her frown grew deeper. "*Both* of them thought I had killed those men?"

"Yes."

"But w—why?" Tabitha's voice broke.

"They had overheard us talking in the kitchen before dinner, and they thought the worst."

Tabitha bit her bottom lip as a tear slid down her cheek. "How could he think that I... um, I mean how could *they* think such a thing?"

"That's what hurts so badly. I don't know how they could believe that. And what makes things worse, I cannot change Tristan's mind. He's a determined man."

"I thank you for trying to defend me," Tabitha said in a choked voice.

"Of course I defended you. Tabitha, I know you did not do the crime. Unfortunately, Tristan feels having you arrested and locked in prison is the only way for him and me to finally be together." Closing her eyes, she shook her head. "But I cannot possibly love a man who doesn't trust my word."

"How can you *not* love him, my lady? He's been in your heart for years."

Diana wiped her eyes again and met her maid's gaze. "I'm going to have to bury my feelings for him. It's impossible for me to make it through life this miserable."

Tabitha was silent for the longest time as more tears fell down her face. She swallowed hard and nodded. "I do understand, but I shall make it so you don't have to be unhappy. I shall make it so that you and Lord Tristan are happy together as it should be."

"What do you mean?"

Taking a deep breath, Tabitha straightened and lifted her chin. "I will turn myself in for killing Lord Hollingsworth and Lord Elliot."

AFTER TABITHA HAD said the words, ice-cold fear sliced through her. The magistrate would certainly take her word, arrest her and lock her away in the Newgate prison without a second thought. Or perhaps Sir Felix would decide prison was too good for her and have her hanged instead. It wouldn't matter if Lord Hollingsworth and Lord Elliot were vile, scoundrels who had deserved to die. Because they were gentlemen, that quality alone would protect them in England's eyes.

Diana gasped and clutched Tabitha's hands. "What are you saying?" She shook her head. "No! I will not allow you to do such a thing. You are innocent!"

Another tear slid from Tabitha's eye as she studied the panic etched on her friend's face. "I might not have stabbed them, my lady, but in my heart and mind I have killed those men—as well as others like them."

"That is not the same and you know it." Diana's lips trembled as if she tried to hold back a sob. "If you turn yourself in, the real killer goes free to murder others, and that is not justice at all!"

"But my lady, how else will you and Lord Tristan ever be together? It's like you said…until I'm arrested, you and Lord Tristan cannot show your love in public. Nobody can know or they will accuse you of the murders."

Diana wiped her eyes. "There is no love now, Tabitha. Even when the killer is arrested and Tristan sees how wrong he was for blaming you and tries to come back to apologize, I cannot forgive him. He did not trust me and that is something I'll never forget." She took a deep breath and exhaled slowly. "So I will have no more talk of you turning yourself in to the magistrate. Is that clear?"

Nodding, Tabitha glanced down at her lap, surprised she didn't see her broken heart lying on her lap. It crushed her—nearly suffocated her, in fact—to hear that Lord Hawthorne had thought she was the killer, when only a few moments ago she'd been wrapped in his arms enjoying his heated kiss. How could a man kiss a woman so passionately if he thought she was a killer? Surely, there must be an ounce of kindness in that man for him to have such emotion. Yet now she knew it was all an act. Just as she'd suspected before, all he wanted was to seduce her and she couldn't believe she fell for his trickery!

For a brief moment, she'd actually thought there might be a chance that the illegitimate daughter of a nobleman could fall in love with a lord and have him love her in return. Curse Lord Hawthorne for making her so vulnerable! Curse him for making her remember things like that were just fairytales and would never happen in her life.

Ever!

She swallowed the knot in her throat that was due to either anger or sadness, she wasn't sure which right now, and looked back at Diana. "You have always been so kind to me. You have put your life and reputation on the line for Sally and me, and turning myself in would be a way to repay you for your kindness."

Diana shook her head. "Not if you're innocent. That proves

nothing. Besides, I need you now more than ever. Because I will die a lonely old woman, I shall need your companionship."

Tabitha tried to smile, but her quivering lips were making it hard. "We shall die together lonely old women because I shall never find happiness, either."

"I doubt that, Tabitha. You are a lovely young lady and you shall find a man who will cherish you and treat you like a queen."

Tabitha blurted out a laugh. "You are very humorous, my lady. A *queen* maybe not, but I'll be happy if a man treated me with respect. That's all I want."

"One day it will happen." Diana smiled.

They stared at each other for a few more seconds before a frown claimed Diana's face once again. She moved off the bed and walked to the window. Rain pelted the glass and still sounded fierce as the wind howled through the trees.

"As much as I hate doing this, I think I need to stop Tristan and Lord Hawthorne from traveling in this weather. I'd rather not speak with him, but I must let Tristan know that he and Hawthorne can stay here the night and leave as soon as the storm passes."

Anger filled Tabitha stronger this time when Lord Hawthorne's name was mentioned. How she wanted nothing more than to claw his face off... or spit on him, or... cry. Instantly, she shook that last thought from her head. No! She would *not* cry any longer. She'd known what kind of man he was when she first met him, so it was her own fault for falling for his trickery. Yet now she wanted to get back at him for some reason.

But how?

"My lady, let me go do it." She snapped her mouth close quickly. Why in the devil did she say that?

Diana turned and looked at her. "Really? You don't mind?"

She really did, but it was the least she could do for her mistress. "I'm your maid, so I shall do even the most loathsome task you give me, even if it means telling Lord Tristan and Lord Hawthorne they can stay the night. But keep in mind I might make their stay very uncomfortable because of my hatred for them."

Diana smiled again even if tears filled her eyes. "Perhaps you should not, Tabitha. After all, they are convinced you killed those men. Perhaps I should have Sally do it."

Tabitha nodded. "I think maybe you are correct. I will go fetch Sally for you."

"Thank you, Tabitha."

As Tabitha left the room, irritation grew inside her, higher and higher from her gut until it burned her throat. Diana was right. Tabitha shouldn't go tell the men for fear they'd want to take her to the magistrate themselves. However, if Tabitha didn't say something to Lord Hawthorne the malice collecting inside her might explode and kill her.

She couldn't let that happen.

Quietly as she could, she crept to the guest bedroom and pressed her ear against the door. The room was too quiet, so she knocked softly. Still quiet.

Perhaps the men had left after all. Yet, as much as she believed them to be fools, they weren't stupid enough to travel in this kind of storm.

On her way down the stairs, she listened for men's voices, but all she could hear was the raging storm outside. When she reached the lower floor, she grabbed her cloak and shrugged it on, heading for the back door.

Before stepping outside, she gathered the cloak's hood tight around her head and then dashed out into the rain. Immediately, the light from the stable caught her attention. Since Diana didn't have a groom, there could be only one explanation for someone being in with the horses.

She ran to the stable and peered in the window. Lord Hawthorne and Lord Tristan were arranging the hay to make themselves beds. Both men wore frowns on their gloomy faces, but neither of their expressions was angry. In fact, if she were to put a name to it, she would think they were melancholy. Could she dare hope that they were both re-evaluating their accusations?

Rolling her eyes, she moved away from the window. Not likely! They were probably just sad because they were kicked out of a house with a warm fire to sleep in a cold stable. Well, it served them right!

She turned and hurried back to the house. As much as she wanted to lash out verbally at Lord Hawthorne, she didn't want Lord Tristan to be present. So, she either had to wait until he fell asleep or hold her tongue and never voice her thoughts to that *irritating man* again.

Unfortunately, Tabitha was never the kind of person who could hold her tongue for very long.

Chapter Twenty-Nine

NIC LEANED AGAINST a bale of hay as he stared at the stable wall. How many hours had passed since he and Worthington had entered this foul place, he didn't know, but with nothing to keep him entertained, the minutes seemed to drag.

Tristan, however, adjusted to the environment a little better. Of course his friend had slept many nights in a stable since he found himself struggling to find his memory and most of the time drunk. So naturally Tristan would fall asleep easier in a place like this. It helped that they took the bottle of port with them and Tristan drank most of it.

Nic glanced at his friend who indeed had already fallen asleep. The steady pitter-patter of the rain hitting the roof probably helped lure Worthington to sleep, Nic was certain. But he was yet to feel the same exhaustion. His mind was a constant whirlwind of thoughts that wouldn't rest. Heaviness had settled in his chest as well, making him completely miserable.

He blamed Tabitha.

Why had he allowed that slip of a woman, a *maid* no less, to control his thoughts at a time like this?

Guilt washed over him in drowning waves. Never had he regretted kissing a woman in his life, but remorse dug a profound hole in his mind and heart now. He shouldn't have kissed her. He shouldn't have *acted* like he enjoyed the moment she was in his arms and her mouth eagerly met his in one of the most passionate kisses he'd ever experienced. Then again, he wasn't acting. He *had* enjoyed every second of their heated moment.

Grumbling softly as not to wake Tristan, Nic rose from his makeshift bed and strolled to his horse. He picked up a brush and began stroking the animal's mane.

This night couldn't end fast enough for him. Not only did he hate being here, but he hated feeling this way and thinking about Tabitha.

Is she really a killer?

He hadn't met many people with enough hatred in their soul to murder another person, but deep down inside, he didn't think Tabitha could do it. Could she have really killed Hollingsworth and Elliot or was she merely voicing her thoughts and feelings when he'd overheard her and Sally?

What if I'm wrong?

Although he didn't like admitting when he made a mistake, worry grew inside him like a festering boil. What if, by chance, Tabitha wasn't the killer? What if she was just an angry and hurt servant like Sally?

Or what if Sally was the true killer?

A noise from the back of the stable jerked him from his thoughts and had him swinging toward the shuffling sound. From the darkness, a shadow emerged and slowly formed into a woman wearing a cloak. The closer she came toward him, the harder his heartbeat slammed against his chest.

Tabitha drew nearer and lowered her hood. Her eyes blazed a deep hatred as she aimed her glare at him. Nic scanned over her cloak to her hands for fear she would be holding a knife. But as his eyes adjusted, he could see she didn't have any sort of weapon. He breathed a sigh of relief.

"Lord Hawthorne, forgive me for startling you. Lady Hollingsworth wanted me to make sure you and Lord Tristan were warm enough."

Nic arched a quizzical eyebrow. "Your ladyship actually

wanted *you* to see to our welfare?"

"Actually no, she wanted Sally, but Sally was asleep. Lady Hollingsworth is aware that she instructed Lord Tristan to leave, but after she thought about it and realized the storm was too strong, she had wanted to let you know that you could stay the night as long as you left first thing in the morning." She glanced at their beds in the hay. "Although, I see you have already settled here just fine."

"Tell Lady Hollingsworth we appreciate her kindness, and we plan on leaving first thing."

"Yes, my lady is very kind, much more generous than I would have been, I'm sure."

Tabitha's tone was very harsh, yet softly spoken as if she tried to keep the conversation between them and not awaken Tristan. Nic glanced at his friend to make sure he was still sleeping before looking back at Tabitha. Her heated glare could cut through glass, Nic was certain. It tugged at his heartstrings to think he contributed to her extremely unpleasant disposition.

"Tabitha, I realize what you must be thinking—"

In three long strides, she stood directly in front of him. Tears glistened in her angry eyes, but she appeared too upset to cry.

"You have no idea what I'm thinking!" She took a deep breath. "How dare you accuse me of something you know nothing about?"

His fingers itched to reach up to her face and smooth out the wrinkles around her luscious mouth, amazing eyes, and tight forehead, to bring back her natural beauty once again. He gulped down the guilt sneaking back into his heart.

"How *dare* I?" he asked. "I think considering the conversation I had overheard between you and Sally, that I have every right to *dare* accuse you. Tell me, Tabitha. If you were the bystander listening in on that particular conversation, what would you have gathered from it?"

"You see, my lord, this is one of the differences between men and women. Men jump to conclusions whereas women will seek to find the truth."

"Indeed? Are you certain about that? I know women are meddlesome, but I highly doubt they are seeking to find any truth. They'd rather gossip and spread false rumors."

She rolled her eyes. "Spoken by a *true* gentleman, I see." She folded her arms. "But I can assure you, if you and Lord Tristan continue your pursuit to have me arrested for those murders, you both will be convicting an innocent woman."

"I think I shall let the magistrate come to that decision." He lifted his chin to show her his stubbornness.

"Just know this," she snipped, "because I am indeed innocent, if I should die, my wrongful death will be on yours and Lord Tristan's head."

She spun around and marched toward the back door of the stable, toward the shadows. He hurried after her, grasped her arm and turned her around to face him. A few tears had slid from her eyes making her cheeks gleam with wetness. Once again, his chest clenched with indecision for his actions.

"If you are innocent as you proclaim, prove it," he said softly, hoping not to disturb Tristan's slumber.

She gasped. "Prove it? Why should I prove my innocence? You should be the one trying to prove my guilt."

"Then prove to me that what I overheard was wrong." He pulled her body closer to his. "I truly want to believe you are not a killer, Tabitha. I may not know you well, but what little I do know about you, I cannot believe you would purposely stab two men to death while in a highly intoxicated and undressed state."

She placed her palms on his chest and pushed to move him away, but he wouldn't budge. Heaven help him, but he enjoyed this closeness entirely too much.

"Were you aware that Lord Hollingsworth beat his wife?" she asked. "Diana was as much a victim in her home as Sally and I were victims in Lord Elliot's home. If I—or her ladyship or Sally—would have stabbed those men, it would have been to break free of our cage—our hellish prison. So tell me, Lord

Hawthorne, if *you* were in *my* shoes, would you want to kill someone who repeatedly did that to you? And when the person responsible was finally dead, wouldn't you be relieved to know they would never be allowed to bring harm on another person again?"

Nic's chest clenched. She'd been beaten. He couldn't imagine that, and out of nowhere, anger filled him for Lord Elliot. "I am very sorry to hear that you were treated poorly, and if I were in your situation, I would probably feel the same. But you are forgetting one thing. It's not up to us to bring punishment to those disgusting people. It's up to the courts, and God."

"Then I suppose my only crime is that I'm satisfied knowing that someone helped God and the courts by hurrying the process."

Shaking his head, he loosened his hold, but instead of removing his touch from her, he stroked her arms lightly. "Please, Tabitha. I wish to believe in your innocence. Help me."

"I don't know how I can except by telling you I did not do it."

"That's hard for me to believe since I overheard you saying that you *would* do it."

She shrugged. "Then that's your problem, not mine. At least I'm being truthful, whereas you don't know how to be."

He scowled. "What do you mean by that?"

"Think really hard, Lord Hawthorne. Think what we were talking about, and doing in the sitting room while Lady Hollingsworth and Lord Tristan were away from us."

Embarrassment crept over him, along with shame. He scolded his feelings. He should *not* be ashamed for kissing Tabitha and enjoying it. So then why did he feel this way? "Why don't you believe I was truthful?"

"Are you jesting?" She snorted what sounded like a laugh. "There you were trying your hardest to seduce me, all the while suspecting me of murder. For a brief moment, your actions earlier showed me what a kind, gentle, and understanding man you were. For a brief moment I actually thought you were attracted to me, impossible as it may seem. Yet that was all a lie. I had known what kind of man you were, but you tried to convince me otherwise. Now I know I had been right about you all along."

"How do you know I was lying?"

"Ha!" She shook her head. "You honestly think I'm that foolish?"

"What if I tell you that for a moment I had been attracted to you, and I had enjoyed our kiss?"

She snickered. "Then I would say you were a great performer, because why would you enjoy a mere maid's kisses when you have seduced many women over the years?"

Nic bit his tongue to keep from saying anymore. He shouldn't have said what he had to begin with. He didn't want to admit, especially to her, how much their kiss had meant to him. "Then it appears we are both talented performers. Does it not?"

"I, my lord, am not a performer."

"Then neither am I." He pulled her closer as he lowered his head. His attention dropped to her lips—lips that tempted him to sample them again.

She sucked in a quick breath and her mouth parted in invitation. *Good heavens!* What was he thinking? He couldn't possibly kiss her even as much as the idea lured him.

"Lord Hawthorne," she whispered, "I beg you not to do that."

"Do what?" he asked quietly.

"You know exactly what I'm referring to. Kissing me will not solve a thing. You still believe I'm a killer, and I still think of you as one of the most despicable rogues in England."

He swallowed hard to moisten the cotton that had formed in his throat. She was correct again, blast it! He could not kiss her. He could not also understand why her statement hurt so badly, like a knife through his chest.

"Indeed, it won't solve a thing." Reluctantly, he released her and stepped back.

She gathered the cloak tighter around her neck before pulling on her hood. She turned to leave, but hesitated. For some foolish reason, anticipation shot through him, quickening his heartbeat.

"Lord Hawthorne," she whispered and looked at him over her shoulder. "If you really cared about your friend, you would try your hardest to find the *true* killer so that Lord Tristan and Lady Hollingsworth can be together. They have waited too long to share their love, and until the real murderer is caught, they will never be fully happy. I'm just a mere maid so there isn't much I can do to help my lady in this dire situation, but you can. Lord Hawthorne, if you put your mind to it, you can help your friend finally obtain happiness."

She didn't wait for his answer before hurrying outside. Nic stared at the closed door for the longest time as her words ran through his mind. The more and more he thought about what she said, the more doubt filled him.

Would a killer be so selfless and think about her friend's happiness more than her own?

Deep in his heart, he knew the answer.

"Who was that?" Tristan's voice came from behind him.

Nic jumped and spun around. Tristan was still on his bedroll, but sitting up looking Nic's way. "That was Tabitha." He walked closer to his friend.

"What was she doing here?"

"She came to tell us that Diana has invited us back in the house for the night because of the storm, but we are to leave first thing in the morning."

Nodding, Tristan adjusted himself on the ground, draping his arms over his bent knees. "I'm glad to know she has come to her senses, at least about that."

The confusion thickened in Nic's head, giving him a headache. He grumbled and strode to his blanket before plopping down on the covering. "Worthington? What if we're wrong?"

Tristan's head didn't move, just his gaze as it rested on him. "Wrong about what?"

"About Tabitha."

"What makes you think we are wrong?"

Nic sighed as he picked off some of the hay from the blanket. "During my talk with Tabitha earlier tonight, I saw a part of her I hadn't noticed before. And, just a moment ago," he motioned his head toward the stall where they'd talked, "I noticed the same thing." He lifted his gaze and met Tristan's. "Would a cold blooded killer think of others when her life hung by a thread?"

Tristan didn't say anything for the longest time before shaking his head. "No. A cold blooded killer would only think of themselves, not others."

"Well, Tabitha was thinking of you and Diana. Do you know what she told me?"

"What?"

"She told me that if I cared about you, that I would try to find the real killer so that you and Diana could be together, as you both deserve." Sighing heavily, he pushed his hair back away from his eyes. "Oh Worthington, I think we both jumped to conclusions when we overheard her and Sally. I honestly feel deep down in my heart that Tabitha is not the killer."

Tristan laid back and looked up toward the rafters. For several minutes he was quiet, and Nic didn't want to say anymore, either. Blaming Tabitha had been very wrong, and even if Tristan didn't realize that, Nic would have to apologize to Tabitha soon or the guilt would eat him up.

"I can't do this," Tristan muttered.

"Can't do what?"

"I cannot allow things to be unresolved between Diana and I. And I especially cannot go on with this doubt in my head." He met Nic's gaze. "I, too, have felt that blaming Tabitha was wrong, but with everything we'd heard and the way the maid acts, it's hard not to think that way." He scrambled to his feet. "Now that I've had more time to ponder on this, I realize that Diana would discern the girl well enough to know if she was a killer or not." He breathed deeply. "I have been too quick to judge when I should have trusted Diana more."

Tristan marched to the stall's gate and picked up his overcoat. "I'm going back to the house to speak with Diana. Things need to be resolved tonight!"

Chapter Thirty

TRISTAN TREADED AS softly as he could up the stairs toward Diana's bedroom. The house was quiet, and he feared everyone would be asleep. He didn't care if the maids were asleep, but he needed Diana awake. They needed to talk this thing out.

He reached her door and stopped, lifting his hand to knock, but hesitated. What if she wouldn't allow him entrance? He couldn't very well carry on a conversation with a door between them.

Instead of knocking, he grasped the handle, turned it, and entered. The room was dark, but in the corner near her bed was a lamp that had been dimmed, illuminating Diana's body as she sat at her vanity table and stared in the mirror. She didn't look his way, so he assumed she hadn't heard him. He waited a few brief moments before taking a step inside.

She wore the same nightgown and wrapper that she'd been in the first time he saw her after his kidnapping. Although he still thought she was the loveliest woman he'd ever seen, her eyes were swollen from crying and her desolate expression nearly brought him to his knees in agony. She was this way because of him.

"Diana," he whispered.

Gasping, she swung toward him but remained on the chair.

"Tristan! What are you doing in here?"

He walked in further, closing the door behind him. "We need to talk."

Her surprised expression turned hard as anger appeared. "No we don't. We have said everything that needs to be said." She turned back toward the vanity mirror. "I would appreciate it if you left my room."

"I fear that I cannot do as you request. You see," he paused, stepping closer to her, "I cannot let things continue like this. It's breaking my heart to see you so distraught, and this matter must be resolved tonight."

"Tristan, please," she said with a heavy sigh as her hands covered her face. "We have nothing further to discuss."

"Yes, we do." He reached her and knelt beside her, resting his hand on her knee. "I still need to tell you how much I love you, and how wrong I was to accuse Tabitha, and especially how wrong I was to doubt your word."

Gradually, she removed her hands as she met his stare. Her green eyes glistened with moisture. "You were wrong?"

"Indeed, I was. Men don't like to admit that, I know, but when I'm wrong, I say it." He caressed a lock of her silky auburn hair as it hung on her shoulder. "I was desperate and grasping at anything as a means to bring us together. I'm so very tired of hiding my feelings for you. I want the whole world to know how much I love you and how badly I want to be your husband."

A tear slipped down her cheek. "But why did you blame Tabitha?"

He shrugged. "Because of what Hawthorne and I had over-heard. But I understand now how angry and hurt the maid was for my cousin's violation against her, and I realize now why she is so disturbed with men in general. I'm sorry I jumped to conclu-sions and blamed her." He moved his hand up and stroked her wet cheek. "As I pondered our conversation while in the barn, I realized I hadn't trusted your word. If I love you as I have proclaimed then I need to believe in you. Forgive me, my sweet

Diana, for having a weak moment. It will never happen again."

"Oh, Tristan."

She turned toward him more and wrapped her arms around his neck. He pulled her close as she cried silent tears against the crook of his neck. Moisture gathered in his eyes, and his heart ached with sadness for causing her so much pain. He kissed the side of her head and held her tightly.

"Tristan, I know Tabitha didn't do it," she said brokenly as she lifted her head and met his eyes. "She was too weak and her soul was broken. She wouldn't have had the strength to kill Ludlow. And your cousin…" She shook her head. "Tabitha was here at the cottage watching over you the night Lord Elliot was killed. We gave you a sleeping draught because we both feared what you might find if you had awakened and caught us." She sniffed and pulled back slightly. "You see, I had left Tabitha here to watch over you so I could ride out to get Sally from your evil cousin. I was there the night he was killed."

Her words poured through him like ice as shock vibrated through his body. "You?"

"He'd beaten Sally and I had gone to his townhouse to rescue her. When I walked in on your bath the next morning, I had just returned. That's why my boots were dirty and I looked so tired." She took a deep breath. "Tabitha had been here the whole time and was still in her room."

"Oh, Diana." He grasped her shoulders. "How could you put yourself in danger like that? Do you know what he would have done if he caught you?"

She nodded. "I'd prepared myself, I assure you. I had my pistol with me, but not a blade. I didn't kill your cousin, but if he would have tried to attack me, I would have pulled the trigger."

Blowing out a frustrated breath, Tristan stood and paced the floor. Several thoughts flew through his mind, and all of them were not good. "Diana, you should not have done that. Do you know what would happen if the magistrate ever found out?" He stopped and faced her. "Oh, my sweet love, he would not understand at all. He would believe you killed both men."

"Yes, I know." Her voice shook. "I fear every day that he will discover something and come arrest me. The two times I rescued maids from their monstrous lords, were the times someone decided to kill them."

Groaning in despair, he hurried back to her and pulled her into his arms. She wrapped her arms around his waist and pressed her head against his chest.

"Tristan, we must find the real killer so I don't go to prison."

"We will." Closing his eyes, he tightened his arms around her, praying to the Almighty that something would happen and Tristan would be able to save the woman he loves. He *must* save her this time since he hadn't been able to three years ago.

He exhaled slowly, trying to release the panic rushing through him. "Diana, does the magistrate know about this cottage?"

"Yes." She lifted her head and looked at him. "I don't believe he knows the exact location, but I did tell him this was where I was when Lord Elliot was killed."

"Then we need to hide you somewhere else. If the magistrate finds any evidence that you were at my cousin's townhouse that night, you will be arrested. Until Hawthorne and I discover what really happened, we need to keep you safe."

A small chuckle bubbled up from her throat, even though humor was not the expression on her worried face. "As hard as I've tried to rescue abused maids and keep them hidden, it now looks like I'm the one who needs the protection."

"You are, and this time I will guard you with my life."

Slowly, a smile touched her mouth. She lifted on her toes and placed her lips against his. He crushed her in his arms and kissed her with all the love and emotion inside of him. He didn't want to think that this might be the last time they would be together. Even if it meant breaking the law, he was determined to keep her safe.

Diana was the one who broke the kiss. "Tristan, I love you so very much."

"You are the light of my life, and I will do all I can to keep you here in my arms."

"I think I have an idea."

"What is it?"

"Lady Dashwood has always supported me and helped me in my endeavors. If I tell her of my plight, I know she will help. She has many estates and cottages all over Britain. She might be able to hide me."

Bit by bit, relief eased into Tristan's chest. He nodded. "Then let us go talk to her tomorrow."

"No, only I must go. Remember, we still cannot be seen together."

He frowned. "You are correct. But please, inform me or send me a missive after you have talked to her so that I know where you will be staying."

"I promise."

When he kissed her once again, he savored the moment. Kissing her had always been so right, so perfect. Indeed, they were meant to be together. Forever.

He just prayed fate had the same idea.

DIANA FIDGETED IN her carriage seat as she stared out the window. She couldn't arrive at her destination soon enough. It had been one very long night, and most of it she hadn't slept. She thanked the Lord that Tristan had returned to finish their talk, and it pleased her to know he was now on her side.

Tristan and Lord Hawthorne left early this morning, and once Diana and Tabitha were ready, they took the coach and rode toward Lady Dashwood's estate. Claudia would know what to do, Diana just knew it.

The carriage bounced Diana on her seat. She scowled and

glanced up to where the coachman would be since she couldn't see it from inside the vehicle. Because she didn't have a driver, Tabitha donned the same clothes she'd used when she kidnapped Tristan and was now acting as Diana's coachman. She just prayed that when they arrived at Lady Dashwood's estate, Claudia's servants wouldn't get suspicious of the feminine looking driver.

Worry of the unknown wouldn't leave her and gave her a tremendous headache. Groaning, Diana leaned back in her seat and rubbed her forehead. *Would this nightmare ever end?*

Trying to think positive, she sat up straight and stared out the window. Her life had to get better soon. She'd been living in hell for so long, it was time to bring things to a happy ending... with Tristan, of course.

She smiled, remembering their talk, and especially the loving words he'd said. And their kiss. She smiled. The kiss that could have lasted all night if he hadn't pulled away and left her room. He was such a gentleman, because if it had been up to her, that wonderful man would have not left her room at all.

The coach hit another bump in the road, jerking her on the seat. "Tabitha! Will you watch where you're going?"

"Sorry, my lady," she called back.

Diana frowned. Tabitha hadn't been the same after last night's events, even when Diana told her of Tristan's confession. Something had happened between the maid and Nic, but Tabitha would not discuss it. Diana noticed the fun-loving energetic woman was quiet and withdrawn from everything this morning as they'd readied themselves to travel. It broke Diana's heart to see her friend that way, and she wondered if Nic had apologized to Tabitha as Tristan had done.

When the carriage slowed to a stop, Diana peered out the window and looked upon Claudia's grand estate. At least Claudia's husband was generous enough to leave her money and the house when he died. Ludlow's excuse to Diana was that because she hadn't given him an heir, she didn't deserve any of his money. But the truth of the matter was that she didn't *want* his money. The quicker she could break free of that miserable life, the better she'd be.

The door opened and there stood Tabitha, still dressed as the coachman, offering to help Diana out of the vehicle. Once she was out and the carriage door was shut, Diana leaned into Tabitha and whispered, "Stay low until I'm ready to leave."

"Yes, my lady."

She missed seeing the twinkle in Tabitha's eyes and her adorable quirky grin. One day the maid would get them back, Diana hoped.

She was shown to the sitting room and within minutes Claudia swept in, wearing a beautiful yellow day gown with scooped neck and puffy sleeves. Claudia always wore the latest fashions and was the envy of most ladies of the *ton*. Her blonde hair hung in ringlets and was decorated with pearls and a golden ribbon.

"Lady Hollingsworth, what a pleasure it is to see you." She hugged Diana. "Let's sit and have some tea and biscuits. My cook has just made a special batch that I haven't sampled yet."

"I thank you for the refreshment. I'm eager to taste what your cook has made. He's always creating such mouth-watering treats."

The ladies sat together on the sofa as a maid brought in the tray of tea and another servant carried in a tray of biscuits. Lady Dashwood poured Diana a cup of tea before pouring her own and sipping.

"Thank you, Gladys and Junie. That is all for now." Claudia dismissed the other women.

Diana watched the two servants leave, and once the door was closed, she switched her focus back on her friend. "Claudia, I apologize for the unannounced visit, but it was urgent that I speak to you."

"Good heavens, dear. What has happened?" Claudia set her teacup down.

"Lord Tristan and I fear that the magistrate will find evidence that I was at Lord Elliot's house the night of his murder and he'll arrest me." Tears spiked her eyes, and she wished she wasn't so emotional all the time. "Claudia, you are the only one that can help me."

"Oh, my dear Diana." Claudia reached over to take Diana's hands. "You know I will do anything to help."

"Sir Felix knows about my grandmother's cottage, and so that is not a safe place for me—or Tabitha and Sally—to stay. I apologize for being so desperate, but I beg you to help me. Do you have a place we can go to hide?"

Claudia narrowed her gaze on Diana. "Is Lord Tristan not going to help you at all?"

"He is going to try and find the real killer, Claudia, but if we are seen together, the magistrate will suspect we are in cahoots together."

The other woman nodded slowly. "Does Lord Tristan believe he can find the killer?"

"I don't know." Diana shrugged. "He's going to do all he can to find this person. Once the person is caught, then Tristan and I can be together." She smiled softly. "It's been too long, Claudia. I want a real marriage, a marriage where the husband and wife love each other."

Flipping her hand in the air, Claudia pulled away from Diana. "My dear friend, that is not a real marriage at all. Most of the *ton* marriages are loveless. You know that."

"Yes, but I also know that marriage can be one of unconditional love. That's what I want, and it's just within my grasp. Please Claudia, help me achieve this."

"Of course, my friend. You know I will help you any way I can." She sat back in her chair and tapped a finger on her chin. "One of my estates in Essex is not in use right now. I will need to get a few servants over there to ready the place for you and your maids, but it will take at least a week."

Relief flooded Diana. "Thank you, Claudia. That will be perfect."

"But until that time comes, you must stay here with me. I

cannot have you at your grandmother's cottage unprotected. My servants are devoted to me and they know what hell you went through, as well. They will not say anything, I assure you. Both Tabitha and Sally can be maids here during our wait. They will have nothing to fear."

"Oh, Claudia." She reached over and hugged her friend. "You truly are a gift from God."

Lady Dashwood chuckled. "I don't have many close friends, and I will do anything I can to keep my friends protected."

At long last, Diana's future was starting to look clearer. Now she needed to pray that Tristan and Hawthorne could find the killer quickly.

TABITHA HUDDLED IN the corner of the coach house and pulled her overcoat around her neck a little tighter before lowering her hat. A few of the grooms mulled about and only glanced at her a few times. Thankfully, they didn't act as if they knew Tabitha was a woman.

She prayed Lady Dashwood had ideas of where Tabitha could hide. She didn't want to bring harm or more suspicion on Diana, but Tabitha also didn't want to go to prison, either. Diana was correct when she said Tabitha turning herself in was not the right thing to do because the true killer was still out there and might kill again.

A servant walked into the coach house carrying trays of food. The young woman stood with the other two men as they partook of the meal. Tabitha pulled her gaze away from them as she looked out into the grand gardens of the estate. Although she had only been to a few estates in her life, one of them remained foremost in her mind. The Dowager Duchess of Kenbridge had the most beautiful flower gardens imaginable. Tabitha didn't know the woman personally and had certainly never met her, but just that one time of seeing the gardens was enough to stay in Tabitha's memory.

Blowing out a frustrated breath, she glanced back at Lady Dashwood's servants, still chatting and chomping down food. In a way, Tabitha wished she could talk with them just to keep her mind occupied. It was hard to think of other things when the fate of her future hung by a thread.

It had almost been a week since she talked to Lord Hawthorne. Hurt and anger still ruled her emotions and fueled her melancholy. She'd thought he would do the right thing and convince Lord Tristan not to turn her in, yet because neither she nor Diana had heard anything, or even seen the magistrate, she still worried that at any minute Sir Felix would come to the door and arrest her.

She blamed Lord Hawthorne for her fear and sleepless nights.

Feeling restless, she strode out of the coach house and into the yard, but there was nothing there to keep her busy, either. She turned and slowly walked around the coach house, trying to waste her time. When she passed by one of the open windows and heard Lady Hollingsworth's name, Tabitha stopped and moved closer to the window. Slowly she peeked inside. The driver, another man and the woman who'd brought the food were standing together talking.

"I feel sorry for that wee woman," Lady Dashwood's driver said. "The lass has lived in a home where her husband hated her and her servants loathed her as well."

"Impossible!" the other man said. "That kind, sweet woman? It's unbelievable the servants wud give 'er grief."

"Aye, that is true," the woman spoke up. "I heard that her lady's maid had been raped by Lord Hollin'sworth because his wife cud not satisfy him."

"Just horrid!" the driver exclaimed. "That monster should have been horsewhipped."

"Aye," the other man said.

"But that's not the worst of it for Lady Hollin'sworth," the woman continued. "The reason her servants hated their mistress was because she *wud not* go to her husband's bed. If she had given him an heir, his lordship wud not have taken the lady's maid or the other women workin' in the estate."

"Was the lady's maid Martha Whitehead?"

"Aye," the woman answered.

"I 'ave 'eard of Martha."

"She has a daughter who worked for the late Lord Elliot. I've heard that her daughter, Sally, wasn't treated kindly by that lord, either."

"How utterly sad."

"'Tis sad, indeed," the woman continued. "I have heard that Martha is now a very angry and bitter woman."

"And who would blame 'er?"

Tabitha sucked in a quick breath and moved away from the window. Good Heavens! This explained a lot. But not only did it explain the older woman's hatred for Diana, pieces to the unknown puzzle started fitting together in Tabitha's mind. Martha could have killed Lord Hollingsworth, and because Martha's daughter had been abused by Lord Elliot, the mother could have killed him as well. Everything was so very clear now!

Hope budded in Tabitha's bosom as she hurried around the coach house and to the carriage. She needed to tell Diana, and she didn't think she could wait for her to finish with her visit first.

Tabitha prayed this was the answer to the end of their torment. She also prayed that Martha wouldn't lie to the magistrate when he dropped by to ask her questions.

As she paced the drive, she thought for sure she'd wear out the bottom of her boots before Lady Hollingsworth came out. She was ready to scream with frustration, and if she had to hold this information inside her for much longer, she would be barging in Lady Dashwood's house just to let them know what the servants had said.

From up the drive, another coach came her way with two riders beside it. Immediately, she recognized the emblem on the vehicle, and one of the men. What was the magistrate doing here? Her heart sunk, and fear expanded in her chest.

As the coach neared, she gradually stepped back underneath a tree and lowered her hat on her forehead so they would not be able to see her face. The footman hurried out to greet Sir Felix and they chatted for a few moments. Although she couldn't hear what was being said, she was anxious to get away, and to find Diana and get her away from these men as well.

Just as panic consumed her, she turned and darted toward the back of the house, but because her hat was blocking her vision, she ran into a low hanging limb. The branch knocked the hat from her head, and immediately, her long hair tumbled down her back and over her shoulders.

She held in a frightened cry as she bent to retrieve the hat. But as she peeked toward the magistrate, he and the footman, along with the third man, were staring at her with wide eyes.

"That's her!" the footman stated. "That's Lady Diana's maid."

Sir Felix flew off his horse. "Halt, Miss Tabitha," he yelled as he hurried toward her.

She wouldn't give up without a fight, and a good run. The chubby man was definitely not fit to run as fast as she was.

Tabitha turned and sprinted across the lawn as fast as she could. Terror pumped through her legs and helped with her flight. She came closer to the corner of the house, and just as she darted around the bush, two strong arms reached out and grabbed her.

"Sir Felix, I got her."

Groaning, she struggled against his hold. Tears burned her eyes. She couldn't understand how she had forgotten about the third man—the one who'd come with the magistrate.

He pulled her toward the front of the house where Sir Felix met her. His scowl was fierce.

"Miss Tabitha, I have come—"

"What is the meaning of this?" Diana demanded as she flew down the front stairs, Lady Dashwood close on her heels. Diana rushed to Tabitha and tried to pry her wrist from the magistrate's grip. "Release her at once, Sir Felix," she demanded.

"I fear, Lady Hollingsworth," he said, lifting his chin arrogantly, "that I cannot release her. I have come to arrest her for the murders of your husband and Lord Elliot."

"No!" Tabitha yanked her hands, but the other man's grip was too strong. "I didn't kill them."

"We have witnesses that say otherwise." Sir Felix arched a bushy eyebrow.

"They are wrong!" Diana folded her arms over her chest. "My maid did not kill those men, I assure you."

"Forgive me, my lady," he replied smugly, "but your *assurance* holds no strength this time. Now, if you will step aside so I can do my duty, I promise not to arrest you as well."

Lady Dashwood huffed. "This is highly irregular, my lord."

The portly man threw a glare at the other lady. "And I suggest, Lady Dashwood, that you stay out of my business as well."

The portly man and his partner tugged Tabitha to the coach. Horror like she'd never imagined clawed its way from her stomach to her chest, squeezing the air from her lungs. She turned pleading eyes to Diana. "I didn't do it." Her voice broke.

"I know you didn't." Diana cried and clutched her hands to her chest.

"Not to worry, dear Tabitha," Claudia assured, "I will hire a lawyer and have you released."

Helplessly, Tabitha was shoved into the windowless coach as a chain secured the door. There was no escaping now. If Diana couldn't find a way to release her, Tabitha would surely die in prison.

Chapter Thirty-One

LAUGHTER CHIMED AROUND the room as the Worthington brothers and their wives sat at the dowager's large dining table for a family dinner. Tristan tried to smile, but it was so hard when his mind was occupied on trying to figure out this mystery of who killed the two lords. What made him that much more upset was not coming up with any leads. Tabitha wasn't a suspect on his list any longer, but Sally was. Now he wondered how he could find out what really happened that night after Elliot had beaten her.

Tristan glanced around the table, trying to act as if he were involved with the conversation. The oldest Worthington brother, Trevor, sat near his wife Louisa, their eyes sparked with love when they gazed at each other. Louisa was midway through her pregnancy, and simply glowing. Trevor and Louisa had a rough patch at the beginning of their relationship, but now Tristan could see they were destined to be together, forever.

The youngest brother, Trey was just as happy with his wife, Judith. The two of them were either holding hands or Trey's arm was around his wife's waist. Sometimes they were this way in public, which made all the matrons' tongues wag with gossip. Tristan wasn't around when Trey and Judith were courting, but apparently it was quite the scandal.

Earlier tonight, Trey had announced Judith was pregnant.

Tristan's mother was as ecstatic as any woman could be as she clapped cheerfully as tears of joy swam in her eyes. Tristan prayed that one day he and Diana would have children, yet for some reason fate had not been smiling on either one of them lately.

Tristan frowned. Maybe fate was never going to be a ray of sunshine in his life. Mentally, he shook the thought from his head. He must stay positive. Diana was destined to be his wife. And Tristan would do all he could to see it happen.

"What is going on with the murder investigation, Tristan? Do you know?"

He snapped out of his thoughts and looked at Trevor who'd asked the question. All eyes around the table were now on Tristan, so he tried to replace his forlorn expression with a cheery disposition, although he knew he failed miserably.

"The last I have heard, the magistrate has no leads to the killer, I'm afraid."

"Does he still suspect you?" the dowager asked softly.

"Yes Mother, but I'm doing my best to try and change his mind. We all know I didn't do it, but for some reason, the magistrate now has it in his head that Lady Hollingsworth and I were working together to rid the world of her husband and my cousin." He shrugged. "What a wild imagination that man has."

Murmurs of agreement went around the room.

"However, just this past week, Hawthorne and I overheard a conversation between Lady Hollingsworth and two of her maids."

Both Trey and Trevor's wide-eye gazes bounced back to Tristan.

"It seems," Tristan continued, "Lady Hollingsworth has a maid who was recently in Lord Elliot's employ. He had been very abusive to this girl. Hawthorne and I are suspecting she might be the one who killed Elliot, but were not sure if she had the motive to kill Lord Hollingsworth."

Gasps burst through the room. "Did Diana's maid confess to

anything?" Trevor asked loudly.

"Her name is Sally, and she didn't confess, but she did state how she'd wanted Elliot dead."

"Did you say anything to Lady Hollingsworth?" Judith asked, swiping a light, chestnut ringlet away from her face.

"Indeed, I did. Unfortunately, we still need to find the proof before anything can be done."

"Oh, dear." His mother fanned her face. "Tristan, you must make certain the girl is indeed the killer before you lay blame."

"Yes, Mother. I know this, but I heard her practically confess."

"*Practically?*" Trey asked. "But that's not going to hold up very well with the magistrate, my dear brother."

"Have you even talked to Sir Felix yet?" Louisa asked before she sipped her dinner wine.

"No." Tristan sighed heavily. "It's like I had said before, I need proof first. I don't want to cause any undue problems with Diana or her maid."

"Are you still in love with her?" Judith asked softly.

He arched an eyebrow. "Sally? Of course not. I have never held those feelings of such nature for the maid."

"No," Judith corrected, "I was referring to Lady Hollingsworth."

Louisa leaned forward as if waiting for his answer. It seemed his sisters-in-law were more interested in that particular aspect of his life than his brothers, or even his mother. "Yes, I am still in love with Diana."

Knowing grins shaped Judith and Louisa's mouths. His brothers, however, nearly scowled at Tristan, enough to burn holes through him.

"No wonder you haven't said anything to the magistrate," Trevor barked. "I think you are trying to protect Diana more than you are trying to find a killer."

"Now Trevor, dear," Louisa said as she patted her husband's hand. "Have you forgotten how confused you were when you realized you were in love with a thief, only to discover how wrong you were?"

Not very often did Tristan get to see his brother blush, but Trevor's cheeks darkened a pinkish color.

"You are correct, my love." Trevor brushed his fingers lightly against her blonde curl by her ear.

Tristan quickly continued before the two of them became any more zealous in their love. "I haven't said anything to the magistrate until I have something that backs up my theory."

"That's a wise thing to do," his mother said.

"Do you think she might be innocent?" Judith asked.

Tristan shrugged then took a drink of his wine. "I don't know. I just know that I if I were in her place and had been beaten like she had been, I would have wanted to kill the man responsible." He shrugged. "So I have two different arguments pulling at me. I have logic that says once the true killer is put away, Diana and I can live our lives the way we've always wanted to. And then my heart tells me that I shouldn't blame the maid because she was so abused and mentally broken."

"Tristan?" Louisa asked. "Why don't you follow your heart?"

Inwardly, he sighed. He should have known she or Judith would say something like that. And for the life of him, he couldn't hold back from telling her the truth. "My heart tells me Sally is innocent, but it's only because Diana trusts her maids, and I trust Diana."

"Oh, Tristan dear." His mother bunched her hands on the table. "Please do not do anything rash. Please make certain of your feelings before you pursue Lady Hollingsworth any further. You mentioned that Sir Felix thinks you and Lady Hollingsworth are in this together. I would hate him to have his suspicions confirmed if he saw you and the widow together in public."

"I'm very much aware of how it would look, Mother." He rubbed his forehead, hoping the pounding in his skull would disappear. "But I don't think you will have to worry about that any time soon. Until the true killer is caught, Diana and I will not be seen together at all. I just hope this ends quickly because I cannot see going through life without Diana as my wife."

"Tristan," Louisa said, shaking her head, "don't give up. If you love her, fight for her. I would not be married to your brother if he had given up on me so easily."

"Same here," Trey added as he gazed into Judith's eyes and smiled. "I don't know what kind of man I would be right now if Judith had given up on our love."

Judith returned the tender smile and grasped Trey's hand. "We certainly would not be here and starting a family together."

Everyone around the table chuckled and nodded. Except for Tristan. Once again, all he could manage was a weak smile. Maybe it was jealousy, or maybe it was just that there were too many obstacles keeping him from love.

Perhaps what his family said was true. After all, they had all been through trials in their lives, and they were now all very happy. *Blissfully* happy, which was what he wanted to be.

After dinner, he returned to his room. His mind was churning with ideas. Between Hawthorne and himself, they would find Lord Elliot's servants and question them all, even if they had to bribe them with money. One way another, they'd find something to use that could lead them in the killer's direction.

From the corner of the small table near his bed, his attention caught something different. A letter sealed with Lady Dashwood's crest embedded in the wax. He snatched the letter and broke it open, his heart beating with anticipation.

"Dear Tristan. Something dreadful has happened. Earlier today the magistrate arrested Tabitha and took her to Newgate Prison. We are beside ourselves and don't know what to do. Please meet me late tonight in Lady Dashwood's stable so that we can discuss what to do next. My heart is broken for this terrible injustice that has happened, and I pray that you and I can figure a way out of this mess. Please burn this letter once you have read it so that Sir Felix doesn't think we are planning something. Most affectionately yours, Diana."

Tristan groaned and sank on the edge of his bed. *Poor Tabitha.*

Indeed, she was not guilty, so what made the magistrate think she was? Surely Diana could speak to the man and assure him of Tabitha's location during both murders. Tristan could even attest to being in the cottage when Tabitha was there. Even if he had to stretch the truth a bit, he could explain to Sir Felix that he'd been sick and Tabitha was nursing him back to health. At this point, he'd say anything to get her released.

Yet, would that bring more suspicion on Diana?

He growled and hit his fist into the mattress. This would drive him insane! He definitely needed to be with Diana, because that put him in better spirits. He could think better around her as well.

Turning his head, he glanced at the clock on the mantel. It was only thirty minutes past eight. Still too early to meet her, and if he left now, he'd surely get caught by someone.

He took the letter to the fireplace and threw it inside. The flames licked the paper quickly, turning it to ashes.

As he stared in the fire, his mind wandered to Hawthorne. What in the devil was that man doing, and would he be able to help Tristan find the killer? When they had left Diana's cottage that morning over a week ago, Nic hadn't been talkative, which wasn't like him. By the faraway look in Nic's eyes, Tristan could see something bothered him greatly, but the man never said anything.

Tristan decided to pen a note to Hawthorne to have him come to the house tomorrow so they could plan a way to contact all of Elliot's servants. They needed to get on this posthaste.

It didn't take very long to write the note, seal it, and have the servant take it to be delivered. Tristan left his room to go in search of something to do that would keep his mind occupied until it was time to go to see his Diana. Unfortunately, his brothers had left and his mother had already retired to her chamber.

Grumbling, Tristan marched into his study and straight to his decanter of rum. It had been a while since the drink had become his best friend, before his kidnapping, in fact. Still, he needed something to settle his nerves, so he poured a generous amount into a glass and sat in front of the small fire.

No matter how often he tried to think back over everything Diana had told him about her husband's death and Elliot's, there was something that niggled in the back of his head. Something he should know, or at least figure out.

He took a drink, and then grimaced. What was that nasty taste? True, it had been a little while since he had used the bottle to help calm his nerves, but it had never tasted this bitter before. Or had it?

"Pardon me, milord, but will you be needing any more rum tonight?"

The servant's voice startled him and he swung toward the door. "Oh, Gibbs. I didn't hear you come in."

"Forgive me, milord." The older footman bowed. "I thought to check in on you before you retire."

"I thank you, Gibbs, but I am fine."

"Will you need more rum?"

Tristan couldn't help but grin. This servant knew him well, but why hadn't he noticed that Tristan wasn't a roaring drunk any longer? Didn't servants know things like this? "No, Gibbs, I'm fine—"

Suddenly, an idea struck him and he quickly stood. "Gibbs, would you like to join me?" He held up his glass.

The older man chuckled. "What humor you have, milord. You know me by now, and know I can't refuse a good drink."

Tristan motioned his hand. "Then please come in and I'll pour you a glass." He moved to the liquor tray. "I fear I'm quite bored this evening and I need someone to talk to. Do you mind?"

"Of course not, milord." Mr. Gibbs shuffled in and to the chair nearest to the fireplace. The older man had been with the family since Tristan was a young boy. Gibbs was like part of the family.

Tristan poured Gibbs a healthy dose of rum and brought it

back to him. The servant mumbled his thanks and took the glass. Both men tipped back their drinks at the same time, and Tristan studied the servant over the rim of his glass. Bushy white eyebrows arched over tired, withered eyes. The man was always smiling and willing to please the family.

Grimacing again at the bitter taste, he glanced into his glass. What was wrong with the rum? "Gibbs, I hope you can help me out." He looked back to the footman.

"I'll do anything I can, milord."

"You have been with our family for a long time, and you were my father's footman for many years."

"Aye." He took another drink.

"I'm sure you know a lot about what goes on in society, as well."

The older man's wrinkled mouth lifted in a grin. "Aye, I do."

"And I'm sure that servants know what goes on in the house-hold—even if things are meant to be kept a secret."

"Once again, you are correct. Loyal servants do not spread gossip, but unfortunately, there are many servants I have met over the years who are not so loyal."

"Are you friends with servants from other estates?"

Gibbs chuckled. "We all seem to know what goes on in other houses, I'm afraid."

Tristan nodded. "Have you heard any of these other servants saying things you deem to be inappropriate?"

"Plenty of times."

"How about from Lady Hollingsworth's estate?"

Gibbs took another gulp and nodded. "Sadly, yes. The serv-ants blamed her for not giving their master an heir."

Although Tristan was grateful she hadn't given Hol-lingsworth children, Tristan's heart wrenched for the pain she must have endured because of the servant's treatment. "Yes, that is very sad, indeed. What about Lord Elliot?"

"I fear your cousin wasn't very kind to his servants. I believe many of them wanted him dead, especially the maids."

Tristan nodded. "Yes, I had heard the same thing." He paused in thought until a name popped into his head from nowhere. "What about Lady Dashwood's household. Have you heard anything about her servants who may not be very loyal?"

"Oh yes, milord. In fact, Mr. Tucker was ready to punch Lady Dashwood's driver in the face not too long ago."

"Really? I wonder why."

"It wasn't too long after you had been kidnapped. Mr. Tucker had visited a pub that night and Lady Dashwood's driver was into his cups quite a bit and telling everyone that he had driven his ladyship to Lady Hollingsworth's cottage... and that the viscountess had kidnapped a man. You, milord."

Tristan had tipped his glass up to his lips for another sip, but quickly dropped his arm. "Me? The driver told everyone that?"

"Aye. That is why Mr. Tucker wanted to punch the man in the face for spreading such gossip, but Miss Amanda wouldn't allow it. She is engaged to Mr. Tucker, you know."

Anger filled Tristan, making him want to plow his fist through the man's face as well. "No, I didn't know this. Has the coachman ever been to this place to visit Miss Amanda before?"

"Aye. A few times."

"When was the last time?"

"Yesterday, I believe."

Tristan grumbled under his breath. "How long has this driver been employed with Lady Dashwood?"

"Only since her husband died."

"Interesting..." Tristan allowed himself to take a drink this time. The wheels in his brain were turning faster now as ideas he'd never thought of before surfaced. When he'd returned after being kidnapped, he'd wondered how some people—the magistrate in particular—knew that Tristan had been at Diana's cottage.

Now he knew.

As quickly as that thought ended, another hit him. Diana was there, at Lady Dashwood's, and Tabitha had been arrested. With a loose-lipped driver such as this servant, Diana was not safe at all.

With his heart pumping in an irregular beat, he jumped to his feet. "Gibbs, I must be going. Thank you very much for the talk. It helped me immensely."

"Is something amiss, milord?"

"I have a terrible feeling…" He paused as panic jolted through him. The love of his life was in danger. He just knew it.

Chapter Thirty-Two

TRISTAN RODE HIS horse hard and fast toward Lady Dashwood's estate. The closer he came, the more his head filled with clouds and he became lightheaded. He shook his head and blinked, trying to focus better. This didn't make sense. He'd only had a few sips of his drink, so why was he acting in such a way?

He finally reached the stable, and dismounted. Hurrying toward the structure, the walls seemed to dance in front of him and the ground slanted as if he were walking on a ship.

Tristan stopped and squeezed his eyes closed. What the devil was happening to him? Cotton felt like it was growing in his mouth, but along with it came the stale, bitter taste of the liquor he'd consumed earlier with Gibbs. In all the years Tristan had been drinking, never had he had such a reaction.

What were the odds the rum was laced with some kind of drug that made him feel as if he was floating right out of his body?

Groaning, he fought against his mind trying to come alert—to snap out of this haze he'd been put under. Why had he taken the vile drink in the first place? Now he cursed the spiked rum for making his head swim and his stomach twist. He vowed never to touch liquor again.

He took in a deep breath and moved into the stable. Gradually, his limbs weakened. Finding the strength, he lifted his hands and scrubbed his face, trying to get the blood flowing through him enough to bring him alert. His muscles began to ache and his body felt stiff. Indeed, someone had put some kind of drug in his drink!

He opened his eyes and tried to focus. Darkness surrounded him at first, and then a small amount of light came from the far end of the stables. Slowly he turned his head, but the movement was still too fast and his stomach lurched in protest. Closing his eyes, he gritted his teeth to keep the contents of his stomach down where it belonged.

In the silence of the room, a horse snorted and shuffled his feet. Once again, Tristan blinked open his eyes and this time things appeared slightly clearer than before, but not much.

Tristan took his time moving toward the light, only because the blasted barn wouldn't quit spinning around him. Right here and now he made another vow—never to touch the vile drink again!

Mentally, he shook his head, remembering he'd already made that vow a few seconds ago. *The vile drink be deuced!* He would swear off liquor forever.

He inhaled deeply, and then exhaled slowly hoping to force his mind to be more attentive. He could overpower whatever drug he'd taken since he only had a few sips.

Taking small steps, he continued to move his feet, keeping his hand on the wall as an aide. The light he'd seen earlier had been the back door that was still open, and thankfully the moon was full tonight which helped make the pathway out of the stable brighter.

As he came closer to the stable door, he wondered why it was still open. Usually the stable hands closed it when they put the horses down for the night. He blinked a few more times, but still his eyesight wasn't as focused as he'd wanted.

Shuffling of footsteps was heard, so he stopped, as did the footsteps. He trained his ears to listen for other sounds, but he couldn't detect anything unusual.

Just as he took another step, a shadow appeared at the door.

He rubbed his eyes, hoping to see better. It hadn't worked. His vision was still blurred.

"Who goes there?" he asked with a dry throat.

The longer he stared at the shadow, the form finally took shape into a person. A woman, actually. His heart lifted. Was it Diana? He could only pray.

"Who are you?" he asked again as he took another step closer.

All he could tell was that the woman wore a black hooded cloak. Although the hood was over her head, the sides of the cloak were pulled back for him to see her silver and white dress. He couldn't see her face at all. Yet she seemed too tall to be Diana. So who was this visitor?

"I demand you tell me," he spoke louder this time.

The woman's hand moved away from her body and she was holding something long and pointy. The moon hit the steel just enough that it shined.

He sucked in his breath. She held a knife! Hollingsworth and Elliot were stabbed to death. Was Tristan to be next?

He came to halt and flattened himself against the wall to hold himself up. "I demand to know who you are and why you are here."

"I am here to kill you, my lord."

The woman's voice was low, and he didn't recognize it. Perhaps if he got her to talk to him a little more, he would be able to tell who this person was.

He swallowed the lump of fear in his throat. "You wish to kill *me*? Do you know who I am?"

"Not to worry, Lord Tristan. I have not confused you with anyone."

"Why do you want me dead?"

She took a step closer. "Because you are getting too close to the truth, and I can't have you turning me in to the magistrate."

Confusion left his brain groggy. "Are you the one who killed Lord Hollingsworth and Lord Elliot?"

"Those men had to die because of their ill treatment of their servants. You, Lord Tristan, have not beaten or raped your servants as these other men have, but you still must die. I need to continue to rid the world of people like Hollingsworth and Lord Elliot."

"You are not making any sense, madam. I beg you, please tell me who you are."

The lady laughed. "I see you are all out of sorts. I'm happy to know my servant drugged your rum as I'd asked him to."

"Please, Madam. Tell me who you are."

"You had thought Tabitha was the killer, but she's not, and because you put ideas into the magistrate's head, he had her arrested. And because you are giving the magistrate false ideas, you are in turn hurting my friend. I cannot have that at all."

I know this lady! Now her voice was starting to sound familiar, but because his hazy mind was not quite alert, he couldn't pinpoint this lady's identity.

"Then allow me to ease your mind," he told her gently, soothingly. "I promise you I have not gone to the magistrate with any information. I had accused Tabitha, but within a few hours I realized my mistake. I assure you, I will not speak to the magistrate until I have solid proof."

"Not if you are dead." She came closer.

Silently, he prayed he would be strong enough to hold her off, or at least take the knife from her hand before she stabbed him. Unfortunately, the room still tilted and he couldn't get his bearings.

"Is it money you want? Tell me how I can convince you to leave me alone?"

A low chuckle rumbled through her. "I am not in want of money, my lord. Only revenge." Lifting the knife higher, she lunged toward him.

Instinctively, he raised his hand to protect his face, and at the same time scrambled to get out of her way. His limbs were too slow. The sharp blade of the knife sliced through the skin on his right arm. Burning pain ripped through him, turning his stomach quicker than alcohol had ever done.

When she pulled back and raised her hand again, he took the opportunity to move away from her. Unfortunately, he feared because of his drugged stated, she would eventually overpower him.

Oh Lord, help me!

DIANA WANDERED OUTSIDE, unwilling to sleep. How could she when her friend was in prison?

Since the moment the magistrate hauled Tabitha away, Diana had been doing all she could to get the maid released. Both she and Claudia had been busy today, calling on people to get statements from them, and collecting anything they could that would prove Tabitha's innocence. Most of the evening, Diana had spent talking to the magistrate, pleading with him to free Tabitha. She'd explained to him about Tabitha's beating two nights before Ludlow had died and that she couldn't possibly have killed him. Diana also explained how she had kidnapped Tristan and that Tabitha had been keeping watch on him the very night Lord Elliot died. So why hadn't the magistrate believed her?

The whole day had passed in such a state of confusion and left her mind in a dither that she had forgotten to send Tristan a note. Now it was too late. But she really wanted to see him. She *needed* to see him. She needed to be in his arms while he comforted her.

She glanced toward the stable. Hopefully, Claudia wouldn't mind if Diana took a horse. She just couldn't wait any longer.

As she walked toward the stable, she wondered why a lantern had been left on. Perhaps a stable hand was still in there putting the horses down for the night. But the closer she came to the stable, voices rang out from inside. She couldn't quite discern who was speaking, but whoever it was, they were arguing.

Perhaps she shouldn't go in and disturb them. It would be

hard, but she'd have to wait until tomorrow to see Tristan. But then Tristan's voice rang through the air, strong and laced with panic, almost *demanding,* her heart jumped in fear.

Something was wrong. She just knew it.

Within seconds, he cried out.

Lifting her gown to her ankles, she sprinted down the grassy slope toward the back of the stables. Finally, she reached the edge of the structure. Out of breath, she quietly tried to step toward the voices as she listened intently.

"You, Madam, are mad! If you kill me, *you* would surely hurt your friend, a friend you have claimed to care so much about," Tristan said.

Diana inhaled sharply. *Kill him?* Someone was trying to kill him?

Fear sliced through her, and she knew she must do something quickly, although running back to the house to get help was not the right thing to do. Somehow, she must interfere.

"Oh, Lord Tristan, you are certainly full of yourself tonight if you think that your death will hurt Diana."

Stumbling, she couldn't believe what she heard. This was about her? *Impossible!*

"Contrary to what you believe, Diana loves me as much as I love her."

Tears stung her eyes and her heart melted from his words, but panic still made her limbs shake. One way or another, she had to help him.

"Not to worry, my lord. I will be there for her and soothe her when she hears of your death. I assure you, she will forget about you soon enough."

That voice! Oh, good heavens. It couldn't be…

Diana took quick steps and rushed through the back door. The woman wearing a dark, hooded cloak turned toward Diana with a knife raised in the air, ready to swipe at her.

"Claudia, no! It is I, Diana."

Her friend gasped and quickly brought her arm in back of her to hide the knife. The movement knocked the hood from her friend's head, and the woman's blonde ringlets gleamed in the moonlight.

"Diana… Wh—what are you doing here?"

"I'm here to stop you from killing the man I love." She looked at Tristan. He stood against the wall as if he were trying to hold it up. He gazed at her through hooded eyes, as if he were intoxicated, and he was carrying his right arm… His *bloody* arm. "Tristan, you're bleeding." She rushed past Claudia and to Tristan. With one hand, he reached out to her, pulling her beside him.

"It's just a scratch," he said softly.

Although it was dark and shadows danced everywhere, the moon's light let her see that the blood on his arm was not from a little scratch. Anger filled her, and she swung toward her friend. "Claudia? Did you stab Tristan?"

"I had to," she replied in a pleading voice. "Don't you see?"

"No, I do not. Please enlighten me," Diana demanded.

"Lord Tristan was telling things to the magistrate that were false. That's why Tabitha was arrested. And he's getting too close to the truth. I will *not* allow this man to damage all of the good I've been trying to do by helping girls like Tabitha and Sally escape their hellish nightmares. Men like Lord Tristan are thorns in my side, and do you know what I do with thorns? I *remove* them!"

"Oh, Claudia." Diana's heart wrenched. "You cannot be serious. Are you the one who killed Ludlow, and Lord Elliot?"

Claudia straightened, standing her ground as she lifted her knife again. "I did, and I would gladly do it again. England is much better without monsters that enjoy tormenting women like us."

"Like you?" Tristan asked. "Pray tell, Lady Dashwood, how do you fit in to all of this?"

"I lived with a father who beat me, only to marry a man who was worse. After I killed my husband, I vowed to find all the lowlife men who were like my husband, and do away with them."

A few tears leaked from Diana's eyes. Her poor, misguided friend. What had caused Lady Dashwood to go mad like this?

Diana glanced at Tristan. His gaze met hers and he pulled her tighter against his side. Comfort washed over her, yet she knew he was losing too much blood, and he wouldn't be strong if they couldn't convince Claudia to stop this insanity.

She looked back at her friend. "Claudia, please put the knife down. Killing Tristan will not help cleanse the world of ruthless men, because he is nothing like your husband or Ludlow. Tristan is a kind and loving and *gentle* man, unlike any I've met before."

Claudia stepped closer and into the moon's light. Her scowl was deep, and frightening. "Diana step away so I can do what I came here to do."

Diana moved in front of Tristan. He tried to pull her away, but his grip wasn't as strong. Definitely, he was losing his strength fast.

"If you still intend on killing him then you shall have to kill me first. I refuse to move!"

"Diana," Claudia said in a harsh voice, "I beg you, move away from Lord Tristan."

Diana lifted her chin stubbornly. "I will not." She studied her friend closely and although Lady Dashwood was determined, her bottom lip quivered.

"It will sadden me greatly to kill you."

"Then don't, Claudia. Just leave us be."

"You know I cannot. Especially now. If I don't kill Tristan, he will have me put in prison. And if I leave you alive, you will hate me." Lady Dashwood shook her head. "Both of you must die!"

Just as Claudia lunged toward them, Tristan pushed Diana to the ground and stumbled in front of her. He captured Lady Dashwood's wrist and struggled with the lady to make her drop the weapon. Diana could tell Tristan was losing his strength, but he tried his hardest to fight Claudia.

Diana's vision blurred from her tears, and she swiped the liquid away as she stood. Claudia and Tristan had moved farther away as each one fought for control. But just as Diana feared, Tristan's weakened body crumbled to the ground. Victory shone on Claudia's face as she raised the knife toward Tristan.

"No!" Diana screamed, and could have sworn someone else had screamed with her.

From out of nowhere, the sound of a pistol boomed through the air. Seconds later, Claudia cried out as the knife dropped from her hand. She fell to the ground, clutching her bloody hand.

Diana swung toward where the sound of the pistol had come from as Tabitha ran closer, holding the still smoking weapon.

"Tabitha?" Diana gasped. "What are you doing here?"

Tabitha peeked down at Claudia lying on the ground and kicked the knife away from the woman, and then turned her focus on Diana. "Is that the only thing you can think of to say at this moment?" She arched an eyebrow.

Diana wanted to laugh, wanted to cry, wanted to run to Tabitha and hug her. But before she did all that, there was one thing more important to do.

She hurried to Tristan. He was very weak but still alert. She fell to the ground beside him and lifted his head to place it on her lap. She grasped the end of her petticoat and ripped a long piece off the garment. "Give me your arm, Tristan."

Without waiting for him to fully raise it, she carefully wrapped the strip of her cloth around the wound tightly.

More footsteps padded on the dewy grass followed by wheezing of air flow coming from a man. Diana looked up and met the wide-eye stare of Sir Felix, the magistrate.

"It's about time you showed up," Tabitha snapped. She pointed to Lady Dashwood who appeared to have passed out. "There is your killer."

"Yes, I know," Sir Felix huffed.

Diana shook her head. "How… how… when did you release Tabitha?" She looked to the maid. "What is going on?"

"Not too long ago, I received a visitor," the magistrate began. "Sally, a former servant of Lord Elliot's, came to see me, begging for Tabitha's release. Sally had witnessed Lady Dashwood killing Lord Elliot, but feared to tell anyone because the young girl thought she would be the next to die." He took a deep breath, his large chest lifting and falling slowly. He knelt beside Claudia and slapped wrist irons on her arms to keep her from doing any more harm. Letting out a slow breath, he turned his attention to Tristan. "Worthington? Are you all right?"

"He has been stabbed," Diana answered for Tristan. "He will need medical help immediately."

"I shall fetch a doctor," Tabitha said before taking a step to run.

"Tabitha, don't go yet," Tristan said weakly.

The maid slowly turned back as her gaze fell on Tristan. "Why?"

"Sir Felix, will you please go fetch a doctor for me?" Tristan asked. "Now that Lady Dashwood has wrist irons on, I don't think she'll be going very far."

"Yes, my lord. I'll hurry." He stood and rushed up the hill toward the house.

"Tabitha," Tristan continued, grimacing as he held his hand tighter. "I want to know why you saved me when I was the one who accused you of murder last night."

"Because… because I knew Diana loved you with all of her heart and you two deserve to be together."

Tristan shook his head. "It's more than that. Tell me, Tabitha. What made you change your mind about me when I know you have always loathed me?"

Diana watched as different emotions flittered across Tabitha's face. Tears filled her eyes and she bit her bottom lip. Diana also wanted to know why her maid had saved Tristan's life. "Please Tabitha, tell me. Tell Tristan. I have known for a while now that something has been bothering you, and I think it's time to let us know so we can help you."

A tear slipped from Tabitha's eyes and her expression changed to relief. Diana held her breath, anticipating Tabitha's confession.

TRISTAN WAITED FOR the maid to speak. His arm hurt terribly, and he had lost a lot of blood already. He really should not worry about Tabitha and seek medical help as soon as possible, but something in his heart told him to hear her out.

"Please, Tabitha," he said. "I would like to know. You have done a very heroic thing by saving my life. Will you not think of me as a friend now?"

Indecision played on her expression for the longest time, and he wondered if she would say anything at all. Finally, she took a deep breath. She remained standing as she stared down into Tristan's eyes.

"For many years," she began, "I thought of you and your brothers as irresponsible men who didn't have a care in the world. I wanted to believe all three of you were carefree, foolish men with no sense of decorum. In my mind, you were all worthless creatures who slithered along the ground and it wasn't worth my time to even spit upon you."

Shocked, Tristan's eyes widened. What on earth could have made her feel that way toward his family? "Go on," he urged, wondering if he even wanted to hear more.

"But then I got to know you a little and I realized you were not as I had expected. I heard stories about your brothers, but they were different as well."

Shaking his head, he still couldn't understand. "But why, Tabitha? What have I ever done to make you think that I was such a terrible person?"

"Because growing up, I'd heard how much you and your brothers were just like your father. Forgive me for speaking ill of the dead, my lord, but your father was the scum of the earth, and since his sons were supposed to be just like him…" She shrugged. "Naturally, my first instinct was to hate you."

"Tabitha," Diana inquired, "why would you even care about the Worthington brothers, and more importantly, their father?"

"Did you know my father?" Tristan asked warily.

Hesitantly, Tabitha nodded. "When I was a little girl, he visited my mother quite frequently."

Tristan groaned as sadness filled his heart. He figured he knew her story already, but he decided not to say anything, and to let her continue.

"My mother was extremely naïve, and she believed the old duke when he told her he would leave his wife and marry my mother." Tabitha rolled her eyes. "Even as a girl I knew he would never leave a wife of good-breeding to marry a servant. Regardless, my mother continued to wait for the time she and the duke could be together. He would bring me trinkets and try to win my love and acceptance. At first, I wanted to since I had no father. Thankfully, within a few years I learned the truth." A tear slipped down her cheek and she quickly wiped it away.

"What truth?" Tristan asked.

"That the Duke of Kenbridge… was my f—father."

Stunned, Tristan lay still not believing what his ears had heard. She couldn't possibly have said what he thought she said—that she was his sister? Beside him Diana gasped as her hand flew to her mouth. Her shocked gesture confirmed everything. He hadn't imagined the words coming from Tabitha.

"M—my *sister*? You, you are my s—sister?"

"Yes."

Tabitha pushed her fingers through her dark brown hair, pulling it off her face. Tristan could now see her facial features, eyes that resembled Trey's, a mouth that reminded him of Trevor's. And he couldn't forget her stubbornness that was too much like *his*.

"I have a sister," he muttered to himself, still not quite believing. Yet looking at her now, he knew without a shadow of a doubt that she indeed was his relation.

"I have a sister," he exclaimed and struggled to sit up. Diana helped him until he was steady to stay aright by himself. He held out his good hand toward Tabitha. "I *finally* have a sister!"

A sob tore from Tabitha's throat as she fell to her knees and grasped his hand. He pulled her in for a hug and she wrapped her arms tight around his shoulders, burying her face into his neck. Hot tears dampened his skin, but he didn't care. Emotion clogged in his throat and he didn't dare say anything without his voice cracking.

Diana sat back as she let brother and sister share a tender moment. He smiled at her and gave her a wink. Tears streamed down her face and she covered her mouth with her hands, but he could see her happiness through the twinkle in her eyes.

Tabitha pulled back and wiped the tears off her face. "For years I hated you and your brothers because you were living the life I would never have. I knew the old duke wouldn't tell his family about his illegitimate daughter, and I really didn't want to claim the Worthingtons as family, either."

He cupped her face. "Can I share a little secret with you? I had a difficult time claiming my father, as well."

Tabitha hiccupped a laugh.

"However, I shall be very proud to tell all of England that you are my sister."

Tabitha shook her head as color left her face. "Oh no, my lord. I don't want you to do that. I wouldn't be able to handle the ridicule."

"We shall talk about this later." He smiled through the pain in his arm that made his limb turn numb. "But right now, if the two of you will help me into the house, I would love to lie down as I wait for a doctor."

"Oh, Heavens." Tabitha stood and dried her face. "I shall go help the magistrate fetch the doctor—"

"No." Tristan quickly grabbed her hand. "Stay. I would like

my sister to assist Diana."

As Tristan struggled to stand with an arm around each woman, he felt complete for the first time in his life. On his right he held the woman who would always be in his heart, and soon to be his wife, and on his left, he held the one thing he'd wanted when he was a young boy.

A younger sister.

Epilogue

TWO DAYS LATER, Tristan was finally able to move around. He didn't like feeling weak, both mentally and physically, and he was very happy when he found the strength to dress himself and leave his bedroom.

Since the night he was stabbed, his beautiful Diana had been coming to the house every day, caring for him. More so than the good doctor, thank Heavens. Indeed she was an angel. *His* very own angel.

When he walked into the dining room and saw his two brothers sitting at the table, Tristan paused at the door. His brothers wore expressions that Tristan didn't like. They didn't appear gloomy, but more confused or frustrated.

"Good day," Tristan greeted and he walked in and took his seat at the table.

The other two nodded greetings.

"I must say, Trey, I'm surprised that Hawthorne isn't with you. In fact, I haven't seen him since after we left Diana's cottage."

Trey shrugged. "Nic was called away suddenly. Something to do with his family in New Castle. I don't know when he'll return."

"I shall have to write him a letter, then." Tristan smiled.

"How are you faring today my dear brother?" Trevor asked.

"So much better than before." Tristan's smile dropped as he eyed his brothers warily. "Why do you ask? Are you both going to tell me something I don't want to hear?"

"Why would you say that?" Trey wondered.

"Because of your expressions."

The oldest brother and youngest brother traded glances with each other before looking back at Tristan.

"Actually," Trevor began, "Trey and I have been discussing something very serious."

Leaning back in his chair, Tristan folded his arms across his chest. "Something I'm not going to approve of?"

"Well," Trevor scratched his chin, "the subject matter is a very delicate one. I think you will have a different opinion from mine and Trey's."

Tristan shook his head. "What are you talking about?"

"Our sister." Trevor sighed heavily. "Since you told us about Tabitha the other day, Trey and I have been thinking about her constantly. We are very happy to discover we have a sister, but we think we should keep the secret from our mother."

"What?" Tristan sat forward in his chair. "Pray tell, why wouldn't you want our mother to know? She knew what kind of man our father was. Do you really believe she doesn't suspect there is one illegitimate child—or more—running around England somewhere? Do you really think our mother is that naïve?"

Trey shrugged. "She's had so much scandal and heartbreak in her lifetime. I think keeping Tabitha's secret is necessary for Mother's health as well as her state of mind."

"And," Trevor added, "since Tabitha doesn't want everyone to know who she really is, I think it would be all right to keep the family secret from our mother."

Tristan scowled as he stared at his older brother for a few moments then turned his glare at Trey. Blast it all, Tristan really hated when they were right and he wasn't. Perhaps it wouldn't hurt to keep their sister a secret after all. Of course sooner or later

Tabitha might want people to know how she's related to the Worthington family, but until then…

He nodded. "Fine. We will keep it from Mother and the rest of society, but if and when Tabitha wants people to know…"

"Yes, we will tell Mother when that time comes," Trevor agreed.

"Have you thought over that other matter I asked you about the other day?" Tristan asked.

"What other matter?"

Tristan rolled his eyes. Sometimes he felt his older brother never listened to him. "I don't want Tabitha to live the life of a servant any longer. I would like to set her up in a cottage somewhere away from the *ton* and give her an allowance so she can live her life as she sees fit."

Once again Trevor and Trey traded glanced with each other before returning their focus to Tristan.

"Agreed," the brothers said in unison and smiled.

"Splendid." Tristan grinned. "Now, I'm hungry." He pushed away from the table and moved to ring the servant to bring in his breakfast.

The rest of the morning passed in relaxation. His brothers left and Tristan had a nice visit with his mother. Tristan tried to read a book, but he couldn't concentrate. His mind kept wandering to the woman he loved more than life itself.

"I must see Diana," he muttered in frustration as he closed the book and stood. He took a step toward the door, but his mind halted him from going any further. He wasn't sure where she was staying. Was she still at her own home even though Mr. Lusk had now assumed the title of Viscount, or had she returned to the cottage? Tristan knew she wasn't at Lady Dashwood's any longer. The woman was locked away in Newgate prison, and her servants were looking for other employment.

Groaning, he sat back down again and flipped open his book. He had to believe Diana would come today after all she had been to see him every day since the stabbing.

Memories of what happened that awful, yet wonderful, night flashed through his mind. He couldn't believe Diana would risk her life to save his. It thrilled him beyond words to know she loved him that much. He would risk his life to save hers without a doubt, and it pleased him to know she loved him just the same.

The door to the sitting room opened and the butler stepped inside. "Lord Tristan, Lady Hollingsworth is here to see you."

His heart cheered and excitement shot through him. Grinning, he nodded to the butler. "Splendid! Please show her in, Bentley."

Tristan stood and waited for her to enter. She looked so lovely in her lavender day-gown with matching bonnet. Her auburn ringlets hung nearly to her shoulders but still showed him a perfect view of her slender neck. When she met his gaze, her eyes sparkled and a smile stretched across her tempting mouth.

"Diana, my dear." He held out his good hand for her to grasp. "I'm so very happy you came."

"Really? Why is that?"

"Because I can't make it through the day without seeing your beautiful face and hearing your gentle, caring voice."

She arched an eyebrow. "Tell me, Lord Tristan, what is it that you want now? For some reason, you are acting very suspicious."

Chuckling, he pulled her to the sofa and they sat. He kept her hand in his as he caressed her fingers. "I would be lying if I told you I didn't want something, because I do."

"Ah-ha. I knew there was a reason for all the flowery words, my lord."

"Indeed, there is." Before saying another word, he leaned forward and brushed his lips across hers. "I hope you do not mind if I kiss you first." He didn't give her time to answer, and pressed his mouth lovingly against hers.

A deep sigh escaped her throat as she threw her arms around his neck and responded exactly how he wanted. He held her close and kissed her like a man starved for attention... or in this case, like a man who was thrilled to have been given a second chance at love. His heart burst in his chest, and he knew for certain she was the woman he wanted to love. Always.

Tristan broke the kiss and only pulled back enough to gaze into her lovely green eyes, the same pair of eyes that caught his attention when they first met. Eyes he has seen in his dreams for three years, from the moment he awakens until he drifts off to sleep.

"Diana, I want you to know how much I love you. Never has there been a woman who has touched me as deeply as you have touched not only my heart, but my soul as well." He stroked his thumb along her cheek. "Circumstances have kept us away for too long, and I want to rectify that situation now."

She smiled although moisture filled her eyes. "And pray, how can we rectify that?"

"Marry me as soon as we can obtain the license. I want to claim you as my wife and treat you like a queen. I want you to bear my children and be the wonderful mother I'm confident you'll become. And I want to love you endlessly and be by your side forever."

"Oh, Tristan," her voice broke, "I would love nothing more than to be your wife, but…"

"But?" He held his breath, not knowing if he was going to like what she was about to tell him.

"I cannot give you children. I am barren. One of the reasons Ludlow beat me and hated me so was because I could not give him a child. Although I would love to have your children, I fear I cannot."

His mind scrambled with thoughts. Having children with her would be wonderful, but he would be happy to be her husband even if the Lord didn't bless them with a large family. "My love, you will always be special to me whether you are infertile or not. However, I do believe that it was Ludlow who had the problem. Not you."

Her forehead creased. "What makes you think that?"

"As many times as he had slacked his lust on other women, not one of them became pregnant." Tristan shrugged. "If he had sired any children, legitimate or not, he would have been boasting all over town."

She sat in silence for the longest time as her gaze traveled over his face before finally resting on his eyes. Slowly, she smiled again. "Tristan, I do believe you are correct."

"Of course I am." He winked and kissed her again, wishing this moment never had to end. He broke the kiss and brushed his lips across her cheek and down her neck. "So my sweet Diana, will you consent to becoming my wife?"

"Oh, Tristan," she sighed. "I have loved you since you first thought I was blowing kisses to you that day we met, and I will continue to love you until I take my dying breath when we are both old and gray. You have always made me feel so special and loved, and I want to spend the rest of my life making you feel the same joy."

Love burst inside his chest and emotion filled him so full he could scarcely breathe. He kissed her again, sealing their bargain. Happiness finally flowed through him like he'd always dreamed it would.

At long last, he had found the very thing he'd always dreamed about having… the sweetest love.

Find more stories by Marie Higgins

authormariehiggins.com

mariehigginsbooks.com/

mariehigginsbooks.etsy.com

Join my Newsletter

www.authormariehiggins.com/newsletter

About the Author

Marie Higgins is an award-winning, best-selling author of clean romance novels that melt your heart and have you falling in love over and over again. Since 2010, she's published over 100 heartwarming, on-the-edge-of-your-seat romances. She's broadened her readership by writing mystery/suspense, humor, time travel, and paranormal, along with her love for historical romances. Her readers have dubbed her "Queen of Tease" because of her twists and unexpected endings.

Website – www.authormariehiggins.com
Facebook – facebook.com/authormariehigginsbooks
Instagram – instagram.com/author.mariehiggins
Bluesky – bsky.app/profile/authormariehiggins.bsky.social
Bookbub – bookbub.com/authors/marie-higgins
Pinterest – pinterest.com/authormariehiggins